Beach Heart Cottage
Book one

This is a fiction work. Names, characters, places, buildings, and incidents either are a product of the author's imagination or used as fiction. Any resemblance to persons, living or dead, events, or structures are entirely coincidental.

Cover design by Diana Baxter. The small mermaid photo on this cover underwent extensive research and recoloring by Diana Baxter.

If anyone has knowledge or proof of the origins of this mermaid photograph, please contact me at. DianaBaxterbooks@gmail.com

By Diana Baxter
www.DianaBaxterNovels.com

Steve, no matter where we are, our Beach Hearts are always on Hatteras. ♥

To Keith, Kaitlynn, Addison, Aaron and Asher. May you all thrive and have a Beach Heart! Let your toes find the Hatteras sand and a smile find your hearts!
♥

Beach Heart Cottage

By Diana Baxter

Ah, it's **August**. That glorious time of the year. It's when the soft whispers in the breeze find North Carolina's Hatteras Island. Stop by and listen to the generational tales that are unveiled at the Beach Heart Cottage.

Under the brilliant radiance of the full moon, as the golden sparks of a bonfire reach the stars, dance the women who celebrate the newest mermaid in their sisterhood.

Step up onto the porch.

Ghost crabs burrow into the cool sand, seeking refuge as the rising marmalade sun ripples over the Atlantic Ocean. Feathery sea oats atop the dunes sway lazily in the soft breeze as mellow waves roll onto the sandy shores, leaving behind empty shells of sea creatures. Scampering sandpipers chase retreating waves, while a handful of pelicans skim the surface of the sea.

Thankful for this glorious morning, Caroline inhales the briny air as the sea mist tickles her skin. Her bare feet sink into the cool, silky sand as she turns and makes her way through a narrow, rugged path tucked between the dunes. She stops and smiles at an old friend. The Beach Heart Cottage.

Caroline continues, aware that the aged porch lined with white rocking chairs has patiently waited for her return. It has been a year since laughter, tears, and tales mingled with Hatteras's welcoming breeze.

Stepping onto the porch, Caroline opens the wooden door. Wiggling her toes, she crosses the threshold onto the worn pine floor. It is then Caroline, is known by her crowned *mermaid's* name.

Releasing her past inhibitions, she allows the sweet celebration of summer magic to begin as Hatteras Island calls her mermaid sisters to the Beach Heart Cottage.

One

"Hey, Caroline, in a few hours you are free from this madhouse!"

A classy brunette, thirty-five years old, Caroline Woodard had her hair in a ponytail, that accented her high cheekbones, heart-shaped face, and citrine eyes.

She removed her glasses and looked up at Sharon, her co-worker, with a calm smile. "I think someone is jealous," Caroline teased as her eyes circled her empty office and back to Sharon. "I'm so ready to get the heck out of here. You can come with me. I'm hiring at the new PR firm. And as partner, you are my number one choice."

"I know, and your offer is more than generous, thanks. To be honest, I'm jealous you are leaving this zoo. I wish I could, but with a new condo, my hubby's hectic job commuting, and the baby on the way. You understand."

Caroline glanced at Sharon's blooming belly. "I understand. But the offer is always open."

Sharon patted her belly bump. "Thanks. Two months to go and little Aaron will arrive."

Caroline pushed her chair back and got up. "You will stay in touch? I want to know the moment he's born."

"Wilmen is a mere pain in my..." She pointed to her rear end. "I am so over this presidential election and it's only the end of July. I am exhausted!"

"We are having drinks tonight at Sansweets and you can relax. I'm buying!" Caroline reminded Sharon. "You are going to my goodbye hurrah?"

Sharon nodded. "Yup, eight o'clock. It's your farewell to the insanity of this office. See you later. I'll be the one with a swollen appearance, drinking Calypso Temples." She studied Caroline. "I am sure gonna miss you. It won't be the same here."

Caroline couldn't wait to exit the building and her boss to start anew. As a senior publicist at Wilmen & Brown in Dupont Circle, Washington D.C, she led a more than hectic life. The public relations firm was representing Senator Colton Jameson, the front runner in the upcoming presidential election. Mastering many departments, her skills were well seasoned-and she was long overdue for a change. And a big change it was!

It had not been easy climbing up the arduous ladder over the past twelve years and making sacrifices. She started out as an intern, fresh out of Loyola with her master's degree in hand. She had burned the midnight oil, downed double-shot espressos, and felt the jab of B12 shots by a doctor who enjoyed his yacht. All thanks to overworked, stressed White House interns. A position she had gotten with a little help from her famous father.

Eyedrops were a common solution for Caroline's bloodshot eyes. With occasional dozing and nonstop yawns, she had stayed up until dawn to get ahead. Success found her, but was it worth it? Yes, without a doubt. She needed more than a life being controlled by her inflated, loud boss, who had no problem calling her 24/7.

The election was going to be tight. All hands on deck, as Wilmen requested. No, he *ordered*. Caroline chose the worst time to leave the firm and partner with Gary Lawson. He was a former colleague who had left months earlier to start his public relations firm. He had made Caroline an offer as a partner that she could not turn down. Her life belonged to her.

No longer Lawson. She was now a partner. *Lawson and Woodard.* The name Woodard had deep roots in DC.

"Are you gonna miss our fearless, loving leader?" Sharon glanced over her shoulder and back at Caroline. "Wilmen is in his lovely mood today. He's not happy you're leaving. You are fortunate not to have witnessed the outburst this morning on a conference call. Wilmen paced like an angry bull in a pen. You know your shoes will be difficult to fill, right?"

"Hey, I'm a Galantine Vartoni shoe. What can I say?" she teased. "His fat foot will never fit. He's a big boy and will get over it."

Sharon looked down at her beige heels and back at Caroline. "You got that right. I'm sure by now you know Senator Jameson dropped slightly last night in the polls after the debate with General Fletton. Rumors are spreading that you are taking Jameson with you to the new firm. Don't do it. Wilmen will go after you and in for the kill. Be careful, this ice is thin, and fissures are forming."

Caroline was a superb marketer and at landing new clients. She was assertive, with a calm approach that Wilmen had used as an asset to grow his firm. She tirelessly dedicated herself to her clients, mostly politicians and a handful of celebs. It hadn't hurt that her father, the late Weston Parson Woodard, had been a lifelong politician. A senator who had once run for president and lost by a slim margin.

DC bigwigs and socialites had surrounded Caroline since birth. Her parents often hosted political cocktail parties at their elegant colonial home in the tony DC neighborhood of Berkley. As a child, with her father holding her hand, she often walked the echoed halls of the Capitol and White House. She knew all the influential people one had to know.

Single, handsome, forty-five-year-old Senator Colton Jameson of North Carolina, who had been her father's protégé, was now the presidential frontrunner. He was Caroline's client and would remain so. It did not matter how hard her soon-to-be ex-boss wined and dined the senator.

Years earlier, Caroline had met up-and-coming Colton at one of her father's fundraisers. Their eyes had locked, and in an instant, sparks went off. Overflowing champagne and flirtatious conversations led to a whirlwind romance. They were an item for a while, but life got in the way as Caroline worked night and day while Colton ran for senator. Although their romance had long since burned out, smoldering embers remained. Warm enough to ignite? Neither was sure.

What mattered was Caroline getting him into the Oval Office.

Caroline removed her reading glasses and looked up at Sharon. "I watched the debate, and my phone is still blowing up. It was a slight fall back. And as far as Wilmen, he can yell all he wants. He doesn't scare me. His deals are all on handshakes. Senator Jameson can go where he feels is best. You know, Wilmen is a mere yapping, ankle-biting poodle in a pit bull's body."

Sharon shook her head. "That is a disturbing visual. I may need a moment."

"Oh yes, so take all the time you need to digest it."

Sharon glanced at the door. "The mailroom kid dates an intern at Jameson's campaign headquarters. He has intel, and I trust this kid. He can't stand Wilmen."

"So, who can? Okay, already, tell me."

"Jameson assured Wilmen he's staying with the firm. He's not going with you. You're out. They are having lunch today at Brunetti's. I put a call out to my favorite private investigator."

Caroline inhaled and exhaled. "No. I have the inside scoop, and Jameson is blowing smoke. Trust me, he's not staying with Wilmen."

Sharon glanced around the vacant walls. "Are you confident about this?"

"I *am*, and seriously, Jameson will take his fight where he wants. It's late in the game now. I'm his best line of defense, and he knows it." She went over to a small closet and removed a handful of blouses and a blazer. "My offer still stands. If you want lunch on the go, rallies, traveling, and cold calls, I'm hiring, and please say yes. I need people like you. I really need you, Sharon. You can even bring the baby. We can have a small daycare!" Caroline said as she brushed past Sharon.

"I'll talk to my hubby again."

Caroline knew Sharon would never leave the safety and comfort of the firm.

With her phone in hand, Sharon raised it to the ceiling. "Ciao!"

"Adios! See you tonight!" Caroline said, and she was out the door for the last time.

After a bittersweet goodbye celebration at the local pub, Caroline went home to her condo. She had to put her mixed emotions aside and pack for her beach work-cation on Hatteras Island with her mom, grandma, and aunties—girls only. This was a vacation of celebration. A celebration that had gone on for four generations. The next mermaid in the bloodline was to be crowned. Silly, perhaps. Heartfelt, yes. For them, the August retreat was an annual event, but for Caroline, it meant a two-week stay.

Caroline was overdue to inhale the salty sea mist, bury her toes in the sugar sand and sip coffee as the golden orb of the sun rose over the Atlantic.

She was almost finished packing when she picked up her phone and called her mom. "Are you packed? We leave at seven in the morning." She tossed her red bikini into her suitcase. "Dunkin' at seven-fifteen. My treat on the chocolate munchkins."

"Oh, honey, you and your tight schedule. Munchkins sound wonderful, and Grams Dorea likes the plain ones. No jelly or chocolate, her gallbladder, you know."

"Yeah, I know." Caroline picked up the TV remote and clicked on the weather.

"Your aunties are so overjoyed our newest mermaid sister is to be inducted. We picked your name. Great Grandma Ida told it to me in a dream just the other night. Oh, she is *so* happy. And I nearly forgot, I went to my neighbor, you know, the psychic, and Ida showed up with her sisters. They are dancing in heaven and have many secrets to reveal once you're crowned as the newest mermaid."

Caroline rolled her eyes as she rifled through her closet. "Mom, not that nutty neighbor. She said I was going to find my true love, and you were going to win the lottery and sail off into the sunset."

"Well, I won two dollars in a quick pick. And people make mistakes, honey. Besides, she said, in *my* near future. Anyway, I know Ida was here. I could smell her perfume. So sweet."

Caroline fought back, making a joke. "And about that mermaid ceremony? And strange dreams of Great Grandma Ida and her sisters dancing? I've been thinking." She frowned, knowing this would hurt her mother's feelings. She feared that her new partner, Lawson, or potential clients in their new firm, would ruin her career if they found out about her beach dance under the full moon. Wearing a mermaid costume, with a seashell crown, summoning deceased relatives. What if Wilmen hired a private investigator to follow her?

"Caroline Woodard," her mom's voice cut into her thoughts, "you have a responsibility to continue the tradition of the cottage. We have been planning your induction for months. If your great-grandmother and her sisters heard you, they would roll over in their graves. Oh, they probably just did! Your cousin did it four years ago when she turned thirty-five, and now it's your turn. This August is Ida's birthday. She would have been one-hundred-and-five this August. It's a double celebration. And your great grand aunties are singing to the sea."

"Mom, Ida died in 1987. They all died a long time ago. Give it a rest." Caroline waltzed into her kitchen and took a wine glass out of the cabinet. With her phone wedged between her ear and shoulder, she poured a glass of Pinot.

"Caroline Woodard, may I remind you this is your duty to continue our sisterhood tradition and Ida forgives you!"

Caroline took a sip of wine and put the glass down on the counter. She needed to chill out and go with the flow. Enjoy the fact that her family was so close. It was time to shift the topic. "I can't wait to cross the bridge to Hatteras Island and feel the sun on my face, let my hair down and allow the summer winds to mingle with suntan lotion. And live in my bathing suit and walk along the beach at sunrise."

"We are all so thrilled." Her mother said.

"Oh, Mom, are you taking Archie? Last time, not only did he fling cat litter all over my SUV, that fat cranky cat ran off and hid under the cottage. Then that weird man next door was crawling under the house, trying to save him."

"No, honey, Archie is not going, and he's on a diet. And the weird man has a name. It's Earl," Caroline could hear the cat purring as her mother stroked the cat's head. "This time, he will stay with my neighbor, whom you refer to as the nut psychic."

"That's a relief."

"Auntie Lorelei arrived yesterday and was airing the cottage out. She brought Wilbur with her."

"Really, Mom? Wilbur, the always drooling mutt that humps pillows. Okay, thanks for the heads-up. Wilbur, the only male allowed in the cottage, is a horny dog."

"Oh, honey, he is older now and has arthritis, like the rest of us. Well, I mean, us elders."

Caroline glanced at her end table, at the photo of her and Gracie, her English springer spaniel who had died years earlier. "I know, Mom. It's just that Wilbur has zero manners. He is not allowed near my pillows."

"Caroline, you need this vacation. You are getting to be terribly negative."

Caroline inhaled. "Stress, Mom. This is a big election, and my leaving the firm and taking this vacation has my head spinning. I need to take a break. I do. But of all times?"

"Your father was the same way before the election. Let's leave that behind. I nearly forgot. Bring linens and pillows. I need to pick up Grams Dorea soon. I was at her place yesterday and helped her pack. She had a tear in her eye. Her granddaughter, the newest mermaid, is to be crowned."

"Yeah, me a mermaid and Grams Dorea and the rest of you cheering me on." Caroline shook her head. "I get dibs on the north-facing bedroom. It's cooler and I will have to work." Caroline went into her bedroom. "Mom, I have so much to do. See you bright and early. The weathergirl said it will be humid and in the low nineties for the first week."

"I know, honey. Auntie Lorelei said it is egg-frying hot, and she is finally having Earl put window air conditioning units in the bedrooms."

Caroline did not understand why her mother and her aunt were such tightwads about the cottage, steering away from modern conveniences.

"Why doesn't Auntie Lorelei put in central air? It is so dang hot in there. Window units are loud, and those dusty fans don't help either. For heaven's sake, Grams Dorea can't be in that heat. You know how cranky she can get."

Their true intention was to honor the traditions of their beachfront cottage that had been passed down through generations, making sure it stayed unchanged. A warrior protected by an invisible shield. The structure, on the frontline of battle, took on each storm and always won. And yes, the six-bedroom, two-story rustic cottage showed its age, even after a few small additions and renovations.

The wooden roof shakes, and cedar siding had been long weathered. Inside, the once light blond, now golden-hued tongue-and-groove walls embedded many secrets, along with tears, joy, and laughter. The red-brick fireplace had warmed many hearts on chilly fall nights as tall tales of hooking the big one were told. Not forgetting who got the best tan over the summer.

"Mom, wait, weirdo Earl is putting in the window units? Ugh, he's such a strange man. The last time I was at the cottage, he was having a belching contest with Auntie Calypso on the porch. It was *so* gross!" Caroline burst into laughter as she poured another glass of wine. "Remember?"

"Yes, honey, I remember, and your Auntie Calypso had a wonderful time, as you may recall, singing and dancing the night away. And that so-called weirdo, Earl, rescued Archie for me. He's a nice man, and I wish there were more like him. A true Southern gentleman."

"Whatever. I'm sure belching gentleman Earl is more bizarre with age."

"Earl is helping your Auntie Lorelei get the cottage opened as we speak. I will see you in the morning. Love you. Sleep well and sweet dreams of the cottage. Oh, and Great-

Grandma Ida's heart is bursting with joy, singing to the sea from above."

"Night, Mom."

Her mother got up from the bed, went over to her dresser, and picked up the latest report from her doctor. Her frightened eyes followed the threatening words that screamed at her. They had to be silenced. She placed it in a drawer and grabbed a hairbrush before heading to her full-length mirror. After a few strokes, she tossed the brush on the bed and turned side-to-side, pressing her nightgown down against her thin body, forcing a brave smile. "You can do this. You *will* do this."

With a heavy sigh, she stepped into her walk-in closet, flicking on the light switch. Her eyes narrowed on a small wooden chest against the back wall. She made her way to it and sat down on the floor. Removing a skeleton key from her pocket, she opened the lock and flipped back the latch. She lifted the lid, then pulled out a smaller box wrapped in sequined fabric. The bright blue and green sequins flickered. Blowing the dust off the fabric, her face brightened.

As she removed the fabric, her heart raced, revealing the twelve-by-twelve glass box. Inside rested the cottage's heartbeat. The meaning of their bloodline. The glue that kept the women strong and close. Looking up at her was the mermaid crown, adorned with seashells, that Ida and her sisters had made in 1939. Dotted with pink and white pearls, calico shells, and tiny starfish, it had been first worn by Ida and her two sisters, and then by many women in the bloodline as the years passed.

Inside the ring of the crown was a worn, green velvet box. She reached in and picked it up. A chill rushed her as she opened it. The object seemed to smile at her as she held out her right ring finger and slid on the gold ring with a large pink pearl that found a home snug in its prongs.

Her mind took her back to a sacred August night. She was twelve years old, vacationing at the cottage with her mother and sisters. The sky dotted with glowing stars, and the balmy air was pleasant as calming waves rolled ashore in the moonlight.

On that night, while her feet were sinking into the cool sand, she learned of the mermaid crown as the bonfire's sparks met with the stars. The responsibility it carried and the respect it commanded.

As the beacon from the Hatteras lighthouse guided ships at sea, the women celebrated the magic the crown held.

Three

It was in the summer of 1939, on North Carolina's Hatteras Island, that it all began. The newly built Beach Heart Cottage, with its sturdy porches and large windows, provided breathtaking views of the Atlantic Ocean. Tucked between the natural vegetation and dunes, the cottage would embrace generations of family.

Ida and her sisters, Marie, and Dorothy had moved into the cottage with their parents. Ida's mother, a local seamstress for the Coast Guard, was never without mending. Her father, a fisherman, owned a fleet of small boats. Life was ordinary for the sisters. Attending the local school, fishing, playing tag, and helping with chores.

Ida, petite and always smiling, was a fearless adventurer. She was the oldest at seventeen. She used thin hemp rope to tie her wavy, light chestnut hair at the end, keeping it in a single braid. Marie, the middle sister with freckles and long saffron hair, had a passion for singing, sewing, and playing the piano. Dorothy, the youngest sister with lanky dirty blond hair, enjoyed painting portraits of locals, documenting the changing landscape, writing poetry, and recording tall tales in her journal.

The tradition began in August, two days after a hurricane had passed the Outer Banks and stirred the sea. As the sun rose, Ida and her sisters, carrying tin buckets, combed the beaches, seeking treasures along the storm-battered shore.

Fragments of whelks, augers, scotch bonnets, and Ida's beloved pink calico scallops were abundant. A few broken sand dollars and colorful bits of glass found a home in her bucket. Ida's bucket was brimming. She knew it was time to return to the cottage and begin her chores. Gingerly, she stepped around the waterlogged debris. She could not help but reach down and pick up some more unique shells.

She was about to pick up a broken sand dollar when Marie shouted, "Ida! Ida! Look what I found!" Marie waved a large black whelk in the air. "Hurry, there may be more."

With a smile and a tight squint, Ida rushed over, splashing through the water, chasing away hungry sandpipers.

Dorothy was busy following a chubby sand crab when she noticed Ida running toward Marie and joined them. "What is all the hubbub about?" Dorothy asked, as one of her sand crabs found its way out of her bucket and skittered off.

"Oh, look, look how big it is! I saw this whelk and had to catch it. There are more, I know it." Marie dipped her shell into the water, washing off the sand. Her eyes sparkled at her find. "It's grand! Why is the inside orange?" She held it up to the sun. "Imagine the life it had under the sea."

Ida gleefully gazed out at the sea, then back to her sister. "It's beautiful, Marie!" She backed away from an incoming wave. "A real keeper for the cottage." She looked up at the sun and at her sisters. "It's a glorious morning and I love it here with all my heart!" she cried out, slowly spinning around as sea foam from a receding wave tickled her ankles. "Put the shell to your ear and close your eyes. Daddy said you can listen to the sound of the ocean."

Marie's hair blew across her face as she pressed the whelk to her ear. "I *can* hear the ocean. It sounds like a beautiful song. It is as gentle as the tip of an angel's wing." She said as she swayed, closing her eyes.

Dorothy frowned, creasing her forehead. "Of course, you can hear it, silly. The ocean is right next to you. Look." She pointed at Marie's feet. "And thanks to you, one of my crabs escaped."

Marie's eyes popped open as she stuck her tongue out. "Oh, hush. I can hear a siren's song. And I'm glad he got away. Tying a crab to a string and parading it around is not normal."

"If I can't have one of the neighbor's new puppies, then I will have a crab!" Dorothy forced a smile as her eyes narrowed on the find. "Okay, that is a pretty shell you found. Can you really hear a siren's song?"

"Yes, and her voice is soothing, as if she's a gentle angel. The angel's mama talks about when we say our nighttime prayers."

"Ida, Marie is making up stories again! The only angels singing is in church, not in a seashell." Dorothy, the grand tattletaler, snickered, holding her bucket filled with oyster shells and wilted dead crabs. She watched her silly sister press the whelk shell against her ear, then looked over at the cottage and back at her sisters. "Ida, Marie, I have an idea. Let's give the cottage, our home, a name." She put her bucket down and dipped her hands into the waves to wash the sand off. "Daddy worked hard to build the cottage with love for us and Mama."

"What a splendid idea, Dorothy. What are you thinking?" Ida asked, holding her hand over her brow as a receding wave tugged her feet deeper into the sand.

Dorothy looked up at the sun and then back at her sisters. "This is our home now. It's where our love will shine, and we can bring our husbands, children, and their children. It warms my heart. How about... hmmmm?" She tapped her cheek. "Beach Heart Cottage?"

"Oh, yes! I *love* it!" Marie cried out and splashed the remains of a wave on her sisters. "What do you think, Ida?"

Ida slapped her hands over her heart. "Yes, yes, and Daddy will love it, too. *Beach Heart Cottage,* it is."

Marie spotted a broken piece of wood by a battered dune and dashed off. She returned and drew a large heart in the sand. "Let's make a sister circle and stand inside the heart."

With squinting smiles, they stepped in. Their salty hands met as Marie cleared her throat. "Thank you, Hatteras, for allowing us to be here. Thank you, Sea, for the fish you provide us. Thank you, Sand, that holds us up. Thank you, Sun, which warms us, and the stars at night that guide us. And lastly, thank you for the wood that built our cottage. And thank you for each of us, for sisters. Our sisterhood. May we laugh, love, and cry at our Beach Heart Cottage. Oh, one more thing, Dorothy likes skinny Tommy Bob up the road, and I hope they get married cause she is cranky and plays with stinky crabs." Marie looked up as Dorothy stuck out her tongue and kicked sand at her.

Ida reminded them, with a heartfelt smile, "Don't forget to be thankful for Mama and Daddy."

They threw their hands in the air and spun around while their parents watched from the porch. The sisters cheered until Ida saw something brown bobbing in a rolling wave and followed it as it came close to shore.

"Those girls are up to something." Their mother folded her arms across her chest. With fondness, she looked at her husband. Finding his lips, she kissed him. "Time to start breakfast. Call the girls for chores."

"Yup, I gotta catch the sea-going bus to the Oregon Inlet ferry."

"Is it running after the storm?"

He watched a pelican skim a wave. "I suppose I will find out. I gotta be up in Elizabeth City by dark. The hardware store up there just received new rope, crab traps, and boat parts I need. Be home tomorrow late."

Her husband went over to an old ship bell he had attached to a post on the porch and rang it three times.

Dorothy looked up at the cottage. "Daddy wants us home. Come on, we have chores to do."

"In a minute." Ida focused on the dark brown bobbing object. She had to have it. Chasing it as each wave rolled in with a tease, it went back out to sea. Barefooted, Ida hiked up her skirt and made her way into the warm water just as a wave was aiming for her. She ran in as the wave broke and grabbed the glass object. With it in her hand, she dashed back to the shore as her sisters cheered.

Ida held her treasure up to the bright sun. Barnacles surrounded the bottle's swollen cork. The sisters' eyes lit up as Ida tipped it back and forth and gave it a shake. It tapped back. Something was inside! Could it be a message in a bottle? How ridiculous was that?

"It's ancient." Ida said as she studied the dark, pitted glass. "I think this is from a pirate ship."

"Blackbeard!" Marie cried out. "It's his rum bottle, filled with treasures and secrets of the sea." Her eyes narrowed on the bottle. "Oh, remember when Daddy told us that a

Spanish ship vanished offshore, taking a queen's dowry with it? What if it's from that ship?"

"Maybe! Let's get back to the cottage and open it," Dorothy suggested eagerly. "But don't tell Mama and Daddy. It's our secret."

Pressing their fingers to their lips, they nodded.

Clutching the mysterious bottle, Ida picked up her bucket of shells, and they made their way back to the cottage. Ida kept one arm behind her back and the other holding the bucket. Their parents observed the suspicious threesome scurry into the cottage amid giggles and whispers.

That night, after their mother went to bed, the sisters were determined to figure out how to open the bottle without breaking it. They held it up to the lantern light, only to find the glass was too dark to see what was inside. They used molasses, hot wax, and lard on the cork and neck of the bottle. They used plyers, and a fishing knife, all to no avail. The cork was stuck.

Frustrated, Ida pushed the bottle under an oak side table in the living room and sat on the floor with a lantern. She stared at it until her eyes were heavy. Giving it one last spin, she said goodnight to it and went up to bed.

Ocean breezes and the sound of crashing waves drove Ida into a sleepless night as she tossed and turned, much like the ocean. The bottle occupied her mind. What if the bottle belonged to Blackbeard? With sword in hand, would his tall, angry, headless ghost rise out of the waters of Ocracoke and make his way to Hatteras? What would he do if he found her? Pressing her eyes shut, curled up in a ball, she pulled her blankets over her head.

As the warm ginger sun rose, Ida woke up and stretched. It was six, and she needed to make the mile trek down the sandy road for fresh eggs. But Ida's first chore that morning was to check the bottle. Quietly, she made her way down the narrow wooden staircase, rubbing her eyes as early sunbeams passed through the windows, leaving the living room in a soft glow.

Ida stopped at the oak side table and kneeled. Her eyes landed on the bottle. Much to her surprise, it was open! She picked up the barnacle crusted cork and studied it. It appeared to have never been stuck. She went to look inside when something peeked out.

Above her, Marie whispered through the stair spindles. "Ida, what are you doing?"

"Shh," Ida put the bottle into the light of the morning sun. Softly, she whispered. "It's open, but how?"

Marie crept down the stairs and stood next to her. "Did Daddy open it?"

"Daddy is in Elizabeth City."

Marie's eyes grew wide. "I forgot. What is sticking out?"

"It looks like a piece of paper." She tipped the bottle back and forth. Something was rolling around.

"Well, take it out."

Ida hesitated. "It's peculiar, Marie. It popped open by itself. And the cork remains undamaged. The barnacles are intact." She turned to her sister. "How did this happen?"

"Ida, Blackbeard was here!" Marie rolled her lips. "We must toss it back into the ocean or he'll curse us. He will come looking for us!"

"Blackbeard is dead, and he has no head. How could he find his way here? And if Blackbeard's ghost wants the bottle, we'll give it back to him, but first, we have to read the note. Then we'll toss it out to sea."

"I suppose you're right. Pull out the paper, before tattletale Dorothy wakes up to grind the coffee beans." Marie glanced up the staircase and back to the bottle, wiggling her toes. "Hurry."

Ida felt the tip of the paper tickle her fingers. She pinched it and slid it out with ease.

With the bottle in hand, they made their way to the back porch. Ida was holding the bottle upright when the girls heard something. They peered down into the dark abyss.

Marie twisted her hands together. "Turn it over."

A round, brownish object rolled out onto the porch floorboards.

Marie's eyes narrowed on the object as it traveled in a small circle. "What do you suppose it is?" She picked it up. She looked at the crusty round object and wiped it against her nightgown. Pinched between her fingers in the morning sunlight slanting through the dunes, the pink opalescence of the object greeted them.

Ida's eyes grew wide. "I think it's a pearl! What should we do with it, Marie?"

"Put it back in the bottle. It belongs to a crazed pirate. Remember when Daddy told us of the terrible fortune if you find a pirate's treasure? And what if it is Blackbeard's?"

Ida twisted her lips. "No, this is not a pirate's treasure. It is a pearl that somehow got stuck inside a bottle during a storm."

Marie's eager eyes met Ida's. "Let's wash it off in the sink."

"First, I want to see if there's anything written on the paper," Ida unrolled the find. Her heart sped up.

Marie agreed as she tucked the pearl into the pocket of her nightgown. "Wait. Ida, if it fell into the bottle during a storm, how did the top get back on?"

"You ask too many questions."

The sisters sat on the wicker sofa as warm breezes and raucous seagulls woke Hatteras Island.

"Ready, Marie?"

Marie quivered, nodding as Ida delicately unfolded the brittle paper. Her eyes met the faded ink written in scroll script.

Ida handed it over to her sister. "What do you say? Should we read it?" She gave it back to Marie.

"I wonder if this is a treasure map," Marie said as she took the brittle paper.

Ida rubbed her hands together. "What if it is?"

"Let me read it." Marie's lips moved. "Well, this looks like it might be a spooky tale. I don't want to continue. Let's get rid of it. Where's the cork?" She got up.

"Stop it and sit down," Ida insisted as she reached for the paper. "What do you mean, spooky? And why throw it away?"

"I think we should put the cork back on and toss it into the ocean where it belongs." Marie struggled to smile as she looked at Ida. "It's a... how can I say this? It's about a mermaid, and she guards the waters off Hatteras Island. She is a ghost from long ago."

"No!" Ida bent over, covering her mouth, smothering her laughter. "The *ghost* of a mermaid? First, there is no such thing as a mermaid, no less her ghost. Keep reading. I bet there is a map to a chest filled with jewels, coins, and pearls."

Marie felt a chill creep up her arms and the back of her neck. She shook it off and continued. "It says there was a sailor on a ship in 1878. The ship had sunk off the shore during a storm off the island."

Ida looked out at the ocean. "How could that bottle have survived?" She crossed her arms, looking out at the ocean and back at her sister. "It must be a prank by those mean, smelly boys up the road."

"No, Ida, it's ancient. It says that the sailor loved her. An eternal love deeper than the ocean and brighter than the sun."

"Loved who? A ghost of a mermaid?"

Marie let out a sigh. "Yes, the mermaid. She rescued him amidst the devastating storm, leading him to safety on Hatteras Island, guided by the lighthouse beacon." Marie pursed her lips. "This is so beautiful, Ida. It is true love." She pressed the letter to her chest.

Ida twirled her long braid. "I bet Tommy Bob did this to get Dorothy's attention. A love letter he wrote to trick her."

"Trick who?"

Dorothy appeared!

"What are you two up to?" Dorothy crossed her arms. "Ida, it's time to get the eggs."

Ida looked up at her. "I will in a few minutes. Let the chickens lay more plump ones. The kind Mama likes. And if you must know, we are talking about Marie's crush on Arnold Simpson. You best start grinding the coffee beans."

"Ewe, Arnold, who snorts when he laughs. He reminds me of Miss Dixie's little pig. Oink, oink!"

"That's not nice," Marie scrunched her face. "I admit. He does laugh like a little piglet!"

"It's true, and Mama needs eggs, Ida, to make the pancakes, so you better get going. And you both need to grow up." Dorothy crinkled her nose as she shuffled back inside the cottage, glancing over her shoulder. "You are two peas in a pod of mystery."

"Whew, she's gone. We don't want her blabbing our secret around," Ida whispered. "Is that all? Come with me to get the eggs and tell me more."

As they went down the sandy road, Marie continued reading. "The mermaid brought this sailor to the surface and to shore during a storm like the one we just had. He wrote that it was a full orange moon in August when she kissed his cold, salty lips to wake him up."

"Go on! This is so romantic! Wait. Orange moon?"

Marie shrugged. "She told him her name was Seraphina." Slowly, she sounded out the name. "Seraphina is a mermaid who swims the waters off Hatteras around the time of large swells and Gail Force winds that toss and sink the strongest of ships. She brings struggling sailors to shore and sings into their souls." Marie looked out at the ocean. "Imagine if this were true?"

"True? It sounds like a child's fable, don't you think?" Ida tapped Marie's arm. "Keep reading anyway."

"Stranded, this sailor was on the island with other sailors who swam to shore. At night, huddled around a fire, they could hear the mermaid singing out over the waves. And in the lighthouse's beam, her shimmering tail was flipping close to the shore." Marie looked at Ida and whispered, "I am in love with this sailor."

Ida giggled. "Do you think he was handsome? I bet his eyes were as blue as the sky, with pools of navy blue deeper than the ocean." She leaned her head on Marie's shoulder, closing her eyes. "His lips are as soft as a summer breeze and tickle like the foam of a wave."

"Oh, Ida, how I want to meet him. And Seraphina is beautiful, with long, golden, red, and brown hair braided with seaweed. I bet her eyes were the most brilliant emerald green and as big as clamshells. And she lives in a castle of pink coral and plays with giant seahorses."

Ida gazed out at the ocean. "I bet Seraphina wore pearls she found in lost treasure chests at the bottom of the sea." A chill rushed around her body as her eyes twinkled. "That's where the pearl came from! A treasure from deep in the sea. Maybe from the shipwreck the sailor was in."

Marie broke Ida's revere. "Ida, stop being so silly and kissing the air."

Ida's eyes twinkled. "I'm in love with the sailor. Go on, read."

"Me too!" Marie felt a chill as she continued. "One night, under the full moonlight, the sailor, named Erasmus, after hearing singing, ventured out into the ocean, into the breaking waves. He was pulled under the water, where he found his lips pressed onto Seraphina's. She cried and begged him to go back to the shore. She put the pink pearl in his hand and whispered if they were to be together, the pearl would find her. He did return, only to tell his tale to his fellow sailors, who scoffed and laughed."

"Then what happened?" Ida asked.

"It was days later another ship rescued them. While on the ship, he wrote this letter and put the pearl and letter in the rum bottle. He then tossed it into the deep ocean in hopes she would find it. Once found, he would hear her siren song and come for her to be together forever. Even if he had to die to become one in spirit with her, he would."

Absorbed in the dreamy tale, Marie gently put the letter in her dress pocket as they collected the eggs and headed home, finding themselves on the back porch.

"Read the rest." Ida's eyes were eager.

"That's all he wrote." Marie placed the paper on her lap. "I guess she never found the bottle. He must have died broken-hearted."

"And now we have the bottle and pearl."

Marie noticed something on the other side. She flipped it over. "Look, it's a very faded drawing." She handed it to Ida. Ida pulled it close to her eyes.

"Why, it's not words, it's a drawing. It looks like a crown, a crown of seashells, with pearls and gems. It's so beautiful! There is something on the bottom. Can you read it?"

Marie squinted, reading. "Seraphina, I made this crown for you and left it on Hatteras Island, knowing I will find you and our souls will be one."

"Here? On the island? Does it say where?"

"Yes, Ida. By the lighthouse."

A soft breeze picked up. The oyster shell wind chimes Dorothy had made clattered. The sisters looked at the swaying shells and back to the faded drawing.

"Do you think this is a true story?" Ida whispered, with eyes that longed for it to be true.

"We need to go to the lighthouse later," Marie said, "and—"

"Ida, Marie, look!" Dorothy cried out as she dashed onto the porch and pointed at the ocean. "What is it?"

In a breaking wave, a large fishtail twinkled in the sun and flipped around, sprinkling the waves. Its aquamarine, gold, and teal blue colors were unlike anything the girls had ever seen. It went underwater and resurfaced near the shore, where the tail fluttered slowly over the tips of the waves.

The girls raced down the sandy path to the breaking waves. The flashy tail dove under and came up one more time. A beautiful, high-pitched voice seemed to carry over the tips of the waves.

"Seraphina!" Ida gasped. "She's here!"

Marie cried as she placed her hands over her heart. "Ida, it's true, the story is true! Seraphina is here after the storm."

"What are you talking about?" Dorothy asked as she met them on the path.

"She's looking for Erasmus," Ida said dreamily. "She heard us reading the letter. We have her pearl."

"What are you talking about? You girls and your imagination." Dorothy headed back to the cottage.

"Oh, the coffee smells wonderful, Dorothy." Their mother stopped at the open porch door. Yawning, she looked past the dunes. "What are those girls up to?"

"I don't have a clue. They are being their silly selves. Will Daddy be home today?"

Her mother ran her hand through Dorothy's long hair and pulled it off her shoulders. "Tonight, I hope. He will be home late, with new crab traps and nets." She heard Ida calling out over the ocean. "What is that girl up to?"

"We saw a whale or a dolphin tail. It was so beautiful and so close to shore." Dorothy rested her head on her mother's arm. "They sure have been acting strange. Marie even went to get the eggs with Ida."

They watched the silly sisters dancing on the sand. Their mother sighed, then shouted, "Time for pancakes, girls! Come on up here now." She rang the ship bell.

Early the following morning, as mermaid tales were told, the sisters celebrated Seraphina's and Erasmus's love. The tale even intrigued Dorothy.

Later that day, as the sun warmed the island and their hearts, it began. The girls spent hours at the lighthouse in search of the crown. Empty-handed and disappointed, they came up with a plan.

Ida took shells from her collection and Marie removed beads from an old necklace. When they read the letter to Dorothy and made her promise not to tell anyone, she gathered vines and flowers. It was at that point that the mermaid crown was created. Marie was busy sewing mermaid costumes adorned with beads and sequins. Along with a yearly mermaid celebration under the stars, they hoped Seraphina would return.

The sisters eventually had the single pearl made into a beautiful ring that each new mermaid would wear until they passed it to the next. As each sister turned thirty-five, they placed the crown on the newest mermaid and they gave her a special name. A mermaid name. Once she stepped into Beach Heart Cottage, that became her only known name. Whether a fabricated fable by three sisters, passed down, they celebrated it with love and care.

Caroline would be next to wear the great-grand sister's crown and slide the pearl ring over her finger as the sparks of the bonfire reached for the orange (blood) moon. It was said that you would find joy and eternal love.

The August winds whispered, anticipating the next mermaid, while the lighthouse beacon guided those at sea. Those who stayed at the Beach Heart Cottage for the annual ceremony swore that if you listen as the wind caress the sea, you may hear Seraphina's delicate voice.

Four

"Mom, how many suitcases do you need?" Caroline focused on her mother as she wheeled the last one out to the SUV. She held up five fingers. "Really, Mom."

"Yes, really. This is it, honey. Grams Dorea is on her way out."

"Mom, we're heading to Hatteras, not boarding the Queen Mary."

"Oh, stop it. You know I like to be in style. Be back in a minute. I almost forgot the most important thing." Moments later, she came out, carrying a brown wooden box. "Caroline, look what I have!" The sequins glimmered in the morning sun.

"Here we go," Caroline muttered. "The Hatteras mermaid folly madness."

Petite Grams Dorea, in her floral dress and sunglasses, leaning on her cane, looked toward Caroline. From under her wide brimmed straw hat, her white hair peeked out. "Did you say something, honey?"

"No, Grams Dorea." Caroline wiped the sweat off her forehead. "It's so humid."

"You have air conditioning in that fancy foreign car, don't you? I can't be in this heat for long periods of time. I'll get a rash."

"Of course, Grams Dorea. And you sit in the front. No rashes, I promise." Caroline was used to her grandmother's unfiltered remarks.

Her mother rolled her eyes and instructed. "Caroline, put the special mermaid box on the floor in the back. And be careful with it. It's very fragile."

"I got it, mom!" Caroline did so, then put on her sunglasses and got behind the wheel. She inhaled, stretching wide, wiggling her fingers, and let out a long needed ahh. Finally, her list of the good life was being checked off. Beach vacation, no dictator boss, new business, and a new partner.

At noon, they entered the left lane of Route 12 in Nags Head, following the familiar sign to Hatteras Island National Sea Shore. Caroline could feel her body decompress once they passed the Oregon Inlet as her tires found the concrete of the bridge that spanned the Atlantic Ocean and Pamlico Sound. With the windows rolled down, they smiled as the sea air rushed over them. Seagulls circled fishing boats as pelicans skimmed the tip of the water. Island time was not far away.

"Caroline," her mother was leaning forward from the back seat, "you know how great granddaddy used to tell us stories of life on Hatteras, back in the thirties?"

"You have mentioned a few of them, Mom."

Her mother pointed out at the emerald waters as they crossed the bridge. "There was a two-car ferry that took great granddaddy and his family across the water. Talk about patience."

Grams Dorea nodded. "It was twenty-five cents back then and took some time to cross."

"And only in pleasant weather!" Caroline noted. "Gramps used to tell me tales from his dad when we would vacation when I was young. Life was tough. They were tough people."

"Yes Caroline. You come from a tough lineage. We know how to survive," Grams Dorea nodded as she rubbed her arms. "I'm cold. Turn the AC down."

Caroline did. "We are almost at the cottage, Mom. I cannot wait to see everyone, and the weather is gorgeous!" Caroline ran her fingers through her hair as she looked at Grams Dorea. "Mom, Grams Dorea, can you feel it?"

"Sure, honey, sure," her mother nodded. The letter with those destructive words tucked in her dresser drawer troubled her. She gripped her daughter's shoulder. "I need this vacation more than you know. Your father always said I was a different person when I returned home from Hatteras."

"We all were," Grams Dorea agreed. "And I need to pee."

Caroline glanced at Grams Dorea. "We're close. Can you hold it?"

Grams Dorea squirmed in her seat. "I hope so. Thank God you have leather and I have a new hip." She burst into laughter as they all joined in.

"Should we call Auntie Jean to let her know we are almost there?" Caroline asked as she watched a pelican glide over the top of a party fishing boat.

"No, honey, I'm sure she and Earl are busy getting the cottage ready. And remember, she is Auntie Lorelei. And I'm Halia. We all use our mermaid names once we cross the threshold of the cottage."

"Except me," Grams Dorea said. "I am always Grams Dorea. And except you, Caroline, because you don't have one yet, but you will, soon. Before the August full moon fades."

The aunties had taken part in the rituals most of their lives, given their mermaid names as each one turned thirty-five. A request that was stated in Ida's will when she left the cottage to her daughters. Jean, the oldest, with her dyed, mid-length, wavy ginger-blond hair, was the spitfire of the sisters. Never married, and a retired nurse was now a Reiki and spiritual healer. She is Lorelei.

The next aunt, Kathy, with her blazing dyed auburn hair, was a gossiper and worrywart. She was also a chatterbox. Married and the owner of several hair salons and day spas. Her nails, hair, and makeup are always flawless. Her crowned name is Calypso.

Shirley always kept her black hair in a pixie cut. Petite, with a sparkling smile, had owned a landscaping and construction company with her late husband. They crowned her Pearl.

Caroline's mother, Margaret, the youngest of the four sisters, kept her blonde hair shoulder-length and makeup always on. Once a host to her husband's high society political pals, she had spent much of her life campaigning with her late husband. She is crowned Halia, which means the remembrance of a loved one.

"Mom. I nearly forgot. We all lose our identity and our minds once we cross the bridge."

"I will ignore that," her mother said. "This is so special for you. We will celebrate your birthday on this trip."

"Mom, don't remind me. I'm getting fillers for my birthday."

Grams Dorea turned to Caroline. "Oh, for heaven's sake, you don't need to make yourself look like a plastic clown. Leave your face alone. You are a Woodard, not a mannequin."

"I agree, honey."

"Mom, I'm kidding."

"Enjoy your youth, my dear granddaughter." Grams Dorea shook her head. "Wrinkles are the map of life's journey. The roads of love, sorrow, and joy we travel. Look at my face and you will see I have traveled the world of life and to the moon and back."

Caroline looked over at her. "I know, Grams Dorea. How many trips around the world have you traveled? Looks like a lot! I'm thirty-six in two weeks."

"Always a brat. Eyes on the road." Grams Dorea blew a kiss.

"Now, thirty-five is *young*," her mom reminded her. "Wait until you get to be in your late fifties, like the rest of us on the trip. Hot flashes, belly fat, body aches."

"Fifties? Try seventy-eight or nine. Oh, heck, I forgot." Grams Dorea chuckled. "I'm getting shorter. My hair is white as snow, and my legs swell up, and now my parts are being replaced. And FYI, young lady, you need a man soon, and we need a baby. I need another great grand baby before I die. It's your turn."

Caroline shook her head, knowing she had two weeks of this chatter ahead of her. Ignoring the baby comment, she said, "Last September you turned seventy-eight on your birthday, Grams Dorea. And I'm in no hurry, and you will not die anytime soon." She pressed the accelerator as she drove on the infamous ribbon of sand. Her mind drifted between the presidential election, her new partnership, and a cottage full of her chatting women. "Have you heard from my aunties?" she asked as she observed all the RVs heading north.

Her mother cleared her throat. "Yes, they will be here later tonight. Auntie Lorelei arrived two days ago. Remember the rules: shoes off, flip-flops on. Auntie Lorelei made us decorative flip flops for this year in rainbow mermaid colors with painted shells."

"Mermaid flip-flops? I'm sure she was busy with her metallic paints, sewing machine, beads, and shells all winter."

"Caroline, if she desires to paint flip flops and glue shells to them, so be it. Honey, you need to chill out. Gosh, you are so tense."

"And sarcastic," Grams Dorea injected. "Stop it *now*, young lady."

Caroline tapped the steering wheel with her thumbs. "I know, Mom, and I'm sorry, Grams Dorea. Time to relax. This election campaign has me on edge. I promise to lighten up."

"Good, no grumps on this trip. I hope you will not be glued to that phone and laptop," Grams Dorea said as she adjusted her seat. "Caroline, please close your window. It's hot and windy." She remained silent for a moment as she faced Caroline. "That senator won't be pestering you, will he?"

Caroline closed the window and answered. "Grams Dorea, I must work on the election, but I promise only a few hours a day. And *he* is my client. If I don't, then I must be back in DC," she smiled pleasantly at her grandmother. "I promise to limit work time."

Grams Dorea raised her thin eyebrows. "Can we bet on it?"

"Maybe."

"Vacation is vacation. I told your mother that years ago when she was married to Mr. Big Shot Senator. He never wanted to get away. His vacation was his office with the other cronies."

There was a moment of awkward silence. Grams Dorea had never cared for Caroline's father or politics.

Caroline's eyes found the rear-view mirror. Her mother shook her head, changing the subject. "It's too bad your cousin Tracy couldn't make it. It is her responsibility to crown you since she was the last one to receive it."

"Mom, no way can she come down to the island eight months prego with twins." Caroline looked back at the road. "I spoke to her last week. They confined her to bed with water retention and high blood pressure." *Better her than me,* she thought.

Her mother ran her fingers through her hair. "Yes, I know. Her husband gave me the crown box weeks ago. I did promise I would have the honor of placing the crown on you and giving you your mermaid name."

Caroline wondered if it was for fun born of a fable, or was it what kept the family together? Seriously, how many families wear mermaid costumes, dance around a bonfire in the middle of the night and wear a crown of shells?

"I know, Mom. You told me we will hear the siren song down those blue mermaid martinis as Auntie Lorelei tosses whatever chemicals she uses to make the bonfire flames turn colors. Ta da!"

"Oh, that reminds me. I need to stop at the grocery store and get a few things, and I need to go to the ABC store for our mermaid martini ingredients." Her mother took out a shopping list. "Do you need anything, honey?"

"Just a little peace and quiet, Mom. I'm sure metallic flip-flops and rainbow drinks rimmed in colorful salt will seduce the mysterious mermaid."

"Seraphina!" Grams Dorea cheered. "I have dreamed of seeing her since I was a child. She *will* surface this year; I feel it in my bones."

"Who?" Caroline squirreled up her face.

"The mysterious mermaid written in the letter. Her name is Seraphina."

Caroline rolled her eyes as her phone rang on the SUV's blue tooth. Wilmen's name throbbed on the screen. She shook her head and cursed under her breath. Her neck and face tightened.

"Aren't you going to answer it?"

"No Mom. I'm done with that jerk." She let it go to voicemail.

"Will you lighten up, Caroline? You've had a chip on your shoulder since you picked us up this morning. I almost forgot to tell you. Yesterday I saw on the Early Dawn Show that Senator Jameson is bouncing back, and you should be happy." She tapped Caroline's shoulder. "Are you going to take him to your new firm? You should. Remember when you dated him? You had love in your eyes."

"Mom. Too much information. Not now. Okay?"

Her mother sighed. "Your father knew he would run for president." Her mother looked out over at the waters of the sound. "He's perfect husband material. And he's right for the country. And the country needs a first lady who had a prominent father, who has shaken the hands of many presidents and met with foreign leaders. You two were so in love. What happened?"

"Mom, that is old news, and that was years ago. Now my job is getting him into the Oval Office, not standing by his side in it."

"Caroline, you need to settle down with a man outside of politics," Grams Dorea said with a rigid smile. "*All politicians lie.*" She turned to look at her daughter in the back seat.

"Not true, Mom," Halia replied quickly.

Caroline shook her head. "How about we be on vacation and no talk of politics? I'm the one who has a plate full of it."

Grams Dorea had to have the last say. "Did you see the cover of one of those magazines by the checkout at the grocery store? Your Senator Jameson in the arms of that reality tramp? The one who made a nude video and was married to that mobster," Grams Dorea said as she held back a smile. "The mobster who was gunned down while shopping for new shoes."

"Grams Dorea, ha ha. It is called photoshopping, and I nixed it. There is no reality star, no mobsters, no murders, no videos." Caroline sighed, knowing all too well Grams Dorea liked to stir the pot. "It's all fabricated by his rival. You, if anyone, should know that."

Caroline's mother reached over and patted her shoulder. "Your father believed strongly in him. He knew he would go places. A single president is *not* what this country needs."

Grams Dorea added. "They're all bloodsucking villains, single or not."

"Mom, Grams Dorea, stop. I have a lot on my mind, and Wilmen has the balls to call me. We are done with this conversation. We're at the beach and here to celebrate."

"I agree." Caroline's mother nodded. "Truce."

"Zipped." Grams Dorea ran her index finger along her lips.

Caroline pulled up to the ABC Liquor Store and parked. Her mother took out her shopping list. "I need to get pirate rum, coconut rum, blue curacao, and Auntie Lorelei got the green and blue salt. She also brought red and yellow hibiscus plants. They're full of blooms to garnish our libations. I'm already thirsty!"

"Wow, mermaid party, full speed ahead!" Caroline looked at her mother in the rear-view mirror. "I know you were a wild teenager. And worse in college."

She laughed. "You have no idea, honey. You know, I met your father at a Rolling Stones concert. He sat next to me with his college party pals. He was so handsome and high as a kite, and I flew with him." She wore a reminiscing smile. "And what a kisser. You have his eyes and his business mind."

"Mom, you've told me about a hundred times."

"I miss him, honey. It's been three years, and it seems like yesterday since he left us to be in heaven." She tapped the window. "He always thought we were crazy women coming down here for our getaway while he stayed up in DC, schmoozing with other politicians. He did so much for this country." She sighed. "He fought so many battles and won all except for a diseased heart."

"I know, Mom. How about you get what we need for our mermaid party?"

Her mother agreed. "Be right out. Do you need anything, Mother?"

"Just a toilet," Grams Dorea said, watching her daughter go into the ABC store. "I say no more." She folded her hands in her lap and turned to Caroline. "Don't you dare get romantically involved with Senator Jameson again? He will hurt my baby." She leaned over. "I love you, honey. No man is worth the pain he put you through."

"I love you, too, Grams Dorea. Don't worry about me. I'm a lot tougher than Mom. Can we leave it there?"

"Yes. But I have to say one more thing. You are tougher and smarter."

Caroline nodded as she paid attention to the picnic tables occupied by people enjoying fish tacos and downing cold, frothy beer. Her stomach growled just as her phone buzzed with a text. She picked it up. Her new partner welcomed her. As she read, her smile morphed into a frown when she saw that Senator Jameson had just phoned to let him know he would stay with Wilmen until they proved themselves worthy. She knew what *worthy* meant. So that's why Wilmen had phoned her earlier. To boast of his victory. The text ended with: We need this, Caroline.

She tapped her top lip, thinking about what to answer.

"Is everything all right?"

"All good, Grams Dorea."

She texted:

I'm on it, Gary. Give me a few hours.

I'm driving. Jameson did not re-sign with Wilmen.

I know that for sure. He is ours.

Wilmen can stick it.

Wilmen is all talk, rattling my cage.

He thinks this is a game of chess.

Check mate. Jameson is ours.

She hit send.

Five

Caroline made the left turn onto Sea Glass Lane. As the tires met the crushed shells, she put her window down, allowing the soothing ocean breezes to caress her. There it stood, wearing a welcoming smile. The Beach Heart Cottage.

Caroline stopped the car. "Ahhh...we're here! I'm so happy!"

"I can't hold it!" Grams Dorea grabbed her cane and swung the car door open. She made her way to the front porch, opened the door, and vanished inside as Auntie Lorelei slid past her.

"Hi, Mom. Bye, Mom," Auntie Lorelei laughed as she stepped out onto the deep, inviting front porch. Behind her, Wilbur barked at them. "Guess Grams Dorea's new HurryCane has put a bounce in her step."

"It sure has! As did her new hip," Halia agreed as she opened her car door and inhaled. "It's so good to be on Hatteras, girls! Can you feel it?"

Lorelei's freckled face beamed in the sun. "Yeah, and get your butts out of that car." Her newly pink-dyed hair mingled with the remains of ginger in the long braid that traveled down her back. Wearing an embroidered white tunic, wide khaki linen pants, and flip-flops, she rushed over to the vehicle. "Welcome! Oh, how I missed you both!" She glanced over her shoulder at the cottage. "And Grams Dorea."

Wagging his tail, Wilbur sniffed Halia's legs and trotted back into the cottage.

Caroline got out, stretching as she inhaled the briny sea air.

Auntie Lorelei gave her a warm hug. "You look marvelous." Her eyes met Caroline's. "You are our next mermaid. Oh, how the sisters are glowing with delight. I finished a splendid meditation at sunrise on the very spot Ida found the bottle. She wants *me* to tell you they are full of joy that you are here. I just finished the last of the sequins on your mermaid dress. I can't wait to see you wear the crown!"

Caroline gave her aunt a kiss on the cheek, ignoring the bit about the deceased aunties glowing in delight and a sequined disco mermaid dress.

"Lorelei," Halia cheered as she got out of the car. "I've missed you and this place!" They hugged. "How is my sister on this glorious August day?"

"I'm over the moon, sun, and stars." Lorelei pulled Caroline close, and the three hugged.

"Caroline, I have a basket of mermaid flip-flops with our names on them by the front door. And, my dear niece, you are Caroline until we crown you under the full moon. And according to my calendar, that is in ten days when we reveal your mermaid name." Happily, she clapped her hands. "This is so wonderful!"

Caroline gave a slight tilt of her head. "Sounds delightful. Hey, let's get the luggage inside and I need a nice, tall, cold lemonade to start my vacation."

"Perfect. I made a fresh squeezed brew this morning just for you. I added the raw brown sugar you prefer, and how about a shot or two of Tito's in it?" Lorelei's eyes lit up as she said. "After your trip with Grams Dorea, you need two shots!"

Caroline smiled. "Awesome!"

"Wait 'til you see the ice cubes I made using organic blue and green food coloring! They look like real scallop shells and starfish."

"Wow, Auntie Lorelei, let the vacation begin! And make it with two shots. It *was* a long drive with all the stops Grams Dorea needed."

"Girls!" Grams Dorea called from the front porch. "Let the celebrations begin! I'll be on the back porch in my chair. Lorelei, is there cold beer in the fridge? And Caroline, bring in my bags."

"Of course, Mom, there's beer. I got you, Bud bottles." Auntie Lorelei said, as she rolled her eyes. "Grams Dorea and her beer. She seems happy. She usually gets so melancholy the first few days."

"Grams Dorea told me last week she feels Grandpop is in the cottage," Caroline mentioned softly. "That could be why she is so happy. She's near his ashes."

Auntie Lorelei looked over her shoulder and back to Caroline. "She spent all her summers here with him. The last trip down here, all she did was stare at his ashes on the mantel as she sat in his old recliner. She chatted to him as if he were beside her."

Caroline removed her sunglasses and looked toward the cottage. "We need to keep her spirits up."

"Uh... speaking of spirits, we need to talk about Grandpop's ashes." Auntie Lorelei dropped her head and backed up, twisting her lips. "We had a slight accident yesterday."

Halia's eyes widened as she asked. "What accident? Are you okay?"

"Yes, oh, never mind." Auntie Lorelei gave a wave of her hand as she looked over at the cottage and went back to Halia. "It's nothing."

"No, *not* never mind, you brought it up now. Finish it." Halia insisted. "Well?"

"Please don't get upset or angry. It was an accident. It could happen to anyone."

Caroline tilted her head. "It can't be that bad. Can it?"

"Well, you know our kindhearted, wonderful cat-rescuing neighbor, Earl?"

"Weird Earl?" Caroline and her mother replied in unison.

"I was helping him carry the air conditioning unit from the shed into the house for Grams Dorea's bedroom. The large one. Well," she wrung her hands, "he tripped over Wilbur and crap happens."

"What crap happened?"

Her eyes met Halia's. "First, Earl stumbled over Wilbur's chew bone, then Wilbur lunged forward to save it and Earl stepped on Wilbur's front paw. Good golly did that dog yelp! I screamed, Earl panicked, and his foot slid off his flip-flop." She put her hands on her hips. "I feel terrible."

"Did Earl break his leg?" Caroline's eyes grew wide. "Did he?"

"Oh no, he's fine. I had set Grandpop's urn on the old piano by the window since I was dusting earlier. The darn urn landed on the area rug when Earl stumbled and fell into the piano keys. It tipped over and the lid flew off. We had the windows open, and a breeze snaked in. I swear a cloud of ashes blew across the room as if his ghost swirled around." She looked at Halia. "Daddy was everywhere. I think he is in the sofa cushions and the area rugs."

Caroline put her hand over her mouth, stifling her laughter. "Grandpop's ashes blew around the room?"

"Yes! Poor Wilbur, Earl yelled at him like there was no tomorrow, and dragged his motley butt outside and hosed his mouth out. He swallowed some ashes; I just know it." Lorelei looked over at the cottage and back at Caroline. "In retrospect, it was funny. Go ahead and laugh!"

Halia chuckled as she took her sister's hand. "Oh, now Daddy will find his way out of Wilbur's back end." She burst into tearful laughter.

"Or haunt us through ole' Wilbur," Caroline smiled.

Auntie Lorelei did not find it funny. "Do you know how many times I have told Grams Dorea to put him in a metal box with a screw-on lid? But no, she had to keep Grandpops in that aqua blue glass Ball canning jar with the loose zinc lid. I told her it was not the best decision. All I got was the stink eye."

Caroline put on sunglasses. "A canning jar? Not an urn?"

"Grams Dorea and your grandfather loved to can muscadine preserves here at the cottage. And wild blueberry jam with blueberries they got from a farm stand. It's nostalgia for her."

With a fond expression, Caroline looked at her Aunt Lorelie. "That is a beautiful story!"

Halia had to ask, "Is Wilbur's paw okay? Is Earl okay? And did you sweep Pop's ashes under the area rug?"

Auntie Lorelei's face lightened as she held back her own laughter. "For heaven's sake, no. Daddy is not under the rug. We swept up, used the hand vac, and put back into the urn what we could. Earl took a pile of ashes from the fireplace, and we emptied the vacuumed contents into it to make the jar look full. We vacuumed and wiped down the rest. It's a very fine dust, you know, and impossible to gather up. I did not know how messy Dad is." She shook her head. "Do you know Grams Dorea keeps his wedding ring in that jar?"

Caroline shuddered. "That's creepy."

Halia's mouth dropped open. "You vacuumed our father's ashes and mixed them with the remains of a fire. That is hysterical." She leaned against the SUV and laughed so hard her ribs hurt. "I need to give Wilbur a kiss! I'll buy him a new bone. Daddy loved to joke around. He must be up in heaven belly laughing."

"Halia, it was something else! And by the way, Earl feels terrible. Wilbur has a slight limp in his left front paw. Earl took him to the vet this morning and thankfully, no bones broke. Earl feels so bad he bought Wilbur a ribeye steak."

"Wow, a ribeye." Caroline shook her head. "Only at the Beach Heart Cottage!"

They broke into contagious hilarity as tears ran down their cheeks. That was until Grams Dorea appeared at the front door.

"Girls, I'm hungry. I need to eat soon and have my nap. Is the cable turned on? QVC is having a therapeutic sandal show at three-thirty."

"Yes, Mom, the cable is on," Auntie Lorelei replied, nodding. "Sandals. Velcro ones, I bet." She looked at Caroline. "How was the ride down here with Grams Dorea?"

Caroline sighed. "It wasn't as bad as you think. After several bathroom stops, we were back on the road."

Halia rolled her eyes. "It was not as bad as it has been. Thankfully, we brought a case of beer. That will make her happy. Daddy loved to drink beer with Mom when they were here."

"I recall. Mom loves her beer at the beach, cornmeal-floured fried pickles with hot sauced sour cream, and shrimp macaroni salad with pimentos," Lorelei cheered. "If it makes mom happy, then we all are happy."

Caroline opened the liftgate to get the luggage. "Auntie Lorelei, I brought a jug of pickles from Costco and a pound of cornmeal. This will keep Grams Dorea busy frying them."

"Splendid, I'll clean up the old cast iron pan."

The threesome smiled at each other as a gentle breeze tickled the sea oats. In the distance, the sounds of the ocean danced in the air. Caroline inhaled again, and with bags in hand, she made her way up the six sandy steps onto the deep front porch. The open wooden door painted in soft aqua welcomed her.

A weathered wooden sign to the left of the door framed in small seashells had a hand-painted message: *Only Mermaid Magic Happens Here. Just Believe!* In the days prior to the ceremony, the new mermaid-to-be is to ask the sea for a special shell. After the ceremony, she signs her name in white paint and glues the shell to it. It had been four long years since this had happened.

Caroline looked at the list of names, knowing the brushstrokes of her mermaid name would soon be visible. Maybe this would be a fun vacation after all. She needed to find that *special* shell.

The women removed their shoes by the front door, placing them in a wooden box, and slid their feet into the handcrafted mermaid flip-flops.

Auntie Lorelei wore a proud smile. "Oh, Caroline, the metallic aqua sandals dotted with pearls are yours."

"Thanks, Auntie Lorelei. My flip-flops are gorgeous!"

Caroline stretched her freed toes as her eyes adjusted to the honey-colored paneled entry that led to the open living and dining room. At the far end of the living room sat the worn, red brick fireplace. Seeing the Ball jar urn on the mantle, she elbowed her mother. Lorelei put her finger to her lips.

"By the way, Earl put all new hooks here in the entry and added this small bench." Auntie Lorelei pointed at the mermaid shaped hooks. "They are perfect!"

"Whew. It's hot in here!" Caroline fanned her face. "I can bake a potato in this room."

"I know it's an inferno. Go stand in front of the fan," Lorelei suggested. "The air conditioning unit that took the ill-fated tumble won't turn on. Earl is picking up new units today. You can make it until later, can't you?"

Caroline heeded her auntie's warning. "I will be fine. Sorry, I've had a stressful week. Add the ride here for six hours with-"

Caroline's mother shot her a look. *That* look. "One day, God willing, you will be in Grams Dorea's shoes, so clam up. Go unpack, put your bathing suit on, grab a glass of that spiked lemonade, and go down to the beach. I'll make your bed."

"Thanks, Mom, I can make my bed. I'll bring in my new linens. You get unpacked and comfortable, and I'll meet you down at the beach."

"What I need is a glass of ice water." Halia tapped her lips as she entered the kitchen.

Lorelei was about to go into the living room when she stopped. "I bought a canopy beach tent this year for Grams Dorea. Earl promised to set it up in the morning. The water is eighty-two degrees and clear as crystal, and all the beach umbrellas and chairs are in the shed. The shed key is in Ida's copper teapot in the pantry. Second shelf. Oh, your mom tells me you are working hard on Senator Jameson's campaign. She said you left the firm and are now a partner with someone else?"

"I left the firm, and yes, I'm now a partner of Lawson and Woodard." She wore a proud smile. "I enjoy saying *Lawson and Woodard*."

"That is wonderful news! I'm so proud of you. So, tell me, are you and Jameson an item again? He is such a catch."

"Yes, I'm working on his campaign, and *no*, we are *not* an *item*." She pressed her eyes shut for a second. "I have a lot going on. And Mom has a big mouth."

"Too bad." Auntie Lorelei's eyes met Caroline's. "He's so handsome and needs a first lady by his side if he wins. We need a woman like you in that White House with effervescence and a strong backbone. Your daddy would be proud."

"I'm sure he has a first lady already picked out. If not, maybe you should apply. I heard he may have a lottery. Buy your tickets now." Sweat was dripping down Caroline's neck, tickling her back.

"Always one with a fast answer. And honey, I'm too old. Too bad. Now don't forget, we have a meditation circle tonight at ten in the living room, to call in Ida and her sisters. I brought sage, white candles, and peach wine for the sisters that I brewed months ago just for this vacation. Oh, where is the box with the crown?"

Caroline picked up her carryall and headed up the narrow stairs. She stopped midway, looked up and whispered,

God help me with these crazy aunties, Grandmother, and my mother. "The box is on the floor by the back seat in my SUV. I'll get it in a few minutes ."

Auntie Lorelei walked over to the staircase and looked up. "Thank you, Caroline, for getting the crown box and everyone here safely. May I add once again, I'm so proud of you! Go down to the beach and chill out so you are fresh for tonight. Is your SUV unlocked? I'll go get the box. I need to put it over by the great aunties' picture to pick up their energy for tonight."

"It's unlocked, and I will make sure I stay up. Can I wear my PJs?"

"Of course. Now get out of here. And we have Wi-Fi. I know how hard you work and will need your computer."

"Thank you so much. I hate to admit it, but I have to work. Don't mention that to Grams Dorea."

"I know, honey, that's why I cleaned off great Grandpop's desk." She pointed to a corner of the living room. "It's waiting for you."

Caroline looked over to the space with a tall window and wooden vintage desk. She knew it would be so hard to work over there with everything going on around her. She said sweetly, not wanting to hurt her aunt's feelings. "Thank you so much."

"I got your back, honey. You are so much like your daddy," Lorelei tapped the newel post. "There's a surprise in your room."

Caroline made her way down the hall to the dormered bedroom that she had slept in every summer since she was a toddler. It had once been Ida and Marie's bedroom. Caroline loved knowing this; it kept a loving connection, or as Auntie Lorelei would say, *energy.*

Everything remained as if it were a tomb that was opened once a year. The crooked pine floor creaked. White beadboard walls peppered with various framed needlepoints gave the room comfort. Hanging on the walls were Dorothy's paintings. Her delicate brushstrokes brought to life many seaside landscapes and portraits of locals.

The cedar wood ceiling hosted a seasoned copper lantern. It hung above the full-sized white iron bed that was covered in a patchwork quilt. Nestled inside the dormer window was a cozy, blue-cushioned bench, lined with books she had read as a child. Next to it was the recent addition to the room, Auntie Lorelei's surprise. It was a small desk, painted a soft yellow. On top, in one of Ida's vintage vases, sat a thick bundle of colorful flowers.

Caroline put her bags down, went over to the desk, and found a note from Auntie Lorelei: *I found the desk at a garage sale and painted it, knowing it will allow you privacy to work in your room.*

Caroline opened the window to inhale the gentle sea breezes. Feeling something behind her, she turned around to find her mother standing in the doorway. "Hey, Mom. What's up? Mom?"

Halia wiped away a tear. "I love seeing you happy. I see my little girl running down the sandy path with her pink bucket, eager to collect shells, with her daddy not far behind." With a shaky smile, blowing a kiss, she continued to her room down the hall.

Caroline walked over to the door and leaned against the jamb, folding her arms. She had not seen her mother acting so nostalgic since her father had passed away. With a deep sigh, she went back into her bedroom. First on her list, turn on the fan. Next, text the senator.

Six

Caroline finished her emails and phone calls. Vacation time had started, and it was time to dig her toes into the silky sand. She grabbed her favorite beach chair and an umbrella from the shed. Tranquility awaited her as she walked down the sandy path. The sky was cloudless. Her eyes followed the rolling waves as she inhaled the coconut scent of suntan lotion that mingled with the distant sound of children's laughter.

"Yes!" she said as she descended the small slope onto the beach and found a perfect spot near the water. Sandbars became visible as the tide receded.

After applying a second layer of sunblock, she opened the umbrella, settled into her beach chair, and checked text messages. Nothing from Senator Jameson. No surprise. If there wasn't a fire in the building, he was not one to respond promptly. She put in her earbuds, only to listen to the voicemails that had piled up during the drive down to Hatteras. After the sixth one from Jameson's querulous campaign manager, she removed her earbuds and tossed her phone into her beach bag.

Time to chill out. She opened her cooler, removed her tumbler, and took a swig of the icy vodka lemonade. A few kids rode boogie boards, while others attempted surfing. She saw a set of sand crab eyes that popped up and quickly retreated.

A wet tongue startled her, causing her to jerk her head back and spill her drink. "Wilbur, gross! Get out of here!" She pushed him away. "Look at what you did. Naughty boy!" She slid her sunglasses down her nose. "Wilbur, you are gross!"

"Wilbur! Wilbur!" Grams Dorea was yelling and swaying her cane from beyond the dunes. "Get back here, you dumb dog!"

Wilbur, wagging his tail and barking at seagulls, dashed into a small breaking wave.

Auntie Lorelei, out of breath, was next to Caroline. She watched Wilbur romp in the ocean. "Sorry, Wilbur got out the back door to chase those darn seagulls. Grams Dorea left it open. I've told her a hundred times to shut the door. He must be on a leash down here." Lorelei glanced over her shoulder to find Grams Dorea standing on the path with one hand on her hip, the other leaning on her cane. "You know your grandmother, it's her way-"

"Or the highway," Caroline finished the saying, shaking her head. "It's going to be a fun time on the island."

"Good grief, you ain't kidding." Auntie Lorelei sheltered her eyes with her hands. "The sun is strong, honey. Did you put on plenty of sunblock?"

"Damn dog!" Grams Dorea yelled as she vanished up the path.

Caroline pulled her sunglasses down. "Yup, let the madness begin. Grams Dorea and Wilbur. That's a recipe for disaster! And, yes, I'm coated in a seventy sunblock."

"Grams Dorea knows what she's doing. She does these things to drive me crazy. She knows how to play me."

"Has she mentioned anything about Grandpop's ashes?"

"Gosh, no, Caroline. She had no clue and thankfully she has been busy rearranging the dishes and the pantry. The jar looks untouched. A little lighter, I'm sure, but untouched."

Wilbur came dashing toward them, shaking seawater and sand everywhere.

Caroline shielded herself with her hands. "Go away, you stinky mutt!"

"Look at yourself, Wilbur. I need to hose him down." Auntie Lorelei grabbed him by his collar. "Dinner at six-thirty. I picked up some fresh flounder at the fish market. Grams Dorea and I are making flounder almondine, and she wants me to take her to the farm stand for fresh peaches. Guess what's for dessert?"

"Yummy!" Caroline's stomach growled. "Ida's peach cobbler and vanilla ice cream. It is *so* good, and what can I make?"

"A fresh salad would be nice. We have all the fixings I picked up at the Farmers Market on the way down." Wilbur started barking at a flock of seagulls. "Oh, this dog. I gotta get him back up to the cottage. Enjoy!"

Caroline slid her sunglasses up her nose. Finally, a moment to herself. With her head back, she closed her eyes. It had been a long time since she took a vacation, no less felt the sun warm her body. The sound of the ocean and caressing breezes lulled her to sleep.

Caroline woke up as the remains of a wave tickled her toes. The tide was coming in. Half asleep, she leaned forward and yawned. She looked around. *What time is it?*

Reaching into her bag, she took out her phone. The time was four forty-nine. She tossed it into the bag and stretched. Two restful hours of napping were just what she'd needed. A wonderful, dreamless nap. With the advancing tide, it was time to retreat to the cottage.

Chair, bag, and umbrella in hand, she made her trek. Plopping her beach gear on the back porch, she went inside to chaos. It took her eyes a moment to adjust and figure out what the commotion was all about. Her other aunties had arrived.

"Oh, Caroline, dear, you are so beautiful! Kissed by the sun and sea." Auntie Calypso rushed over and kissed her, and stood back. "Auntie Pearl and I have just arrived. We are beyond thrilled to see you crowned!"

Caroline hugged Auntie Calypso. "Thank you, I'm thrilled, too. And glad you made it here safely. I need to take a shower. I'm sticky with sunblock and sand."

Auntie Calypso reached for Caroline's hair and pulled it forward. "Honey, your ends are so brittle and need a trim. Lorelei needs to get your hair ready for your crown. Your mother and I think it would look perfect, in sexy beach curls with strands of colorful metallics woven into it. I brought mermaid glitter gel. Oh, and skin lotion with mermaid glitter, so you sparkle under the moonlight. And aqua glitter nail polish. All from my salon." She squeezed her niece's shoulders. "I'm so excited!"

Caroline ran the ends of her hair through her fingers. "I guess I can use better products. And as far as my hair for the silly ceremony, do whatever you all want."

"Did I hear silly?"

Caroline looked past her auntie to see her mother coming into the room. "Yes, Mom. Guilty. Send me to a timeout in my room." She held back a laugh.

Her mother pursed her lips as she walked over to the mantle and pointed. "Young lady, this photo is of the great aunties. They loved it here and I feel them in every room. You need to get DC out of you and get on island time."

Caroline twisted her lips. She knew she needed to chill a bit and stop being so uptight. She put her hands in the air. "You're right. I know how much this means to you all. I resign to island time."

Her mother sat down on the vintage green brocade sofa, crossing her legs. "Go take that shower. We made more special lemonade."

Caroline flashed a smile at her mother and Auntie Calypso. "You and Auntie Lorelei can give me mermaid hair sparkling with glitter gel anytime. And by the way, you look amazing with auburn hair."

Auntie Calypso touched her hair. "You like it? I wasn't sure if it made me appear older. Do you like it shoulder length?"

Caroline knew she had to stop her aunt's chatter. It could go on for hours if she let it. "You are as beautiful as always. Red, brown, green, or purple hair."

"You are too sweet! Let me get Auntie Pearl so you can say hello. She's upstairs unpacking." She looked up the stairwell and called out. "Pearl!"

"What?"

"Come say hello to our newest mermaid!"

"Auntie Calypso, please let her unpack. I'm sure the drive was long from New York."

"Okay, we'll chat at dinner. Never mind Pearl." She turned to Caroline. "We stayed at a lovely hotel in Cape Charles by the Chesapeake Bay Bridge. I did, however, dodge dragonflies as big as birds. Anyway, the coffee was good, the milk was too cold, and the donuts were stale. We took turns driving. So much traffic in Virginia Beach and before the bridge near Kitty Hawk. I need a glass of wine. I take that back. Where is the vodka?"

"In the lemonade." Halia said. "And it's very good."

Caroline said. "Listen, I'm layered in sunblock and sand. I need to get this washed off. Then we can chat over a bottle of wine before dinner. Deal?"

"Did I hear someone say shower?" Auntie Lorelei called out from the kitchen. "The outside shower is working. Earl hooked it up yesterday. I just put body soaps and lotions out there. All goat's milk and is natural from a local woman. Earl installed new hooks, and the towels are now hanging on them.

Caroline looked toward the kitchen, shaking her head. "How did she hear me?"

"She's always had excellent hearing." Auntie Calypso fanned her face. "Thank goodness she's got Earl putting in AC units! He's such a helper and a good-looking man. It's hotter than hell in here and my hair is frizzing and worsening my hot flashes." Her eyes twinkled. "Remember two years ago when Earl brought over a couple of bottles of homemade scuppernong wine? Well, never mind. Go take that shower. I'm heading down to the ocean to cool off." She reached for Caroline's hands. "Your mother tells me you're working on Senator Jameson's campaign. It's a shame you broke it off with him. Imagine if you were our first lady?"

Caroline couldn't keep up with her auntie's multiple conversation switches.

"Auntie Calypso, I work for him, and that's it. I hope we can pull it off and that he wins. End of story." She whispered into her auntie's ear. "He has a girlfriend, in fact, a fiancée, and we are about to announce it. Not a word to my mother." Caroline gently placed her index finger on her aunt's nose. "Got it? It's shower time."

"Really? Do tell me?"

"Later, Auntie." Caroline promised as she went out the back door to find the outside shower area freshly painted. She stepped inside, impressed by how Earl had fixed it up. There were shelves, hooks, and privacy curtains in the dressing area. And even a shampoo dispenser. She hung up her bikini and stood under the cool water. So much was on her mind, and she needed to spend time upstairs on her laptop and make several calls before dinner.

Halia reached for Calypso's hand, and they sat together on the sofa. "Calypso, I'm so glad to be here. This is a big celebration, knowing this would have been Ida's one hundred and fifth birthday. Can you believe this tradition had been going on this long?"

"It's wonderful." Calypso looked over at the pictures on the fireplace mantle. "We are family, and may our sisterhood go on forever."

"We are a powerful group of women in this bloodline." Halia leaned over and hugged her sister, and she pulled back. "Caroline is so on edge. I have never seen my daughter so uptight. And so sarcastic. It's that job of hers. Of all times to leave the firm and partner with a nobody, well, a somebody. Her father had used Wilmen for years. If it were not for her father, she would never have gotten an internship there. I phoned Wilmen to apologize for her actions." She put her hands in the air. "I reminded her what a wonderful man

Wilmen is having taught her everything she knows. This is how she repays him? Starting a new firm with Gary Lawson?"

Calypso tapped her cheek. "Lawson... how do I know that name? Wait, isn't he... didn't he get fired from a campaign during the midterms for punching the host of the Morning Rising Show?"

"Not punching him, but I think he almost did. He has the temper of a penned bull. Admittedly, he is excellent at his job. But Caroline needs to be loyal to Wilmen. Not go off with a wildcard."

"Now, now, Halia, it's her life. She will learn her lesson and go back to Wilmen. One thing we both know is that she should have stayed with Senator Colton Jameson. Such a nice young man. And if he wins, imagine us at the White House dining with dignitaries!"

"Calypso, I imagine it all the time, and it breaks my heart. She is a *Woodard*, and that means a lot in DC. Her father would never have accepted his daughter *working* for Jameson. She should be by his side as his wife. Her father told me years ago Jameson was a winner."

Calypso tapped Halia's forearm and leaned in. "I have a secret."

"Really? What?"

"Only if you keep a lid on it. Caroline will kill me, but I think you should know." Auntie Calypso looked side to side and leaned toward Halia. Her voice was low. "Jameson is getting engaged and they will release it soon."

"No!" Halia slapped her hands on her chest.

Calypso quickly placed her index finger on Halia's lips. "Shhhh."

"No what? Shhhh? What's going on?" Grams Dorea came in with a bottle of beer in her hand. "Well?"

With a slight moan, Halia stood up. "Nothing, Mom."

"Mom," Calypso said as she was getting up, "is that a new housecoat? I love the color."

"It's a summer dress and Caroline gave it to me for Christmas," Grams Dorea replied. "I saved it for this vacation. I like this coral color more and more. The sea creatures, not so much. Come, girls, we need to sit on the back porch and enjoy the evening. I have fried pickles on the table. It's too hot for me in here." She looked around. "Where is Pearl?"

"Upstairs unpacking. You know she must have everything put away, and her closet is color coordinated before she can relax. She even has dates on her shoeboxes." Calypso said.

Grams Dorea cracked a knowing smile. "She inherited that from your father. Mr. Organized. How I miss him." She went over to the Ball canning jar on the mantle. "Hi, honey." She stroked the jar and picked it up.

Halia felt her heart stop. *Do not pick him up.* Fearing Grams, Dorea would discover her husband could be on the rug, or worse, they might have sat on him.

"Mom, why don't we all go outside now? Let Daddy rest."

"I suppose you're right, Halia. It's dusty in here. I thought Lorelei cleaned." Grams Dorea ran her finger along the windowsill. "There is so much fine dust."

"Well, it's an old house," Halia was quick to answer. "We can clean again tomorrow."

"Put glass cleaner on the shopping list," Grams Dorea mentioned. "I get the porch swing. We need to discuss the ceremony and tonight's meditation circle. It is Pearl's turn to read the letter from the bottle and call on Seraphina and Erasmus."

"Yes, Mom." Calypso coughed. "It *is* awfully dusty in here." She tapped her tongue on the roof of her mouth as she headed toward the porch.

Halia's eyes were wide as she followed, brushing ashes off the back of Calypso's sundress.

Seven

Caroline spent the rest of the afternoon in her bedroom, working on her laptop. She was relieved her new seasoned assistants were proving to be an asset. She now had an assistant to her assistant. Hearing the ship's bell ring, she closed her laptop.

She stretched, got up, and slipped into a blue gingham sundress, pairing it with her mermaid flip-flops to bring delight to Auntie Lorelei. She ran a brush through her hair, put it in a loose bun, then headed downstairs. Standing at the foot of the stairs, she listened to the laughter and conversation emanating from the dining room. The soulful voice of Etta James singing "Steal Away" played on the vintage stereo.

"Caroline, you look like a little girl in that blue dress," Auntie Calypso said fondly as she came out of the kitchen with a mac and cheese casserole.

Wilbur ran around the corner of the table and jumped on Caroline.

"Wilbur! For heaven's sake, get down!" Auntie Lorelei shouted. "Wilbur, mind your manners!"

"It's okay, he's just saying hello." Caroline patted his head and pushed him away. "Go."

"She looks like Dorothy from The Wizard of Oz in that dress. All she needs to do is put Wilbur in her bike basket," Halia suggested happily as she poured herself a glass of wine.

"Really, Mom? Wilbur is too big."

They all laughed.

"Look at you!" Auntie Pearl reached for Caroline's hands. "Our mermaid!"

"And you look amazing, Auntie Pearl," Caroline smiled at her. "In fact, gorgeous."

"Thank you, honey." Pearl turned to everyone. "Doesn't Caroline mirror Ida when she was young? Just like the photo over the mantel?"

"I know Ida is beside her." Halia looked at her daughter.

"A spitting image," Pearl insisted.

"Thank you, Auntie Pearl. How about we sit down to eat? I'm starving."

"Honey, you sit next to Grams Dorea at the end of the table." Halia signaled with her chin.

Caroline's eyes circled the table, finding a wooden bowl full of fresh greens. "Oh my gosh, I was supposed to make the salad."

"We knew you were busy on that laptop, and we didn't want to disturb our little worker bee mermaid, so I made it," Calypso said as she shook the bottle of dressing.

"Wow, thank you, Auntie Calypso. I've been playing catch up. I promise, tomorrow I will make sure my feet are in the kitchen at five p.m." She pulled out a chair and sat down next to Grams.

Auntie Lorelei brought in the flounder almondine and set it down on the table. "Does anyone need anything before I sit my tired rear end down?" She looked around at the hungry group.

"No," Grams Dorea replied. "Just give thanks. We are all here. Three generations of women, and many before us, who have sat at this table to celebrate. They used these dishes and silverware, laughed, and found joy here at the Beach Heart Cottage. With that, I give thanks to the sisters who started this. Our sisterhood. May they be with us this evening during meditation to guide us. I know this time we will hear Seraphina's sweet voice ripple over the tips of the waves."

Everyone cheered and raised their wine glasses as the chandelier above flickered. Caroline's eyes met the bulbs. "Grams Dorea, tomorrow how about I change the bulbs?"

"Oh, no, honey, that is Ida saying hello! This always happens the first night the women gather at this table. Just a hello from the other side," Grams Dorea responded, looking up at the flickering bulbs. "It's in the sacred journal."

Caroline silently inhaled, knowing not to disagree. *If Grams Dorea isn't happy, nobody is.* "Where is the journal, Grams Dorea? And why is it sacred?"

Grams Dorea's smile radiated with love. "It's in a special place, Caroline. What the sisters wrote in ink is why we are a close sisterhood. We will read a passage from it tonight during the circle, and you will come to understand. This year, your crowning is special."

"This is glorious! And it's a blood moon this year," Lorelei reminded them as she dished a piece of fish onto each plate. "Wow, I just got chills up and down my arms. Ida is here!"

"A what?" Caroline asked as she picked up her fork. "A bloody moon? Sounds like my former client, that actor from England. A bloody pain in my arse!"

"Peter Bretton?" Halia asked as she dished out coleslaw. "Best to stick with your Senator Jameson. He's our man."

"Mom, it is best I stick with who pays my bills, although that actor was an awful creep and a womanizer. And yes, dear Pee-tah paid well."

"We've never had a mermaid crowned under a blood moon," Auntie Pearl said softly. "This is the celebration Seraphina has been waiting for. We will hear her voice singing to us, tickling the tips of the waves. Oh, my arms. I have goosebumps!"

Caroline put her fork down, shaking her head. "What are you all talking about? A blood moon, singing mermaids, chilled arms, am I the only sober one here?"

Halia looked around the table. "In time, you will learn."

"Mom, will you please tell me what I'm in for? I have heard about this for years, and you never explained it. I only knew we came here in the summer to swim, sunbathe, and eat blue crabs. But then again, there were always whispers that stopped when I walked into a room."

The aunties looked at each other.

"You forgot to drink and get away from men." Grams Dorea's smile was from ear to ear as she lifted her mug of beer.

"Hear, hear!" the sisters laughed.

Halia got up and stood behind Caroline. "My sweet daughter Caroline, the blood moon is when there is an eclipse, and it illuminates the red color by the sun, turning the moon an orange color, during which we have one hour to take advantage of it. It has magnetic, magical, and healing energies. It is a gift from Ida and her sisters, and you are the only one in the bloodline to celebrate under it. Ida believed such a moon was a sign of infinitive love."

Caroline looked around the table. "Wow, this *is* special to all of you, isn't it?"

"Yes, honey, it is." Halia kissed her daughter's cheek, squeezed her shoulders, and sat down. "It is all in Marie's journal. She became a teacher and wrote their story. Ida and Dorothy wrote in it as well. But it was Marie who dedicated to leaving a legacy,"

"Why have I never heard of the journal?"

"You will, Caroline. We only use it when the next mermaid is ready. It's part of the great aunties' request."

"I want to read it." Caroline leaned forward. "It sounds so mysterious."

Auntie Lorelei cleared her throat. "You will tonight. That is part of our circle. You will read the entry where Ida was alone as she searched for Seraphina after she and Marie found the bottle and they-"

"What bottle?" Caroline asked.

The women looked around the table at each other, and Grams Dorea nodded. "Caroline, my dear granddaughter, the three young sisters found a bottle with a note in it that washed up near the beach after a hurricane brushed the shores of Hatteras. It was after the storm and a blood moon that they found the bottle. This is how it all began. The sisters were sure they glimpsed a large tail in the waves close to shore that next morning, but they never saw it again."

Caroline tried not to smile. "It could have been a dolphin."

Auntie Pearl answered confidently. "Oh, honey, there is so much more. It was not a dolphin. The large tail, as told, was shimmering in the morning sunlight in colors of the rainbow. Ida and her sisters claim it waved at them before it vanished."

Grams Dorea picked up the story. "They searched for Seraphina, to reunite with Erasmus, the shipwrecked sailor who spent days here on Hatteras. The sisters spent endless days and nights looking for Seraphina. Even as they aged, to no avail. It's all in the journal. They believed that when a mermaid is crowned on her thirty-fifth birthday under that moon, the magic of their love will collide, bringing that mermaid never-ending love."

"Wow," Caroline turned to her mother. "Mom, I never knew this. I thought this was all brouhaha. Daddy dismissed it as female nonsense, as men could not enter the cottage during a summer mermaid ceremony." She put her napkin on the table.

"Your father was a chauvinistic pig!" Grams Dorea blurted out. "Only Earl can cross the threshold. He is helpful and kind."

Halia inhaled with her head back. With an exhale, she picked up her wine glass. Grams Dorea never cared for her husband.

"Grams Dorea, please don't start. Daddy was a hardworking man. He did so much good in this world and country, and with that being said, can we keep the peace?" Caroline reached over and patted her grandmother's hand. "Please? For me. I'm next mermaid."

Grams Dorea smirked at Halia and paid her attention to Caroline. "All right. I need another beer. Pearl, can you get me one from the fridge?"

"Mom," Caroline asked, "why thirty-five?"

"According to the letter that was in the bottle, the lost sailor spent thirty-five days shipwrecked. So, the story goes. And Ida was thirty-five when she finally fell wildly in love and married. Ida, as you know, became a marine biologist and-"

"Mom, c'mon. A marine biologist back then? Be serious. That's a very modern profession."

"Actually," Auntie Lorelei said, "the first marine biologist was Captain Cook in the seventeen-hundreds.

"And not only was Ida a marine biologist," Halia continued, "she married a biologist. They traveled the world and lived on a boat for many years. According to the journal, Marie believed her sister chose that career to find Seraphina."

"This is intriguing." Caroline leaned forward with her elbows on the table, her hands cradled her chin. "This is turning into a fun vacation. I wish I could have met them."

"You will!" Lorelei announced. "I can feel it! The cottage knows. The island knows."

Caroline bit her tongue. *The cottage knows. The island knows. Who else knows?*

Pearl came into the dining room and filled Grams Dorea's beer mug, put it on the table, and looked at her three sisters. "I can't even express how much joy I have in my heart." She broke into a waterfall of tears.

Calypso reached for Pearl's hand. "Me, too. I love all of you."

"Well, now, this calls for my peach cobbler." Grams Dorea lifted her chilled beer mug. "And no talk of politics at this table, and all phones off, and for the rest of the evening. That means you, Caroline. I know you are itching to check your phone and see what *he* is up to, but family first."

Caroline nodded at Grams Dorea. She knew *he* was Senator Jameson. She was learning how much this meant to her family. How it was a bond, their glue.

Pearl brought out the peach cobbler, and behind her was Halia, with a half-gallon of vanilla ice cream.

After an hour of laughing and carefree conversation, Lorelei looked at the vintage clock above the buffet. "Oh my goodness, it's almost nine! We need to get ready."

Pearl and Calypso picked up the dessert dishes and the half-melted ice cream.

"I need you all go out of this room while I sage, to clear the energy." Lorelei opened the desk drawer and took out her sage stick wrapped in lavender, a white feather, and a large scallop shell.

Halia and Grams Dorea were out on the back porch. Caroline helped Pearl and Calypso in the kitchen, cleaning up pans and dishes. Finally, Pearl finished washing the last dish, Caroline dried it, and Calypso put it away.

The heat was going to make it difficult to sleep, with hardly a breeze. Pressing her back against the green Formica counter, Caroline wiped her forehead with sweat and looked around the vintage kitchen. To her left was the 1950s green marble-swirl kitchen table with its polished chrome edges, and the six matching vinyl chairs that made a home with it. Fading yellow and white checkered café curtains with white pompom trim, Grams Dorea had hand-sewed, were in remarkable shape. The blonde tongue-and-groove walls, darkened by age, gave the kitchen character and warmth, as did the double-bowl, white porcelain sink. Its scratches and chips proved it had decades of scrubbing. The pine cabinets, layered in white paint, showed their history.

Caroline wondered if Ida, Marie, and Dorothy looked out those windows with racing hearts in search of their mermaid. Did they touch the walls, leaving their fingerprints behind? Did they laugh at the dining room table as they constructed the mermaid crown under the light of a lantern?

After a lengthy yawn, Caroline put her dishtowel on a hook and excused herself, intending to run upstairs and check her phone and laptop.

"Caroline?" Grams Dorea called out from the porch. "We start soon. I have eyes behind my head. No business tonight."

Caroline stopped at the foot of the stairs. Her hand gripped the newel post. "Yes, Grams Dorea. I need to freshen up and put on my pjs." She hated to lie, but she had to get in touch with the world. She regretted her decision after seeing at least twelve voicemails and a handful of emails. It was going to be a long night after the circle.

An email caught her eye. CJameson@pdmail – URGENT. It was his private email that only a select few had. Her heart raced. This could be it. Had he told Wilmen? This email had to be opened. Even if it ruined her night. She pressed the key. Her eyes followed each word. He was staying onboard with Caroline and Lawson! This was fabulous news! She had to respond fast, before Grams Dorea sent out a search party.

She needed to get in touch with her new partner. They need to move ASAP. Nothing would be on handshakes. Contracts had to be signed. She glanced at her phone. It was nine forty-seven. Her mind was swirling. She might have to rush up to DC.

Eight

Using a seagull feather she had found on the beach years earlier; Auntie Lorelei waved a smoky sage stick. She smudged the thresholds and all the downstairs rooms. She always thanked the spirit of the seagull for leaving the feather for her. With every nook and cranny infused with pungent smoke, she asked Pearl to open the windows and doors, to let any negative energy find its way outside and into the universe.

Pearl coughed as she opened the windows. "Lorelei, for heaven's sake, it's like a bonfire in here. Why must we do this?" She waved her hands in the air. "Yuck. Now it's in my hair!" She sneezed. "I'm going to open the door."

"Good and bless you. It's keeping us safe." Lorelei said and continued her smudging. "Shhhh... I have a wonderful cleansing burn going. After, I will seal the thresholds with my new black sea salt."

Pearl continued to wave her hands around as she made her way to the front door and opened it. She screamed and jumped back.

"Well, butter my butt and call me a biscuit if it ain't purty, Miss Pearl! Golly, I didn't mean to send a shiver up your spine."

"Earl!" Pearl put her hand over her heart and narrowed her eyes at the familiar face. "For heaven's sake, you scared the bejesus out of me!" She broke into a welcoming smile. "How are you?"

"I'm dandy, Miss Pearl. Yourself?" He leaned into the screen door. His khaki baseball cap with an embroidered swordfish rested on his graying hair. His tee shirt was soaked in sweat, as were his drab olive cargo shorts. "Why, of all the sisters, you sure are the prettiest flower in the patch. I gotta confess, all you sisters are so pretty it's hard for me to tell you apart."

Pearl blushed. "Earl, you are always the gentleman."

"Yes, ma'am." He pulled a blue bandana from the back pocket of his shorts and wiped the sweat off his forehead.

"Earl, you need to sit down. Your face is redder than a lobster done boiling."

"I'm awright. I need to bring these air conditioners inside before I melt." Beads of sweat bubbled on the back of his neck and forehead. He looked at his handcart with a box on it and at Pearl. His olive-toned eyes circled her face.

Pearl opened the screen door. "Please, come on in and bring those air conditioners with you."

"Yes, ma'am." He struggled to get the handcart up the front steps. "I got the other three in the truck. Four in all. This heatwave has been hotter than blue blazes. Dang, humid air is thicker than the molasses my mama cooked with." He removed his baseball cap, fanning his face with it. "Whoa, wee!"

Lorelei confronted him on the front porch. "Stop! Not one more step, Earl."

Earl stopped and put his baseball cap on. His eyes met hers. "Miss Lorelei, ma'am, sorry I'm late. I went up the beach. I've got the last four in the sizes you need." Smoke was snaking out the open door. "What in tarnation is going on? Y'all smoking pork butt in the fireplace?"

"Of course not!" Lorelei said as she eyed the air conditioning box on the cart at the bottom of the stairs.

Earl leaned in and whispered. "Is your mother okay? I mean the urn, jar, and all. Ain't any dust lingering, is there?" He fanned the smoke around with his hands.

"Hush up, Grams Dorea has ears all over her head. She has instinctual radar. I think we missed some ashes. It is a little dusty by the sofa and the area rug."

He tightened his face. "Dang."

Pearl tapped Lorelei on the shoulder and asked. "What about Daddy's urn?"

"Nothing, Pearl, I'll tell you later. Earl honey, I must sage you before you enter," Lorelei pointed with her feather, "hat off, arms up, legs spread."

"Anytime for you, Miss Lorelei."

Pearl put her hand over her mouth as she held back a smile.

Earl was no stranger to her ritual. Lorelei had saged him the day she arrived before she had let him in the cottage to help her open the place up.

"Oh, now, Miss Lorelei. How long have we known each other?"

Lorelei shot him with a stink eye. "Too long, Earl."

Earl knew it was seldom that they permitted men inside when the sisters came for their August vacation. He had permission because he was the cottage caretaker and had become a dear friend over the years.

Sixty-five-year-old Earl, a widower for the past several years, enjoyed it when the sisters arrived. Yes, they teased him and gave him a tough time, and he loved every minute. Earl lived in his family home on one side of Beach Heart Cottage, and on the other side sat a vacant, storm damaged place.

Earl owned a handful of vacation rentals and other real estate ventures on Hatteras and Ocracoke Island. When he wasn't waist-deep in fishing gear and boots, with a fishing rod in hand, he spent his time on his old pontoon boat, catching fish and entertaining tourists with exaggerated fishing stories. He liked to think he looked like a seasoned sea captain. And he did.

Earl knew by the odd way Lorelei acted that there was something brewing. Something big. He wondered if they were a mysterious coven of witches from up north. *Who else would wave around a smoky stick and enjoy it?* He also wondered, *where do they keep the cauldron? Worse, why is the grandfather in a Ball canning jar?*

"Earl, I told you I would have to sage you again," Lorelei pointed at his head. "Baseball cap off." She started waving the smoky stick at the top of his head.

He sneezed twice.

"Bless you." Pearl said.

"Careful now." He looked at Pearl. "Miss Pearl, is she gonna roast me or something crazy?"

"Maybe," Pearl giggled.

"What in the world is going on?" Grams Dorea came into the room, tapping her cane and parting the smoke with her hand. "Earl? Lorelei, for heaven's sake, you've set the poor man on fire!"

"Yes, ma'am, she makes me so hot I smoke. Truth is, your daughter here is harassing me with her smoke stick."

"Quiet, Earl." Lorelei poked his nose with her feather.

Grams Dorea stared at Earl. "Lorelei, you know that is not how to get a man by blowing smoke around his crotch."

"Mom!" Pearl gasped.

Lorelei shook her head. "Ignore that comment."

Earl thrived on their attention. "Am I done?"

Lorelei got closer, peering into his eyes. She stepped back. "All negative energy is gone. You get an all clear."

He put his arms down, baseball cap on, and went out to take the air conditioning box off the hand truck.

"Oh, no you don't." Grams waved her cane at him. "We have a private party in five minutes. No men allowed. Leave the cart there. Come back tomorrow." She handed Earl a cold beer and reached into her pocket and gave him a five-dollar bill. "Thank you, Earl, go home now. Out the door with you. We will see you in the morning. Good night." She shut the door. "Girls, it's time to start the circle."

Earl stood on the front porch with his nose to the door, a beer bottle in one hand and five dollars in the other.

"Grams Dorea, it's so hot in here. I can't believe you kicked him out." From the staircase landing, Caroline fanned her face. "We need those air conditioners tonight."

Grams Dorea mumbled as she made her way to her recliner.

Calypso came in from the back porch. "Lorelei, why is there so much smoke?"

"We needed a good cleanse. I'll put the fans on now." Lorelei extinguished her sage stick in the shell. "Where is Wilbur?" She looked around. "Wilbur? Come here."

Pearl pointed at the door. "I think he's outside."

"I'll get him." Caroline ran over to a sideboard and reached for a flashlight.

"You better hurry," Grams Dorea reminded her. "It's almost ten."

"Caroline, cover up. Put my sweater on. It's by the door." Pearl pointed. "I can see clearly through that skimpy nightgown."

It was too hot for a sweater, but Caroline knew better than to argue. She grabbed the sweater off the hook and rushed out into the night. "Wilbur, Wilbur! Come on, boy. Wilbur, get over here. I'll give you a ribeye!"

She heard rustling in the pampas grass. Earl was bent over while Wilbur licked his face. "Git." He pushed him away.

"Wilbur!" Caroline clapped her hands and whistled. "Come on, boy."

Panting, Wilbur came out of the pampas grass and ran up onto the front porch, wagging his tail.

"Where did you go? Get inside." Caroline ushered him in and shut the door. "Naughty boy. And stay away from my pillows!"

With the dog safely inside, Earl twisted the cap off and whispered as he lifted the bottle of beer, "Thanks, Grams."

It was time to find out what was going on. Earl made his way out of the pampas grass and up to the cottage. He kicked off his sandals and silently stepped up the steps to the side porch. He crouched near an open window. Slowly, he lifted his head above the windowsill. Through the screen, he squinted.

The women were settling into a circle in the living room. Caroline was sitting on the floor, while Grams Dorea sat in her late husband's recliner. The others were on the sofa and chairs. White candles flickered. As he stood up, pressing his back against the house, the brim of his cap bumped the wind chimes.

"Crap," quietly escaped his lips as he stumbled down the steps. Abandoning his sandals, he made his way over the dune to his own cottage, not without a few sandburs digging into his feet.

"What was that?" Grams Dorea looked toward the window.

"It's the wind chimes. Thank God we finally have a breeze," Caroline said as she fanned her face.

"The Grand Aunties are here!" Calypso cried out. "Oh, they're here! It's a sign when the chimes ring."

"It's time," Lorelei instructed Pearl. "Please light the three large red candles on the coffee table."

Caroline watched Pearl as each candle found a flame. "Why red?"

Her mother smiled at her. "It's the color of love, honey. The white candles are for purity."

Caroline nodded, unsure.

"Now for the special lantern to be set in the center of the coffee table and lit. Caroline, this is the actual oil lantern Ida used when they found the bottle." Grams Dorea said as she got up, and leaning on her cane, made her way over to the sideboard. She removed the deep brown, pitted bottle from its hiding place. She set it down on the coffee table as the flame from the oil lantern flickered in harmony with the white candles. Echoes of distant crashing waves filled the air.

Caroline sat back, crossing her legs. "What is happening, Mom?"

"Shhhh..." Halia pressed her index finger against Caroline's lips.

"Okay." Caroline wanted to lose herself in the ritual, but her mind was on the emails waiting for her upstairs. Contracts, meetings, debates, Lawson, campaigns. She hoped this would not take too long.

Lorelei opened the antique oak desk and came back to the circle with a thick book and put it near the lantern.

Grams Dorea looked at her daughters and granddaughter. "Tonight, we begin the celebration of the newest mermaid in our sisterhood. Caroline, my dear, it is our privilege and obligation to our bloodline and sisterhood that we honor you. Let us be silent for a moment as we ask the Great Grand Sisters to be by your side."

No one spoke or moved as they closed their eyes. Nothing happened. With one eye open, Caroline looked around as everyone waited for something. But what? Blowing curtains? More wind chimes. A slamming door? A levitating table? A tickle? A boo? Hyper-alert, she waited. Nothing.

Outside, the balmy breezes were picking up, allowing the rocking chairs to move as the sea oats swayed. Caroline closed her eyes and relaxed when something tickled her left ear. She swatted it away, figuring it was a mosquito.

"Caroline, it's okay, it's Ida. She is here by your side," Lorelei said quietly. "We can begin."

Caroline turned her head. "What? Grams Dorea, you did that. You are behind me."

"My dear granddaughter, it was Ida. The crown on your head has brought her overwhelming joy. Calypso, can you hand Caroline the journal?"

Calypso picked up Marie's journal and handed it to Caroline.

Caroline looked down. In her hands rested the delicate, leather-bound journal. It contained the story of life at the Beach Heart Cottage. She looked around at the eager eyes on her.

"I don't know what to say. This is so beautiful." At that moment, she forgot about the emails waiting upstairs. It revolved around being present and gaining knowledge of the past. "How do I know what to read?"

Pearl's eyes lit up. "Open it. The page will fall where the sisters want it to."

Calypso picked up the lantern and held it over the old book.

"Here goes." With hesitation, Caroline opened the journal, allowing the pages to fall. To the left of the page, she could make out a detailed pencil sketch of a mermaid's tail. Her voice was low and soft as she read:

It is August, and the sunny days have been such that the heat has once again found us. There is no sign of Seraphina. I never believed my silly sisters. They are merely creative and imaginative. That was until last night. With Mama and Daddy at the oyster gathering on the Hatteras dock, and Ida and Marie in a deep slumber, I learned never to doubt.

"Stop," Lorelei held out her hand, wiggling her fingers. "May I see the journal?"

With care, Caroline gave it over.

Lorelei read it and handed it back to Caroline. "This isn't Marie's writing. It is Dorothy. This has never happened before. She must have written a passage."

Caroline felt chills rush through her body as if Dorothy was reading beside her. She continued:

I had removed the crown and the letter from under Ida's bed earlier in the day and hid them in the shed. I went out of the cottage, and quietly I entered the shed and took them down the sandy path to the beach to toss them into the sea. As the full moon rose, blanketing the ocean in a stream of white and shone on me while I was sitting on the cool sand, I put the crown of shells on my head.

I sat near the water's edge. The sea was calm as little ghost crabs scurried past my toes.

I read the letter by the moonlight, then closed my eyes tight and waited for Seraphina to call out to me. Time had passed, and the moon was now over my shoulder as I was ready to throw the silly things into the ocean. I heard her. I opened my eyes to see, in the crest of a wave, a large tail painted in brilliant colors flip about in the moonlight. Her voice is just as Ida claimed it would be, soothing as an angel tickling the night air. Seraphina is real, in search of her sailor. I know deep in my heart that when she finds his spirit, they will live happily ever after. Until then, their souls are restless. Dorothy Conrad, August 29th, 1939.

The lantern light flickered and blew out. Gasps rippled through the room. This had never happened before. The room, now aglow with white candles, illuminated Caroline's face as she closed the journal and looked over at her grandmother.

"She's here," Grams Dorea declared. "My namesake, Dorothy, is here. She is smiling at us!"

Caroline felt a rush of emotions. "Grams Dorea, I was *there* with Dorothy, sitting on the beach under the full moon, wishing to hear the siren's song." Caroline put her hands on her heart as her eyes traveled over to her mother. "Now I understand your passion, the legacy. I *am* so sorry I doubted all of you. I feel privileged to be the next member of the mermaid sisterhood and wear the delicate crown of seashells. And you can glitter me up all you want!"

"That's my girl. I knew you would come around." Grams Dorea's face beamed with love. "Now, Caroline, put the journal on the table. It is time for Calypso to read the letter Ida found in the bottle, and then we meditate and close the circle."

Caroline had to ask, "Can I read more later when I'm in bed? I want to know how they lived, who they were."

"It is best we put it in its safe place. It is so brittle and holds such secrets." Pearl twisted her hands together. "We find it exciting when a new entry is read. It surprises us."

Everyone nodded in agreement.

With a slight frown, realizing the rules, Caroline agreed. "I understand, and now I can't wait to be crowned."

Lorelei stood up and said, "The lantern has to cool, but let me put these items away and we can continue." She picked up the journal and the letter and, with care, placed them back inside the sideboard. On her way back to her chair, she stopped and looked down at Caroline. In the candlelight, Caroline's face glowed as if she were a child on Christmas Eve. "The crown has been waiting for you."

Calypso picked up one of the several photographs from the mantel, from 1975, when the sisters were together for the last time. The picture was taken on the cottage's back porch. In the center was Ida, the crown resting on her short gray hair. Her smile was as brilliant as the sunrise. Age may have changed their bodies and faces, but they wore the same joy they had as young girls holding hands. Another was the sisters in costume posing on the beach.

Calypso brought the photos over to the coffee table and set them down.

"They had such love for each other. If only photos could talk..." Pearl sighed. "Caroline, look at Ida back then. You are her mirror image."

Caroline picked up the photo and pulled it close. Under the flickering light of the candles, her eyes met Ida's. "This is amazing. She looks like me so much it gives me chills." She could not stop studying Ida's face as she traced it with her index finger.

"You see why this is so special, my love?"

"Mom. I do. It's as if they have cast a spell over me and I'm about to take an adventure. I feel like crying." She fanned her eyes. "Gosh, I am. What is happening?"

"Love, honey, pure love only found here at the Beach Heart Cottage." Grams Dorea sat back, folding her hands in her lap. "You will wear the crown proudly, my dear."

"I will, Grams Dorea." Caroline put the photo back on the coffee table.

They held hands and entered the meditation that closed the circle.

Nine

Everyone retired to bed. Caroline blew out the last candle and went into the kitchen for a glass of ice water. Lorelei followed her, Wilbur by her side, wagging his wiry tail.

"That was amazing tonight. I feel utterly calm for the first time in years."

"There *is* a calming, Caroline. The sea, the tradition, the cottage. This has been a long day, honey. Wilbur, time for bed." She yawned. "Yoga on the beach at sunrise and I'm adding a chakra aligning."

"Maybe. Night." Caroline yawned as she put her empty glass in the sink and looked out the window into the darkness. "Chakra what?"

"Honey, not maybe. Just be there." Auntie Lorelei slapped her thigh, and Wilbur trotted beside her.

Alone, Caroline wandered into the living room. It was quiet, with only the simmering scent of blown out candles and the distant hush of the ocean. She looked up the stairwell and back to the sideboard, tapping her lips. Who would know if she took the journal and put it back before dawn?

With light steps, she made her way over to the sideboard and opened it. She reached in and pulled out the journal. Holding it close to her chest, her heart sped up as she tiptoed up the stairs.

"Night, Caroline. Sweet dreams."

Caroline froze. "Night, Auntie Pearl." She continued to her room and closed the door. Resting her back against it, she looked down at the brittle book with a smile.

Waiting for her on her desk, her phone and laptop pulled her to the present. Eighteen new emails welcomed her. Regretting her true responsibility for a while, she hid the journal under her pillow.

The first email to open was from Colton Jameson. She sat down to read it. He was counting on her to win the election. It was *all* up to her. It was *her* job. He was her employer. She sat back, puzzled. Was he serious? He was a notorious teaser with a sense of humor, but seriously? This was not how Colton spoke to her in person or in emails. So cold. So authoritative. Was he annoyed that she took a vacation? He knew that her vacation was not just leisure. She had a complete staff a call away and a new partner. He knew Lawson would be an asset.

His next email had the subject line *fiancée announcement*. Her heart sank. They'd had their fling. No, it was more than a fling. That was a few years ago, and they remained close for business reasons. She knew who the *fiancé* was and had her reservations after her private investigator had revealed dirt on her. Dirt could turn into mud. Worse, quicksand. She had told Colton what they had discovered. With a tight smile, he said everything was under control.

The email said Colton wanted to hold off the announcement. Caroline knew it wasn't easy to keep things under wraps. Nothing had leaked. A young, hunky guy in the Oval Office? Hundreds of women were sending love letters, often with provocative photos, to Wilmen's firm that were always passed to Caroline. Some were so raunchy, even the men on staff blushed.

A fiancée would solve a lot of the problems, but for this one, the Band-Aids were going to fall off soon. She sat down at her desk, exhaling a stressed sigh, talking to herself. "Okay, think this over. What is Colton up to? Are we all set to release this to the press in two days?"

She knew he was a night owl, in his office on the computer, or watching the endless news feeds. She picked up her phone as a mellow breeze snaked into the room while she dialed his number. "Colton, pick up."

"If it's not the rogue PR woman lounging on vacation, slathered in sunblock, frolicking in the sea when she needs to be in DC getting me into the White House."

Not sure how to take this, Caroline replied, "That would be me. We need to discuss this fiancée matter. We, meaning that my team and I have been working on this."

"Who's we? Wilmen's team? Or Lawson's team?"

Caroline shook her head. "Lawson, of course. You know how hard I'm working."

"Yeah, just like your father. As far as the announcement is concerned, I need to work things out before we go public."

"What things? I need to know what is going on, Colton. Rumors are airborne, and I'm not comfortable with this."

"It's under control. I'll get back to you when I'm ready."

"Colton, ready? Ugh, where are you?"

"At my parent's condo, pacing around the kitchen, pouring a bourbon, swirling it in a glass. I looked at a photo my mom kept on the fridge of you and me, during your dad's first senate campaign."

"Are you in North Carolina? Emerald Isle?"

"For two days. Then I'm off to Ohio, Michigan, and I forget where they are sending me. Your *team* is building my brand."

"And we have built your brand like no other."

"Caroline, there is a job for you when I win. How about being my press secretary when I win?"

"Thanks, but no thanks." Moving to her bed, leaning back against her pillows, she shook her head, looking at her glittery coral pink painted toenails.

"Your father would be proud of his little girl. Hold on, there's somebody at the door."

Caroline could hear his security personal call out for him.

"Listen, Caroline, I gotta go. I'll email you later with the details. Put on your sunblock. I'll call you from Ohio." He hung up.

She looked at her phone. This was Colton Jameson, always in a hurry, as if there were a fire in the building. She guessed it was his fiancée. She had a feeling that the woman was becoming a liability, and she knew Colton felt the same.

Caroline put the phone on the bed. Feeling something jabbing in her back, she sat up. The journal! How could she forget? Running her fingers over the leather cover, she inhaled. Marie and Dorothy's stories had to be on hold until she finished answering emails and listening to voicemail.

After the last email, she ran her hands through her hair. She had to get some sleep. She crawled into the soft cotton sheets. Her head sinking into the pillow, she drifted off.

"What was that?" Caroline sat up. Squinting, she looked around the bedroom that glowed in an amber halo of morning sunlight. She picked her phone up off the end table. It was after seven. She heard the bang again.

"Ooopsy, sorry there, Miss Caroline. Did I wake ya?"

Caroline looked over at the dormer window. "What the... Earl?"

"Your Grams Dorea instructed me to be quiet. She is asking for a miracle." Earl pressed his face into the screen, covering his eyes. "Ya decent, ain't ya?"

Caroline pulled her sheet over her chest. "What is going on? What is all the banging?"

"I'm up here on the side roof putting brackets in for the air conditioner for this window and fixing a leak in the roof. I gotta use this here drill." He held it up. "And tell them they need a new roof."

She squinted. "Brackets, drills?"

"Yes, ma'am, ya all gonna have a new AC unit blowing cool air into this room in about an hour. It'll be colder than a witch's–t."

"I know the rest. But seriously? Why so early?"

"It ain't early. The sun has been up for hours. Ya missed a brilliant sunrise. If ya were fishing, it'd be late."

Caroline's tired eyes were wide open by now. "Oh my gosh, okay, wow, AC in this room? This is awesome news."

"Didn't mean to startle ya. I gotta get my drill a new bit. Grams Dorea is making buttermilk waffles and they sure are good. She put brown-sugared pecans in 'em and topped 'em with wild raspberries. That filled my belly for the day."

Caroline nodded as her stomach growled.

"Be back in a bit." Earl vanished.

Caroline waited a minute before she got out of bed to the sweet aroma of waffles snaking up to her room. She arched her back, adding a loud yawn. Her eyes still heavy, she lay back down for a moment and drifted into a light slumber that was soon interrupted by the whine of a drill.

"I guess it is time to get up." She sat up, noticing Earl was gone. With no delay, she reached for her cotton robe and picked up her phone. A flood of voicemails came in. "Too early for this," she murmured as she shuffled down the hall to the bathroom. She knocked.

"Be out in a minute."

"Okay, Mom." Caroline crossed her arms and leaned against the wall. "Mom, I'll go downstairs and use that bathroom." Downstairs, she used the bathroom and dashed out the back door.

Auntie Calypso, sitting on the wicker settee, called out. "Grams Dorea has yummy pancakes and waffles for you in the kitchen. Honey, are you okay?"

Caroline spun around and said. "I'm feeling terrific, Auntie Calypso!' Barefooted, she made her way through the sandy path between the dunes.

Auntie Calypso stirred her sugared coffee. "I think Caroline is feeling the energy. We need to keep her off that phone and laptop."

Auntie Lorelei agreed as she sipped her lemon tea. "That girl is obsessed with her job, just like her father. That worries me. We need to toss her devices into the ocean."

Halia joined them on the porch and asked, "What worries you?"

Lorelei sat back. "Your daughter is a workaholic."

Halia sucked her cheeks in as she sat down. "Caroline is happy, and I'm so proud. Her father instilled so much in her. She and Senator Jameson made such a perfect couple."

Auntie Lorelei looked at Halia. "Key word, Halia, *made*. That was then."

Halia raised her eyebrows and looked away.

Grams Dorea joined them, not holding back her opinion. "Oh, hogwash! My granddaughter needs a nice man and to settle down. Her clock is ticking, and it's nearly midnight, if you know what I mean." She sat down in a wicker rocker, keeping her eye on the ocean. "I pray she is not seeing that Jameson. *Him* and his White House shenanigans and cronies. Good gosh, the media will be here looking in our windows, causing a raucous worse than those darned laughing seagulls finding roadkill."

"And if she is seeing Jameson?" Halia pressed, hoping she was.

Grams Dorea ignored Halia's question. In the silence, only waves breaking on the shore filled the air.

"How about we avoid starting the morning out on this sour note?" Pearl shifted the conversation. "We are here to celebrate."

Halia's face tightened. "I need coffee." She got up and went inside to find Earl standing outside at the kitchen screen door. "Morning Earl. Would you like a cup of coffee?"

"Sure would. I'm ready to put in the downstairs air conditioning units. But I need to check one thing that we sort a neglected."

"What is that?"

"We gotta make sure this cottage can handle these units. I mean, she ain't young, and your fuses are ancient. The wiring could be a real problem."

"Oh, dear." Halia frowned.

Earl scratched his forehead. "I need to get to the fuse box. I know I ain't allowed in, since it's a lady's place here and all."

"Let me check with my mother. She's the boss. Be back in a sec."

Earl's eyes widened as he saw Pearl outside, coming around the corner of the house. In her hands were his sandals.

"Earl, are these sandals yours?" She held them up. "I found them this morning here on the ground by the porch."

"Oh, oh, why yes, they are." Earl came down off the porch to get the sandals. "I took them off earlier to put on my sneakers. Guess I forgot. I'll take them and put them by my toolbox."

With a warm smile, she handed them over.

"Thanks, Miss Pearl. And may I say, you are lovelier each time I see you."

A sunburn rushed into her cheeks. She giggled bashfully. "Earl, you are such a charmer!"

"Perhaps, but ya sure are one beautiful woman." His face wore the same blushing sunburn. "I have a few bottles of Scuppernong wine, if ya might be interested."

Pearl tapped her lips, dropping her head, and then looked up. "We could have a picnic down on the beach. I'll make a basket of appetizers. Crab stuffed mushrooms and a charcuterie board with delicious cheeses and fruits."

Earl was quick to answer. "Yes, ma'am. How about around four today? After I'm done here with Gram Dorea's list of chores. If ya don't mind me asking, what in the world is a chartie board picnic?"

Hands on her hips, Pearl said in a pleasant voice. "Never you mind. You'll find out."

Neither said another word as the oyster shell wind chimes cackled in the soft breeze.

"Earl, you can come in," Halia called from the kitchen window. "Fuse box is in the broom closet. I'm making a fresh pot of coffee."

"Sounds mighty fine. I'll be there in a few." With his sandals in hand and a kick in his step, he found his way to the kitchen.

"Psst... Pearl, what is going on? Scuppernong wine?" Halia teased her sister through the window screen.

With the giddy smile of a teenager, Pearl headed down the sandy path to the beach.

Caroline let her feet sink further into the wet sand with each receding wave. The sun warming her face, she watched a school of dolphins playing close to shore. A flock of seagulls fought over a long dead blue crab and two kids on boogie boards tumbled into the waves.

How she needed this vacation! She inhaled the briny, light sea mist as it broke through the sun. She let out a long ahh and began finding fragments of scallop shells as she made her way along the beach as a morning mist rolled in. Still in her pjs, she decided not to venture too far. Splashing in the fringes of waves, she was feeling a sense of peace until she heard the ship's bell. Her breakfast must be ready, and Grams Dorea was not someone to keep waiting.

While making her way to the path, Caroline bumped into Auntie Pearl, who was sitting on the beach.

"Hi Auntie Pearl, are you taking in this glorious morning?"

"Ahhh, yes, I am. It is splendid." She tilted her head back and inhaled. "Once the sun breaks through the morning mist, we will have a glorious day!"

Caroline looked up toward the cottage. "We better get back or Grams Dorea will give us the infamous stink eye." She extended her hand.

"Yup, that stink eye!" Pearl reached for it and popped up, brushing sand off her shorts. "Thanks. You know Caroline, I could live my retirement out here. I'm so tired of New York."

"You have a beautiful home on all that land."

"It's too much for me, and the taxes in Westchester are out of control. Your Uncle Marcus left me plenty to live on, but when is it all too much? I need to live my life without all the stress. I could even do landscaping on the side."

Caroline nodded. "That would be wonderful. Maybe you could live here at the cottage."

"Now that's a thought!"

Ten

"Grams Dorea, tell Mom I'm going for a bike ride into town to get salad stuff for tonight." As she went out the back door, Caroline asked, "Need anything? I'm going to the Red and White Market."

"No, we brought plenty. But a few green tomatoes from the farm stand would be nice. Make sure they are firm." Grams Dorea, leaning on her cane, reminded Carolina. "If the shed is not open, the key is-"

"I know, above the stacked wood, top shelf in the pantry, in the copper pot. Thanks, Grams Dorea."

Grams Dorea made her way outside onto the back porch to a cushioned chair at a card table and sat down. She had just started on her seascape puzzle when there was a knock on the screened porch door.

She looked up. "Morning, Earl. What can I do for you now?"

"I ain't' here with cheerful news. Ya gonna need an electrician. Didn't consider all these window AC units would suck up energy. Ya don't have enough juice." He took off his baseball cap and wiped the sweat from his forehead. "I got a buddy who owes me. He can be here in an hour."

Grams Dorea put her puzzle pieces down and looked up. "Then call him. Go on. No fussing."

"Ya sure ya don't want an estimate first?" He squinted into the screen door.

"If you say we need it, we need it. And for Pete's sake, do not break my screen squishing your entire face into it."

Earl pulled away from the screen. He put his baseball cap on and hurried off, checking his watch, anxious about his date with Pearl, which wasn't for hours.

"Mom, have you seen Caroline?" Halia asked as she made her way onto the porch and looked out over the dune. "Gorgeous day."

Grams Dorea looked up. "She's out for a bike ride to the Red and White Market to pick up fixings for supper." She patted the cushioned chair beside her. "Sit down and relax. It's hot today. Thank the sea gods for the breezes."

Halia sat down, expelling an exaggerated sigh, gazing out at the ocean.

"I know that sigh. What's going on?" Grams Dorea asked as she crossed her arms over her chest. "Speak."

"Nothing, Mom."

"That sigh was *not* nothing. I know you better than that. Talk to me."

"It's Caroline. She is taking on too much work. Partnering with Lawson is a huge mistake. I can't talk sense into her. Did you see how thin she's getting? She is snappy, on edge, and always checking her phone."

Grams Dorea waited a moment. "Halia, as you know, once a woman in our clan is crowned, they soon fall in love and begin a family. If it is her intention. Look at all the women before her. The mermaid's magic will find her. Her job is her passion, and I hate to admit, she reminds me of your late husband." She bit her tongue before she let loose on politicians.

Halia patted Gram Dorea's arm. "I know. I wish she would marry Colton."

"Don't you start with that. Moving on, speaking of thin, you are thin as a rail."

Halia pressed her sundress against her body. The doctor's words and report still clung to her. But now was not the time. She said, "I haven't been sleeping well. I'm considering selling the house in DC. It's far too big. It served as great entertainment for Weston's political friends. Now it's an empty, cavernous shell with nothing but echoes of the past. I'm thinking of buying a nice townhouse, maybe in Manteo, here in North Carolina."

"Manteo?"

"Yes, Grams Dorea, then I can be closer to the ocean and relax. I love that village and I can be within walking distance of so many things, even a cup of coffee."

"Well, now don't forget, I don't have nine lives and this cottage is in you and your sisters' names. Don't you dare sell it or I will come barreling down from heaven and poke you all with my cane!"

"Never, Mom, never. This cottage holds the hearts of generations."

★

After some struggling, Caroline got the bike out of the shed. It had a little more rust on it than last summer. She used the ancient bike pump and put air in the tires. Reaching onto a shelf, she got a can of lubricant and gave the chain a squirt. The wicker basket had held together, and even the bell worked.

She pushed it out to the driveway and adjusted the seat. With her straw hat and sunglasses on, she put her foot to the pedal and down the road she went. What freedom! She was happy to see the new sidewalks and followed them to the coffee shop. She put her bike on the bike rack and walked inside. The alluring, deep, earthy aroma of freshly ground coffee filled her senses.

The man in front of her ordered a two-pump café mocha raspberry latte with extra whipped cream and a sprinkle of brown sugar on top. She wanted to laugh, thinking to herself, *extra whipped cream and sprinkles.* Such a girly drink. The young girl behind the counter was new, flustered, and slow, so a coworker helped.

The man turned to Caroline. "Sorry."

The new girl grinned painfully at Caroline.

With a tilt of her head, Caroline replied. "I'm in no hurry. I can stand here for hours inhaling the wonderful aromas."

The man ordered a thick cinnamon bun piled with icing. Caroline's eyes wandered around, looking at seascape watercolors by local artists. When it was her turn, she ordered an organic coffee and located a side table to grab a packet of raw sugar.

"Excuse me." She reached for a packet.

"Sure, hey, am I in your way?" the man asked as he shuffled his fluffy coffee and bun aside.

"Nope," she looked at his cinnamon bun. "That looks delicious."

"They make them fresh daily. It's what brings me here."

Staring into his Prussian blue eyes, heightened by well-groomed chestnut hair, Caroline stirred her coffee. She did not see a rambunctious kid until he careened on her leg, jolting her to the side. Some of her coffee splashed onto the man's white Van dock shoes.

"Oh, shit! I mean..." Wide eyed, she looked down at his shoes. "Oh, gosh, I'm *so* sorry."

The kid ran outside, with his frazzled mother not far behind, yelling at him to stop.

"Did your foot get burned?" Caroline grabbed a handful of napkins and handed them to him.

"No, it was a splash. It's fine. No problem. That kid is always running around. No big deal. I have more shoes." He stooped and blotted his shoe and tossed the napkin in the trash.

"Oh, gosh, that kid needs to be disciplined. If my Grams Dorea saw that, he would be over her knee." She watched the kid run in circles in the parking lot. "Wow, he needs to calm down. Sugar high or what?"

He chuckled as he stood up. "She gives him iced coffee. I swear it is espresso. I'm Dillan, by the way."

"Hi. I'm Caroline."

"Nice to meet you, Caroline. Are you here on vacation?"

"Yes... no... sort of. A working vacation," she laughed. Why was she acting like an idiot?

"Awesome. Glorious weather ahead and no hurricanes forecasted." He tossed the napkins into the trash. "Where is home?"

"DC," Caroline answered, not realizing she was opening a second packet of sugar. "I'm here for a while to decompress. And spill coffee on people." Her face flushed. "Let me at least pay for your coffee." She reached into her purse.

He put his hands up. "No way. It's not your fault."

She squeezed her face. "You sure?"

His phone rang. He looked down, but he didn't answer. "Work. I live in a vacation paradise, but always work. An oxymoron if there ever was one, right?"

"I know the feeling." She stirred her coffee and moved over as a family with little kids made their way inside. "Oh, you mean you live here? On the island?"

"Moved down a few months ago from the city. New York, that is."

"Wow, big change. For sure. I better go, I'm buying salad fixins, as Grams would say." *Oh my god, can I sound any lamer?*

"I hope I see you around, Caroline, from DC. Stay cool."

"Thanks, I will."

She watched this enchanting man with a coffee-stained shoe go out the door. This could be an interesting vacation, after all.

Eleven

Caroline continued her bike ride to the Hatteras ferry dock. Cars, motorhomes, and SUVs lined the street on their way to Ocracoke Island. Vacationers wandered around as they waited for the next ferry. Glad she was not in those long lines, she pedaled to the farm stand. With her bicycle basket filled with fresh vegetables, she made her way back to the cottage to find several vans parked outside and chaos inside.

"What is going on, Mom?" She put the bag on the kitchen counter. "Who are all these men? Is it a party I'm not aware of?"

Halia shook her head. "Ask your Auntie Lorelei. She and Earl put in all those new air conditioning units. Earl told her *not* to turn them on until his buddy checked out the electrical box. You know your auntie, the know-it-all. She did and blew out all the fuses. Now these wonderful men are here putting in a new fuse box. We have no power and almost had a house fire."

"Fire? Oh crap, what did Grams Dorea say?" Caroline asked as an older man with a toolbox passed by with a nod.

Halia lifted her shoulders. "You know, Grams, Dorea. She is glad it's being fixed. She stomped her cane a few times and mumbled a few words of holy hell discontent."

"Wow. This is big and Grams Dorea only did a cane stomping?" Caroline said as she looked around, wiping beads of sweat off her forehead. "It's brutal in here. Where is everyone?"

"Auntie Calypso is down at the beach; Grams Dorea is on the porch and Pearl is with Earl on his boat."

Caroline put her hand over her mouth and burst into laughter. "A boat? As on a date with Earl?" She cracked up. "Pearl and Earl. Sounds like a country duet. The Pearl and Earl Party Boat Hour."

"Oh, honey, your sense of humor is back! It's not a date. I would call it a boat ride. Pearl left here with a basket of food, and Earl picked her up in that topless lime green jeep of his, with that skull of a pirate painted on the hood. Pearl told me they were supposed to have a beach picnic, but Earl surprised her with an afternoon on his boat."

"Wow, hey, does Earl have a hound dog, too?" Caroline snickered as she took the vegetables out of the bag.

"Don't open the fridge. Just leave the vegetables in the bag. Ice for drinks is in the Yeti cooler." Halia pointed to the corner.

"Thanks, Mom." Caroline poured a glass of tea from the big pitcher on the kitchen table and reached into the cooler for ice. "I need to spend some time upstairs working. Don't tell Grams Dorea, or she will read me the riot act."

"It's going to be a hundred degrees up there, but go. Get our Colton in that oval office." She ran her hand through Caroline's hair. "Go."

Caroline flashed a smile. *Our Colton.* In her bedroom upstairs, the air was suffocating. The humidity had settled onto everything, leaving her files limp. Fortunately, a gentle ocean breeze provided slight relief. She set her glass on the end table and sat down on her bed, where she felt a lump.

"Oh, crap!" She pulled the covers down and found the journal. She picked it up and held it to her chest. What to do?

"Caroline?" Her mother tapped on the door. "Honey?"

Caroline stuffed the journal under the pillows. "What's up?"

"I have a nice young man here who needs to get in to look at the wall plugs."

"Yeah, sure come in."

He spent a few minutes with a tester kit examining the plugs. "No power in here."

Caroline looked at her mother, then at the pillow. "I can't get a minute's peace here." She picked up her laptop and files. "I'm going to the coffee shop to work. I cannot focus here with all these repair people and heat. My laptop needs a charge too. Call me when the cottage is cool."

Halia's phone dinged. She took it out of her pocket. "Oh, dear. Oh, my."

"What's with all the oh dears and mys?"

"Auntie Pearl just texted me. Earl's boat broke down out in the sound and is being towed into a marina. She's a nervous wreck."

"Are you serious? Is she okay?"

"They weren't very far out in the water, and the motor died or something. He's getting a tow. Thank goodness it did not sink. I hope she wore a life jacket."

"Mom, knowing Auntie Pearl, she is wearing two life jackets. She is, okay?"

"Yes. You know Auntie Pearl, a drama queen. I'm heading down to the beach to read."

"Have fun, Mom!"

Caroline heard her mother's footsteps on the squeaky stairs and looked at the pillows. The journal under them. It was a close call. She made her way downstairs, grabbed her keys off the sideboard, and headed out to her SUV. With the AC on full blast, she put her face close to the vents. Cooled, she put the car in drive.

Just past eleven, she discovered a secluded corner in the coffee shop to establish her mini office. With her earbuds in, she dove into the emails. Back in her room, as if it had a pulse, the journal was calling out to her. She knew it was wrong. Who would know? Except Ida, Marie, and Dorothy. *What am I going crazy?* Shaking it off, she read her emails.

Lawson was not happy with her being away from the office, but it had been part of the deal. Lawson needed Caroline's connections and name. Caroline and her team had worked hard to develop Colton's stump speech. Why is he running? What he can and will do for the country. Now Lawson was adamant that they would change their strategies and break from the Wilmen brand. This could get ugly extremely fast.

There was no reason to derail this train. Tweaking his platform, yes. Not changing it. Voters needed to hear the same message over and over. People believed in him. He was young, single, handsome, and philanthropic. He had no dirt on him as far as they knew, and his romance with Caroline never existed. But all that could come crashing down in one news cycle by his opponent.

The problem was his recent engagement with that popular morning news anchor with her own show on the horizon.

Being divorced and six years his senior, she built a reputation on her relentless drive to destroy anyone who disagreed with her. Colton had put himself between a rock and a hard place. Caroline let out a loud sigh. A few people enjoying iced coffees looked over at this pretty woman moaning over her laptop. She flashed them with a smile and started typing.

An hour passed as the bright sun entered her space.

The barista came over to close the window shade. "You need anything? We close at three today."

Caroline squinted. "No. And can you leave mine half down?" She looked at her phone. It was after two. "Wait, a coffee refill, thanks."

Her phone rang.

"Hello Colton." She sat back, looking at the nautical art across the room.

"I'm in Cleveland. There was no standing room. We take off for Indiana in twenty minutes and then Wisconsin."

"Colton, we need to talk."

"Yes, we do. I picked my vice president."

"It's getting very late in the game, and I hope it's not flighty Marrison from Arizona. She is the ball on a heavy chain with too much controversy, and her husband is bad news. We talked about this, Colton."

"That's why I'm calling, and you are the second to know." He paused. "It's Gary McMillan."

Caroline's eyes widened. "Wow, from Maine? That came unexpectedly. Excellent choice! This is going to be one hell of an election."

                    Diana Baxter

"We are going to be in the White House, babe. Lawson and I spoke this morning. His team has everything under control. I'm on the plane, ready to take off. And uh, Wilmen is out, and you don't need to worry. I got him."

Caroline drummed her fingernails on the tabletop. "I should be in DC."

"No, enjoy your vacation. I'll call you tonight after the rally."

Caroline sat back, relieved Wilmen was not her issue.

"I believe in you, Lynnie. *You* will get me in the White House."

Caroline pushed her hair behind her ear. He'd nicknamed her Lynnie when they had dated. She recalled the first time, the exact moment. They were hand-in-hand at Lighthouse Beach in Buxton. They'd stopped to watch the sun sink behind the Hatteras lighthouse. As the waves crashed around them, their lips met in the fading light.

Twleve

Caroline hung up with Colton just as the barista brought her iced coffee. She added sugar and stirred, staring out at the busy marina across the street. Her mind was swirling. She took a sip and did a double take—on the dock, getting out of a pontoon boat. Was that Auntie Pearl with Earl? Yes, it was. Earl tied up the boat as a flashy boat that must have towed them also docked. She watched as Auntie Pearl, picnic basket in hand, got into the lime green Jeep with Earl and drove off. She knew at dinner they would all learn of the chaotic boating disaster.

Earl, she thought, was a pure character, straight out of a slapstick movie. He might be odd, but he kept her mother, aunties, and Grams Dorea entertained. And in his own way, he was a good-looking man. Smiling, Caroline went back to work. She was in the middle of writing an email to Lawson when the door opened and closed. Caroline looked up. There he was! The man from this morning who not only drinks girly coffee, but she ruined his shoe.

She ducked down behind her laptop, her eyes following him. He ordered and sat down at a small table across the room. The flirtatious and giggly barista let him know his raspberry iced tea was ready. She brought it over and set it down, chatting away as she twirled her long hair. He smiled at her.

Caroline ducked lower in her chair as she watched them. She kept her head down when he got up and made his way over to the counter for a few napkins and left. She watched through the window as he got into a hi-end SUV.

I knew it. He looked out of place with his fancy shoes and clothes. I'm so done with that type. She crossed him off her list. Watching him drive off toward Hatteras Village, she thought, *wait, an SUV? He most likely has five kids, a wife, two dogs, and a nanny.* She inhaled and returned to work.

The barista reminded Caroline that it was almost closing time. After drinking the last drop of iced coffee, she packed up her laptop and files. She discarded her empty cup and entered the blistering summer heat. Having forgotten her sunglasses in the car, she shielded her eyes and put her bag in the back seat. She let the SUV run with the doors open for a minute to cool it off. While waiting, she noticed a boutique across the street with vibrant sale signs all over the windows. She couldn't resist.

"Welcome!" An older woman in a tropical patterned maxi-dress, graying hair in a bun and hot pink lipstick greeted her. "Are y'all here on vacation, hun?" She made her way over to the counter and opened a box. "It sure is hot. They are saying it's gonna be like this for a while. I sure wish the wind goddesses would lend us a hand."

Caroline's eyes adjusted. "Hi, yes, it is hot, and I'm here on vacation." The store was wall to wall with bathing suits, cover-ups, beach hats, and jewelry, and of all things, fishing poles and boogie boards.

"Y'all looking for anything special?" the woman asked after a quick glance at Caroline's ring finger. "You here with family?"

"Yes, my mother, aunties, and Grandma. A full house."

"Why, that *is* special, a girls' vacation. Where y'all stayin'?"

"In Hatteras, in our cottage." Caroline picked up a navy-blue polka dot bikini with gold trim from a round table of bathing suits.

"That's a pleasant color." The woman moved over to Caroline. "I have a matching navy cover up with pom-poms and gold trim." She lifted it off the rack and put it next to the bikini. "It sure looks real pretty together with your eyes and hair. It's a man lure for sure."

"That's the last thing I need!" Caroline laughed, stepped back, and looked over the sexy combo.

"Oh, now, you never know. And we have a fifteen percent sale on swimwear this week. Your husband or boyfriend will love it. Does he fish?" Her attention shifted to the back of the store. "My husband sells fishing gear, everything y'all need."

"I'm not married. And, uh," she glanced at the row of fishing poles, "I don't fish."

"Boyfriend?"

"Uh, no, not right now. No time for that." Caroline was becoming uncomfortable with the nosy woman's questions.

"Why, this bikini will catch you a boyfriend or husband faster than a hungry fish to a baited hook."

Caroline broke into a slight laugh at the silly comment.

"Don't laugh, that's how I caught my Emery." Her face lit up. "I once had a fine, perky figure like yours. Well, that was some thirty-seven years ago, or was it thirty-eight?" She tapped her bottom lip. "Then I had two wonderful boys. My oldest was over ten pounds at birth. Did me in, so I thought. Then, two years later, in the back of my mama's cottage, in my old bedroom, the next one flew out, practically landing in his bassinet. Now I'm a grandma to seven. Oh, golly, how time flies."

This was too much information. Caroline did not want a husband, a boyfriend, or babies flying out of her in a back bedroom landing in bassinets. She wanted her client to win the election.

"I'm sure time goes by fast. My Grams says one day you are young and the next day you look in the mirror and ask who is looking back at you."

"Y'all sure got that right," the woman agreed just as new customers opened the door, sounding the chime. "Welcome, be with y'all in a sec. Please close the door. Don't want my cool air getting out."

Caroline tilted her head and decided. "Do you have a size ten in this bikini?"

The woman wasted no time thumbing through the rack, humming. "Sure do." She pulled it out. "Now, the cover-up is one size. This would look good on y'all and your perky figure. And your skin is flawless, with a few freckles on your perky nose."

Caroline never liked the six freckles near the tip of her nose.

"I'll take both and some of your best sunblock. The sun is like fertilizer to my freckles."

"Fertilizer to a freckle. Why, if that isn't the funniest thing, I've heard all summer!"

The woman led Caroline to the counter while she kept an eye on new customers. "Seventy sunblock it is, and it works fabulously." She plucked a green jar off the shelf behind her. "Dermatologist approved and you won't get liver spots when y'all get old like me. Make sure to put it on your hands and ears." She was ringing up the items when the door opened.

"Afternoon, Miss Dottie." A barefooted older man in cut-off jean shorts and a fishing cap with hooks dangling from it appeared. "Hope ya don't mind. We had to tow ol' Earl's pontoon boat to your dock. I told him it ain't a smart idea to take that dang old thing out. The engine gone and died, and the left pontoon is taking on water. We patched the right pontoon a month ago. Anyway, we tied it up at your dock. He promised to have it towed to the marina later today. I know Emery will be back tomorrow and will want his boat in its slip."

"Now y'all are telling me crazy Earl took out that pontoon? Emery told him it was not safe after the hurricane last September, when it rammed into the dock. Darned thing is ready to sink. He had no business taking it out."

The man at the door laughed. "I told him that Gorilla glue ain't the best way to tape up a pontoon. Earl ain't one to listen. He had a fine-looking woman with him, and he scared the bejesus out of her. Tucked into a lifejacket, she was shaking like a rattle."

"You tell Earl to get that boat out of there by morning or my Emery will sink it! Heck, it may sink itself."

They shared a laugh.

"Will do, Miss Dottie," the man waved, adding a nod as he left.

Caroline shook her head. "That was my Auntie Pearl in the boat."

"You sure?" Dottie's eyes grew wide. "He knows better than to be taking visitors out on that raft, for heaven's sake!"

Dottie leaned across the counter. "Earl is harmless, but he sure keeps us laughing. His family goes way back here on the island. He has a kind heart and tries hard since his Betsy passed a few years back. She was his rock and my dear lifelong friend. May she rest in peace."

"Oh, I'm sorry to hear that. Earl is our neighbor."

"Y'all don't say. You are stayin' at the house next door? The old cottage? That belongs to...?" She closed her eyes and snapped her fingers. "Golly geez, my memory can't help me." She opened her eyes. "I'm embarrassed. I can't find her name in my old memory."

"That's okay. She is my grandmother. Her name is Dorothy Henson, and her late husband was my Grandfather Wayland."

"Well, I'll be!" Dottie came out from behind the counter and gave Caroline a bear hug. "Wayland and my Emery used to go out fishing when the Red Drum were running. Why, your grandmother is a pip. Tell her Miz Dottie says hello. I must bring her one of my coconut layer cakes with rum-soaked blackberries. She loved them."

"My Grams Dorea sure is a pip," Caroline laughed. "Please stop by. I'm sure she would love to see you."

"I will make it a point to stop over. How is she?"

"Hanging in. A new hip this past spring, and there is no stopping her."

"Bless her sweet little heart." Dottie put her hands on her chest. "I recall her being tough as nails and could she clean up a fish!" She made a face. "That was never my passion." Dottie leaned close. "Those four daughters of hers were wild back in the day. Parties on the beach under the full moon. Something sacrilegious about mermaids?"

"No, no, they just like to have fun telling tall stories from long ago." *Do the townspeople know? How embarrassing!*

"So Pearl is your aunt? Well, tell her to stay away from Earl's homebrew. Scuppernong wine, he calls it. Lord a 'mercy, that will land ya flat on your face." She looked around and back at Caroline. "Gossip at church has it that Earl is looking for a new wife."

"Auntie Pearl?" She pulled back. "No... no. She's here on vacation."

Thankfully, the door opened.

"Afternoon, Dillan." Dottie greeted him with her booming voice. "I left your bag out back. The kitties need some more dry food, if y'all don't mind feeding the critters. I can't go outside with customers here."

There he was. The man with the stained Vans. Was he a spy for Wilmen? *No, how silly is that?* Or was it?

He noticed Caroline and waved. "Hi again, DC! Hey, I got the coffee out of my shoes. Miss Dottie suggested a remedy, and it worked."

"Isn't that just wonderful?" Dottie said with a bright smile. "The only way to get a stain out is with my mama's old recipe."

"I picked up a twenty-pound bag of cat food for you as thanks for the shoe tip," Dillan said as an orange tabby cat slid past him. "And a can of Friskies for Miss Alley. Is that okay? It's chicken and dumplings."

"Ah, thank you, hun. Miss Alley will enjoy that." She turned to Caroline. "Here's a tip. A little peroxide, baking soda and borax does wonders for anything white except linen and silk," she explained as she folded Caroline's items and carefully put them in a bag. Caroline ran her credit card through the machine.

"See you later, Miss Dottie," Dillan flashed a smile. "You, too, DC."

Caroline turned her attention to Dottie. "Wow, good to know about the cleaning secret. It was my fault," she admitted as she watched Dillan outside. He bent over and petted a cat.

Dottie looked from side to side. "Why does he wear those fancy city shoes? I keep telling him flip-flops are the way to go down here, but he's good to the cats. The strays on the island are hungry critters, although I know they are getting plenty of fresh fish scraps at Oden's Dock."

Caroline smiled at this kind woman.

"Miss Alley, she is gotta be eighteen by now. That gal gets to eat first. Poor ole' gal wandered onto my doorstep at home one day and never left. Like my Emery! I fed him and he stayed." She snorted. "I bring Miss Alley here to work. She lounges out back, soaking up the sun. Today I saw her under the old Camilla bush. That ole' girl won't come inside. Lord knows I have tried." Dottie handed Caroline her receipt. "Thank you for shopping at my boutique. Send your family in for the sale! It ends next week. I will stop over to visit with my cake!"

"Thank you. I'll tell my grandmother you will come by," Caroline made a beeline for the door. Outside, she caught Dillan, throwing a bag of cat food over his strong shoulder and disappearing around the corner to the back of the store.

She tossed the shopping bag into the back of her SUV and headed to the cottage. Her phone was dinging. Messages from her team. Colton. Lawson. Wilmen. Her mother.

Another long night ahead of her.

Thirteen

"Hi, Grams Dorea." Caroline cheered as she breezed into the cottage infused with cool air. "Wow. It feels good in here."

"The electrician hooked up a generator to keep the window unit on, so we did not bake in this heat. He told us another day to get the electricity up and running. The upstairs is still an oven on convection, and we are gonna camp out downstairs tonight. Your aunties and mother are down at the beach." Grams Dorea looked at Caroline's bag. "You were shopping, I see. Anything good?"

"Yup, a new bikini." She plopped her bags down. "A sleepover party downstairs tonight?"

"Yes, and Earl is kind enough to let me stay at his place tonight. You can join me. We called around. There were no rooms available."

"I would guess the hotels are slammed this time of the year on the island."

"Everyone except Pearl is down at the beach. Go join them and get some sun!"

"I will, Grams Dorea. I need to jump into the ocean but, back to you staying at Earl's. That should prove interesting. Earl may wind up back here!"

Grams Dorea narrowed her eyes. "Perhaps he will."

"I nearly forgot, Miss Dottie says hello and she will stop by with a coconut cake and rum-soaked berries. She owns a boutique in town where I got my new bathing suit. She said you and she spent much time here and Gramps fished with her husband."

Grams Dorea wore a fond smile. "Mizz Dottie is a wonderful woman. I haven't seen her in well over twelve years. Time goes by so fast. She and I spent hours here at the cottage, chatting and playing cards while our husbands fished. I did all the fish cleaning, and Dottie did the cooking." Grams Dorea sat down in her recliner and looked up at her husband's urn jar. "Ain't that right, honey?"

Caroline watched Grams Dorea talk to her husband's ashes as if he were sitting beside her. She wondered if she would ever have a relationship like that. Or did she even want one? She kissed her grandmother on the cheek and went upstairs to change.

Dinner conversation at the table that evening was entertaining. Pearl regaled them with her adventures with Earl, as everyone laughed. Caroline and her mother finished drying the last of the dishes.

Caroline tossed the dishtowel onto the countertop and let out a heavy sigh. "Night, Mom, I'm tired. I need to get my air mattress ready."

Halia put her glass of water down. "Me, too. It is time we get the air mattress pump and more candles out of the closet. We have one lamp working, thanks to the generator."

"Grams Dorea told me that the hotels are full."

"Yes, Caroline. It's that time of the year. Earl offered to let Grams Dorea sleep in his guest room. Auntie Pearl is taking her over to Earl's place soon. Can you make sure she has her orthopedic pillow and medications?"

"Sure, Mom. I know the hum of the generator will put me to sleep."

Halia's eyes widened. "Earl is supposed to stop over and put more gas in it." Over at the back door, she looked at the outside thermometer. "It's eighty-seven degrees, and even the breezes off the ocean are warm."

"Lovely," Caroline made her way into the living room. "Grams Dorea, are you really going to stay at Earl's?"

"I cannot sleep on the floor on an air mattress. I can't get down on the floor, no less get back up."

There was a knock on the door.

Pearl rushed over to answer it. "Hi, Earl. When Grams Dorea is ready, I will take her over."

Earl took off his cap. "My front door is open. I'm here to gas up the generator to get you ladies a few hours of relief. I have five bedrooms, and y'all are welcome to stay. It's sure nice and cool over at my place." He looked at the tired group. "I got plenty of refreshments!"

Pearl blushed. "Thank you, Earl. I think we will be fine here. You don't want a house full of women, do you?" She raised her eyebrows.

"Why, I sure do. If I get a platter of those fancy cheeses out of it."

"Earl, you come on over for breakfast once we get our electricity back and I will make you one of my Western omelets as a thanks for letting Grams Dorea stay at your cottage."

Earl looked side to side, then to Pearl. "Deal. I will see y'all tomorrow. I gotta turn off the generator to gas it up. No power for a few minutes, so don't panic. Y'all better have candles and flashlights ready." With a skip in his step, he left the porch.

The Beach Heart Cottage night seemed to stretch on forever. Caroline spent much of it at her grandfather's old desk in the living room, working on her laptop until the battery died. The generator began to sputter and use its last drop of gas.

The dark skies were lighting up as the morning sun was breaking through a bank of low clouds. Someone knocked on the front door. Lorelei answered it. She squinted at the group of men.

"Morning, ma'am. We are here to get your electricity up and running."

"Oh, wonderful! You sure are early."

"Yes, ma'am. Earl is a buddy of mine. We owe him and are here to help y'all out. We'd like to get started early since today is gonna be record-breaking heat."

Lorelei stepped back. "Sure, come on in and ignore our campground in the living room. Is there a possibility of it being fixed by this evening?"

The man glanced into the living room. "By late this afternoon. If we start now. And, uh, we need to get into all the rooms."

Lorelei sighed in relief. "Thank goodness." She needed to get back to her sewing machine and piles of sequins.

The repairmen stepped inside, not without peeking at the temporary bedroom that took over the living room. It did not take long before the hammering and the yelling back and forth woke everyone up.

Yawning, Caroline, with a pillow and blanket, made her way upstairs to her stifling bedroom. She opened the window for a slight ocean breeze to soothe her as she changed into a sundress.

Back downstairs, she found Grams Dorea sitting in her recliner. "Morning, Grams Dorea. How was your night at Earl's? Did you rest?"

"My dear granddaughter, never judge a book by its cover. Earl is a pure gentleman. A little horny, though."

"*What*?"

"We played a round of strip poker. Down to our skivvies."

Caroline slapped her hand over her chest. "You did not!"

Grams Dorea burst into laughter. "Oh, honey, the look on your face was priceless."

"You had me going! Then again, some things that happen at Earl's stay at Earl's."

"We stayed up playing pinochle and drinking beer. You know he can fry green tomatoes better than your mother. They were delicious. He told me so many tales of his great granddaddy and our family. How they fished and partied. His lineage goes back to England. And pirates." Her face softened. "Hand me Grandpop's ashes, honey."

"Pirates, Grams Dorea? He's putting you on." She reached for the Ball jar urn, praying Grams Dorea did not notice the contents were less and the jar lighter.

"Thank you." She held the urn on her lap. "Earl is sharing dinner with us tonight. And yes, I'm breaking all the Beach House Cottage rules." She rocked and spoke to the urn. "I miss you. I know you're here with us at the cottage." She hugged the jar. "Caroline, Grandpops feels a little lighter. Here, hold him."

Caroline reached for the jar and looked at it. "I'm sure he is fine in there. He's on a diet!"

"You are funny!" Grams Dorea snorted. "I hope those men can get the power on today. Go ask Lorelei what is going on with them. And tell the girls they need to clean. The living room is full of dust."

Caroline felt her heart sink as her eyes landed on the canning jar. "I will. How about I get you a glass of orange juice?"

"Sounds good. And with the generator running, can you put on the fan?"

"Yup!" Caroline returned and handed her grandmother the glass of juice. She took her grandpop's ashes and put it on the mantel.

Fourteen

It was after three when Caroline was sitting on the beach and got a text message from Auntie Lorelei: *they restored Power. All the new air conditioners are on.* Relieved she could now take a shower and get some work done in the coolness of her bedroom; she headed up to the cottage.

Caroline's mood was light as she dropped her beach bag on the floor. "Oh, this feels wonderful, Mom!"

"It's refreshing, isn't it?" Halia agreed as she entered the room with a glass of iced tea. "The air conditioning units have been running at full blast since they restored the power. The thermometer reads ninety degrees out there in the shade."

Caroline checked her phone. "Mom, I need a shower and to get some work done. I have a conference call at four-thirty."

"Okay, honey, but a few workers are upstairs finishing up." She put her glass down and made her way over to

Caroline, pushing her hair past her shoulders. "Honey, you get him in the White House, and you *will* be by his side."

Caroline reached for her mother's hand. "Mom, look me in the eye. No blinking. I'm hired to help him secure the presidency, not to be his wife. I believe in him. Our country needs him, and it is my job to get him there. Please, let the idea go of a grand wedding in the Rose Garden."

Her mother looked out the window at the swaying sea oats and back to Caroline. "Your father would be so disappointed."

"Mom, Daddy is gone. This is my life, not Daddy's." She pulled her mother close and hugged her. "Okay, Mom?"

"Well... can I still pray that you will reunite?"

"Pray all you want, Mom. Pray he becomes President Colton Jameson. I will not be First Lady Caroline."

"Listen to how wonderful it sounds when you say First Lady Caroline. It naturally rolls off your tongue. So regal."

Caroline shook her head. "Mom, stop."

Her mother slouched her shoulders, sighing loud enough for Pearl to hear it as she entered the room with a bottle of cleaner and a cloth.

"Why the long face, Halia?"

"My daughter is as stubborn as her father was."

"Truce!" Pearl held up her white cloth, waving it around. "Grams Dorea said the fireplace area and sofa are full of a gray fine dust and we need to clean better. It's making her sneeze. Must be ashes from an old fire."

Caroline and her mother looked at each other and burst into laughter.

"What's so funny?" Pearl asked as she made her way toward the fireplace. "It's a mess over here. I need the vacuum. And a mop."

"I'm sure Grandpop would approve of a little dusting!" Caroline said, then dashed up the stairs.

Pearl moved the fireplace screen when something caught her eye. She bent over to pick it up.

"Huh? This looks like Dad's wedding ring. Why would it be out of the jar? Halia?" She held it up. "Look at this."

"If I were you, I'd stick it in the jar and forget you ever saw it."

Caroline sat down on her bed and lay back, looking up at the ceiling. She hastily slid her hands under the pillow. The journal wasn't there! *Oh my god, somebody took it! No, wait. I took it.* Where was it? Then she realized she had placed it not only under the pillows but also under the comforter. There was the journal!

"I can't believe I forgot about you. Thank God! I would have been so dead! How about I take a quick shower, and we have a little sneak read before my call?"

She tucked the journal under the pillows, pulled a pair of shorts and tee shirt out of the dresser. When she removed her bikini and threw it onto the side chair, she noticed a pair of blue eyes staring back at her through the window.

Startled, she screamed and instinctively used her arms to cover her body. The eyes vanished. She moved backward and hid behind the closet door. She was sure it was the man with the Van shoes. Dillan. No, it couldn't be. She peeked out. He was gone.

"Mom! Where did that peeping Tom go?"

No one heard her. Downstairs on the back porch, everyone was enjoying cocktails and music.

Caroline reached for anything in the closet to cover up. She found a sundress, wrapped it around her body, and dashed down the hall to the bathroom. Breathless and still stunned, she sat on the edge of the clawfoot tub. She chuckled inwardly at her own awkward appearance and his surprised reaction.

Over at the window, she peeked through the mini blinds and gasped. There he was with a ladder over his shoulder. At least he wasn't looking up. From that high angle, she couldn't tell if it was the same man. And he had work boots on, not white shoes.

Someone knocked on the bathroom door. "Crap!" she cried out.

"Caroline, are you okay? Are you taking a shower? We have hot water again. And your mom said you have a call at four-thirty. After, can you spare a few minutes so I can get you fitted for your mermaid dress?"

"Yes, I'm fine, Auntie Lorelei. I'll be there as soon as I can for my fitting." Caroline kept her eye on the man on the ground as he helped Earl lift the ladder onto Earl's truck.

"Isn't it wonderful to have the cottage cool again? I'll see you downstairs."

Caroline looked in the mirror. Her nose was glowing with new freckles. She studied her face and body. *He saw me naked.* She covered her breasts with her hands. *It can't be him. What would he be doing here on the roof? I'm working too hard.*

She turned on the water, stepped into the shower, and cooled off. With her hair up in a towel, she was sitting on the edge of her bed when her phone rang.

"Caroline, we're gonna win. I can feel it. You're my girl. You always will be."

Caroline sat back, not saying a word.

"Hello? Did you hear me?"

"I'm here, Colton. What's going on?"

"We rock, Caroline. The Midwest voters love us. Big rallies!"

"Great!"

"Florida and Georgia tomorrow, then Virginia Beach. How about you sneak away from your vacation and join me in Georgia? The governor has a beautiful beach house on Jekyll Island. He graciously offered it to me. We can stay there, and no one will know. Then we can *personally* go over a few things."

She gave him credit. He was trying. "We?"

"Of course!"

"Not the best idea. The past is the past. Let's leave it that way. And you are engaged. What are you thinking?"

"I wasn't."

Caroline shook her head. "When do we announce your engagement? We need to move on this. Get it out there before somebody else does."

He was silent.

"Well?"

"It is over and-"

"Holy shit, Colton!"

"No, listen, it was amicable."

"I bet! A woman scorned by a presidential candidate! Heavens, what did you do? And she is a well-known news anchor. Hot mess."

"She did it. Last night. She wishes me well."

"Okay, my gut? This will explode, and she'll get a book deal and a Netflix mini-series. Watch your back. Do you want my private eye to watch her?"

"No, no, don't do that. And she doesn't need a book deal since she has her TV anchor gig, the wealthy ex who does not want controversy, and her kids. She doesn't want to drag them through the mud. Besides-"

"Colton, never trust an ex. Don't be so naïve." Hiring the P.I. was now on her mental list of calls. This would be in everyone's best interest. "Wait, what did you say? Besides what?"

"You're never gonna believe this—she's donating to my campaign."

"I'll believe that when I see it."

"She already did it. Now, do you believe me?"

"Listen, I have work to do. I'll be up 'til dawn." She said as she adjusted the towel on her head. "Working on your image as the hot single guy candidate. Are we still on for our call in," she looked at her phone, "twenty minutes?"

"That's why I'm calling you. Lawson rescheduled it for tomorrow." She knew he was running his fingers through his hair. "Remember when we stayed up 'til dawn at your grandmother's cottage? And how we snuck down there one October. You opened the cottage up and roasted coconut marshmallows in the fireplace, and we smoked the place out, setting off the fire alarm? I had to slip the fire captain a few bucks not to tell your grandmother."

Caroline knew he was playing with her heart. Evading his trap proved challenging. "I remember." She smiled into the phone. "Colton, that was then. This is now. I'll talk to you, I'm sure, at some early hour in the morning."

"Always a worker like your father. If not for him, I would not be where I am now. And a suggestion: you need to chill. You are on vacation. Before you go, I wear that pin your father gave me when he was running for president. I know he lost by a small margin, but I find it to be good luck. Bye, Lynnie." He hung up.

Caroline stared at the phone. "Lynnie?" She shook her head. It was past five. Dinner was at six, and making the salad was her responsibility. She closed her laptop, put her phone on silent, stuffed it into her shorts pocket, and made her way to the kitchen. Everyone had already had a little too much happy hour.

"Wow, are you all a little buzzed?"

"We are, Caroline!" Auntie Calypso pinched her cheek. "We are on vacation on Hatteras Island!" She danced away. "Turn up the speakers. I love Van Morrison!" Calypso sang along to *Into the Mystic*.

"Ouch," Caroline rubbed her cheek. "No more pinching, please."

Auntie Calypso clapped her hands. "We are having blue crabs and lobster for dinner. Earl is bringing his famous potato salad and the scuppernong wine he brews. We're having a feast. I'm making my world-famous fried green tomatoes!"

"Wow, you guys are high!" Caroline laughed. "I better catch up! Wait, are you smoking something funny too?"

They burst out laughing right when the doorbell chimed.

"Caroline, can you get the door?" Auntie Pearl asked, holding a bowl of coleslaw.

"Got it." She opened the door, and there stood Earl, arms full, a bag in one hand and a large pot in the other. Behind him, a familiar face. Caroline wanted to cover herself up with her arms.

"Evening, there, Miss Caroline! I got my hands full," Earl announced with cheer.

Caroline's eyes remained on the man behind Earl. He stepped forward with a funny smile. "Hey, if it isn't DC! Wow, is this your place?"

Caroline's mouth dropped open as she stepped back. "Uh oh, hey yeah, my place. No, my Grams." She looked down at his feet. There they were, gleaming up at her, the notorious white Vans. "How did you know I live here?"

"I didn't. I mean, I don't. I mean, do you?"

Earl looked at them. "Y'all know each other?"

"Not really." Caroline was quick to answer. "Oh, come on in."

"Hope ya don't mind me bringin' my son along. Grams Dorea invited him, too, as a thanks since he worked his butt off helping install those AC units today." He looked over at the white bowl in his son's hands. "Dillan made the potato salad, just like his mama used to."

Caroline stumbled into a chair. "Uh, okay. Grams Dorea, our guests are here!"

Pearl greeted them and gave Earl a gentle kiss on the cheek. "Caroline, let these handsome men inside. The cooled air is getting out."

"Sure," she ushered them into the living room while Pearl shut the door.

Caroline felt naked. Her eyes darted around the room, then to Dillan. "Thanks so much for all the food."

Dillan's magnetic blue eyes found her. How could Grams Dorea have invited him? If she only knew.

Fifteen

Auntie Pearl led Dillan into the busy kitchen. "Caroline, show this handsome young man where to put the lobsters." Winking at Caroline, she helped Earl.

Dillan looked at Caroline and said. "Dad and I picked the lobsters and blue crabs up an hour ago at the fish market."

"Okay, how about you follow me?" Caroline kept her head down. She stopped at the kitchen table and pointed. "Put them here. Looks like the cooks are busy."

Halia came into the kitchen. "Welcome, Dillan, is it? Right?"

"Yes, ma'am. Thanks so much for inviting us. It sure smells delicious in here."

"The last time I saw you, you were a gawky teen with a surfboard. It seems not that long ago." Halia turned to Caroline. "Grab a few beers and you and Dillan go sit in the living room with Grams Dorea."

Biting the inside of her cheek, Caroline watched him make his way to the sofa. *Earl's son?* It seemed impossible. *What are the odds?* She grabbed a few beers from the cooler and stood with her back to the pantry door, counting to ten, then made her way to join them in the living room.

"Thanks, honey, this young man is Earl's son, all grown up. He is so polite. And he has muscular legs." Grams Dorea said as her face lit up. "You need a man with muscular legs. If you know what I mean. I was young once."

Shocked at Gram Dorea's bold comment, Caroline nodded and left the room to get a glass of wine. She came back and found a chair and settled into it.

Giggling, Auntie Calypso strolled in, having had a little too much libation. "Here you go, Grams Dorea. Freshly fried pickles and hot sauce." She looked at Caroline and Dillan. "Do you kids need anything? And thank you for the lobsters! A real treat."

From the sofa, Dillan smiled at her. "You are most welcome."

"I just wanted to say thank you for assisting your dad in installing the AC units upstairs. This cottage was unbearable. I thought we would have to move into your dad's cottage."

Caroline sank into her chair as she gulped her wine. *It was him!* Dillan was kind enough not to look in her direction.

"Time for Neil Diamond!" Auntie Calypso took out her phone and set Pandora to her favorite artist as she danced into the kitchen, singing *Sweet Caroline*.

Caroline sank deeper into the chair. Of all songs!

"Young man, try one of these fried pickles. It's my recipe and I add coarse cornmeal. Gives it that extra crunch." Grams Dorea pointed to the platter and asked Caroline to take it over to Dillan. "Did you know my granddaughter is very important? She is a celebrity in Washington, DC."

"Grams, I am not!" Caroline furrowed her eyebrows and shook her head as she got up and brought the platter to Dillan. He put a few on a small plate. She sat back down.

"See how modest she is? It's mind-boggling that she is still single. She is so beautiful and smart. I want a great grandchild before I croak and wind up like my late husband up on the mantle." Grams Dorea glanced toward the mantle. "Hi, honey."

"We're all a little drunk, er, high," Caroline muttered as she shrank into her chair.

Dillan, wanting to break the awkwardness, bit into a pickle. "Delicious and, yes, crisp. Thank you."

"It's the cornmeal and special spices." Grams Dorea explained as she reached for another one. "Have more, young man. Try the dip."

He did, "Dip is delicious." He turned to Caroline. "What is it that you do, Caroline?"

Grams Dorea was quick to answer. "She is a publicist for Hollywood types and politicians. Even once a famous musician. Some big rock star who rides on a flashy bus."

"Wow." He picked up his bottle of beer and took a long swallow. "Anyone I would know?"

Caroline replied in a polite voice. "The Walton Eastman Band. Grams Dorea. I'm sure Dillan is not interested."

Dillan's eyes grew wide. "I am. That is so impressive. They are a huge country band and just won the country album of the year."

Caroline felt her face warm up.

"My daughter is the publicist for Senator Colton Jameson, the presidential candidate." Halia said as she came into the room, "and her father had also run for president."

Grams Dorea dipped her pickle in the spicy sauce. "He lost."

Dillan could sense the tension and decided not to say another word.

Caroline jiggled her foot. "Enough presidential talk. I need more wine." She got up and walked into the kitchen. Pots of boiling water filled the steamy room, as did music and chatter. Earl was busy shucking the corn, dancing around with Auntie Pearl. It was a wild sight.

"Mom, where are the new bottles of wine?"

"On the back porch in the blue cooler."

Caroline went out to the porch. She tripped and looked down. Wilbur was snoring away. "Sorry, Wilbur."

She reached into the cooler for a chilled bottle and opened it. She sat down on an Adirondack chair. Of all people to attend a dinner party! The man in the living room who saw her in the raw. Earl's son, no less. *Oh my God, did he tell Earl? Good grief, how embarrassing.* She swatted a mosquito and lit the citronella candles.

The screen door from the living room opened and slammed shut.

"Hey, I was getting a lecture from your grandmother about politicians. Guess she is not fond of them."

The flickering of the candles illuminated Dillan's face. She wondered if Earl was this handsome when he was young.

"Mind if I sit down?" He looked at the chair next to her. "Is it available? It is chilly in the living room."

"You can light more bug candles. Grams Dorea loves her new air conditioners. Now I need to wear a sweater in the cottage." She handed him the lighter.

"Whatever they are brewing in the kitchen sure smells good." Dillan sat back and guzzled his beer.

The hushed rustle of sea oats filled the silence while balmy breezes tickled the candle flames.

Caroline finished her wine and poured another full glass, she gulped it. She rested her head back as her body relaxed. *So what if he saw me? He is damn good looking.* "

So, Dillan," she tilted her head, "what brings you to Hatteras Island?"

He sat back, crossing his ankle over his knee. "My dad is not getting any younger. Since Mom died, he gets lonely and buys more real estate. And I needed to get out of New York, anyway."

She smiled. "What did you do before the big move?"

"I was an acquisitions attorney on Wall Street. It was not for me. After my breakup with my longtime girlfriend, it was time to flee the rat race."

Caroline finished her wine and looked over at Dillan. "I'm sorry about your breakup and that your mom is gone. I can't imagine life without my mom." The wine was softening her mood. "You help your dad with repairs?"

"When he's shorthanded. I have my real estate license and have been buying fixer-upper properties and turning them into rental properties. I sell them too and absolutely love it." He lifted his beer bottle. "I grew up down here and left for college and came down occasionally to party with my buddies. Then work consumed me."

"I thought I heard a slight Carolina accent. Hey, if you need another beer, they're in the red cooler next to your chair. Blue cooler is wine."

"Thanks," he helped himself. "Don't you love it here? The sunsets are amazing in the winter. Colors are out of an ethereal sky."

Caroline agreed. "Ethereal, yeah. You had a long-time girlfriend?" The wine was talking.

"Yeah. She was a furniture designer and took off with her business partner." His tone was flat.

"I'm sorry. It can get ugly. Being single is the only life for me. I mean, one day, maybe kids and a white picket fence. Grams Dorea pesters me, and my mom complains she wants grandkids. It is not in my life right now. I need to get Senator Jameson into the White House."

"You really are Jameson's publicist? Wow, that is a heavy job. How can you be on vacation with the election not far away?"

"Long story. I can work remotely for now, before the election heats up. I have a rather large team. They are awesome." She tapped her index finger on the armrest. "After dinner, I must head up to my room and work. 'til dawn. The upside is I get to watch the sunrise."

"It must be exhausting." He sipped his beer. "It must be an amazing job."

"It's such a high. I've been around politicians and campaigns all my life. I love the pace. The tension. The wins. And the losses hurt like hell, but then the next race comes along."

Auntie Pearl stuck her head out the door. "Time to eat, kids!"

Dillan got up and offered his hand to Caroline. She accepted. It was tender yet strong.

Grams Dorea sat at the head of the table, with Earl at the other end. She made it clear to Earl and Dillan that men were rarely allowed in the cottage. She expressed gratitude for his hospitality in letting her stay at his house and helping her with the installation of the air conditioners.

In the center of the table sat a plate piled high with blue crabs, and next to them, the lobsters, with garlic butter in a gravy boat. A basket with damp hand towels and a roll of paper towels was close to the salty crustations. Side salads and sweet corn muffins filled the sideboard buffet. It was time to delve in.

Caroline was fighting with a lobster tail when it squirted her in the face as she yanked the tail off. Dillan was quick to offer her a handful of paper towels.

Halia kept a keen eye on them. For her daughter, she was determined there would be no other man but Colton Jameson.

Grams Dorea, who had referred to her granddaughter as a DC spinster, was happy a new man *'with muscular legs'* was paying attention to Caroline. *Finally!*

Halfway through dinner, with conversations about how wonderful the food and company were, Grams Dorea saw Caroline pull her phone out of her pocket.

"Caroline, that had better not be Jameson or his political cronies. This is family time."

Caroline frowned. "I know, Grams Dorea. Sorry." She slid the phone back. It was Jameson and urgent.

"I am impressed to be sitting next to Caroline. I mean, she may get our next president into the White House." Dillan said as he looked at Grams Dorea. "That is a major undertaking."

"Hogwash, young man. Politicians are nothing but cheating dogs. Left, right, they all bite! Give em a fire hydrant and they will all lift their legs."

Halia gasped.

Dillan kept his head down to avoid anyone seeing him smile.

Caroline wagged her finger, adding a smile. "Grams Dorea! Oh my gosh, not at the table. If I can't text Jameson, you can't talk naughty at the table."

Grams Dorea rolled her eyes. "Touché."

Dillan had to stir the pot. "Caroline, tell us the *naked* truth about Jameson. Is he as clean as they say?"

Caroline nearly fell off her chair.

Earl looked at Caroline, then went to Dillan. *He knew*!

Caroline was quick to answer. "Yes, he's a wonderful man. He'll make an excellent president. There is much on his agenda."

Grams Dorea passed the potato salad to Earl, insisting that there would be no political talk at the table.

She looked around the table. "That's a rule here, Dillan."

"Sorry," Dillan reached for his beer. "I didn't know. I'll respect that." He dipped his lobster into the warm butter.

Caroline dropped her tense shoulders. She was relieved.

Earl and Pearl had been sharing smiles while Auntie Lorelei and Calypso chatted about painting the bedrooms a new color. Halia and Grams Dorea were busy picking apart blue crabs. Caroline could not stand it any longer. She excused herself to get more wine.

Stepping out onto the back porch, she looked at her phone.

> Come with me. I need you. Meet me on Jekyll Island.
>
> She texted Jameson.
>
> Colton. Not a wise idea.
>
> Stay on course.
>
> You have momentum. Don't blow it.
>
> Call you later. Dinnertime here at the cottage.
>
> He texted:
>
> Got it.

Sixteen

Everyone enjoyed dinner. Earl sat back and patted his belly. Dinner plates filled the sink as Auntie Pearl brought out a key lime pie and Irish coffee to the living room.

Auntie Calypso looked out the window. "It's a half-moon and soon the orb will glow, filling our hearts."

"Calypso." Grams Dorea's eyes met Auntie Calypso's. She put her index finger to her lips. She feared that after too many glasses of wine, Calypso would reveal the upcoming crowning of the mermaid.

Caroline could not relax after the text from Jameson. What was he thinking? She had to escape and intervene. Just as she was about to announce she needed to rest because of a headache from rich food and wine, Auntie Lorelei sashayed into the room. She was holding a white pillowcase.

"What are you up to?" Auntie Pearl asked as her eyes narrowed on the pillowcase. "Is that?"

"Yup. Ta da!" Auntie Lorelei pulled the pillowcase off.

"Is that a crystal ball?" Earl asked as his eyes drifted over it. "Ya ain't some witches, are ya? Gonna do weird stuff and we never be seen again?"

"For heaven's sake, Earl, no." Auntie Lorelei hugged the large glass orb. "This is Conchita, my crystal ball. She needed to say hello. My guides are telling me she must get fresh air being inside this stuffy pillowcase."

"Okay, son, it's time to get back home. These ladies are gonna turn us into lobsters and boil us up in some cauldron of sorts."

"Dad, chill. I'm sure there is an explanation."

"Caroline, can you get Grandpops off the mantle?"

"Sure, Grams Dorea."

"You keep Grandpops on the mantel?" Dillan asked as his eyes landed on Grams Dorea.

Earl chuckled, recalling the afternoon they dropped Grandpops. "They don't allow men in here for this reason. These purty women turn all the handsome men that come here into dust after boiling them, and into a Ball jar we go."

Dillan elbowed his father. "Keep your voice down."

"Grandpops looks pale, doesn't he? And lighter." Grams Dorea examined the jar and gave it a slight shake. "Are you feeling okay, honey?"

Earl's wide eyes met Lorelei's.

"Why is Conchita not in her blue velvet box?" Pearl asked as she picked up her glass of wine.

"It's in for repairs. The latch broke." Lorelei gently stroked the glass orb. "Conchita is okay with just a pillowcase."

With her grandmother talking to her late husband in a canning jar and her aunt having a crystal ball named Conchita that needed air, Caroline was wondering if they sounded crazy.

Auntie Lorelei reached into the pillowcase and took out a set of brass prongs and set them on the coffee table. She rested her crystal ball on them. Her gaze shifted to Grams Dorea. "Put Daddy to bed. It is getting late, and you know he was never a night owl. Let's ask Conchita what the future brings, then I can put her to bed."

Caroline reached for her coffee. "Night, Grandpops. Sleep well."

Dillan watched this interesting group.

The hairs on Earl's arms and the back of his neck rose, fearing old Grandpops' face was going to glow in the crystal ball and tell the truth—that Earl had let him out of the jar! He leaned over and whispered into Dillan's ear. "We can make a run for it now. They haven't locked us in yet."

Dillan whispered back, "Dad, shhhh. Let's see what happens."

Auntie Pearl leaned forward from her chair. "Earl, did you say something?"

"Oh, I'm getting tired." He looked at his watch. "I ain't the spring chicken I used to be."

"You are as young as you feel," Auntie Pearl said with a sweet smile.

Caroline's fingertips were restless. She could not help but tickle the phone in her pocket. She elbowed Dillan. "Welcome to after dinner at the nuthouse. I'm getting a glass of brandy. Would you like one?"

He smiled. "It's cool. Yes, on the brandy. Just so you know, I'm really enjoying myself. Your aunties, mom, and Grams Dorea are a trip."

"Trip, yeah. You have no idea!" Caroline got up and asked if anyone else would like anything and returned with glasses filled with brandy on a tray.

Auntie Lorelei sat down in front of the coffee table, inhaled, and let it out. "Ahhh..." She placed her hands on the cold glass orb. "Does anyone have a question? Nothing political, I might add, since Conchita has already revealed the end result of the election. You won't hear a peep from me."

Everyone exchanged glances except Grams Dorea. She was asleep. Soft snores escaped from her.

Halia asked. "Will Caroline settle down?"

"Mom!"

"I had to ask."

"Shhhh... I need Conchita to focus." Lorelei closed her eyes for a moment, then popped them open toward Dillan.

Being amused, he smiled at her.

"Wake. No, Wade. Wade is to slog through shallow waters on the shores of oceans and seas. His sea. Their sea. He once traveled the seas."

Earl's eyes landed on Dillan. "Huh?"

"Whoa!" The hairs on the back of Dillan's neck rose. "Okay, Dad, you told one of these fine ladies, didn't you? Pearl, right? Come on, Dad, you put the ladies up to this. Fess up."

"I ain't having nothing to do with this witch stuff." Earl's face was flushed. "Nope."

"What's the matter?" Caroline asked. Her eyes narrowed, watching Dillan's strange reaction.

Auntie Lorelei continued her stare into the glass orb.

Dillan frowned. "My middle name is Wade."

"*What?*" Caroline squealed. "Seriously? I need another brandy. Auntie Lorelei, what is going on? Is this a joke? You set this up, didn't you? Admit it! And Earl, you were in on it, weren't you?"

They were all shaking their heads, murmuring innocence as Grams Dorea let out a snore.

"The orb has spoken. Caroline, this is nothing new. Conchita is always correct. Well, almost." Lorelei slid her hands over Conchita. "Dillan Wade. A lovely name, and it suits you living here. It rolls beautifully off the lips, like the ebb and flow of the tide." She clapped her hands. Grams Dorea stirred in her recliner. "Girls, it is best to call it a night." She covered Conchita with the pillowcase.

Caroline felt chilled and embarrassed.

Earl and Dillan looked at each other as they got up and said their goodnights. Caroline led them to the door. Earl ran off the porch and through the path.

Dillan watched him with a shake of his head and said to Caroline. "That was one of the most interesting evenings I've had in a long time. Maybe ever. Thanks, and now the secret of my middle name is out. She looked it up, didn't she?"

"I honestly don't know." Caroline crossed her arms. "Well, you never know what will happen here at the Beach Heart Cottage." She pointed to the sign that hung to the right of the door. "Those are all the women before me. I'm sure they too had great times here."

He glanced at the sign and back to Caroline. "Before you? What do you mean?"

"Oh." She realized she had said way too much. "Um... I can't tell you. And I don't want to lie."

"Pretty much always the correct choice. Thanks again for dinner and entertainment." Dillan made his way off the front porch.

"Anytime!"

He stopped. "Hey, anytime you want to spill a latte on my Vans, let me know. Dad has my number."

Caroline waved. Once inside, she picked up the brandy glasses from the coffee table and asked, "All right, what was that all about? Seriously, a crystal ball? Is that how you scare men out of here?"

The sisters burst into laughter.

Grams Dorea opened her eyes. "Oh, honey, yes, we did that to get those men out! They were lingering far too long. I can feel the testosterone oozing off the walls."

"What? Grams Dorea, were you faking you were asleep?" She turned to Lorelei. "How did you know Dillan's middle name?"

"It was an educated guess," Auntie Lorelei joked. "As soon as I saw his face, I knew I'd hit pay dirt."

Gram Dorea sat up. "Earl's great grandfather was a man named Dillan Wade. He built Earl's cottage way back, just before Ida's father built this one. Through the slits of my eyes, I could see ole' Earl twitching. Why, he ran out of here like a bat out of hell!"

"You weren't asleep? You were faking the snoring?" Caroline was not sure whether to laugh along with them or cry. "I feel bad for Earl. The man was looking over his shoulder as he dashed off the porch."

"How come I don't know him? Them?" Caroline asked.

"They weren't around when you were growing up," Auntie Lorelei explained. "We were here in August. Earl was busy with his family, and we were busy as well. His wife was a sweet woman. It was sad to know she had passed away." She picked up her crystal ball. "Night, ladies. Conchita and I had so much fun on this lovely evening. I have sewing to do. Grams Dorea, I nearly completed your costume, needing only a sprinkle of beads on the bodice." With her crystal ball snug against her body, she blew a kiss and went upstairs.

"I'll clean up," Caroline offered as she picked up the last brandy glass and the empty pie dish. "Night all."

Caroline, alone in the kitchen with her headphones, listening to music, was cleaning up the dishes, smiling at the night's events. It *was* slightly funny to see Earl's face and how he ran off. She also could see Dillan's face. His strong features, assuring voice, and polite manners. He was an interesting man, for sure.

With the dishes dried and put away, Caroline made her way upstairs to her room. She glanced at her phone. It was past one. On the desk, her laptop was calling her. She ignored it, yawning. *There's always tomorrow.* Slipping into pjs, she sank into the bed and felt the journal under the pillow.

"I forgot about you." It would be a perfect time to sneak downstairs and put it back. It would be cheating. Breaking tradition. Caroline ran her hands over the cover of the old journal. "One paragraph. Would that hurt? Who would know?" She twisted her lips. "Nope, you are going back to that desk. If I got caught with you, I could lose my crown, and the great aunties would send me to wherever they send those who cheat." She smiled at the brittle book filled with secrets. "Come on, downstairs we go."

She delicately slid the old journal into place. As she turned to go upstairs, the back door blew open!

C'mon, it's just the wind. She went over to shut it and stepped onto the back porch. With her head tilted back, she inhaled the gentle sea mist. The soft hush of the ocean waves against the shore soothed her. She was going back inside when she heard something. She stopped. What was that?

At the edge of the porch, she looked around. An ethereal voice lifted off the ocean. It was as if an angel were singing a solo in a choir. Mesmerized, she opened the screen door and stepped off the porch onto the cool, soft sand. The voice sang in gentle whispers, leaving her skin chilled. She listened until the wind chimes chattered.

"Whoa, too much brandy." She stepped up onto the porch and inside and shut the door. Once in her room, she got into bed and fell into a deep slumber.

Seventeen

"Has anyone seen Caroline?" Auntie Pearl asked as she flipped a western omelet. "This is for her. She needs all her strength to not only be our newest mermaid but to keep her energy up with this election. And I brewed her decaf. She needs to chill a little."

"I agree, and I'll check on our mermaid." Halia knocked on Caroline's door. "Honey, are you up?"

Finishing her last email, Caroline replied, "I'll be down in a minute."

Halia smiled as she opened the door. "Pearl is making you a special breakfast. We are biking on Ocracoke today to go shopping and check out that fun restaurant by Silver Lake. Do you want to go with us?"

"Who is us?"

"Everyone, even Grams Dorea. She's renting us a golf cart. We are taking the walk-on passenger ferry and we leave in an hour."

"No, Mom, I can't. I want to, but I have too much to do. It'll be on me if he doesn't get elected. That will be his mantra. Caroline's fault."

"He'll win, don't worry," Halia assured her daughter as she stood at the door. "It will be wonderful for the country. And for us. And for you. Please eat before your breakfast gets cold."

"I will." Caroline closed her laptop. Colton was *not* listening to Lawson. He wanted to change so much of what Caroline had built for him. Her way was working. She had to get him back on track. Was it the ex-fiancé who was feeding him poor advice?

After breakfast, Caroline went out to Auntie Lorelei's SUV. To her surprise, they secured their bicycles to the back of it. "I thought you were taking the walk-on ferry."

"Change of plans. Grams Dorea decided she wants to come home whenever she wants and feels better if we drive." Auntie Lorelei rolled her eyes. "We're off. Oh, before I forget, can you walk Wilbur? And make sure he has water." She kissed her dog's head. "Mommy will be back soon. You be a perfect little boy for Caroline."

Caroline watched them drive off. "It's me and you, buddy. Be well-behaved for me, please?"

Wilbur barked and ran up onto the front porch. With a wide smile, Caroline tilted her head toward the sun. "Ah, we have the cottage to ourselves all day, Wilbur. How about we go for a beach walk? But first, I need to finish an email."

Caroline warned Colton that going rogue was risking it all. "Senator Jameson," she typed, "if you refuse to listen to me, I'm taking the day off." Then she added, "Colton, I'm begging you, do nothing stupid!"

She handed him over to Lawson and their team. Let them manage his stubbornness for a few hours.

She got into her new bikini and did a twirl in front of the mirror. With her hair in a bun, she applied sunblock and put on her coverup. In the kitchen, she filled a thermos with a lemonade cocktail and another with cold water. Inside her beach bag, she had a towel, a phone, sunblock, and a water dish for Wilbur.

With Wilbur on his leash, she made her way down to the beach. Anchored close to the dune was the new tent for Grams Dorea, complete with beach chairs.

The day was glorious, with humidity at its lowest. The crystal-clear water beckoned with gentle emerald waves, leaving shells in its wake. Earl's house was next door, and the one on the other side of Beach Heart had been boarded up due to storm damage. She had the beach to herself.

After pouring Wilbur some water and tying his leash to her chair, she settled down. Her toes sank into the sugary sand as the calming sounds of the ocean allowed her to unwind. With her head resting back, it did not take long—she dozed off as the balmy breezes swirled around her.

Wilbur's barking put a rude ending to her ten-minute doze. "What is wrong with you? Shut up, or you go back in the house." She studied the mutt's chocolate eyes. "You are so cute, but a pain in the butt. You want to go for a swim?"

He barked at her. "Wow, you are one smart little guy. Give me a minute." She was leaning forward to grab her straw hat out of the beach bag when she thought she heard a voice. Someone said her name. She looked around. No one was there. "What is that, Wilbur? Odd."

With Wilbur on his leash, they waded into the breaking waves. She stooped, running her fingers through the warm, salty water, then stood up. "Come on, Wilbur, let's go for a walk!"

The tide was receding, allowing sandbars to pop up. She looked around at the empty beach. Wilbur's tugging was too much. "I give in, Wilbur! Let's have fun!" She let his leash go and tossed a stick as he splashed around in the waves. Caroline was picking up a couple of pink calico scallop shells when she spotted a full black whelk shell. She chased it as a small wave took it out. Hearing the soft voice again, she popped up and glanced around. Wilbur was nowhere to be seen!

"Wilbur! Wilbur!" She cupped her mouth. "Wilbur, get your doggy butt back here!" Looking over at the dune, she saw Wilbur trot out. He was not alone. Squinting, Caroline could see someone holding Wilbur's leash and being tugged.

"Crap."

"I found your dog peeing on the dune."

"Hi, Dillan. Sorry. He's a pain, and I'm babysitting. Doggie sitting. Everyone headed out to Ocracoke." She reached for his leash and pointed at his nose. "Thanks to you, Wilbur, I lost that fat black whelk."

Dillan looked out at the sandbar. "I think I see it." He took off his white tee shirt, kicked off his sandals, and dashed into the breaking waves. Caroline watched him while Wilbur barked. Dillan waded out into deeper water, dove, and surfaced triumphantly, holding the black whelk in the air.

Caroline thought, *is he for real?*

He followed a wave to shore. "I believe this is what you were looking for? It is in perfect shape. A real find."

Caroline's eyes, hidden behind her sunglasses, lit up. "Yes, wow, what a way to impress a woman. You were like a Hatteras merman!"

Dillan, dripping wet, swished the shell in the water to wash off the sand. "Merman? No. Wanting to impress you? Yeah." His eyes twinkled as he ran his hand through his thick, wet hair. With a slight squint, he handed Caroline the shell and picked up his tee shirt. "Are you impressed?"

She reached for it. "Hmm... if you found an emerald necklace from a queen's treasure chest, *that* would impress me. Kidding. Thanks so much. I'll put it on my desk, and every time I look at it, it will remind me of the gorgeous day on Hatteras when Wilbur peed on the dune, and a merman rescued my whelk." She smiled, adding a slight, flirtatious sway.

He put on his tee shirt. "Have you been out here long?"

She put her hand over her brow. "A little over half an hour. I know he's supposed to be leashed. He got away. Well, I might have helped. No one is here by our cottage, and he was pulling my arm out of the socket, the beast." Wilbur was tugging on his leash. "I had better get him back up to the cottage." She turned to leave.

"Caroline?"

She stopped. "Yes?"

"Uh, I'm not... you know... stalking you. I just saw Wilbur, and I recognized him from last night. I wanted to make sure he wasn't on a lost dog post on Facebook."

"Ugh, last night, don't remind me of that!"

"Would you like to have an iced coffee or sweet tea later?"

She slid her sunglasses down to the tip of her nose.

"I would like another pair of coffee-stained Vans. How about it?" He looked out at the ocean and back at Caroline. "Over at the coffee shop?"

Caroline bit the inside of her cheek and looked at the glistening ocean and back to her shell. "Sure, why not?" She could not believe that she said yes. With all the work she had to do. *I said yes to Earl's son.*

"How about we meet at two?" His smile was a mile wide.

She noticed his eyes, deeper blue than the depths of the ocean. His hair was dark as coal.

"You want me to pick you up?"

"Sounds great." She pushed her sunglasses up her nose. "See you then." With a lilt in her step, she took Wilbur and headed up to the house.

Her mind was swirling. Her new bikini must have magical powers, since it had been a long time since she shared anything with a man, as her work had her cemented.

He is very handsome. Helpful. Kind. There had to be a catch. Mid-afternoon coffee would be a pleasant break. She held her whelk snug, forgetting about yesterday when he saw her naked in her room.

Eighteen

There was a knock on the front door. Wilbur barked as he jumped on the sofa, slobbering the window. His wagging tail knocked the throw pillows onto the floor.

"Be there in a sec! Wilbur, be quiet!"

Caroline was working downstairs at her grandpop's desk. She was about to close her laptop when another URGENT subject line screamed at her. She replied, "For heaven's sake, Colton, I will talk to you in an hour. Everything is under control. Call Lawson." She hit send.

She adjusted her sundress and opened the door. Wilbur was behind her, pushing his head against her leg. "Wilbur, please take a nap." She pushed him away and looked up.

From behind his back, Dillan handed her a bunch of orange and yellow flowers. "It's so impromptu, so I hope you like them."

"They are lovely." Caroline said with a smile. She had seen the flowers, thousands of them, growing all over the island. The gesture was heartwarming. "Give me a second. I'll put these in water."

"Sure." He said as he walked inside.

She put her hand up. "Stop! You are not supposed to cross the threshold. You are a male species, as Grams Dorea puts it. But heck, no one is here. Come on in. Stand right here. Don't go any further. I think Grams Dorea has eyes everywhere. And thanks for the flowers, they're so pretty." Wilbur sniffed Dillan's legs, then trotted over to his bed.

"They're Joe Bell flowers. At least that is their mythical name. Their horticultural name is gaillardia."

His eyes enticed her, his voice soothed her, his physical being excited her. But there was something different about him.

"Mythical?"

"Folklore may be a better term."

She went into the kitchen and found a vintage milk glass vase in the cupboard. With a sunny smile, she put them in the vase, and they went outside to his SUV.

They drove to Hatteras Village. "Busy day." Dillan stopped to let someone walk on the crosswalk. "I heard the car ferry traffic is backed up for over two hours. Thankfully, I don't take the ferry."

"Really? You don't go to Ocracoke?" Caroline turned the AC vent to low. "I love going over there and riding my bike. Getting a cold smoothie and the beaches are amazing. I would love to go to Portsmouth Island and go shelling."

"That's cool. I took my boat over to Portsmouth last month. Lots of sand dollars and millions of pesty mosquitos."

"That wouldn't be the pontoon boat your dad took Auntie Pearl on, would it?"

He burst into laughter. "No way. I towed that thing into a dock. I think Dad is trying to patch it again. It has a serious tilt to the left. He loves ole' Honey."

"He *loves* honey?"

"Oh no, he named it honey, because he and my mom spent their honeymoon cruising around the sound on it. It has wonderful memories for Dad."

"That's so romantic." *Crazy Earl isn't so crazy after all.* "I'm sorry about your mom."

"It's tough to lose your mom. It's been a few years." He pulled into the coffee shop's crushed shell parking lot.

Caroline had to ask. "How do you like living here?"

"Honestly? I'm getting used to it. It has taken me time to, as you say, chill. You learn life doesn't have to be lost in a maze. To answer your question, yeah, it is growing on me. Living in New York City was a tremendous change for me. Being back home here, yeah, I'm learning to get back on island time."

They sat at a table in the far back. Dillan asked her how the campaign was going, and she admitted that working with Colton was driving her crazy. She wanted the election over last week.

"Okay, my turn." Dillan tapped his index finger on the tabletop. "How did your aunt know my middle name?" He sat back, crossing his arms.

"Should I tell you? And ruin it? They know your whatever long-ago relative was Dillan Wade. So, Auntie Lorelei made a guess."

Dillan gave a guttural laugh. "I should have known. A charlatan!"

"Yup, the charlatan and Conchita. Sounds like a sitcom. All jokes aside, it was fun. Your dad's face was hysterical. He ran off the porch so fast! Like he'd seen a ghost!"

"It was funny! And those damn sand burrs assaulted his feet."

"Ouch!" Caroline squeezed her face. "I have had my encounters with them."

"Tell me, is your aunt a witch? I mean her crystal ball and all."

Caroline laughed, adding a wave of her hand. "Gosh, no. But she is different. She can look at the lines in your palm and tell you about your past and future. She does tea leaf readings, too. It's all for fun. No harm in it. Although she is a *gifted* person."

"And you inherited this; shall I say, *gift?*"

"No, thank heaven," Caroline replied, hoping it was not a lie. "I assume to someone who is not used to it, my auntie can appear freaky. She predicted everything that happened when my dad ran for president. Dad never listened or cared. He later regretted it, and she said *I told you so*! Auntie Lorelei gave palm readings to his staff at a fundraiser party my mom gave." She giggled at that memory of it. "He scoffed at Auntie Lorelei. She told him she would put a spell on him. I think she did!"

Dillan laughed, taking a slurp of coffee to hide the feeling of being unnerved. *Did she say her father ran for president?*

In the awkward silence, Caroline noticed a flower in a small vase on the next table. "Look, a Joe Bell flower."

"Did you say Joe Bell?" a raspy voice asked. The elderly gentleman sitting at a nearby table pushed his chair out.

Dillan leaned in and whispered, "That's Haddy. A boat captain and local old-timer. He's always bursting with stories."

Haddy's wrinkled face had verified many years in the sun, sea, and salt. He pulled his chair over to their table. "Afternoon, Dillan, and who is your lovely lady friend? I ain't seen ya with a woman since y'all moved down here." He sat on the edge of his chair.

"Haddy, this is my neighbor, Caroline. And Caroline, this is Haddy."

Caroline said hello.

"Hello, Miss Caroline. I heard y'all say what we refer to as *Joe Bell*. There's a story behind those pretty gems that most youngsters don't know 'bout. It goes back." He took a deep breath. "In the early part of the last century, as the story goes, a love-sick fella named Joe Nash Bell, Jr. lived on Ocracoke back at the turn of the century. He was a man of superb taste and enjoyed all things beautiful. Even his women."

He stopped to catch his breath, and in his raspy voice, continued. "A sharp dresser back then he was, often seen in a collarless, long-sleeved white shirt, gold collar button adorned with a garnet or two, khaki pants, and bright red suspenders. Fancy shoes for an island fella." He glanced at Dillan's shoes and back to Caroline.

Caroline smiled. "He sounds like an interesting character."

"That he was. Until the love of his life left him for another man. Broke his tender heart."

"Then what happened?" Intrigued, she sat forward.

"Like any man in love, it devastated young Joe Bell, Miss Caroline. He officiated a handful of weddings, and none were his."

Caroline looked at Dillan and back to Haddy.

"He brought flower seeds to the island from the mainland, some say, from as far away as California. He scattered them in honor of his love, in hopes their beauty would win her back. She never returned to the island, leaving Joe a broken man. As you can see, the flowers prospered."

"What happened to Joe Bell?" Dillan asked.

"Well now, the poor fella never married. Died young in 1930 on his brother-in-law's porch. It was there that he had a stroke, so the story goes. They planted Joe Bell flowers next to the grave, but they no longer grow there. You can see by the colorful flowers thriving all over the islands, his legacy lives on."

Caroline sat back. "Thank you for sharing that with us."

"Y'all are welcome." He looked up at the clock and back at Dillan and Caroline. "I've been taking up your time. I hope I didn't bother you kids. My wife over there told me I had to tell the tale. When you find the one love of a lifetime, you had best keep 'em. No seeds, no flowers will bring 'em back. Only love can be planted in your heart. Good day." He got up, tapped on their table, then walked out the door.

"That was so heartfelt. Poor Joe Bell." Caroline put her hands over her heart. "That is so romantic, sadly."

"You know what's even sadder?"

"What?"

"Haddy's wife died ten years ago."

"He said she was over there." As she looked around the room, a chill rushed through Caroline's body. "Dillan, there is no one here but us. Ewe, creepy."

"Yeah, creepy is an understatement. Last night with Conchita, now this. It's time to go." Dillan looked over at the empty table and then outside, at the sky. "Looks like rain might be coming. I think it's time to head back. What do you say?"

"Perfect idea. I need to get to work. Thanks for the coffee. I will never look at those flowers the same way."

Nineteen

Dillan pulled up to the cottage just as the winds from the south picked up. "I enjoyed our iced coffee and the tale of Joe Bell."

"Me, too. Back to work. It never ends. Thanks again. Maybe I'll see you on the beach?"

"Maybe. Keep an eye on those clouds and-" Dillan's phone buzzed. "Oh-oh, I better get over to one of my dad's cottages. A drain is not working."

"You can do plumbing?"

"Jack of all trades. Let's say I'm learning on the job."

"I'll keep that in mind. Have fun." Caroline opened the door and dashed inside the cottage just as the first fat raindrops fell.

With the rain pouring outside, Caroline worked. The sun emerged from the clouds after six-thirty, creating a full arched rainbow over the ocean. Her phone rang.

"Caroline! We need you to come get us."

"Mom?" Her heart sped up. "Is Grams Dorea okay?"

"Yes, she's just fine, but thanks to her and her stubbornness needing one more glittery starfish ornament, we missed the walk-on ferry."

"Can you get the next one?"

"Nope. We just missed the last one out of Silver Lake. We're stuck on Ocracoke."

"Ocracoke is a wonderful place to be stuck, Mom. Is it raining there?"

"No, it was a gorgeous day. If there were somewhere to stay here tonight, it would be fine. Unfortunately, all the places I've called are booked up. You need to take the car ferry over here and get us. The last boat leaves here at midnight."

"Seriously? I'm confused. I thought you drove your SUV over to Ocracoke?"

"Nope. Grams Dorea was thrilled to see the walk on passenger ferry and wanted a fresh experience. We left my SUV at the Hatteras dock lot and walked on."

"How will you all fit in my SUV?"

"We will make it work, even if we stick Grams Dorea on the roof!"

"Mom!" Caroline looked at her phone. "That bad, huh?"

"You have no idea. She is complaining left and right. The rest of us are having a wonderful time here at a restaurant! They make the best Manhattans, and they go down easy!"

There was a knock at the front door. Caroline got up and looked out the window. She saw Earl's truck.

"Mom, Earl is here. Why?"

"For heaven's sake, I do not know. Come get us before I gag your grandmother and make her walk the plank!"

"Okay, I'll leave in a few minutes. I need to get the door." She hung up and hurried downstairs and opened it. There stood Earl and Dillan.

Earl smiled. "Hi, Grams Dorea sent us over to replace the upstairs bathroom shower head. Is she here?"

Dillan stood behind Earl, giving a slight wave.

"No, she is not. If Grams Dorea said replace it, then go ahead. I got to run over to Ocracoke."

"Ocracoke?" Dillan asked, holding the new showerhead.

"They missed the last passenger ferry. And they can't get a room anywhere. I must drive over there, squish them in my SUV, and rescue them."

"Y'all ain't gonna fit in that toy SUV of yours. The weather's cleared up," Earl looked back at Dillan. "Why don't we take the boat and fetch them?"

Caroline's face dropped as she asked. "The pontoon boat? I don't think-"

"Dad means my boat,"

Caroline shook her head. "Oh, no, Dillan, you don't have to. That's asking a lot."

"We can install this showerhead tomorrow. Come on, let's go on a rescue mission." Dillan said.

"Seriously? You don't mind a boat of women?" Caroline timidly asked. "You sure?"

"Seriously, Miss Caroline, that's the best kind of boat," Earl grinned. "Now follow us to the marina."

"Dad, I'll go with Caroline. We'll meet you there."

"Wow, thanks, let me call my mom and let her know." She pulled her phone out of her shorts. "Thank God for cell phones. Oh, when do you think we'll be there?"

Earl held his hand up. "Two hours, if we leave now."

Dillan's eyes met Caroline's. "Don't worry, I can get us there in just over an hour."

"I'll tell them to get dinner and sit tight." Caroline's face softened with amusement. "They'll be a fun bunch when we get them!" Her eyes met Dillan's. "Let me grab a sweater."

With Dillan at the helm, they made their way out to the sound. Earl was on the phone with Pearl as she chattered about daiquiris, a live band and crab cakes. They were in no hurry to get back to Hatteras.

Caroline stood beside Dillan, rubbing her arms.

"Grab a blanket. Dad will show you where they are."

The cabin was luxurious. Earl gave her a blanket. Up on deck, the sun was sliding down on the horizon.

Dillan reached for the blanket. Unfolding it, he draped it around Caroline's shoulders. "Better?"

Caroline smiled at him. "Thanks." Her voice was soft.

The sun was ochre against deep pink and deep orange clouds that filled the sky after the rain. Pelicans skimmed the water's surface. The wind rushed through her hair. She looked over at Dillan. Their eyes locked. She moved closer.

"Hey, kids!" Earl boomed. "Gorgeous sunset! Sailor's delight! Look over there. You can make out a school of dolphins frolicking."

Dillan glanced over his shoulder, "Frolicking, Dad?"

Earl looked at his phone. "Caroline, your family is whooping it up at one of restaurants. They want us to meet them there for drinks."

Caroline bit her bottom lip, wishing Earl would go below deck. Dillan had the same thought.

"Dad, go have a beer. I restocked the fridge last night."

"Sounds like a plan." Earl inhaled the briny air as he noticed how close they were. "You kids wanna be alone?"

Neither said a word as Earl grinned and went below.

Caroline felt a hand reach for hers. This was so unlike her. What was it about Dillan? Was it the sunset, or the magic of Hatteras?

Twenty

Dillan pulled into Silver Lake and docked his boat at a friend's house. They got out and found the restaurant off Irvin Garrish, where they could hear a loud group at the bar.

Under the strings of Edison bulbs, the castaways were having a superb time. Earl was quick to join the ladies at their table.

"Mom, are you drunk?" Caroline looked at the colorful cocktail in her mother's hand. "You are!"

"No, honey, we are having so much fun. We've made new friends from Virginia and Ohio. Let me introduce you." She reached for Caroline's hand.

Caroline's eyes roamed the crowded bar. A band played as her eyes found a familiar face. No, it couldn't be! "Shit! Hey Dillan, Mom, I'll be back in a sec."

Caroline weaved through the boisterous crowd, over to a table in the back. "Alton? What are you doing here?"

"Caroline! Hey, how are you? I should ask the same. What are *you* doing here?"

"Jesus, Alton, my family has a summer place over in Hatteras. You should know that!" She studied the stranger with him. "I hope to God you're not here because of-"

"Your client?"

"Oh, please tell me he's not here!" Caroline looked over her shoulder. "Is he?"

"No, don't panic. He's on the campaign trail in Georgia. Twenty-four seven for me. I was losing my eyesight. I needed a quick break, and my brother-in-law invited me to stay at his place here on Ocracoke."

"If you're here, who's in charge of security?" Caroline felt her face flush. Her heart was palpitating.

"Retman is. I left you a voicemail yesterday."

"Sorry, I did not open it yet. Chris Retman, the old hound dog, is back from retirement? Wow! I have not seen him since my father ran for president."

"Retman is working for Senator Jameson until I return in a few days. Chill out. Sit down and have a drink with us. This is Sam."

Caroline nodded at Sam. "Nice meeting you, but I've gotta get back to my family."

"Say hello to your mother for me. She is a great lady."

Caroline forced a smile. "Thanks, I will. See you around."

Caroline went outside to listen to her voicemails when she felt someone behind her.

"I got you a vodka tonic with a lime slice. Your mom said it's your favorite." Dillan handed the drink to her. "Are you okay? You look like you just saw a ghost."

She clenched her jaw and looked toward Alton and back to Dillan. "Let's go inside and join everyone."

Dillan held back her drink. "Is it something I did?"

"No, no, no," she shook her head. "I really should have stayed home, work and all, but family first, right?"

Dillan smiled. "Enjoy your drink and family for a while. We had better make sure they can all make it to the boat, and no one falls off the dock. From the looks of it, *my* dad and *your* Aunt Pearl might be the first to be fished out."

Caroline broke into a nervous giggle. "You got that right. Look at Auntie Calypso, dancing by herself with a margarita in hand. Wow, she can move her hips."

The boat ride back to Hatteras was uneventful. Everyone was glad to stay below deck, feeling the effects of a day in the sun and the cocktails.

Once inside the cottage, yawns, glasses of water, and Tylenol had a rippling effect. Caroline kissed her mother and auntie's goodnight and went to her room. She sat down at her desk, and she needed to sleep. Her phone dinged; she had a new text message. "What now, Colton!" she huffed as she opened it. A smile found her face.

> Glad I could help tonight.
> Your family is fun.
> Hope to see you on the beach.
> My dad passed out on the sofa.
> Too much partying with your Aunt Pearl
> Dillan

Caroline stared at the text. "I have no time for this. I have work to do. The last thing I need is a distraction from a man." She texted back:

> I had fun, thanks.

She hit delete.

Maybe next summer

Delete.

Coffee tomorrow?

She looked at it. Absolutely hit delete.

Not sure what to say, she put the phone down and opened her laptop. After answering emails, she sank into the soft cotton sheets of her bed.

"Caroline, it's Mom. I saw your light on. Can I come in?"

Caroline sat up in bed. "Mom, why aren't you asleep?"

Halia sat at the edge of the bed, twiddling her thumbs, looking at Dorothy's paintings. Tomorrow, she will get the results from the tests.

"Mom, what is going on?"

Halia sighed. "Several things. One of which is that you need to stay focused. I see how you look at Dillan and how he looks at you."

"Mom, for heaven's sake, he is a nice guy. We had fun tonight, just like you and your sisters did with Earl. We are on vacation. You're the one who says I need to have fun. So, I did."

Halia sighed as she looked down at the floor. "I saw him hold your hand on the boat." She raised her head and looked at Caroline. "He is not for you."

"So, he held my hand. I'm thirty-five, Mom, not five." Caroline rolled her eyes. "I'm allowed, aren't I?"

Halia sighed again. "You know whose hand you should be holding."

"Enough, Mom. You are like a broken record. I'm going to sleep. It's very late." Caroline pulled the sheets up to her neck. "Night."

"I saw you talking to Alton."

Caroline pulled the sheet down. "You *did*?"

"Of course, I did. He was your father's right-hand security man for years. He's aged, like all of us. Why is he in Ocracoke?"

Caroline tilted her head and reached for her mother's hand. "Mom, I'm sure that brought back memories of Daddy. Alton is on a two-day vacation. His brother-in-law has a cottage on Ocracoke."

Halia rubbed Caroline's shoulder. "I wanted to say hello, but it was too hard with your father and all."

"He said to say hi to you, and you are a great lady. Which you are. Now get some sleep. Tomorrow is a new day. The sun will shine on Hatteras, and in several days, you get to dance around the mermaid bonfire as I'm crowned. Go to sleep. I love you. You're the best."

"Night, Caroline. Love you, too."

However, neither of them could fall asleep. Halia with her worries and Caroline thinking about Colton.

Twenty-One

It was late morning when Caroline finally took a break and strolled down to the beach. Lorelei summoned everyone upstairs to her bedroom to try on their costumes. Grams Dorea waved them off, too busy with her seashell jigsaw puzzle on the back porch to fight the stairs.

"Morning, Grams Dorea," Earl called out as he stood at the screen door.

"Morning, Earl, are you here to fix something?" she asked as she put a piece of the puzzle into place.

"You asked me to replace the bathroom showerhead and clean out the firebox. It ain't been cleaned in years and it is dusty." He knew why it was dusty and kept a straight face.

"I did? My memory is lapsing. Guess I had too much partying last night over on Ocracoke." She put her glasses on. "Okay, come on in and don't be messing around too long." She beckoned him with her index finger. "Earl, come here. You see my puzzle?"

His eyes narrowed on it. "You got a lot of tiny pieces."

"I need to find the piece that fits in here. It's the edge of that pink calico shell."

"I ain't good at puzzles, Grams Dorea."

"Then it's time to learn. Pull up a chair." She pointed her cane to the left. "That chair."

"Grams Dorea, I ain't got time with fixin your place and all."

"You ain't got time?" Grams Dorea sat back and slid her glasses down her nose. Her piercing eyes met his.

"Alright. I got five minutes to find that shell piece for y'all."

"Go on, chip in." Grams Dorea said as she sifted through the puzzle pieces.

Upstairs, the four sisters were deciding the final details about the upcoming mermaid ceremony. They stored the mermaid costumes in the cottage's cedar closet next to Lorelei's bedroom-sewing room. Every detail needed to be addressed. The sisters tried on their costumes to tuck in or take out, along with repairs.

Aunt Calypso, with no effort, fit into hers. A few missing sequins were all it needed. She did a slow twirl in the mirror.

"I look like I did fifteen years ago." She pulled on the string attached to her scalloped tail. "It works!"

"Make those ten years," Pearl teased.

"Ha ha. But it fits. My scalloped mermaid tail is so pretty. The teal and gold beads and sequins still appear as if new."

"I'm adding a stronger fishing line on rings on the tail to the back of the costumes," Lorelei said, "so this year we can pull them up and down and not trip."

"Oh, Lorelei, what an excellent idea! I love it!" Pearl cheered as she examined her costume.

"Girls, I have a surprise. Something I have been working on for months." Lorelei stepped into the cedar closet and came out with a large gray dress bag. Gently, she spread it across the bed.

Halia asked, "Is that Caroline's costume?"

With a smile, Lorelei unzipped the bag. Gasps escaped from the sisters.

"Where was it?" Pearl neared the bed. "It's stunning."

"How?" Halia asked. "It can't be!"

Calypso's eyes traced it. "It's a sign from Seraphina!"

Lorelei's face flushed with pride. "Grams Dorea had it in the storage vault with furs up by her place. But when we all stopped wearing fur, she forgot about it. I was in awe when I took it out of the bag."

Auntie Pearl's eyes watered. "It's a mermaid's blessing, if there is such a thing." She wiped her tears.

Lorelei held it up. It sparkled in the light. "It is the original gown Ida wore at her last ceremony. Well, most of it is. I spent months repairing and patching it. This is as close to the original as I can get. Much of the fabric had disintegrated. I spend hours online and in antique shops searching for fabric, and came across it at a textile shop in Virginia that specializes in vintage fabrics."

Halia ran her fingers over it. "I have chills. It is stunning. Grams Dorea never mentioned this to anyone."

"She found the receipt from the storage company when she and I were cleaning out her attic. Grams Dorea's face lit up, and she asked me to go pick up her items. I found this bag with the old coats that I had donated. As a surprise, I have been getting last-minute measurements from Caroline. This is the gown she will wear, and she has no clue! I showed her yours, Halia, and she believes that is hers!" She reached inside the dress bag. "Girls! Look what I found at the bottom of the bag!"

Pearl and Calypso burst into tears.

Halia sat down on the bed. "It's beautiful. What is it?"

"A wand. A *magical mermaid wand.* So, Grams Dorea says." Lorelei twirled it.

Halia got up and put on her glasses. "Magical? Can I see it?"

"Be careful." Lorelei handed it over. "It's original and must be nearly a hundred years old."

"More or less." Halia said as she held it. Her eyes traveled up and down. The handle, made of sturdy cypress wood, was smooth. Shells, pearls, and lace ribbons adorned the top.

"I redid the ribbons. The rest is original. Grams Dorea says it will bring magic and eternal love to whoever the chosen mermaid taps. She told me after her crowning and holding the wand, she met her eternal love, Daddy."

Pearl asked Halia, "May I see it?"

Halia handed it over. "I never heard Mom tell that story. It's beautiful."

"It's amazing." Pearl's eyes welled up. "I can sense the energy it holds. And the love!"

"Let me hold it." Calypso held her hand out as Pearl gave it to her. "It keeps our bloodline, our sisterhood. Can you feel it? It's who we are."

Lorelei smiled. "Ida wants Caroline to hold it. I know it. I feel it. That's why Mom found that receipt after all these years." She reached for the wand and put it next to the costume.

"The full blood moon will be above. As the stars step aside, we celebrate."

Pearl's eyes remained on the vintage costume on the bed. She ran her hand over it and said. "The gown is beyond beautiful. Look at the shimmering gold fabric, covered in sheer teal and pink overlays. And embellished with pearls." Her eyes followed the gown to the tail. Blue and violet sequins lined the tips of the scallops. "Lorelei, you did an outstanding job."

"Notice the large — I mean, *large* scallop shells for the top of the costume? Those are original. Ida was busty! I had to reattach them, and I added mother-of-pearl glitter and tiny pearls. Too bad the other costumes are missing. Sadly, no one knows what happened to them."

"Where is the crown?" Calypso asked.

"Halia brought it down with her. It's in the closet, in its box." Lorelei said as she sat down at her sewing machine. "I have minor repairs on the crown, and it will be ready for the ceremony. But for now, I must finish your costume, Halia. Your tail needs attention."

"And the pearl ring?" Calypso asked, crossing her arms.

Halia replied, "I have it. It's in my bedroom. Grams Dorea wants to give it the once over."

Pearl smiled, clapping her hands. "Splendid!"

"Where *is* Caroline?" Halia asked as she stood by the window. "Is she still down at the beach?"

"Your daughter is out to share a coffee with that sexy Dillan." Calypso replied. "He is a merman! I wouldn't mind being rescued by him. Ladies, we need to tap him with the mermaid wand."

Pearl giggled. "Ah, our merman. His father is the elder merman, in my book."

Calypso looked at her sister. "You are naughty! What book are you reading?"

Pearl blushed. "If you only knew. It must be the sea air."

Halia's face tightened. "Did Caroline really go with him?"

"Chill out, Halia, she needs to have fun and relax. Dillan is a summer romance," Calypso assured her sister. "It is gorgeous outside and low tide. Sandbar time. I'm heading to the beach. Anyone want to join me? I'll be in our tent." She exited, not without stopping to say, "Thanks to you, Lorelei, it's going to be a wonderful celebration of love and life." She blew a kiss.

As happy as Calypso was, Halia was in a huff. There was only one man for Caroline. She left the room.

"What's Halia's problem?" Pearl asked as she watched her sister go.

"Jameson," Lorelei shook her head. "The broken record. She should let it go. Caroline deserves better. Halia is so hung up on this first lady nonsense. We all know that when her husband lost his bid for the presidency, it devastated her. Remember how she had been interviewing designers to redecorate the Oval Office? And she met with that dress designer from California to create her signature style?"

"How can I forget?" Pearl sat on the edge of the bed. "After Weston lost the election, she didn't talk to anyone for weeks. Even Mom."

Calypso added. "Have you noticed how subdued she is? And she and Grams Dorea are barely speaking to each other. When they do, it's snappy."

"We all know how Grams Dorea feels about politicians." Lorelei threw her hands in the air. "Me, I couldn't care less. Help me get this costume back in the bag."

Caroline parked her bike, fluffed her hair, and stepped inside the coffee shop. Dillan was nowhere in sight. She moseyed around, looking at local ceramics and art. Fifteen minutes had passed. She texted him. No response. She was leaving just as he came through the door.

"I'm so sorry, Caroline. Over at one of my dad's rentals, a sink pipe burst, and it was a mess. The guests were flipping out. They rented it for a wedding. The bride's family was not happy. I sent for a real plumber and got out as fast as I could." His face tensed. "I know you are on a tight schedule. If you want to leave, I can drop off your iced coffee at the cottage on my way home."

Caroline pursed her lips. *Is this guy for real? Drop off my iced coffee?* She looked around and back at Dillan. "I can stay for a bit, but I have to be back for a conference call."

His face softened. "Iced coffee, my treat."

At the counter, the flirtatious barista gave Caroline the once over.

They sat outside at a table with a wide umbrella. Soft, warm ocean breezes caressed Caroline's skin. Her hair blew across her face. Dillan brushed it back. She felt uncomfortable. Unsure of where she wanted it to go, with Colton looming in the background.

"That was a fun time last night, over in Ocracoke."

Caroline nodded as she sipped her iced coffee. "Yep, my aunties and mother can be fun. Grams Dorea is a tough cookie. My grandpops called her Cookie. She kept him in line, and I sure miss him."

Dillan felt a connection. He, too, was unsure. He leaned toward Caroline and asked. "Can you tell me about him? I know my grandfather fished with him."

"He did? Serious? Small world!" Caroline sat back and pushed her hair into a messy bun. "Grandpop used to take me fishing over on the sound side. He had a tiny boat, and I was his ore girl. When he wasn't fishing, Grams Dorea had him doing chores. He loved to cook and have friends over. I learned there were many nights that ran into the early morning over at Beach Heart Cottage."

Dillan smiled. "Rumor has it they had some wild parties. My dad has photos all over the walls in his den. You should come over sometime and I can show you. I believe they are your relatives."

Caroline's face brightened. "Really? I would love to see them."

Dillan's focus moved to Caroline's eyes. "My dad tells me your aunties like to dance around a bonfire when they're here." He leaned in. "He thinks they do witchy stuff, and after the crystal ball incident, I have to wonder."

Caroline burst into laughter. "Your dad is correct. We are a coven of wild, warlock-eating witches. We are planning our next sacrifice, and you are looking damn good. My aunts have been collecting firewood and want to know if you would like to come over to dinner tonight. I mean, *for* dinner."

"Ha ha... you are too funny."

Caroline wondered what Earl knew. Did he spy on them all these years? With a tight smile, she added, "My family loves a bonfire. It's a spot to relive our past and discuss the new." She looked at her phone. "I gotta get back to work. After this election, I can exhale."

"I know, work is work, been there, done that, and you have one heck of a job. The stress must be intense." Dillan pushed his chair out.

"It is."

They walked outside and over to Caroline's bike.

Dillan looked up at the sunny sky and went back to Caroline. "It's a gorgeous day. How about burning off some of that stress and going for a walk on the beach?"

Caroline smiled. "I wish I could. I have a conference call, and I need some downtime. Perhaps a rain check."

Dillan put his sexy smile on full bore. "Sweet. Rain check it is."

"And thanks for the coffee invite. I may see you later. Let me see how this call goes." She got on her bike and, with a slight wave, pedaled off.

Twenty-Two

The conference call ended. Caroline sat back and gave into a wide stretch, and looked around her bedroom. Her eyes landed on one of Dorothy's watercolors. The ocean, with a pink sunset and cotton clouds on the horizon, had two seagulls skimming the tip of a breaking wave. She narrowed her stare. "Is that? No, it can't be. Can it? Is that a mermaid's tail peeking out from the crest of a wave?"

Caroline got up and studied it. Nothing was there, no tail. "Guess I need some beach time." She got up and changed into her bathing suit. Covered in sunblock, her hair back in a ponytail, she slid into her cover up.

Midway down the stairs to the living room, she bumped into Earl on his way up.

"Afternoon, Miss Caroline."

"Hey, Earl, what are you doing here? Grams Dorea will give you a beer, five bucks, and a boot if she knows."

He looked down the stairs and back at Caroline. "Oh, she asked me to fix a leak up in the bathroom shower."

"Good, it's getting worse. The cold handle is stuck. Drip, drip all night. Thanks." She dashed down the stairs to find her mother standing by the front window in the living room.

"Well, if it isn't Miss Social Butterfly herself, who had shared a cup of coffee with that *other* man," Halia remarked smartly.

Caroline laughed. *Here we go.*

"I heard you were out with Dillan today." Halia's tone was sharp.

"Mom, I had an iced coffee. You may have forgotten that I work nonstop and sometimes 'til dawn. I *am* allowed to enjoy being out, even with a man. And he's Earl's son, who is harmless. It's my life, if you may have forgotten."

Her mother sucked in her cheeks and looked out the window. "That's what worries me."

"I'm a grown woman, Mom. I'm going to the beach to relax. You know, I have an idea. You should go on the campaign trail with Colton since you are so hung up on him. He is hiring another assistant. I can get you the job," Caroline snapped. "Please let me enjoy a vacation I should not be on."

"That was uncalled for!" Halia nipped. "How could you?" She turned her back to Caroline.

Grams Dorea, leaning on her cane, entered the room. "What's all this bickering about?"

"Nothing, Grams Dorea, I'm heading to the beach." Caroline spun around and went over to the hall coat rack and plucked her beach bag off a hook.

Grams Dorea stared at Halia. "Leave our mermaid alone! You have been sulking and bitter since you got here. Go down to the beach with your daughter and enjoy life. It's short, you know. And stop this nonsense and your daughter. She is an adult if you have not noticed."

"I know. Life is short. She is all I have since my husband died." Halia wrung her hands as she looked out the window at the swaying sea oats. Her eyes filled with tears. "I have cancer."

"What?" Caroline ran back into the room. "Mom, what did you say?"

"She said she has cancer." Grams Dorea felt her body shiver.

"Mom, oh my gosh. Come sit down." Caroline took her mother's hand and led her to the sofa. "Sit." Her heart raced. "Mom, I'm *so sorry* I said what I did."

"Get your mother some tissues," Grams Dorea asked Caroline as she turned to Halia. "What is going on?"

Halia's face was damp with tears. "I had it last year. They treated it. It was gone, but I think it's come back."

Caroline got a box of tissues and sat next to her mother, holding back her tears. "Mom, here's a tissue." She looked at Grams Dorea. "You knew?"

Grams Dorea nodded. "You think it came back? Why didn't you tell me what was going on? I'm your mother, for heaven's sake." Gram Dorea's face flushed as she sat herself in her recliner.

"Mom, why would you hide this from me?" Caroline was shaking.

"I didn't want to ruin our vacation and your mermaid celebration or your arduous work on the campaign. I'm so sorry, I just couldn't hold it in any longer. The doctor's office will have results today."

"Call them now." Grams Dorea said, trying to remain calm.

"No. They said today before five. It started as small, dark growth on my chest that rapidly spread." She unbuttoned her blouse. "Here, they took it off my left side. Look at the scar."

"Hogwash, Halia. These doctors love to scare the nonsense out of us."

"No, they don't," Halia sniffled. "Just the opposite. It may have spread through my lymphatic system. The past week I ached all over."

Caroline felt her stomach hit the floor.

Grams Dorea looked over at the Ball jar on the mantle and to Halia. "Your bones hurt from walking on the beach. You are not that young anymore."

"Maybe," Halia moaned, dropping her head. "I don't know. But I'm scared."

"Mom, please think positively. Do you want me to call the doctor now?"

Halia blew her nose. "No. Do not tell anyone else, please. If it is positive, not a word until after our vacation. I don't want to spoil this for anyone, especially you, my love." She brushed Caroline's cheek, salty with tears.

Caroline looked like a frightened child. Grams Dorea was quiet.

At that moment, Earl came down the stairs, holding a wrench. "What's going on here," he laughed, "a funeral?"

"Earl!" Grams Dorea snapped. "Hush up."

"Geez, sorry. I fixed the faucet leak. You got hot and cold water again. The fireplace flue is now in working condition and the firebox is tidy. I'm heading out. I have a meeting with Dillan. We are thinking of buying the cottage next to yours, the one that's been vacant since the last hurricane. I can bring that cottage back to life."

"Good. Go. And send me a bill for the repairs," Grams Dorea waved him off.

Earl shook his head. "Yes, ma'am. I sure hope you all are okay. You all look like someone died."

"Stop saying that!" Grams Dorea snapped. "Go on now, go home."

Earl took one more look at the teary-eyed women and left, mumbling something about hormones. He bumped into Pearl, who was coming up from the beach. "Afternoon, Miss Pearl. Are y'all having a splendid day?"

Pearl smiled bashfully. "I am now."

Earl looked around, feeling like a teenager. "I got me another bottle of scuppernong wine. Ya wanna meet me down at the beach, say around seven?"

"Why, Earl, yes, of course I do."

"Can y'all bring that chartie board? I enjoyed it. Especially that salami that looks like a rose."

"Okay," Pearl held down her floppy hat as a breeze met her.

Earl looked over his shoulder up at the cottage. "They all seem a bit under the weather up there. Grams Dorea is being, well, a bit rude to me."

Pearl tilted her head. "Huh?"

"Ah, nothing." He looked up at the sky. "Looks like a storm out at sea. It'll pass. I'm heading over to the vacant cottage next to yours. It's going up for sale and I'm thinking of buying it."

Pearl looked over the dune. She could only see the roof. "Looks like it needs a lot of work."

"It's a bargain. If y'all wanna come join me, I could use a woman's eye. Just come on in. Dillan is showing it. If it those rain clouds come to make a visit, how about we share that chartie board at my place?"

Pearl bit her bottom lip to hide her smile. "I may just do that!"

With an ear-to-ear grin, Earl watched her head toward the cottage. "Wait! Join me at the vacant house or my place?"

Pearl stopped. "Why, both, Earl!"

"Hot dog!" With a skip and stumble in his step, he headed to the vacant house to meet Dillan.

Twenty-Three

Pearl put her beach bag and hat on the bench in the front entry. She grabbed an iced tea and strolled into the living room to find Halia pacing and Caroline wiping her eyes.

"It's a gorgeous day. Why are you all so dreary?" Pearl was wondering if Caroline and Halia got into another argument over Colton. "You ladies need some beach time. Calypso is at the beach with Lorelei. Go get some sun. Caroline, go down to the beach and take a dip. The water is beautiful and so warm. We decided on pizza tonight. How about it? Text me what toppings you ladies would like."

No one responded.

"Okay, grumpy girls, I'm going to the outside shower." She grabbed a towel off a hook and made her way out the back porch door.

Caroline looked at her phone. It was almost four. She looked at her mother, who kept her hand on her phone in her pocket.

"Caroline," Grams Dorea said calmly, "call the doctor's office for your mother."

Halia, with a hitch in her voice, turned to Caroline. "No, I want to hear the news myself."

"Mom, think positive. And I should call."

Halia shook her head.

They waited. At four fifteen, there was nothing. At four thirty, still nothing. Halia paced when her phone rang. It sent a shudder down her spine. Grams Dorea's eyes were wide. Caroline felt her stomach in her throat.

Halia made her way over to the fireplace and answered it. She was silent, nodding, asking questions. The call lasted a minute. When she hung up, she rested her forehead on the mantle and broke into sobs.

Caroline dashed over. "Mom, Mom! What did the doctor say?"

Grams Dorea, short of breath, repeated. "What did the doctor say?"

Halia reached for Caroline's hand. "It was negative, and I need to wear more sunblock, get checked every six months. I'm clear of all cancer." Her body shook.

Caroline burst into tears, as did Grams Dorea.

"Thank goodness it's over. I've been waiting weeks for the results. I *am* so sorry I have been on edge and snappy. Especially to you, Caroline. Enjoy your life. A phone call can end it."

Grams Dorea tightened her face. "Now that you nearly put me into my grave, can you please get me a beer?"

Halia dried her eyes. "Yes, Mom."

"I'll get it. Mom, you sit down and relax." Caroline, still shaken, hugged her mother. "Don't you ever do that to me again. Do you hear me? You tell me first." Caroline dried her eyes as she left the room. She returned and gave Grams Dorea her beer. "I'm going to enjoy my cocktail down at the beach. No more doctor phone calls, do you hear?"

Halia nodded as she continued to wipe her eyes.

Caroline brushed a tear off Halia's cheek. "Mom, pizza tonight sounds marvelous."

Grams Dorea chugged her beer and looked at her daughter. "Thank God, Halia. Now we can all enjoy this incredibly special ceremony. Nothing can get in the way."

"I know, Mom." Halia said as she pressed her hands together in prayer and looked up. "Thank you." She got up to get a glass of water.

What a scare! Whatever would she do without her mother? Caroline grabbed her beach bag, and she headed out the door. Her heart still beating fast, she made her way down to the beach to join her aunties under the tent canopy.

"Caroline, there are cups in the Bogg Bag, and the thermos is in the cooler."

"Thanks, Auntie Lorelei."

"I have several cheeses, dip, and chickpea crackers in the cooler as well. Enjoy."

Caroline's stomach growled. "Thanks, Auntie Calypso. How did you know I love chickpea crackers?"

"Your mom told me. Enjoy and take a nap!"

"I will, Auntie Lorelei." With her feet resting on the cool sand, slight balmy breezes caressing her face and the soothing sound of gentle waves filling her senses, she let out an ahhh. With their voices drifting over her, they reminisced about past vacations as she drifted off to sleep. Her aunts grabbed their bags and headed up to the cottage.

"Hey, Caroline, wake up." Something poked her forearm. "Shhhh. It's me."

Squinting, she looked up. A mustached tourist in mirrored shades was kneeling next to her.

"Get away from me or I'll start screaming!"

"Scream away! You're so damn cute when you're mad."

"*Colton?* What the heck are you doing here? Look at you!" she was waking up. "Huh, I'm dreaming." She popped up and looked around. "Yup, I'm having a bad dream?"

"You think I'm a bad dream?"

"Yes! Were you followed?" Panicked, she looked around again. Alton, in the distance, was playing frisbee with Sam, who waved.

"No, it's all good. Do you like my disguise? So Pink Panther. You know, a gray mustache, matching wig. You like the Tommy Bahama hat? The toucan bird shirt is the bomb, as my young constituents would say. *Our* young constituents. And how do you like the black knee socks and sandals?" He pointed to his feet. "I fit in, don't I?"

She burst into laughter. "Your wig. It's crooked, and you this is ridiculous. Those milky-white legs hurt my eyes. And those Caesar Roman sandals are a trip. Wow, you make a funny grandpa."

He looked down at his legs and feet. "Thanks. You know how to bust an ego."

"You must be so hot under that wig and hat. Never mind that. What are you doing here?"

"I wanted to see you. And yeah, I'm boiling. They glued this hat to the wig and clipped it to my hair. Damn thing is like a heating pad on high." Colton shifted his head from side to side. "I'd jump in the ocean, but my disguise will fall off." He looked around, only to see his security, and two young girls playing on boogie boards. "I could jump in. Who would know?"

"Don't! You never know what reporters or weirdos are in the dunes. Even with your guys around you. I *knew* it. Damn it, Alton was over in Ocracoke checking it out, wasn't he? And that is not his brother-in-law, is he?"

"Busted! And I was there, too. You didn't see me in disguise. I was near you, and nobody knew who I was. Sometimes, I need a day or two off. And you were busy with that tall, dark, handsome guy with the fancy speedboat."

"Are you stalking me? Is that why you're here?" She was only half-kidding.

He looked out over the ocean and went back to Caroline. "I figure if my PR woman can take time off, so can I. I need a breather after the breakup and all."

"Ugh, the breakup. Besides, your PR person is not running for president. Get inside the tent." She looked around. "Are you crazy? Wait, speed boat? Dillan? What-"

"My guys checked him out and they have it under control. Any new speeches and media?" He pulled his hat and wig off and sat next to her on the blanket. "It sure is gorgeous here." He scratched his faux mustache and gave it a tug. "This gets itchy in the heat. Look what I go through to see you."

"I didn't invite you, and you shouldn't be here. This is making me extremely uncomfortable." She reached into her bag for her sunglasses and slid them on. "What if the media finds you here?" She glanced over her shoulder. "They could be anywhere. Everywhere. And keep your wig on. Please."

"I'm working my way up the coast. Virginia Beach tomorrow. I love working with you. Caroline, or is it Lynnie? You know I will need a wife in the White House."

"Hold on, mister. Are you proposing? Jesus Colton, first, you need to get elected. And we will find you a wonderful wife. You can have a White House wedding in the Rose Garden. Did a president ever get married while in office?"

"Woodrow Wilson. Maybe others. And *you* are that wonderful wife. You are the someone who will have a cause, a passion! We'll fill the White House with kids and dogs, just like we used to dream we would. Remember those nights we talked about what life would be like if I were president and you the first lady? Caroline, it's all coming true." He plucked off his mustache. "Ouch."

"I remember."

"Call me *Mister* President." Colton added a sexy wink.

Caroline shook her head. "Mr. President!"

"Hey, remember that windy night when the power was out, and we had to light candles in your grandmother's cottage?" He glanced over the dune at the cottage and back to Caroline.

The romantic memory of it lingered in her mind. No, she couldn't allow herself to do that. She had to flip to the present.

"Wow Colton. You *are* living a fantasy. My cause is to get you there. And my passion is working. Kids and dogs are not in my plans; neither is smiling for the press on the White House lawn. Besides, you seem to have recovered quickly from the breakup with what's her name."

"It wasn't what you think. I made a mistake. I don't want to be the modern-day James Buchanan. The only president to stay single. How empty the halls of the White House must have been. Too bad. You are beautiful, talented, and have a political upbringing. A Woodard!" He looked over his shoulder toward the cottage again. "Your mom wants you there."

"My *mom*? She asked you to come here, didn't she?" She shook her head. "Mom is stuck in her own fantasy world since Dad passed away, and you know how badly she aspired to be First Lady Margaret. Hey, I have an idea."

"Stop there. I *am not* marring your mother."

"Why not? She and I look alike. She has the passion to re-decorate, and she loves you. And you can get a romping dog and adopt kids."

"Stop it, Caroline, and be serious with me for a minute."

She flashed a smile. "I am."

With a frisbee in hand, Alton came up to the tent and put his head inside. "Hi, Caroline."

She looked up, forcing a smile. "Hi, Alton. Ocracoke, and now you're here? You get around."

He smirked at Caroline and looked at Colton. "Mr. Jameson, there is a large group of people down on the beach. Stay under the tent until they pass." He remained a few feet away from the tent, pretending to examine the frisbee.

"I should go meet them. Shake hands."

Alton was quick to reply, "No, I don't think so, and you stay put."

Alton walked away.

Colton turned to Caroline. "Caroline, you know blue and gold are your colors! And you know they are my favorite colors. Presidential colors if you add red lipstick."

"Ugh, Colton, really?" She reached for her cover up and slid it on. "Where are you staying?"

"A secret." He pressed his finger to her lips. "Heck, I can't keep this secret."

"Oh, so tell."

"Your mom insisted we can be guests at your cottage. And I can stay in your bedroom with you. In your bed."

"*What? No!*"

"Teasing you. We have a place at the end of Hatteras. All secure under secured names. I'm having a meeting there early tomorrow, before we fly out of Manteo to Virginia Beach. I'd like you to be there."

Caroline tensed as she watched the waves roll in. "Colton, this is not the best decision with you being here on the island."

"Such a nervous nelly. Come on, let's go for a beach walk and talk. Alton and Sam will be behind us. The beach is empty now, and here I am with this gray wig. I'm an elderly gentleman with his pretty granddaughter." He nudged her. "Come on, *Lynnie*, let's go find some sea glass, like we did that weekend when we stayed here and went to Lighthouse Beach for that long walk. Do you still have the necklace I had made for you from that cobalt piece of glass I found?"

"No." It was in her room at the cottage, hanging on a hook.

"I need a break from campaigning, Lynnie. The ocean invigorates me." He got up, put his disguise on, and reached for her hand. She took it.

"As if you need to be invigorated! Just so you know, your outfit isn't suitable for a beach walk. And Lynnie is not my name."

"Lynnie was your name that weekend." He nudged her. "All weekend."

Caroline pressed her eyes closed. It had been a magical weekend. She had fallen in love and believed Colton was her soulmate. Months later, egos and schedules had gotten in the way. Hurtful, yes. Regretful. Could be.

"That was then, Colton. This is now. We had a wonderful time, but those days were long over. It wouldn't work now for the same reasons it didn't work then. I want to do my job and get you where you need to be. It's time to drop the past and pick up the future."

He was silent as he inhaled the salty air and looked at her. "The future. You know what I want."

She ignored his comment, keeping her eyes on Alton.

"Your mom invited me over for pizza."

"*Tonight*? They know you're here?" Caroline gasped. "Seriously? That's why my aunties left me alone in the tent?"

"I guess your mom said something. We talk sometimes. Me and your mom."

"This is crazy, and you talk to my mom? And Grams Dorea, does she know?"

He was quick to answer. "Hell, no! I would get a swift hit in the rear end with her cane. Can you please hide it tonight? And as a peace offering, I'm bringing her a case of Bud."

"Oh, my gosh. This is gonna be an interesting pizza party. And please, Colton, no more Lynnie."

"Killjoy, Caroline. Guess Lynnie does not want to come out to play," he reached for her knee.

She pushed his hand away. "You are tenacious, aren't you?"

"If I did, I would not be where I am now. With you, I'm even closer." His eyes wandered to her legs. "I also know that your birthday is today."

"You remembered?" Caroline had a sudden, disturbing thought. Was it truly a call from a doctor? Or was it Colton on the phone with her mother, setting up the meeting on the beach? Caroline cinched her brows as she reached for her straw hat. "Let's go, Colton."

With many questions swirling in Caroline's mind, they walked south, in search of sea glass, with Alton and his men not far behind.

Dillan, holding a handful of Joe Bell flowers, was coming down the sandy path from Earl's cottage when he stopped dead in his tracks. From behind tall sea oats, he watched Caroline and an older man walking along the shore, skirting the breaking waves.

Alton was aware of Dillan's presence. Jameson had to win not only the election but also Caroline before Dillan did.

Twenty-Four

Dillan was back at his dad's cottage. He put the flowers in an old pickle jar, filled it with water, and set it down on the kitchen counter. He was questioning who the older man was with Caroline. It was most likely one of her aunt's husbands. Yes, that is who it was. Of course. He looked at his phone and had to meet his dad at the vacant house. He texted Caroline.

> Hi, I didn't have time to go to the beach.
> I had to show my dad a house. Be back later.
> Beach walks at night are fun too.

He hit send and made his way over to the vacant cottage. Earl was wandering around the warped wrap-around porch, kicking a loose board here and there.

"Dad, I'm here." Dillan opened the lockbox, and they went inside. "Wow, this stinks of mold. This may be a disaster."

"I smell it. She's been idle. Nothing me and you can't handle. It will take some time, but we can do it. First chore is to open the place up and toss all this furniture and carpeting."

Dillan sneezed.

"Bless you."

"Thanks, Dad, but we may need more than a blessing to get this place ready. Let's open the blinds and windows and get some light on the subject." He sneezed again as he pulled the dusty mini blinds up.

It weathered many storms and survived. Yes, it was going to take work, but it sat beautifully on the lot. Its six bedrooms and four bathrooms have not had a visitor in a long time.

Earl went upstairs and found it in satisfactory condition. It would be a worthwhile investment and only a few houses down from his own cottage. There was no need to prepare it for renting out by next season.

From the bottom of the stairs, Dillan told Earl, "Let me call the owner to see if we can make a deal. You want it, right?"

"I need to spend time and check it out." Earl opened a window, allowing fresh air in. "Feel that, Dillan? This place gets amazing sea breezes. She's a keeper."

"Looks like it has strong bones. Just needs a major cleanup," Dillan replied as he made his way around to the back. It was old, for sure, and held a vintage Hatteras charm. The kitchen and bathrooms had to go. Dillan looked out the side window at Grams Dorea's cottage, then checked his phone for any texts from Caroline. Nothing. He put his phone down and walked out the back door to the porch. The tattered screens blew in the breeze. He inhaled the briny air and went inside.

The front door opened.

"Earl? Are you in here?"

Dillan came over. "Hi, Pearl, what a surprise."

Her smile was warm and friendly. "Your dad asked me to check out this poor old house and give him a woman's opinion. You know, a decorating eye."

Dillan gestured her inside. "You will want to cover your nose. It's not only dusty but also smelly in here, Pearl."

Pearl waved her hands in front of her face. "It sure is and stifling hot. Yuck, you fellas need to open all the windows and get some fans running. There is a fantastic breeze outside. Here, let me." She opened a few windows with Dillan.

"They turned the power off a while back," Dillan mentioned as he struggled to open a window. "These need to be replaced."

"Why, Pearl, I thought I heard your delightful voice, and I'm sure glad you stopped by," Earl came down the stairs. "This is a diamond in the rough, isn't it?"

"That it is." Pearl smiled at Earl. "It reminds me of old sea glass. Warn, but still beautiful and will be crafted into something spectacular."

Earl made his way to Pearl. "Kinda like me?"

She nudged him. "Yes."

"I brought the scuppernong wine."

Pearl squeezed her shoulders to her ears, adding a teenager smile. "I made the charcuterie board and two salami roses."

Earl blushed, patting his belly. "Yummy. If I buy this, I'll name it *Sea Glass*. How about ya wanna help me fix her up decorating and all? Come with me upstairs. It's a keeper."

With giddy nods, they sauntered off.

Dillan, wanting no part of scuppernong wine and salami roses or whatever they were up to, walked outside. From the deck on the ocean side of the cottage, he could still see Caroline with the older man. Wondering if he was an uncle or a business associate, he shrugged it off. They were new friends. Casual friends, he reminded himself. Or were they? With that question in the air, he made a call to get more details on the property.

Caroline stooped to pick up a small piece of dark green sea glass that had washed up between shell fragments. "This is old." She rolled it between her fingers as she held it up to the sun.

Colton smiled at her find as he scratched his neck. "Listen, this wig and mustache are itching in the heat. I need to get back to our rental and shower before I scratch to death. Join me for refreshments?"

"No. I will pass. I need to head back to the cottage and wash off this sunblock and sand and get ready for the pizza bash. Just wait until I have a word with my mother." Caroline was more than annoyed at the fact that they had been secretly in touch. She knew the intentions behind her mother's actions.

"Can I have the sea glass?" He held out his hand. "I want to put this in my pocket so when I'm stressing before a speech, I can chill, thinking of this day and you."

Caroline squinted from under her sunglasses, ignoring his *thinking of you* comment. "Sure. Keep it." She dropped it into his hand.

This impromptu visit had her deep in thought. *Is it because he needs a woman by his side to win? Is that what earworms have been telling him on the campaign trail? What about his ex? What was that all about? What if they followed him?* Or was it her mother constantly stirring the pot? Did he love her? Shaking off all the distracted thoughts, she asked. "What time did you say my mom invited you over?"

"I was told six-thirty-ish."

Caroline laughed. "What until Grams Dorea sees you in her cottage? Oh, call her Grams Dorea, or she will give you the stink eye all night."

"Grams Dorea, gotta love her. She *always* gave me the stink eye, no matter what. I believe by now they all know since my security has been around the cottage, checking things out."

"This is gonna be fun. In fact, I'm going to get a few bottles of wine."

"I'll have Alton pick up some pinot. Is that still what you drink?"

"We've got it covered. Thanks anyway. I guess I'll see you later?" Her shoulders relaxed as her demeanor softened. She still enjoyed his company. Their passion was a mere ember, and she was careful not to put any heat on it.

Not without a kiss on her cheek, they parted. She stepped inside the cottage and dropped her beach bag on the floor. With her hands on her hips, she called, "Mother! Oh, Mother, where are you?"

Halia came into the living room. "Is everything all right, honey?" She fiddled with her hair. "Oh, I forgot to wish you a happy birthday this morning. Happy birthday!"

Caroline's eyes narrowed. "Thank you, Mother. And there is just one minor problem. Colton Jameson is sharing pizza with us. Mom, this is ridiculous. He can't be here. It will leak all over the press, and they will plaster my picture along with everyone else in a rag magazine and on some morning talk show. Damaging my reputation and my new partnership. Please, for the love of Daddy, stop it."

Her mother wrung her hands. "Honey, he's perfect. He was Daddy's protégé. And your daddy would love nothing more in heaven to know you are Mrs. Jameson."

Caroline felt her body shiver with annoyance. "Mom, Mom, Mom, I've had enough today between your impromptu cancer scare and Colton Jameson, dressed as an elderly vacationer, rudely waking me up from a splendid nap. Time for a shower, and then I'm going up to my room to work, and I'll see you at the pizza gathering. Grams Dorea is gonna blow a fuse, so you better be ready." She opened the porch door and headed for the outside shower, not without saying over her shoulder. "And hide her cane."

"Honey," her mother called after her, "wear that floral summer linen dress with the white belt and those cute pink heeled sandals. The ones I picked up at Nordstrom's. A little pink, glossy lipstick too."

Caroline turned the shower on full blast, chuckling over Colton's elderly man disguise.

She put on a pair of navy linen shorts and a white tee shirt. There would be no flirty fairy sundress and seductive heels. Her mermaid flip-flops were fine. Her hair up in a carefree bun and a trace of peach lip gloss, she started down the stairs and stopped at the landing. She looked down at her aunties wearing summer dresses, dolled up in makeup, with anxious smiles. Were they all in on it?

Little *JAMESON for PRESIDENT* flags were stacked on a dining room chair, waiting to be put up. They scattered candles around the room, all lit. On the coffee table sat a vase filled with red, white, and blue carnations. A platter of appetizers was placed right beside it. Van Morrison's music wafted throughout the cottage.

Caroline smiled. "I see you are all dressed up for the pizza bonanza."

With eagerness, they nodded their heads.

Auntie Calypso was wearing a broad smile and said. "The last time we saw Colton was at that Christmas bash at your mom and dad's a couple of years back after he won his senate race. I can't wait to see our future president."

"I do recall that. Ah, the good old days," Pearl joyfully raised her glass of wine. "To good times and more ahead!"

"If I remember correctly, we filled the punch bowl twice at that Christmas bash saturated with gossip and political chatter." Tapping her forehead, Caroline added, "Maybe three times." With a roll of her eyes, she looked around the room. "Where is my mom?"

Auntie Lorelei answered in a soft whisper. "She's out on the back porch, conjuring up the courage to tell Grams Dorea. Bribing her with freshly fried pickles and beer in a frothy mug."

"Oh boy. I need a glass of wine." Caroline made a beeline for the kitchen and was reaching for a bottle of wine when she heard the back porch door close. She squeezed her eyes shut, waiting to hear Grams Dorea's disapproval. Silence filled the air. "Huh?" She poured a full glass and joined everyone. Her eyes met her mother's. "Did Grams Dorea read you the riot act? I hope she did."

Halia smiled at her daughter. "Your grandmother is happy to see him again."

Caroline gulped her wine, then laughed. "I bet she's happy to give him a lecture on elder health care! Did you hide her cane?"

"Caroline!"

"Mom, please. You know how she is. She watches those news programs and all that negativity."

There was a knock on the front door.

"I'll get it!" With a quick step, Pearl opened it. "Pizza's here!"

Earl juggled a pile of boxes. "They're hot!"

"Hurry in and put them on the kitchen table. I have the oven on to keep them warm." With a giddy smile, Pearl led the way. Scuppernong wine was swirling around her body. Wine she and Earl had shared at the vacant house next door.

Halia whispered to Caroline, "Earl has to go home before our next president arrives."

"Mom, he will. Give him a break. He was nice enough to deliver the pizza. Wait, how did Earl get past security?"

"Honey, not only was Earl checked out, but we were, too. And most likely everyone on our street."

After the alarming afternoon, with the doctor's report, Caroline felt that if this made her mom happy, then so be it. What if that report had been different? There would be no celebrating tonight. It was time to let it go.

"I think Pearl has a crush on Earl," Calypso whispered. "They were at the vacant house late this afternoon. Alone."

"Oh, really?" Caroline's eyes lit up. "I wonder what they were up to?"

"I saw Dillan leave and, well, a good two hours later, Pearl came back all flushed and in another world. Like a teenager."

Caroline raised her eyebrows.

Earl was helping Pearl in the kitchen, putting pizzas in the oven, clueless to who the guest was. He hoped the flowers, candles, and party were for him as a thank you for all the help around the cottage. He couldn't have been more wrong!

"Wow, Earl is growing on me," Caroline confessed. "Although, Auntie Lorelei, you scared him with Conchita. And Dillan questioned me about how you knew his middle name."

Auntie Lorelei smiled. "That Dillan is hot. Baby making material."

Caroline almost spit out her wine. "Auntie Lorelei!"

Auntie Lorelei's face brightened. "And I see how he looks at you, with lust and-"

"Whoa...wow...Don't say it," Caroline cut her off. "And Mom, don't start."

"Fine, I won't say a word." Halia looked at her phone. "Our next president will be here soon. Come help me put the campaign flags up. Did you notice I put the American flag out front on the porch?"

"Whatever makes you happy, Mom. This is your night." She gave her mother a soft hug. She looked at her Auntie Lorelei. "And by the way, please don't take your crystal ball out this evening."

Auntie Lorelei laughed. "Don't worry, Conchita is resting. She will have much to say after all the energy we collect tonight. I can't wait to have a chat with her tomorrow at our sunrise meditation."

Twenty-Five

Earl was in the kitchen helping Pearl with the pizzas when Halia walked in.

"I think Earl has done enough." Halia tilted her head as she looked at Earl. "Sorry, Earl, time to leave. You know how Grams Dorea gets."

Earl was confused, assuming he was the guest of honor. He looked at the pizzas and then at Pearl.

"Earl, best you go. Take some slices for you and Dillan." Pearl said as she put slices on a plate when the doorbell rang. "Crap," she said under her breath. "Earl, take the pizzas and go out the back door." Pearl hurried to get the pizza on the plates and pushed him out the back kitchen door.

"Geez, I get the message. You'd think I was the devil."

Halia rushed to the front door. She stopped; holding a small American flag, she composed herself, and with a wide smile, opened the door. "Oh, Dillan?" Her cheer dulled as she stepped back, keeping the door open three inches.

"Hi, is my dad here? I need him to help me unload sheetrock from my truck." He tried to poke his head inside. Halia made sure he could not see Caroline.

Caroline could hear his voice and mumbled under her breath, "Here we go." She met him at the door. "Hi, Dillan. Mom, open the door. I want to go outside for a sec."

With hesitation, her mother did so, reminding her, "Hurry, Caroline. No time for dillydallying."

Caroline brushed past her mother, letting out a sigh. She stepped outside. "Your dad has pizza for you. Come on in."

Halia felt her heart sink. "Caroline." She tapped her watch.

"I know, Mom." She led him into the entryway. "How about I call you tomorrow?" She said, wearing a flirtatious smile. "I think I'm going to need beach time."

His face lit up. "Excellent. Say mid-morning? I'm busy later in the day, working on a project with my dad."

Grams Dorea came inside from the back porch. "What is going on? I saw Earl dashing past the porch with pizza. Is *that* Jameson the rat fink here yet?"

No one said a word.

Grams Dorea looked Dillan up and down. "You ain't the senator. Late as always. Damn politicians. Girls, let me know when the rat fink senator and his entourage show up. Text me." She went over to her recliner, picked up her phone, and ventured out to the back porch.

Dillan's eyes spun around the women and back to Caroline. *Senator.*

"You better be going. Your pizza will get cold," Caroline led him out the door.

Aunt Lorelei spoke up. "Conchita, the crystal ball, is coming out, so you best be on your way. She has eyes, and I may need a lock of your hair."

"What? I'm outta here. Caroline, text me at some point." He popped his head back inside. "You ladies have a wonderful time with Conchita."

Caroline shut the door, pressing her back against it. "Mom, this was *not* a good idea. Grams Dorea let the cat out of the bag, and what if it's feral? Rumors could fly around the island in no time, and gawkers will arrive, and so will cameras." Shaking her head, she made her way to the kitchen and stopped. "Mom, what did you do to the dining room? It looks like a campaign stop. Streamers? Really, Mom. Will confetti rain down?" The patriotic décor in the dining room, now a campaign venue, was ready. Hats, banners, and buttons from Jameson's campaign and her father's past presidential campaign filled the room.

"You worry too much, Caroline. And yes, I decorated for our special guest and made cupcakes iced in red, white, and blue. And there are no confetti-filled balloons. But that is a smart idea." She shrugged, "Too late."

Caroline had heard enough and headed straight to the kitchen and poured a glass of wine. There was a tap on the window above the sink. She jumped back, causing her wine to spill. She wiped off her shorts and slipped out the back door.

"I had to see you, Caroline."

"Dillan. Shhhh, spies are all around. I'm *so* sorry for kicking you out, but-"

"I get it. These are for you." Dillan handed her the pickle jar filled with Joe Bell flowers. "I missed you earlier today. Busy and all with my dad and that vacant cottage." He, too, told a white lie.

Caroline's face lit up as she reached for the brilliant orange and yellow flowers. "Thank you. These have such meaning in so many ways." She held them close.

"Is that who was on the beach with you today? The senator?"

Caroline was stunned. "Are *you* stalking me?"

"No, no, of course not. I was at the vacant cottage with my dad, and I was looking at the property and the decks when I saw you and an older man. I thought he was younger."

She looked up at the stars and back at Dillan. "Yeah, I can't lie. It was him. In disguise."

He stepped back. "Wow, he came all the way to Hatteras Island from campaigning to see you?"

"To pester me is more like it. He has an event in Virginia Beach tomorrow afternoon, and on his journey up from Georgia, he stopped here." Her heart beat a little faster. "I'm dreading this pizza gathering. Soon, it will be over, and he will be in the White House, or back to continue being a senator. Whichever happens."

Out on the dark porch, unbeknownst to Caroline and Dillan, Grams Dorea was sitting in her chair, listening to every word.

"Caroline?" Her mother called from somewhere inside. "Caroline! Where are you? The senator will be here soon."

"Go!" She pushed Dillan away. "Hurry."

He stopped and kissed her cheek and left. Her face flushed and heart sped up as she reached into the cooler on the back porch, pulled out a bottle of pinot, and stepped inside.

"There you are! They will be here any minute. Honey, your hair. It's messy!" She rearranged the loose bun. "Go upstairs and run some gloss on those lips." She tilted her head. "Caroline, you are all flushed, wearing a dreamy glaze in your eyes. It's Colton, isn't it? Thank God!"

Dillan made his way through the dunes toward his dad's cottage. When two black SUVs pulled into Beach Heart's driveway. He crouched down behind a cluster of thick sea oats. Peeking over a dune, he noticed three men stepping out of the first car and they did a circle around the cottage with flashlights. Dillan did not move. After several minutes, one of them opened the door of the second car while the other two stood by the front door.

It *was* Senator Jameson, arriving with his entourage. Dillan wanted to text his dad but decided it was too risky, being that Earl was the island blabbermouth.

Twenty-Six

Wearing a Styrofoam campaign hat, Caroline's mother waved her little flag with pride. Caroline stood behind her giddy aunties. She waited until they had all finished with hellos, hugs, and kisses. It left her to be center stage to usher Colton into the room. He gave her a hug and a kiss on the cheek.

Halia dashed over to the sofa, plumping the throw pillows. "Senator, please, come sit down. Would you like a drink? Bourbon on the rocks, as I recall. Two perfect round cubes." Halia clasped her hands. "This is so wonderful! You have time to share pizza with us. We have sausage and peppers, or do you want the works?"

Colton looked at Caroline and then at Halia. "Sounds delicious, Mrs. Woodard. Yes, I'll have a bourbon and yes, two ice cubes. I'll also take the works on my pizza."

Halia's face flushed as she looked at Caroline. "This is wonderful, right, honey?"

"Yes, Mom, it is."

"Please, make yourself comfortable." Auntie Calypso said as she took Colton's arm and led him to the sofa. The aunts gathered as if he were a newborn in the nursery.

Halia pointed to the coffee table filled with appetizers. "Enjoy! Caroline, go sit next to the senator." She reached for Caroline's elbow. "I'll get you a glass of pinot and, for our handsome senator," she looked at Colton, "a bourbon with two icy rocks."

"Thanks, Mother." Caroline elbowed Colton. "I'm glad you're here. My mom is so happy."

He nodded as he watched Halia dash off to the kitchen. "Me, too. You have a wonderful family." He whispered in her ear. It tickled her. "I'm glad you are here next to me. The air is balmy, the hush of the ocean, and knowing I was going to see you made my day complete. We could take a stroll later and gaze up at the Milky Way. Like we used to do."

"We could." Caroline patted his hand. Seeing her mother so full of joy and her aunt's happiness warmed her heart. He may have been driving her crazy as a client, but those dormant embers were getting warmer. She had better be careful not to melt. Her wall was high, but there was something. Was it the way he looked at her, touched her? His presence was powerful, and his voice commanding yet sexy. His energy, high. Caroline felt it. She had to shake it off.

Colton asked everyone to sit and be comfortable as he reached for a cracker and crab dip. "This is delicious." He took another one.

"I made the dip. Earl, our neighbor, brought over fresh blue crab meat. He caught them this morning. It's an old recipe passed down from his grandmother," Auntie Pearl said softly. "Here you go, Senator Jameson."

"Thank you. It's certainly addictive. And please, everyone, call me Colton, just like old times." He reached for his drink and sat back. "This cottage is so welcoming." He looked around. "And I'm one lucky man to be surrounded by such beautiful women."

Oh, he's got to be kidding! Caroline thought to herself. *Mr. Corny.*

The women were blushing when a thud on the back porch door got everyone's attention. It opened. Caroline's heart almost stopped. Alton held the door open as Grams Dorea entered with her cane thumping as she made her way to her recliner.

"Thank you, young man, for opening the door." Her eyes met Colton's. "Your *man* found me dozing off. I guess you all forgot to text me *that he* is here. I would have missed this event if not for this nice man."

"You are welcome, ma'am." Alton's eyes flashed over to Colton, who nodded. Alton shut the door.

Halia was holding her breath. She took a moment to let it out and asked, "Grams Dorea, would you like anything?"

Her eyes landed on Colton. "I will have some of that dip *he* is stuffing his face with."

"Mom, be polite," Auntie Pearl whispered as she reached for the crackers, put some dip on a plate, and handed it to her.

"Grams and I don't always see eye to eye, do we?" Colton raised his eyebrows, smiling.

"You got that right, *Senator*." She settled into her recliner. "Who made the dip?"

With a pleasant smile, Pearl answered. "I did, Mom. I put a dash of Old Bay and dill pickle juice in it, the way you like it."

Grams Dorea put on her glasses. "I see. It looks good." She paid attention to Colton. "You plan on staying long?"

Colton cleared his throat, a smile in his voice. "Let's start over. How are you, Grams?"

Caroline mumbled under her breath, "Grams Dorea."

"My apologies, Grams Dorea. You look lovely, as always. And that is a beautiful housecoat you are wearing. Is that a new cane?"

Caroline's eyes widened. *Oh gosh, she will hit him!*

"Always a way with words, you politicians. My granddaughter bought this *beach dress* for me," Grams Dorea huffed. "You make sure you don't hurt my granddaughter, or my cane will boot you out of here. One round with you was enough. She cried for weeks."

Caroline sank into the sofa. Her eyes met her grandmother's. "Grams Dorea likes to be herself. Isn't that so, Grams Dorea?"

Grams Dorea stuck a cracker into her dip, not saying a word.

Knowing this could end in disaster, Halia clapped her hands. "Okay, who's ready for pizza? Senator, you want the works, right?"

Colton stood up. "No need to wait on me. Let me get it."

"Now, now. Let us ladies tend to you," Halia, always the gracious host, said. "You sit and chat. And don't forget to help yourself to my caramel espresso brownies. I made them just for you. They will keep your energy up on the campaign trail. And we have a special dessert, too!" Her smiling eyes landed on Caroline. "Our birthday girl!"

"Patriotic cupcakes and cake!" Caroline cheered. It was a cheer only to keep her mother happy. Inside, this was a stressful visit. Her mind was occupied with Dillan.

Colton looked over at Caroline. "Happy birthday, honey." He kissed her cheek. Halia placed her hands over her heart.

Caroline's face flushed. *Oh, just what my mother wanted.*

"Thank you, Mrs. Woodard, for the brownies. I always need a pick me up after the rigorous media events your daughter has me doing." He smiled at Caroline and went back to Halia. "I'll take two slices of pizza." He moved a throw pillow out of his way. "Thank you.

Halia made her way into the kitchen with Pearl behind her.

Colton nudged Caroline. "Your mother is an amazing woman."

Caroline raised her eyebrows. "That she is."

In the kitchen, Pearl whispered to Halia. "Mom is being her *I hate politicians'* self." Pearl, being the soft-spoken, patient woman she was, could never understand her mother's dislike for Colton.

"I know," Halia sighed. "Nothing will change her, except a gag."

"I can't believe you said that!" Pearl shook her head, laughing. "I don't think we have one big enough. We better not take too long, or else it will be damage control."

They broke into soft giggles.

Auntie Lorelei was making small talk with Colton and Caroline when Grams Dorea broke her silence.

"Senator, why should I vote for you?"

Caroline felt her face flush. "Grams Dorea, I think Colton needs a break."

Colton swirled his ice cubes and took a long sip. "Caroline, she asked a good question and let me answer that. Grams Dorea, I'm the best damned man for the job. I promise to make elder care my priority."

Grams Dorea, giving Colton the stink eye, bit into her cracker.

Halia entered the room, her hands full with a tray of plates and napkins, and behind her, Pearl with pizza slices on a large platter.

"I have extra fresh grated Parmesan cheese and hot pepper flakes, too. I can heat it up if it's not hot enough." Halia set the tray on the table. Her eyes met Caroline's. "Honey, help the senator pick a slice. Here, give him a napkin." She handed a pile over.

Caroline took the napkins. "Here, Colton. Mom, he can get his own slice of pizza."

"I got it, Mrs. Woodard. Thank you. Do you mind if my guys outside have some pizza?"

Pearl looked at Colton. "Sure, Senator. Oh, I meant to say Colton. I will get a plate together for them, and they can dig in. We loaded them with cheese and sauce. I would not want sauce on your fancy shorts."

"Or manly bare legs." Auntie Lorelei giggled with one eyebrow raised as she enjoyed her sangria.

OMG! Tapping her wine glass, Caroline got up. "I need a refill." She made her way to the kitchen. Her mother and aunties were driving her crazy. *Help the senator pick a piece of pizza. Oh, he has manly legs.* She grimaced. Her mother was acting as if they were on a first date in high school. As she reached into the fridge for the wine bottle, she stopped. The Joe Bell flowers on the countertop found her. She closed her eyes, recalling Dillan's smile and soft kiss.

"Caroline!"

"Yes, Mother, I'll be there in a sec." She poured her wine, sniffed the scentless flowers, and went back to the living room and plopped down next to Colton. "Mom, you can take the campaign hat off. We are eating."

Halia touched the hat. "Oh, dear, I forgot. I'm so happy to have our guest of honor here tonight."

"Fine with me." Colton's eyes landed on it. "The more campaign hats, the better. Caroline, why aren't you wearing one?"

Grams Dorea's cane hit the floor with a sharp thump. "I will have a slice of plain. Take the cheese off. It gives me big old hemorrhoids. Dairy, you know. Like sitting on a pile of hot rocks."

Caroline covered her mouth, nearly choking on her pizza.

Halia shrieked, "Mother! We have a special guest."

The aunties kept their heads down, holding back laughter as they nudged each other.

"There are two things that give me a pain in my rear: cheese and politicians."

"I had a grandfather like this," Colton laughed. "You say what you want, Grams Dorea. Don't you let anybody stop you."

With wide eyes, Caroline looked over at Grams Dorea. "I'll get you a slice of pizza and scrape the cheese off." She got up and walked into the kitchen. She leaned over the sink, covering her mouth, and laughed silently. *Hemorrhoids.* There was no doubt Grams Dorea wanted Colton gone. Caroline gave her credit for being honest about it.

"Isn't Caroline wonderful?" Halia gushed when Caroline came back with the cheese-less pizza slice.

"I have to agree," Colton nodded. "Caroline is an amazing woman, just like her beautiful mother and amazing father. May he rest in peace."

Halia fanned her face. "Amen to that. Thank you, Colton. Her wonderful father has a lot to do with her upbringing."

Colton nodded. "Amen. He was a fantastic man. If not for Weston, I would not be here today. I owe him so much." He looked at Caroline with a grin. "You know that."

She nodded.

Halia's eyes began to tear up. She had to change the subject. "How is your pizza? They use the best fresh cheese. And the sauce is homemade from the tomatoes the owner grows in her garden."

Colton put the crust on his plate. Wilbur was drooling near his legs.

"If you don't mind, Wilbur loves pizza crust." Auntie Lorelei fondly looked at her dog. "He is such a sweet boy. My baby." She blew him a kiss.

Colton broke the crust into pieces. Wilbur wasted no time and gulped them down.

Grams Dorea harrumphed to herself.

"Grams Dorea, I understand your position on what I do for a living. It is not for everyone." Colton looked at the group of women and back at Grams Dorea. "I promise *all* of you I will do my absolute best if I win this election to bring the country back. With demanding work and an excellent, talented team, we will win, and you can all visit me at the White House. And Mrs. Woodard, you can spend the night in the Lincoln Bedroom. In fact, any time you like."

Halia's face lit up. She picked a small campaign flag from the coffee table and waved it. "To our next president, Colton Jameson!"

"Your support means a lot to me, Mrs. Woodard. I made a promise to your late husband that I would run for president. I know he is watching and will get me there."

"Amen," Halia broke into a wide smile, waving her flag.

Auntie Lorelei and Auntie Calypso whispered something and left the room. Auntie Pearl dimmed the lights as Auntie Lorelei entered with a sheet cake covered in candles. Pearl was not far behind with a coffeepot.

Everyone sang happy birthday as Auntie Lorelei put the cake on the coffee table. Caroline looked at her mother and back at her aunties. "Thank you."

Halia clapped. "Caroline, make a wish!"

Caroline waited, then blew out the candles.

"Honey, was it the wish I think it was?" Halia asked with a curious smile. Her eyes landed on Colton.

Caroline smiled at her mother as she cut into the thick cake.

Twenty-Seven

"**D**ad, do you know what is going on over there?" Dillan asked as he poured a glass of iced tea and reached for a piece of pizza.

"Next door? All I know is I delivered pizza and tossed out," Earl grumbled as he settled into his chair on the screened porch.

Dillan bit into his pizza as he sat down. "So, you don't have a clue, do you?"

"Nope. But they're up to something, Dillan. I tell ya, they're witches. Except Pearl, she is an angel. In my eyes, anyway."

Dillan placed his slice of pizza down. "What? Well, come to think of it, that Conchita incident was strange. I mean, who carries a crystal ball in a pillowcase? And then she talks to it, and it talks to her telepathically, so Caroline told me. I don't think she was putting me on."

"No matter, I like 'em. It's a shame they only come down for August every year, then close the cottage up again. It sure would be nice if they stayed longer. I get lonely, and they keep me busy. I enjoy keeping an eye on the place for Grams Dorea. She is one tough cookie."

Dillan finished his pizza and reached for another slice.

"They are up to something," Earl said as he tapped the arm of his Adirondack chair. "Yup, something really big."

"Do you know?"

Earl shook his head. "Nope. It ain't every August, but every few years, something goes on over there and always under the full moon. Men ain't allowed and they get all strange. As if the cottage and the ladies become one and the cottage has a heartbeat. Just like in a late-night movie I once watched. Burnt Offerings. Scared the heck out of me."

"Dad, I don't think it's the moon or a movie. I bet it's the sangria they make. But I have some insight, and if I tell you, keep a lid on it." Dillan put his pizza on the plate and leaned forward. "I mean it, Dad."

Earl looked over at Dillan. "Fess up."

"You know what Caroline does for a living?"

"I know she works in Washington at some big shot firm doing something. But now ya got me curious." Earl glanced across the darkness at the Beach Heart Cottage, all lit up, and back to Dillan.

"Caroline is a public relations specialist. She is working on Senator Jameson's bid for the White House. And guess who is their honored guest tonight at that pizza party?"

Earl's eyes grew large. "The big kahuna himself? Wow, ya don't say. Are you sure? What in the dickens would he be doing here on the island?"

"He's on his way to Virginia and making a stop. And I am as sure as the sun rises in the east, that's why we were kicked out."

"Well, I'll be darned. That explains that fella staring at me this afternoon when I was cutting back the Russian olive bushes in the driveway. He was sitting in a big black SUV. I was gonna go up to him, but I figured he had enough of his family on vacation and needed air. How about we go spy on them?" Earl got out of his chair. "Come on. I got my night vision goggles. Let's have some fun."

"No Dad. Do you want us to get tackled or shot? His security people, you don't mess with."

Earl sat down. "Guess that would be an issue with my aching hip and my new knee. Those ladies sure can keep secrets! And I see you are taking a liking to Caroline. Reminds me of that song, Sweet Caroline. She's a real keeper. She's much like your mama when she was young. Full of fire and brimstone, with a soft voice. Golly, I miss her."

"I know, Dad. And I see you've taken a liking to Pearl. She looks like a keeper, too."

"I think she might be. She lost her husband a couple of years back. I like her company, and she can make the best chartie boards. And a delicious rose crafted out of salami and ham."

Dillan looked at Earl, puzzled. "A what board?"

"Never you mind. I say we try to see what we can. If we crawl up to the dune and lie low, I can use my night vision binoculars."

"Dad, sand burrs will stab you, and they will see you. Let it rest. In fact, I'm going to go over the ideas for that vacant cottage we were at today. Start the cost projections, and tomorrow, we put a bid in. What do you say?"

"I say we buy it. Go do your projections. I'm going to stay out here. Night, Dillan."

"Night, Dad," Dillan tapped Earl's shoulder, then went inside.

Earl took out his phone and texted Pearl sweet nothings, never mentioning their guest.

Pearl smiled as she felt her phone vibrate in her pocket. Not to be rude, she let it go.

Caroline wanted this evening to end. All she could think about was this impromptu pizza party leaking out to the press. It would cause a ripple. Senator Colton Jameson met with Caroline Woodard and family on Hatteras Island. She imagined all the stories the competition would conjure up. Dragging her deceased father into the light. No one was perfect. Caroline could see the headlines: *What is Jameson's connection to the Woodards? Who is Caroline Woodard? Daughter of Weston Parson Woodard, all grown up. Will she be our next first lady?* It was time for him to go!

It was almost ten o'clock when Colton needed to depart. He had a big day ahead and had a pre-dawn meeting with Caroline and others before he flew up to Virginia Beach.

Halia got up. "It was wonderful of you to take time to visit us."

Colton got up off the sofa. "Ladies, thank you for the pizza, birthday cake, and the conversation. Just the break I needed."

Halia moved over and whispered in his ear. "Caroline will come around. Give her time." She pulled away.

He gave a nod and was saying his goodbyes when they heard a scuffle outside. The front door burst open. Alton dashed inside. "Senator?" He raced over to him.

Caroline turned white and ran to the door. She could see the men struggling with someone. They had his hands zip-tied behind his back.

"Earl!" Caroline screamed. "Don't hurt him! Colton!"

"We found this guy in the dune with night vision goggles." Alton looked at Earl and back to Colton.

Halia dashed to the door, appalled. "For heaven's sake, Earl, whatever are you doing?" She looked at Alton. "It's okay, Earl is our neighbor."

"I'm sorry, ma'am. He needs to be detained while we get the senator to safety."

Pearl, behind Halia, pushed her way forward. "Earl! What on earth is going on?" She turned to Colton. "He's our neighbor and friend."

"I'm sorry, Pearl. I wanted to make sure you ladies were okay. I'd seen these big black SUVs and men gathering outside. Ya all know I watch over the place. Thought ya all were being robbed or held hostage." He dropped his head. "Sorry to cause such panic."

Caroline confidently told Alton that there were no security issues. Earl was the caretaker, she explained, who did indeed watch over the cottage and the women. "We did not tell anyone that the senator would be here. He couldn't have known."

"What is going on out there?" Grams Dorea asked from the doorway.

"I texted you what I was doing," Earl said to Pearl, his eyes pleading for her to confirm it.

Pearl took her phone out of her pocket and read her text. Her eyes met Earl's. He had texted he was coming over, concerned about the men by the front door and the strange SUVs. She showed the text to Caroline, who showed it to Alton. They let Earl go with a warning. Like a dog with his tail between his legs, rubbing his wrists, he apologized to everyone.

Colton came out onto the front porch and looked at Earl and back at Caroline. "See you at six a.m. Alton will text you the address." Alarmed by the incident, and at a fast pace, surrounded by his security men, they ushered him into one of the SUVs. They drove away, vanishing into the night.

Earl watched, picking sand burrs out of his foot. "Ouch!"

"Earl, what were you thinking?" Pearl scolded him. "And no shoes on your feet. Men!"

"I was just doing the right thing. Guess I got off easy. I thought you ladies were in danger. Ouch!" he pulled out a deep burr from under his big toe. It stuck to his finger. He flicked it off.

"For heaven's sake. You must wear shoes, Earl," Pearl chided him as she watched him hobble. "Come on inside and I'll get my tweezers!"

"I lost my sandals when that big guy picked me up. He dragged me by my heels. His guys were gonna rough me up some. Maybe I'd never be seen again. Thank goodness y'all showed up."

"Earl, they would not hurt you. They are not mobsters." Caroline said, with her hands on her hips. "But what you did was dangerous, even if your heart was in the right place. And you must promise not to tell a soul he was here, or they will make sure you don't talk."

Earl's eyes widened. "Yes, ma'am."

Halia was inside, mumbling as she cleaned up, when Caroline came inside. "Mom, what did I tell you? It was risky having him here. What if Earl tells someone, who tells someone, then the media will be here asking questions? I don't like this."

Grams Dorea listened to the drama. It certainly took the boredom out of life. "Listen to your daughter! Allowing a male into the cottage is against the rules. Only Earl has permission to enter. And only on a need-to-need basis. Look at the chaos *his* visit caused."

Halia ignored her mother. "Caroline, it was a wonderful evening. Earl won't say anything. I think Jameson's men scared him enough," Halia huffed as she broke up the pizza crust for Wilbur. "Wilbur won't say a word either, will you? Here you go, boy."

"Mom, you live in a fantasy." Caroline tossed her hands in the air and went out to the back porch. Her body tensed. She let out a deep breath. Her mother was smothering her. Her phone beeped. She had a new text. Jameson? What else was new? She broke into a soft smile when she saw who it was.

> Is my dad over there?
> He is not here and is not
> answering his phone.
> Gone MIA
> BTW, did you like the lowers?

Soft breezes wafted over the dunes, tickling the feathery sea oats. Caroline smiled at the text, curious why he emojied a mermaid. She looked over her shoulder at the chaos in the cottage. Earl was having foot surgery by Dr. Pearl and team to remove burrs while sitting on the sofa with his feet up on the coffee table.

> Your dad is here.
> Having foot surgery. Removal of sand
> burrs.
> The all-women surgical team is busy.
> BTW, I love the

She laughed as she pressed send. What was she doing? She had no right to lead Dillan on. On one side of the scale was Colton, plus her mother, plus her career, plus some of her heart. She had felt it when Colton sat next to her. On the other side was one man she barely knew.

She looked up. Millions of stars surrounded her as the Milky Way stretched across the eastern sky. She stepped off the back porch, inhaling the briny night air, and slowly spun around. In the far distance north, the beacon of the Hatteras lighthouse light flashed every 7.5 seconds.

Tilting her head back, she lifted her arms to the sky and said. "Daddy, I know you are looking down at us, laughing at the comedy that has been unfolding. I know you have something to do with the silly chain of events to lighten my load." She giggled. "I know it. And I must add, Mom is Mom. Let me work on my life. And whisper in Mom's ear, you love her. She needs to know. I love you; Daddy and I *am* doing my best to help Colton win. I know this would mean a lot to you." She blew a kiss into the air.

The wind chimes clattered as a soft female voice sang across the ocean. Chills ran over her body.

"Caroline."

She turned to find Dillan's lips on hers.

Twenty-Eight

After an anxious early meeting, Colton was off to catch his flight out of Manteo to Virginia Beach. Caroline was relieved, knowing he was off the island. With Lawson taking the reins, it allowed Caroline to take the time needed to relax.

She wanted to unwind before the upcoming crowning ceremony. She had taken it more seriously, not wanting to disappoint her aunties or her mother.

Driving back to the cottage, she couldn't help but break into laughter, reflecting on the slapstick events of the night before. In her mind's eye, she could see Earl during and after his sand burr removal surgery. How her aunts had hovered over him, how he hobbled home with Pearl by his side. Earl had been a big baby during his foot surgery, moaning, adding continued cries of ouch. Alton's face as he restrained Earl, while Pearl scolded him. Caroline smiled to herself at how

Grams Dorea spoke of her cheese issues in front of Colton. What a night!

She pulled into the driveway and went into the cottage.

"Caroline! These just arrived!" her mother greeted, holding an oversized crystal vase bursting with a red, white, and blue mix of roses and carnations. Hali's face disappeared behind it.

"Mom, what is going on?" Caroline noticed smaller vases with colorful bouquets and little campaign flags scattered around the living room. "Don't tell me!"

Halia set the vase down on the entry table and read the card. "Thank you for a wonderful evening, fondly, Senator-"

"Jameson. Nice, Mom. He is such a charmer."

"Each of us got one, and this beautiful large one is for you. Grams Dorea got a ten-pound box of Belgian chocolates. Honey, there's a card for you. Read it, go ahead." She plucked it off the plastic holder, handing it to Caroline.

She opened the sealed envelope; Caroline's face said it all as she read the card.

"Caroline," Grams Dorea called out from her recliner, "that senator may be a ratfink politician, but he sure knows his chocolate. You must try one!" She rifled through the top layer of the box and held one up. "Delicious raspberry creams and milky soft dark caramels are the best. They don't stick to my teeth."

Halia looked over at Grams Dorea and back to Caroline. She whispered. "She is poking holes in the bottom of each one with her fingernails. Be mindful when she offers you one. You might even get one half-bitten. I told her those caramels could pull her bridge out. She won't listen, and when it happens, I don't want to know about it."

Caroline smiled at her Grams and back to her mother. "Mom, if it makes her happy, who cares?"

"I do!"

"Well?" Auntie Calypso asked as she entered the room. "How was your meeting with your sexy senator?"

"The meeting was as planned. He *is* sexy. He's *not* my senator, he's ours, and I'm off for two days. Two whole days straight."

"What does his card say?" Halia was trying to read it.

"Same old, same old. Thanks for the pizza blah, blah, blah." The note was endearing. She sniffed the roses.

Auntie Pearl came in from outside. "The flowers are lovely. Oh, girls, Earl told me his foot is better and to thank you all again. He is sorry for the incident last night and he is giving us a bushel of blue crabs to make up for it. I'm thinking we should have a Carolina boil, like the old days. Do we still have the pot from the last boil?"

Grams Dorea was about to poke another chocolate and looked up at Pearl. "Check in the shed. It was next to the grill. We may need a new one. And the propane tank may be empty and rusted out." She squinched up her nose as she examined her chocolate. "Anyone like the jelly filled?"

"No!" everyone answered in unison.

Grams Dorea beckoned Wilbur over. "Here you go, some candy for a nice boy." Drooling, Wilbur gobbled it.

"Mother, no! Dogs can't have chocolate!" Halia reprimanded. "Or sugar."

"He eats everything, even chocolate." Auntie Lorelei said, shaking her head. She called for Wilbur. With his tail wagging, he pushed against her leg. "He once ate an entire bag of M&M's with no side effects except days of terrible diarrhea."

"Would you like another one?" Grams Dorea plucked out a jelly one as she smiled at the drooling dog.

"No, Mom, you enjoy them," Lorelei reminded her firmly. "One was enough. The last thing we need is a dog with watery diarrhea on your vintage wool area rug, do we?"

Grams Dorea ignored her as she picked up the TV clicker. She was stockpiling the jelly-filled rejects for Wilbur.

Caroline stretched. "I'm going to get ready for a day of beaching, biking, shelling, and relaxing." She went into the dining room. "Mom, time to take down your campaign venue, don't you think?"

"Why?"

Caroline lifted her shoulders to her ears as she looked around at the elaborate decorating and the passion her mother put into it. "Mom, you know what? It looks amazing. Keep it. The red, white, and blue streamers give the room flair."

Lorelei was about to make her way upstairs and stopped on the landing. "Two more nights, girls! The weather forecast says clear skies and the blood moon will be above us, glowing. At twelve forty-seven a.m., that's then we set the crown on Caroline's head."

Murmurs filled the room.

"And I have a special addition to the ceremony," Lorelei continued, "but until I reveal it tonight, we must meditate and set our intentions as the moon crests over the ocean. Caroline, tomorrow we begin preparations. Hair, nails, glitter gels." She clapped her hands. "I was meditating earlier, and Ida expressed her joy. She has a special blessing for you, Caroline."

Caroline was too tired to laugh or cry. When her aunties or her mother spoke about talking to the dead, it was a little too much. And she did not want to be covered in gooey glitter gel, imagining sand sticking to her.

She went down to the beach, exhausted from late nights and early mornings. The sound of the ocean lulled her into a wonderful nap under the tent, as she drifted from one dream to another.

A laughing seagull woke her up. With heavy eyes, she saw someone standing in front of her. She smiled at the petite young girl with the long chestnut hair. She had a single braid pulled forward down her chest, tied at the end with twine. The girl gave her a shy smile and waved.

Caroline sat up. "Can I help you?"

The girl swayed and pulled out a small tin bucket filled with shells from behind her back. She picked something out and put it on the blanket near Caroline's toes. The girl moved away, vanishing into the surf. The hairs on the back of Caroline's neck stood up.

"What the heck? Where did she go?" Shielding her eyes with her hands, she looked around. Only an older couple with their dog was on the beach.

She leaned forward and picked up the object worn by the sea and salt. The violet and white shell, the size of a half dollar, was in the shape of a heart. It could not have been a dream—dreams do not leave heart-shaped shells.

Should she tell her aunties and her mother? As she made her way along the sandy path, she heard a woman call her name. Nobody was there. She heard it again; this time it ended in a soft giggle.

"All right, who is it? Mom, is that you?"

The girl with the bucket of shells peeked over the dune and was gone. Caroline dropped her beach bag and ran toward the ocean. Not a soul. "I'm going crazy. Too much sun and spiked lemonade." She picked up her beach bag, sprinted up to the cottage, and burst into the living room. She shut the door. Looking out the large window, she shouted, "Mom, Mom, come here! Quick!"

Concerned by the tone in her voice, Halia ran to her daughter. "Are you okay?"

"I'm not sure." Staring at the dunes, with a strained voice she pointed, "Mom, I fell asleep, and I woke up and this young girl was standing there. Right there, at the opening of the tent. In her hand was a bucket of shells." She tapped her bottom lip as her eyes shifted to her mother. "Her clothing was old-fashioned. A long pale blue dress with some kind of pattern on it. And she had a long braid tied with twine."

"She must have been a Mennonite," Halia was looking out the window. "They like to come down to the ocean."

"Mom, she gave me a shell. She bent over and put it by my foot, and she said nothing. She giggled and vanished into the ocean. Then she appeared again, peeking over a dune, and vanished." She reached into her bag and closed her hand around the shell. "Look." She opened her hand.

Halia's eyes widened, seeing the large heart. She called out to her sisters and her mother. "Caroline, tell everyone what you saw. Show them the shell the little girl gave you."

They gasped and, in a circle, reached for each other's hands.

Auntie Lorelei got a closer look. "This is stunning. It is a wampum shell."

Caroline squinted at it. "A wam what?"

Grams Dorea made her way over. "Caroline, may I hold the shell?"

"Of course." Caroline handed it to her.

Grams Dorea pulled it close to her heart. "My dear granddaughter, I'm the only person who has seen her. Back when I was next in line to be crowned, I too had a visit."

Caroline looked at Grams Dorea. "Visit?"

"Ida." Grams Dorea took Caroline's hand in hers. "That was Ida. Soon after, I met your loving grandfather." She glanced at the mantel and back at Caroline. "It's happening, my love."

"I saw a ghost?" her face tensed. "I had too much of Auntie Lorelei's spiked lemonade."

"You saw Ida, honey." Halia reached for Caroline's hand.

"Grams Dorea, may I?" Lorelei went over to the oak sideboard, reached inside, and took out a small box. She opened it and put something in Grams Dorea's hand.

"This," Grams Dorea opened hand, "is what Ida gave me just before I was crowned."

Caroline's eyes widened. In her grandmother's hand rested a heart-shaped shell. "We have identical shells. How can this be? They are perfect hearts." She looked around at everyone. "I feel intense love emanating from every inch of the cottage." She burst into tears.

"My dear granddaughter, the earliest Native Americans, the Croatans, were inhabitants of Hatteras Island. They collected colorful shell fragments of whelks and clams, known as quahogs, which they would craft into beads called wampum. Ida found this shell back in the late 1930s after a storm. It is a symbol that love, joy, and sisterhood find all the women who come here. Ida believed, as we all do, that one of the Croatan men carved the heart for her. You, my dear, you have the perfect mate."

Halia enveloped her daughter in a warm embrace. The atmosphere in the room shifted, pulsating with the energy of love. Gently, she tucked a strand of Caroline's hair behind her ear. "Sweetheart, this is why we refer to it as the Beach Heart Cottage. It resonates with generations of love."

"Once the crown rests on your head," Auntie Lorelei said as she dried her eyes, "your life will change forever. The magic of love and your true heart will find you." Before

                    Diana Baxter

Caroline could ask, Lorelei continued, "Yes, I found my true love in life, my soulmate. Okay, Wilbur has a canine soul. The truest love there is on this earth."

Hearing his name, Wilbur barked. The women laughed.

"Now, Caroline," Grams Dorea smiled fondly. She brushed her cheek. "You take that special shell and put it in a sacred spot. You will need it for your ceremony, where we will reunite them."

Caroline dried her eyes with the back of her hand. "Mom, thank you for being so patient with me. Everyone, I apologize for acting like this is mermaid silliness. I've spent my adult life working with data, crunching numbers, counting votes. Helping others succeed. I'm ready to be crowned and can't wait to learn my mermaid's name."

Auntie Lorelei instructed, "Caroline, you must bring the shell with you tonight at meditation."

Caroline held the shell to her heart. "I will never let it go."

"This crowning is so special, so rare," Grams Dorea reminded with cheer, "that we may hear Seraphina sing to Erasmus over the waves."

Twenty-Nine

Caroline rode her bike over to the coffee shop to find Dillan sitting at a back table. He got up and made his way over to her.

Unsure if a kiss was okay, she turned her head away.

He reached for her hand.

She put her hand in her shorts pocket.

"Is there something the matter? Did I do anything wrong?" Dillan asked, concerned.

Caroline tightened her lips and looked around the café and back at Dillan. "No, it's... well, it's me. I, oh, I'm sorry if I gave you the wrong impression last night when we kissed. Maybe I should go." She turned to leave.

He reached for her hand. His voice was low. "Caroline, I never meant to upset you. I'm not expecting anything from you. I enjoy your company and I even enjoy your family."

She dropped her head for a moment and looked up into his eyes. "I enjoy your company, too. That's what scares me." His voice, his eyes, his being made her anxious. He was what she dreamed a man would be. He was too ideal. Too perfect. She had to keep reminding herself how broken her heart was when she and Colton had ended their romance.

"Why would I scare you? I don't understand." His eyes found hers. "I'm not here to frighten you."

She looked up. "It's complicated."

"Let's sit down and have an iced coffee and talk about it," Dillan suggested. "If you want to." His eyes lit up. "No commitment."

With a nod, Caroline found a table and sat down. Her neck stiff and shoulders squeezed tight, she let out a sigh.

"Iced coffee, almond milk, two packets of brown sugar?" Dillan, now wearing a cheerful smile, asked Caroline. "Am I correct?"

"One sugar. Two was a mistake." She squeezed out a smile.

"Oh," he went up to the barista and ordered. She had to break it to him. They were simply new friends. She had no time in her life, or heart, for a man. Colton still occupied a space in her heart, leaving little room for anyone else.

The door opened, and in came Dottie from the gift shop. Snug in her arms rested a tiny, shivering chihuahua.

"Why, Dillan, hello!" Her loud voice boomed around the café. "I have a thirty-pound bag of cat food in my storage shed. If y'all can get it, I much appreciate it." She looked over at Caroline and back at Dillan. "Is this why I haven't seen you at my place?"

"Huh?" He looked at the dog and then at Dottie. "Maybe. Nice seeing you."

"Your daddy was at our place just this morning. He told me and my Emery that this lovely young lady is some bigshot in politics. Rumors are spreading that we had some hotshot here last night." She raised her eyebrows as her eyes found Caroline. "A certain senator?"

"No, not that I'm aware of," Dillan was quick to answer. "Rumors, Dottie. They spread like wildfire down here."

"Hmmm," Dottie tapped her upper lip. "Your daddy said security men roughed him up. A big fella hoisted him out of the dune and dragged him to the cottage. Poor Earl got his feet all cut up on sand burrs. Then they zip-tied his hands and tossed him into the back of an SUV. And they told him he was gonna go missing. All he wanted to do was return a bowl." She frowned. "Your daddy will recover."

"What? No." Of all the gossiping people to hear that Jameson was at the cottage! Denial was the best bet. Dillan respected Caroline and her privacy. He wanted nothing to roil the pot. "As you know, Dottie, my dad, is the island's big storyteller. I assure you no one hoisted him and dragged him around or threatened him, no less a big shot politician visiting. I was there with him all night." That wasn't quite true.

With an unsure smile, Dottie replied. "I guess your daddy is quite a storyteller, for sure."

The barista was giving Dillan an uncertain stare as she told him the total.

Dillan gave her a twenty. "Keep the change. Nice seeing you, Miss Dottie, and don't listen to ole' Earl. I will be over later to get the cat's food. I have several errands to run for my dad."

He made his way to the table and handed Caroline her coffee, and sat down.

She smiled. "Thanks. What do I owe you?"

"On me, you get the next one." He tasted his coffee. "Is yours okay?"

"Perfect. Thanks."

"Oh, no," Dillan said.

"Oh no, what?"

His face tensed. "Here she comes."

"Well, now, honey, I apologize. I've forgotten your name." Miss Dottie was closing in, standing inches from Caroline.

Caroline smiled as she looked up at Dottie. "I'm Caroline. I was in your store last week."

"Of course, and you bought the polka dot bikini." She looked at Dillan and back at Caroline. "I told you that blue and gold bikini would snatch a merman. And did you ever catch a handsome one!" Her little dog yawned. "Guess we are boring him." She petted the dog's head. "Well, I do plan on stopping by to see your grandma and bring her my famous coconut cake."

Caroline was grateful for the change of embarrassing subject. *Handsome merman.* "That would be wonderful. Why don't you stop over tomorrow evening? We're having a Carolina boil. Bring your husband. I'm sure my grandmother will enjoy having company."

"Well now, that sounds like a wonderful invitation. We can talk about days gone by. I'll bring a shrimp and pea salad. Plus, the cake."

Dillan was not saying a word as he nodded, twisting his lips.

Caroline shifted the conversation to what Dottie was cuddling. "What a cute little dog."

"Well now, I best let you young folks enjoy your coffee. This is my little Macy. She has a vet appointment." She stroked her dog's little head. "Ain't she the cutest thing? I found her at the shelter up in Manteo last month. Someone dumped this poor little girl up there. She's an old lady, like me, ain't that right, little Macy?" The dog yawned again. "I call her Macy 'cause I plan to dress her up in the finest doggie fashions I can find come cooler weather."

Caroline melted. She loved dogs, even drooling Wilbur. "Macy is adorable, and she's so lucky to have a new mommy to love her. Thank you for saving her and making her fashionable."

Dottie leaned in. "Stop by. I am having another sale. This time it is lingerie. Heavenly spun silks and lace as soft as butter. Against your new tan." Her face lit up as her eyes landed on Dillan.

Caroline felt the blood rush to her face. "Okay, thank you."

"Bye, kids." Dottie strolled off, chatting with Macy.

Dillan let out a long breath. "Thank God she's gone. What a gossiper. She means well, but she must dig into everyone's business. I help her with the cat food bags. She can't lift them, and her husband, he is an interesting man. Full of tall tales of the sea and always out fishing."

Caroline took a sip of her iced coffee and set it down. "Perhaps she's lonely."

"I guess. My dad is friends with them."

Caroline yawned.

"First the dog, now you." He leaned in. "Am I that boring?"

She broke into a wide smile. "No, I'm just tired. Long day. I had an early morning meeting with Senator Jameson." She realized what she had said. "It was a Zoom meeting. Never mind, I can't lie. He was here for a pizza bash last night at the cottage."

Dillan nodded. "Yeah, I know. My dad told me all about his mishap and being detained." He leaned in further. "Will you be honest with me?"

"Depends." She sat back, clutching her coffee cup.

"You can go out the door and never talk to me again, but I have to ask. Do you have a *thing* with Senator Jameson?"

Caroline looked down at her coffee, swirling the ice cubes. He didn't have a right to ask her that. But maybe he did.

"It was a long time ago. I work for him now. He has known my family for what seems like forever. My dad was his mentor, and I promised my dad on his deathbed I would work to get him in the White House one day. I'm keeping my promise."

Dillan was silent for a moment. "That's beautiful."

"Thank you."

"I have a feeling that he must have hurt you."

She tilted her head. "We hurt each other."

He sat back, crossing his arms. "You wear him like a tight glove."

"No, I don't. I don't even understand what that means." She looked at the door and back at Dillan. "It's not your concern. I'm here on vacation and I have a job to do, and that is to get him elected."

"You are right. It's not my concern." He cleared his throat.

She knew she'd hurt him.

"But I feel I have to say that it is time to take that restrictive glove off and find your freedom. I'm saying it because I did it. I was going to get married. It wouldn't have been right. For either of us. I left New York and now I'm free and loving life."

She let out a weighty breath. "Wow. Okay. I understand where you're coming from." She let Dillan inside for a moment. "It's my mother. She drives me crazy, obsessed with him and me since my father died. She clings to me. I feel for her but she wants me to be First Lady Caroline." Slowly, she broke into a smile. "There, I said it."

"Whoa! That is heavy. Do you want that?" He sat back, running his fingers through his hair. "Do you?" He did not know this!

"I don't know. I don't think so. Even if I loved him. I want to be me. And I don't even know who *me* is." She felt tears tickle her eyes. "My mom is trying to live her dream through me."

"Then be you, Caroline. Your mother sounds like she wants to be by Jameson's side."

"She *wanted* to be. My mom lost her bid years back when my dad lost the election, and she has never let it go." She reached for a napkin and blotted her eyes. "I'm so sorry. You hit a nerve. Or several."

He reached over and wiped a tear from her cheek. "You are even more beautiful with tears in your eyes."

Her face softened. "Thanks. I guess. My dad became very ill soon after the election. It was a fierce battle against Sean Warton of Indiana. It was the beginning of his end. He passed away three years ago."

"Wait, your dad ran against Warton? Your dad's Senator Woodard? Wow, you're Virginia royalty." He recalled earlier that she mentioned her father ran for president. Now he knew she was not kidding.

"We don't use his name down here on the island. The cottage belongs to my grandmother, but yeah." She sniffled. "That was my dad. Now you understand why my mother is the way she is. She is reliving Dad's run for president all over again through Jameson. And me."

Dillan sat back, distancing himself from her. "He could win."

"Ask it, Dillan. Does he want me with him? Yeah, he does. But I'm in a different place in my life. A few years ago, yes. I want him to win. I'll do everything in my power to see that happen because I believe in him. But I can't blame my mom for hoping."

"Have you told your mother this is your life, not hers?"

Caroline sniffled again. "All the time. I'm very close to her, and it breaks my heart when I see her face glow when I mention his name. She knows if he wins, she can go to the White House whenever she wants to, and pretend she is the FLOTUS in her mind. That is until he finds a wife. That's another hot mess, and believe me, I'm putting out fires on that one all the time."

"You have your hands full."

"You think? I'm so embarrassed I got emotional and I'm dumping all my problems on you. I've been so stressed out." She looked up at the clock on the wall, in the shape of an octopus, its tentacles reminding her of her mother. "I need to go back to the cottage to finish up some work."

Dillan looked at his phone. "I need to meet with the building inspector. Dad is buying the cottage next to yours, but first I must deal with Dottie and the cat food. Such earth-shaking events, compared to your life."

Caroline smiled, swallowed the last drop of her iced coffee, and stood up. "Hey, come to our Carolina boil! Auntie Pearl is arranging it, and your dad is bringing the blue crabs."

He stood up, too, looked out the window and back to Caroline. "Will the senator be there with his guys, dragging my dad around giving him a fat lip?"

Caroline burst into laughter. "No, just giving him feet full of burrs."

Dillan's face fell. "He'll be there?"

"Jameson? No! Of course not." She realized how tight Jameson's gloves were. Squeezing her. She needed to remove them, finger by finger.

Dillan wanted to kiss her. Instead, he smiled. "See you later. I'm looking forward to the boil tomorrow. What should I bring?"

"Whatever you like to drink." Caroline tossed her cup in the trash. "And uh, bring that potato salad you made last time. Mom raved about it."

Dillan chuckled. At least her mother liked his potato salad. He needed Halia to like *him*.

Thirty

A rainstorm settled in during the night, but the skies were clear by morning. There will be no rain for the Carolina Boil this evening. Caroline, up early, watched the sun rise against a bank of maroon tipped clouds over the ocean, always a spectacular sight.

She had texted Dillan after their talk at the coffee shop, but he hadn't answered. She looked at her hands, wiggling her fingers. They were stiff. She recalled Dillan had suggested she take the gloves off and live her life. Easier said than done when you are working on getting those *gloves* into the White House.

Wiggling her toes, she sat barefoot on the cool, damp morning sand, still moist from the rain. Seeking divine guidance to liberate her heart, she observed the early morning shell collectors displaying their finds in the sunlight, while a sunburned tourist jogged along the water's edge. Feeling the urge to take a stroll, she headed toward the vacant house that Dillan and his father were interested in purchasing. She paused in front of the dune.

"Wow, you are one messy warrior."

A flock of seagulls that had found refuge on the warped roof took flight, squawking as they flew off toward a man surf fishing.

She continued along the beach. As her feet met the silky sand, she looked up, thankful for where she was on Hatteras. A breeze tickled her body, causing the hair on the back of her neck to tingle. Reversing her footsteps, she found herself back at the vacant cottage. She made her way up the overgrown path, careful not to step on the broken, nail-riddled boards of the decaying walkway.

Her attention shifted to the tired cottage. "Well, you will need a serious facelift, my dear." She hoped Earl would buy the place and fix it. She knew her grandmother would have a good neighbor, whoever Earl sold it to. Working her way through overgrown weeds and bushes, she made her way to the side of the cottage that faced Beach Heart. Her eyes lit up when she noticed hundreds, if not thousands, of Joe Bell flowers, illuminating the earth in yellow, orange, and pink as the sun found them.

"Now I know where Dillan got these." She bent and picked a few. Twirling one in her fingers, she smiled at it. "You brighten my morning, little flower. You are so free to grow here and bring beauty."

"I hope I *brighten* your day."

Caroline looked up at the deck. "Dillan, oh my gosh. I... I was..." Her heart sped up.

His smile was as radiant as the morning sun. "Are you freeing up some of those fingers from the glove?"

She looked over at the flowers and back at Dillan. "I think so."

"Be careful, this place is full of nails and burrs." With a slight wave, he vanished inside.

Perplexed by Dillan's appearance and disappearance, Caroline was alone in the middle of the Joe Bells. After picking more flowers, enough to make a bouquet to give to her mother, she made her way to her own cottage.

"There you are, honey." Halia rushed over. "I need to go out and get some items at the store and stop at the farm stand for the boil tonight. Do you want to go with me?"

"Absolutely. Let me get my sneakers."

Auntie Calypso was on her way out the door. She turned to Caroline. "I have the list. I'm going too."

"I'm driving." Caroline said as she reached for her keys.

Caroline drove as her mother and aunt chatted about the boil.

"Earl is letting us borrow his boil pot. Ours seems to have retired, to rust in peace." Laughing, Auntie Calypso held onto her hair to stop it from getting blown by the wind from the open car windows. "Is that handsome Dillan coming?"

"No," Halia snapped from the back seat. "He's not invited."

Caroline looked in the rearview mirror at her mother. "Mom! Don't forget who saved you from the Ocracoke disaster."

Halia let out a loud moan of discontent. "I suppose."

It was almost five-thirty when Earl set up the boil in the backyard. The air was warm, and not a cloud in the sky. They covered the tables on the back porch with newspaper. Outside, torches filled with citronella were ready to be lit. The aunties had spent hours putting up the tropical décor on the porch. Strings of white lights, with battery-operated candles on the tables, were waiting to be turned on at sunset.

Inside, the women were preparing salads. Halia was slicing fruit and filling a punch bowl with sangria when there was a knock on the back porch door. "I'll get it," she rushed to the door.

In Dillan's hands were a large bucket of blue crabs and a smaller one of shrimp. "Hi, where do you want these? The shrimp just came off the boat."

"Wonderful. Put them outside on the small table by the boil." Halia pointed. "Thanks, and uh, oh, never mind."

With a nod, he looked past Halia's shoulder, trying to see if Caroline was there.

"Wait," Halia forced a smile at Dillan. "You know my daughter has a boyfriend, right?"

Her words somehow carried. Everyone stopped what they were doing.

"I'm just here to help my dad," Dillan replied quietly. "Sorry if you think otherwise. Hey, no foul, no harm. I'll take these out to my dad." With his head down, he went to join Earl. He recalled his conversation with Caroline. How her mother was clinging onto her. He let her comment roll off his shoulders.

"Mother!" Caroline hissed when Dillan was out of sight. "How *dare* you intrude on my life? I'm about to pack and head home. No mermaid celebration! Enough is enough. And for your information, I invited him."

"I'm looking out for our future first lady." Halia rushed past Caroline and into the kitchen, grabbing Caroline's car keys off the table as she went. "You are not going anywhere."

With heavy footsteps, Caroline stomped after her. "Stop it, just stop it. You are not living through me. And give me my keys." She held out her hand.

Halia dropped the keys on the kitchen table, crossed her arms, and looked out the window.

"Halia, your daughter is correct. Let her live her life. Enough nonsense." Grams Dorea said, sitting at the kitchen table, cutting the corn on the cob into thirds. "Caroline, go have a drink with that boy of Earl's. He is a gentleman, and what a body."

Caroline looked at Grams Dorea and went back to her mother. "Seriously? Mom, I love you, but you must stop this."

Halia pointed her nose in the air. "What has to stop?"

"I'm not you, Mom." Caroline crossed her arms as tears found her lashes.

Halia let out a long sigh. "I miss my life. I miss your father." She cried as she pulled out a chair.

Auntie Pearl was quick to give her a handful of napkins. "Oh, honey. We all miss him and are here for you. I love you and I am your sister. You need to let Caroline live her life."

"Auntie Pearl is correct, Mom. We all miss Daddy; we loved and still love him, and you need to move on. And I need to live my life. I do not want to live the life you had in politics. Once this election is over, I'm considering leaving Lawson, doing something outside of Washington, with less stress."

"Caroline, don't make a rash-"

"Mom, if you want grandchildren, I'm your only hope, so let me be myself. Give me space to breathe. Colton will always have a special spot in my heart. You know that. Right now, I need to get my job done. And for your information, even though I don't have to tell you this, I will. Dillan and I are friends, nothing more." On the counter sat the Joe Bell flowers Dillan had given her. A reminder she didn't need.

Dillan, outside on the back porch, couldn't help but hear every word. Especially *Colton will always have a spot in my heart*. Ouch. And *Dillan and I are friends, nothing more*. He leaned against the wall. If he did anything on her vacation, he would teach her how to live freely.

Halia hugged Caroline and pulled back. Her teary eyes met Caroline's. "I hope you can forgive me."

"Forgiven. No more drama." Caroline wiped her mother's tears away. "We are here to enjoy ourselves. Two more nights and I to be crowned! I'm so happy. Don't take that from me."

Halia nodded as she twisted the napkin in her hands. "I'll try my best."

"No *trying*, Mom! It's time to stop."

Halia held her head high, hiding a sniffle. "I will stop. Daddy would want me to be strong."

Caroline patted her mother's arm. "Yes, Mom, he would. He does."

Dillan was sneaking off the porch, only to bump into Miss Dottie. In one hand, she had a Tupperware cake holder and, in the other, a bag filled with containers.

"Dillan!" her voice boomed. "Glad to see you are here. Emery, you come here and put that cooler with the shrimp macaroni salad on the table." Then she shouted, "Knock, knock! Hello!" and made her way into the kitchen. "Hi, y'all! I brought my special cake. Multilayered coconut cake with wild rum-soaked blackberries on the side."

"Thank you!" With a wide smile, Auntie Pearl took the cake and set the heavy platter down on the table. She wondered who this woman was.

"Why, Dottie, it's been forever!" Grams Dorea wore a genuine smile. "Sit down. Girls, this is my friend from way back, Dottie. Is Emery here?"

"Yup, out by the boil with the men talking babble. Sucking on his old pipe. I brought you a big bowl of pea and shrimp macaroni salad that you like. I see that handsome boyfriend of yours is here." Her eyes found Caroline. "It was that bikini. I told you it would catch a man. Oh, dear, you've been crying."

Who was this loud woman pushing Dillan on her daughter? How dare she! Halia wasted no time in intervening. "I'm her mother, Halia. Caroline's eyes are red from peeling onions."

"That'll do it every time. It's the fresh onions oozing away, if y'all bought at the farm stand. Use the sweet Vidalia onions next time," Dottie suggested as she greeted the women. "I'm an old friend of Dorothy's. And I mean old!"

"Dottie, inside this cottage, I'm known as Grams Dorea."

Dottie crossed her hands over her heart. "Why, I just love that. Grams Dorea, it is."

"How about putting the salads out on the back side table," Halia suggested, knowing Grams Dorea and Miss Dottie had much catching up to do. "Caroline, why don't you take a glass of sangria and go relax on the beach? You'll hear the bell when the food's ready."

"Great idea." Caroline went out the door with fresh mango salsa and chips. She set them down on the table and looked at the men standing around the boil. Dillan never looked her way.

Pearl came out with a glass of sangria. "Here, honey, go relax. I will deal with your mother." She kissed her cheek. "Go."

Caroline made her way down the path to the beach. She was standing by the dune when she heard a soft voice. A breeze carried it in a gentle whisper. *When you hear her, the magic begins*. She shook her head. What a vacation this was turning out to be. Not only was she seeing dead relatives, but she was also hearing them! Giggling, she sipped her sangria.

Sea foam tickled her toes as she strolled along the water's edge and settled down near a dune. With closed eyes and only the sound of the ocean, she let her shoulders fall. "Ahhh."

A gentle wind caressed her shoulder and worked around to the back of her neck, sending tingles down her spine. Another delusion!

She laughed aloud. "I *am* going crazy! Yup, that's it. My mother has done me in." A seagull flew above, landing close to her. "No scraps here!"

"I'm the one who is crazy. Crazy for you, and I'm not going away."

Caroline dropped the glass, sangria spilling red over the sand.

"Colton! Why are you here?"

Thirty-One

"I was on my way back from Virginia Beach to my place on Emerald Isle when I got an invitation to a Carolina boil. You know me, I'm a Carolina boy and no way was I going to miss a good crustacean feast." He sat down next to her.

"Don't tell me." Her shoulders dropped. "Mom."

"Yep, your mom." He gazed out over the ocean and toward a dune, where Alton appeared.

Caroline squinted at Alton. "Ugh... your motley security crew is here, too? My neighbor claims they roughed him up."

"What? No."

"Colton, please go home. Better yet, let me call a justice of the peace and you and my mom can have a beach wedding so she can move into the White House, and I can move on."

He made a pop sound with his lips. "Ah, no. That is a very creepy scenario."

Caroline burst into laughter. A warm breeze kicked up, tickling her skin. "That would be strange."

"You think?" He let out a chuckle. "Strange indeed."

"Colton, what we had was wonderful. It's difficult for me to see you, and working with you is not easy. I told my dad I would do my best to get you in office, and I'm keeping my word." She looked out over the ocean and went back to Colton.

"That's what this is all about? Keeping your word?"

"Yes. And you are a hard man to say no to. For now, my job is to get you into the Oval Office. Then we can see where we are."

"The other night when I stopped by and enjoyed pizza with your family, I felt it. I felt *us* again. You did, too. I know you did."

"I did, yes, Colton."

"I need us as a team. Caroline Woodard, daughter of late Senator Weston Woodard, by Colton Jameson's side. Can't you see it? We would kick ass in DC. No, we *will*. Your mom can live in the White House and do the decorating and host all the parties she wants."

Caroline swallowed hard as she looked around, crossing her arms. "On tax dollars?" She broke into a curious smile. "Never mind. How did you get here?"

"That isn't important. Did you hear me?" Colton reached for her hand. His energy was intense, on fire. She had to resist. How? Her love for him may have been dormant, but he had intense charisma. It would not take much to rekindle. That glove was not going anywhere at that moment.

In a blink, she could see them stepping out of Marine One. In one arm a baby cooing, her other hand snug in Colton's. Reporters calling out to them. *Caroline, how is motherhood? President Jameson, how is fatherhood treating you? Will there be another baby in the future?* The air filled with flashes from their cameras. Her proud mother tagging behind, dressed up in red, white, and blue, waving her little flags. She laughed at herself, imagining her giddy aunties, with Wilbur wagging his shaggy tail, trotting across the White House lawn. She shivered herself back to reality.

"You want to know a fun fact?"

She looked at Colton. "Sure."

"Your mom told me she named you Caroline after her honeymoon here at the cottage. Hence, your name is Caroline."

"She *told* you that!"

He squeezed her hand. "Caroline, conceived in North Carolina, what a story! The media will soak it up."

"Yuck, why would my mom tell you something like that? On her honeymoon, no less. News to me. What is wrong with her?" She tilted her head back, taking in the dusky sky. "Oh, I get it. Wow, she is something else. Planning my future kids are to be conceived here."

"Your mom is my number one fan."

Caroline looked him in the eye. "And she also *loves* you."

"And you?"

"What about you and the fiancée? I mean, seriously?"

"You got me there. I was mistaken. I'm not wrong about how I feel when I'm with you."

Caroline felt her heart flutter. She looked out over the ocean and went back to Colton. "Time, we need time. Let's get this election over."

The ship's bell rang.

"You are staying to share dinner, I assume?"

"Yes, I am. Is this going to be a problem with your tall, dark, handsome island pal?"

"My *pal*? I told you, he's just a friend."

He tugged her hand as he got up. "Good, now when are we making our announcement?"

"What? No! And if you don't stop, my only announcement is you are leaving with a doggie bag."

"Killjoy Caroline. You will eventually realize I am the one and only one."

She pulled her hand back, and they headed for the cottage. Caroline stopped. "Maybe you are the one, but not now. So, really, how did you get here?"

He snapped his fingers. "Hatteras magic."

Caroline felt a chill rush through her as the voice she had heard earlier whispered. *The magic begins.* "No!" she cried out.

"Are you okay?" Colton brushed loose strands of hair from her face. "Caroline, you look like you've just seen a ghost."

Caroline shook her head. "It's nothing. Let's get some food. I'm starving!"

She knew it was not *nothing*. Grams Dorea spoke of the mermaid magic, the magic wampum shell, and what will happen after the mermaid ceremony. Her thoughts ran wild. Quitting her job could be the answer. She could move to Alaska and go off grid in a cabin. Grow a garden and survive on chickens and goats. *Yes, that's it. No, that is not it.* It was the beach, the aunties, her mother, her stress, and now Colton hounding her. She needed to get away from her getaway.

They neared the group of men standing around the boil and stopped. Caroline's eyes met Dillan's. "Dillan, this is-"

"Yeah, I know. What a surprise." He held out his hand, then turned his attention to Caroline and back to Colton. "Nice to meet you, senator. You've got my vote."

Caroline looked away.

"Every vote does count, thanks-"

Emery's eyes grew wide as he asked. "You really are Senator Jameson?"

"As sure as the sunrises!" Colton said.

"Holy moly, Dottie, get out here!" he hollered over his shoulder. "Where is that woman? Blabbing away, I'm sure about that. She ain't gonna believe this! I'm Emery Straton, senator."

Jameson shook Emery's hand. "Good to meet you, Emery. Caroline, where can I get a beer?"

Caroline felt her face flush. "Follow me." She could not look at Dillan as they made their way to the cottage.

"He *is* gonna win, y'all know?" Emery assured them with a slow nod as he watched them. "He will bring this country back. Did ya see that purdy woman by his side? They make a handsome couple."

Earl and Dillan exchanged glances.

Auntie Calypso called out from the porch asking if the boil was ready.

"Almost!" Earl called back.

Dillan kicked sand around.

"Who is fooling who? I saw how your eyes met hers. She had to turn away." Emery said, as he elbowed Dillan. "Don't let that fish out of your net. You know what to do. Now go on and git her." He looked over his shoulder. "Go on. Git inside."

"Go on, son."

Dillan finished his beer and made his way to the back porch and stopped.

Caroline smiled and said, "Hey, Dillan, I'd like to introduce my client to you formally."

Jameson's face scrunched. *"Client?"*

Caroline ignored that. "Dillan is a neighbor of ours and a new friend of mine. Senator Jameson is a long-time friend of our family."

"And our next president!" Halia appeared with a bowl of coleslaw. She put it on the table and stood next to Colton. Her face was bursting with joy. "Welcome, Senator Jameson." She kissed his cheek. "Honey, sit in the chair near Senator Jameson at the head of the table. He must be tired and hungry."

Colton mumbled to Halia, "Thank you. At least she mentioned me as a family friend."

Halia frowned as she patted his hand.

Dillan went inside for another beer.

"Colton, did you hear my mother? You sit over there." Caroline pointed. "I'll be right back." She entered the kitchen and encountered Dillan, whom she then led to the bathroom by the hand. After locking the door, she leaned against it.

"What are we doing in here?" he asked as he tried to avoid his head hitting the slanted ceiling.

"I want to know one thing—why didn't you want me to come in?"

"In where?"

"The cottage next door. When I was picking Joe Bell flowers. You went inside."

"I went inside, and *you* disappeared on me. I went downstairs to meet you and you were gone."

"Oh." Caroline bit her bottom lip.

"What did you think?"

"Dillan, I'm *so* sorry about the senator being here. My mom did it again. I'm *not* seeing him. In here we can have privacy. Not only am I not seeing him, but it's even worse."

"Worse?"

"Never mind." She waved her hand. "How about we enjoy the dinner and the guest of honor? The senator and his goonies will leave after."

Dillan stroked her hair. "To be honest with you, I overheard you tell the senator that I'm nothing but a friend."

"I didn't mean it. My mom has big ears. Sometimes I need to say things to keep her happy."

"Got it. Now, what do we do? I mean, we are adults hiding in a bathroom."

"We go to Plan B. Get through this dinner. Follow my lead." She went to open the door when his lips found hers. She pulled away. Their eyes met. She wanted to stay. "We better get out of here before my mom sends a search party." She peeked out the door, looking left and right. "Coast is clear." She was gesturing towards Dillan to follow her when Grams Dorea appeared, with Dottie behind her.

"Are you kids having some *young fun* in there?" Dottie's boisterous voice did not go unnoticed as Halia came inside. Their eyes met.

Caroline stopped her mother. "We will talk later. This is the last time, Mom," she continued outside.

Dottie watched Caroline tug Dillan around. "Why? What on earth is going on?"

"Young people and their raging hormones. Remember those days?" Grams Dorea leaned on her cane. "Come on, let's go eat."

"I sure do." Dottie came to a halt on the porch and let out a scream, slapping her hands over her heart. "Emery, it's Senator Jameson!" She fanned her face with her hands. "The rumors are true. You are on the island."

"Dottie, for Pete's sake, I hollered for ya. If ya'd not be flapping those busy lips, ya'd heard me!"

"Lord a mercy, he is really here."

Colton took Dottie's hands and held them. "Nice to meet you, ma'am."

"I'm Ditte, Dot, I mean Dottie. Oh, golly, I'm *so* embarrassed." Dottie's watery eyes could not leave the senators. "You're more handsome and taller in person. Please, call me Dottie. I'm your biggest fan!"

"Yup, she sure is. We even got your bumper sticker on our old jeep and a sign in the store window." Emery said, as he went to open the screen door for Earl.

With the strainer full of hot food, Earl hurried inside. Emery dashed over to help him.

"Clear the deck!" Earl yelled out.

Everyone backed up as they dumped the steaming boil onto the table. Rogue corn cobs and small potatoes rolled around, only to stop by a blue crab, sausage, a few lemons, and large pink shrimp.

"That smells delicious. How about we dig in? Grab a plate, y'all!" Auntie Lorelei ordered. "Senator, you are first."

Caroline went to the end of the line. Lorelei went over to Caroline and whispered, "This was your mother's doing. We told her not to."

Caroline whispered, "It's fine. Eat up and enjoy the evening. Have fun!"

"Great attitude, Caroline." Auntie Lorelei said.

Jameson came onto the porch with a glass of bourbon in hand and sat down at the head of the table. "Surely smells good. Like the old days!"

"I brought shrimp in this morning." Emery said, as he placed the strainer on the deck.

Dottie sat down and chattered as she filled her plate. "Well, now, this looks scrumptious, Emery. You did a good boil. Ain't my husband a hoot in his overalls? I asked him to dress up, but he said nope, I'm doing a boil in my boil wear." She smiled graciously, keeping her stunned eyes on Colton. "I made pea and shrimp macaroni salad. It is divine and you must try some. Fresh shrimp from off the dock. I added a little Old Bay and peas from my garden." She picked up the bowl and passed it down the table. "And I make the best coconut cake on the island."

"I bet it's a four-layer coconut cake?" Colton asked.

"It sure is, Senator Jameson."

"I'll have some of that. Thank you, Dottie."

Dottie fanned her flushed face. "You are very welcome, Senator."

They ate, laughed, and Dottie rambled on about the past. Colton was his North Carolina-born self, and they couldn't get enough. Bragging about his campaigns and how he was ahead in the polls, he thanked Caroline for the media blitz she put together.

They put dessert out when the sun made its final descent.

Dottie boasted, "North Carolina's favorite dessert and I make the best," as she cut thick, buttery slices. Auntie Calypso set a tray of brandy and glasses on the table while Halia brought out a fresh pot of coffee.

"How 'bout we finish our desserts and call it a night? I am tired and sure our *guest* needs to leave sooner than later." Grams Dorea said as she squinted at Colton. "You can take a doggie bag. Halia, go on and make him one."

"I'll make one for Alton, too." Halia got up and went inside.

Colton swirled the ice in his empty glass. "Grams Dorea, you are correct. I must head out. Another day tomorrow, back on the campaign trail." He stood up and looked around. "Thank you all for a wonderful evening. The food was delicious, and the company was outstanding. And Miss Dottie, your coconut cake is the best. Emery, Dillan, and Earl, nice meeting you. I'm counting on your vote."

Dottie put her coffee cup down. "Why, you can take the rest of the cake with you. I'll go get Halia to wrap it up for you." Before Colton could say thanks, but no thanks, Dottie and the remains of her creation had disappeared into the kitchen.

Colton said goodnight and went inside. Dillan, Earl, and Emery settled on the back porch for brandy and island talk.

Caroline took Colton to the front door. Over his shoulder, she saw her mother and Dottie coming with the wrapped-up food. "We'll talk in the morning."

"That we will." He leaned over, kissing Caroline on the lips. "Sleep well, my First Lady, Caroline."

The aunties gasped, Dottie's mouth fell open, Grams Dorea shook her head, and Halia, smiling, handed him two doggie bags.

Thirty-Two

Gentle waves lapped the shore as the sun made its way above a bank of cirrus clouds. It was another glorious day on Hatteras. This was the day that led into the night when the mermaid ceremony would begin. Today, the final preparations were underway.

Caroline had just finished cutting fruit for a smoothie when Auntie Calypso came into the kitchen. She ran her fingers through Caroline's hair.

"Morning, Auntie Calypso. Would you like to share a banana, blueberry, kale, yogurt smoothie with me?"

"No, thank you. I need my coffee! I'm bursting with excitement! Today begins the festivities, and you will learn of your mermaid name as the blood moon sits above us."

"I'm excited about it. I have this sense of belonging. No, more than that. A connection, *a bond, a sisterhood* to the cottage and all of you." Caroline smiled as she hugged her auntie.

"It's our sisterhood," Calypso said.

"Auntie Lorelei mentioned we have a meditation on the beach at..." Caroline looked at her phone on the countertop. "Wow, in fifteen minutes."

"Yes, we do. Grams Dorea has already made her way down there with Pearl's help. We had better not be late. Finish that smoothie and let's get going."

A gentle breeze enveloped everyone gathered beneath the tent. Grams Dorea sat comfortably in a chair, while the others formed a circle on a blanket. Auntie Lorelei lit her sage and cedarwood sticks, gracefully waving them in the air. After extinguishing the smoky sticks, she joined the group. Together, they held hands and took three deep, mindful breaths, inhaling and exhaling in unison.

Grams Dorea picked up the journal that rested on her lap. "Caroline Ann Woodard, my dear granddaughter, it is time for you to join the mermaid sisterhood. I am honored and proud to be the matriarch in our family to set the crown on your head as the energy of the blood moon finds you. It will bring you eternal love and joy. And now, I will read to you what Ida wrote in ink when she was crowned:

As the weight of this crown of shells rests on my head,

I know that only love and patience are ahead.

My eyes are closed as I feel its magic, magic that brings me hope and joy.

Shells that found me so far from the deep will guide me in my sleep.

It is under the full glow of the brilliant orb above that one day I will find my true love. With all my heart, I know this is true, as the waves crash on the shore.

I know one day my love will find me as I walk the cottage floors.

Thank you, Seraphina, for finding me that morning on the battered shore.

One day, your soul will find him, as one day I will find you.

Caroline tilted her head, playing with the words *magic that brings me hope and joy* in her mind. That was beautiful.

Grams Dorea put the journal on her lap and closed it. "I can feel Ida as I read that poem. I never tire of it. Now, Lorelei, will lead us into a meditation that will hold our sisterhood bond."

Lorelei took a deep breath and asked. "Everyone, hold hands and breathe in for three, hold it, and out for four." She set her phone to ring.

For what seemed like an ageless time, Caroline tried to meditate, to be aware of nothing beyond the soft sounds of the sea and wind. Keeping her life under control was challenging. The only way she could accomplish it was by whispering the words repeatedly: *magic that brings hope and joy to me.*

After their meditation, except for Grams Dorea, they held hands and waded into the waves. Each one had the special shell she had found in her hand. They each set a silent intention, and on the count of three, they tossed them back out to sea. Caroline held onto hers a little longer.

"I'm so happy!" Caroline was jumping up and down in the water like a child. "I can't wait to wear the crown!"

Halia smiled at her daughter. "Let's get up to the cottage; we have much to do."

"Do you mind if I go for a little walk on the beach? I still need to find my special shell for the welcome sign outside the front door."

The sisters looked over at Grams Dorea in the tent. She nodded.

"Thanks, Grams Dorea. See you all in a little while." Caroline put on her sunglasses and began her stroll.

"She will make a lovely mermaid," Calypso said, wiping wet sand off her legs. "I need to get my cosmetic case out."

"And I'll get the mermaid dresses out of the closet." Lorelei's face lit up. "This is going to be special. Ida's gown, the blood moon, and Caroline's acceptance."

"Yes, it is. You all do that. Grams, Dorea, and I are preparing the shells that will line the path. We finished painting them metallic green and blue," Pearl said as she went to help Grams Dorea up off the chair. "I love this. It makes me feel young again. Life can be so difficult and short. Why not a path lined with shells? And dress up as mermaids as a bonfire's sparks reach for the moon?"

"I agree. I feel alive and young again." Lorelei threw her head back and inhaled. "This is more than a ceremony. It is spiritual in so many ways, and I know the great aunts will be here. I'm getting this feeling we may hear Seraphina."

They all felt it. The energy.

Caroline stopped and looked over her shoulder. The tent was empty. She debated whether to continue or make a beeline for the path along the dune that was calling her. Why not?

She followed the short path to the back of Earl's cottage. Finding a weathered wooden walkway, and followed it to the front of the cottage. In the driveway, she saw only Dillan's truck.

Tapping her upper lip, she changed her mind and started around the house to reverse her path back to the beach.

"Hey, early bird!"

Caroline froze.

Dillan was on the front porch, holding a cup of coffee.

Caroline bit her bottom lip as she lowered her sunglasses to the tip of her nose.

"Hmmm, I'm guessing you're looking for someone?"

"I think I found him."

"I like that answer." Dillan balanced his mug on the porch rail and stretched. "It's a gorgeous morning for a stroll on the beach."

Caroline didn't answer right away, focusing on a pair of doves sitting on the porch roof, wondering if she should. Today of all days.

"It's also a stunning morning for a cup of freshly brewed coffee." He picked up his cup and raised it in a toast to the day. "And I even have organic brown sugar."

Caroline looked over at her cottage and back at Dillan. "I can't stay long. My family will send out the hounds. Or at least old Wilbur."

He gave a wide stretch. His muscles rippled in the morning sun. "We don't want that, do we?"

As she came up the porch steps, he leaned in and kissed her cheek. "I'm guessing you're taking a break from all that political work?"

"I'm off today. All day." She glanced at his coffee mug. "Hey, how about that coffee?"

"Step inside. Ladies first or is it first lady?" he teased.

She tapped his arm. "Ha ha, you're a real jokester!" Going ahead of him, she removed her sunglasses, allowing her eyes to adjust to her surroundings, which were rustic, much like the Beach Heart Cottage.

"Well, when the senator was leaving last night, he sure made it sound like you will be by his side as his wife."

She shook her head. "He said it to please my mother. New subject."

"Agreed. Have a seat, and I'll get your coffee." From the kitchen, he called out, "I make a potent brew."

"Exactly how I like it," Caroline replied as she studied the walls covered with various-sized framed photos, and she got up to admire them.

Dillan returned. "Here you go." He handed her a mug. "I see you discovered my dad's Wall of Life on Hatteras. My dad is one of those memorabilia guys." He pointed to a photo dated 1974. "That's my mom and dad on the pontoon boat before they were married."

Caroline neared the photo. "Wow, she was beautiful." She drank her coffee as her eyes shifted to each photo. "What are these old newspaper clippings all about?"

Dillan's gaze moved over to the framed newsprint. "Stuff my dad downloaded. We go back to British mercantile shipping. My dad says the salty sea runs through our veins. I think blood does, but heck, I will not argue."

Caroline smiled. "So cool. It says this ship was wrecked back in 1867 off the shallow shoals of Buxton during a late summer storm. There is such a history around here. A treasure is to be found."

"Like a queen's emerald necklace?"

"Yeah, like that," Caroline laughed. "Or a string of black pearls."

"So, you're upping the ante. Too bad I'm too busy with my dad's projects. There's no time to treasure hunt." He looked over at a large, white, vintage clock on the wall. "I have to be in Frisco later to check out a boat for a buddy of mine." He finished his coffee. "Caroline, I gotta ask."

She set her mug down with a clunk on a side table. "Okay."

"How are those gloves doing? Are they finally off?"

"Not really. I'm working on it." Caroline looked at her right hand. "My mom invited Jameson to the boil, and I'm sorry about it. He was campaigning by the ferry dock early this morning. So, I heard!"

"I heard the same. He was walking around the lines of cars waiting for the ferry, shaking hands." Dillan was trying hard not to let the name Colton Jameson upset him. It did.

"Oh, wow. Hey, I'm sorry, my mom said things she shouldn't at the boil. I promise she will not do it again. I want to be angry with her, but I can't. She misses my dad and being in the spotlight. It was her life."

"I get it. My dad misses my mom. Although news flash, he's been talking a lot about your Aunt Pearl. I think he has a teenage crush on her. All he talks about is her chartie board and some sort of rose salami."

Caroline cracked a smile. "I know. My Auntie Pearl talks about your dad. She lost her husband six years ago. I love all my aunties, but she is my favorite. So gentle and soft-spoken. She used to sing to me when I was a little girl, during my parents' parties. She would come up to my room and keep me company."

"I'll sing to you sometime. I play the guitar and piano." He moved closer, reaching for her chin with his index finger. His soulful eyes lured her as if they were pools of blue seawater. Her breath quickened as his gentle lips found her neck.

She worked her hands up his muscular arms to his shoulders, pulling him close. As if they were an orchestrated dance, they moved in harmony. Her moans all but silenced the ocean waves and the hush of the sea oats.

Thirty-Three

"Caroline, that was some beach walk. Look at the time!" Halia scolded, with one eyebrow raised, as she put her phone in her pocket. "I was about to go looking for you."

Caroline's rosy smile met her mother. "Calm down. I was gone for a little over an hour." Some things are best left secret. "I'm going to get something to eat. I'm starving!"

Grams Dorea, in her recliner, was grinning ear to ear. "Caroline, you look flushed. Too much sun and *fun?*"

"Ah... yes, no, what? Huh?" Caroline felt her face flush. Did Grams Dorea know? If she did, she sure had a sound of approval.

"Caroline," Auntie Lorelei asked with a curious smile, "where have you been? We have mermaid hair to do and much more! Your Auntie Calypso has the most wonderful glitter gel in aqua and pink for all of us to put on. Halia, come help me carry the logs down to the beach for the bonfire." And out the back door they went.

Caroline was watching them go when Grams Dorea, with her index finger, summoned her.

Caroline stood next to her.

"Sit, please."

Caroline sat on the sofa and leaned toward her. "What's up, Grams Dorea?"

"I am the keeper of many secrets, and I saw you go next door."

Oh, darn! Busted! Pressing her fingers to her lips, Caroline looked around the room. "Shhhh... Mom will flip out. We shared a cup of coffee."

"Hogwash. I know that glazed look. You're wearing him like a glove."

A glove, Caroline smiled.

"I see it in your eyes. Good! You enjoy your life, my dear, and don't listen to your mother. For Pete's sake, she even annoys *me*." She studied the twinkle in Caroline's eyes. "I think the mermaid magic has already started, and he lives next door. Go with it, honey."

"Grams Dorea, I'm so confused," Caroline said in a hushed tone. "Colton has a powerful hold on me. You do not know how difficult it is to pretend I don't care when I do. I like Dillan, but he is a distraction."

"You need this distraction. You enjoy yourself."

Caroline silently agreed. "Thanks, Grams Dorea. I love you."

"Now go have some lunch because you are about to be the center of attention for the remains of this day. And night." She put her hand out.

Caroline leaned over and took it. "Thanks, Grams Dorea." She got up and kissed her soft cheek. "I do like Dillan. He is kind, caring, and sweet."

"And what a body!"

"Grams Dorea! You *are* naughty!"

"I may get older, but I once wore that same glow. Go on, get your lunch."

Caroline left the room feeling as light as the air. The time she spent with Dillan was straight out of a romance novel.

Caroline spent the afternoon wandering from room to room. Reading books, only to be distracted by the steamy thoughts of Dillan. It was only a kiss. But what a kiss it was. Without work, without the stress of looming deadlines and sudden crises, she didn't know what to do with herself. She went downstairs.

In the kitchen, she could hear laughter. The women were experimenting with Auntie Lorelei's mermaid martinis. They decided on the aqua martini. It had blue curacao, banana rum, pineapple juice, and edible gold powder dusted on the rims, topped with a yellow hibiscus flower.

Caroline volunteered to taste one. "If we drink these, we will pass out before the ceremony."

"We drink these as we light the bonfire, then we toss flame-colored powders into the fire," Auntie Pearl said as she lifted her glass.

Auntie Calypso added, "The colorful flames are beautiful as they reach for the moon and stars. We then go down to the water's edge to listen."

Caroline looked at her Auntie Calypso. "Listen for what?"

Auntie Lorelei pushed Caroline's hair back past her shoulder. "For the siren's song."

"After we hear it," Caroline asked with raised brows, "what do we do next?"

The women looked at each other and back at Caroline.

"We listen and look. We've never heard it," Auntie Calypso admitted. "Your grandmother was the last one to hear it when she was crowned Dorea."

Caroline got goosebumps. "For what?"

"Seraphina or Erasmus! Then we return to the bonfire," Auntie Lorelei smiled at Caroline, "and you read the love letter from the original rum bottle, then you are crowned and at that moment, we give you your sacred mermaid name."

Grams Dorea came into the kitchen. "We celebrate in our circle, each saying our mermaid's name as we call upon Seraphina to bless our new mermaid with her magic. Hatteras magic changes lives. Eternal love will find you as it did for Erasmus and Seraphina."

"Wait, they never found each other again?" Caroline tilted her head. "She couldn't live on land, and he couldn't live under the sea."

"Of course, he did not live in the sea, nor could she live on land," Grams Dorea said. "They would forever entwine their souls once Erasmus found her."

"It's so beautiful." Halia clasped her hands together. "You, my dear, are going to be crowned under the blood moon, and it will intensify the energy. And I hope we get a glimpse of Erasmus."

"To the mermaid and her man. Awesome times ahead." Caroline cheered as she looked at her aunties. "This will be fun!" She dipped the tip of her finger into a jar of gold dust and studied it up close. "Cool. It has an iridescence of blue and gold."

"Hmmm, eyeshadow." Auntie Calypso dipped her index finger into the powder, then onto her eyelids and lips. "What do you all think? Do I look marvelous?" She batted her eyes, adding a pucker.

They erupted with laughter. "I think you did too much martini tasting. I may have had too much, as well." Halia said as she fanned her face.

Caroline took another swallow. "You ladies have fun. It is almost four and I need to..." she was going to say *work*. "I need to take a nap. Why not?"

"Dinner at seven, then we begin," Auntie Lorelei reminded them. "Sweet dreams. Ida, she is waiting to hear from you."

Under the soft cotton sheets, Caroline wondered if this mermaid thing was farfetched. She lost that thought and found herself with Dillan's eternal kiss, as his soft lips traced hers. She had wanted to stay there. Feeling she had known him forever. Her head sank deeper into the pillow.

"Caroline...? Honey...?"

She looked towards the door. "Mom, I need my mermaid nap."

"I just want to let you know Colton was on the news moments ago. Grams Dorea has the TV on downstairs."

She sat up. "Campaigning, I'm sure."

"No, it was about his ex-fiancée and some scandal, and he mentioned us. The Woodards, and how he respected your father. And how he was such a mentor. And he mentioned you."

"Oh, shit!" Caroline was wide awake now. "How bad? Is damage control needed? And why did he mention me?"

"He mentioned how you have been his support during campaigning, just like you had been for your father. It was lovely."

"Lovely, Mom? He mentioned me. Ugh... I have to call Lawson." She picked up her cell phone. Moments later, she hung up.

Halia sat down at the foot of the bed. "What did he say?"

"The office has it under control. Lawson said there was no mention of my name. Is that what you wanted to hear? It was about Daddy. I shouldn't have taken on the job as his publicist. I should have left him with Wilmen. What I need is this nap."

Halia was sure she'd heard him mention Caroline's name. "He needs you. But what about this ex-fiancée? She sounds like a splinter under a fingernail. Wretched woman! What sort of women would do such a thing to *our* Colton?"

"A wretched one! *Our* Colton, Mom? He will be fine."

Her mother smiled. "I speak from my heart."

"For your information, Mom, he has been planning what room you will stay in at the White House. I think it's the Lincoln Bedroom." Caroline burst into laughter. "Love you, Mom."

Thirty-Four

Halia shut the door and breezed down the hall to pluck her mermaid dress out of Lorelei's closet. She pulled out the gray bag with her name on it and put it on the bed. Unzipping it with care, she removed her costume. The cascading pink and gold sequins sparkled in the late afternoon sunlight from the window. Yards of gold fabric from the trailing scalloped tail shimmered. Even after all these years, the bodice remained in near perfect condition, with metallic pink and pearl dots.

In front of Lorelei's full-length mirror, she held her costume up to her body. In some ways, it was silly for grown women to parade around a bonfire in these shimmering costumes, pretending to be mermaids. She tilted her head. It was not silly. It was tradition and sisterhood. She looked closer in the mirror. Yes, she has lines around her eyes and lips. They were lines that could tell many stories and earned. She stepped back, adding a smile. And as far as Ida, Marie, and Dorothy

271

were concerned, there *is* an Erasmus and a Seraphina, and one day they will unite. Smiling at herself in the mirror, she turned from side to side.

"I know what you're thinking, Halia," Lorelei said as she entered the room and stopped. "We are post-menopausal women trying to capture our youth. We have learned this from our mothers, their mothers, and so on. Why not? Age is the number you make it. We are young at heart, holding so many cherished memories here at the Beach Heart Cottage."

Lorelei looked at Halia and her costume. "I know you were never into it as much as we all were, but life is short, Halia. The mermaid gatherings have kept us close. There is magic in the air here. We are strong women. I could not ask for better sisters, aunts, nieces, mother, and even our grandmothers."

Halia placed her costume on the bed and folded her hands. She looked at Lorelei. "I know. It seems like yesterday Mom was yelling out of this window at us not to go out too far in the ocean. Her chestnut hair piled on top of her head, she'd be up here using the same Singer sewing machine, getting our costumes ready. I wonder what happened to our childhood costumes?"

Lorelei laughed. "No idea. The Singer was our mother's sewing machine." She walked over to it and turned to Halia. "Remember when we spent our summers here and Daddy would come down for the weekend and Mom would hand him a honey to-do list?"

"He would look over the list," Halia nodded, "tell Mom he needed to run to the hardware store. Then he'd go to the shed, wearing a big old smile, get his fishing pole and bucket, and make a beeline for the ocean."

Lorelei looked out the window as she spoke. "Remember that time Mom put a hammer and a box of nails on his dinner plate?"

They laughed.

"Good old days gone by. The walls remember." Halia looked around and at her sister. "This was our bedroom. Remember the bunk beds Daddy built for us? I loved the top one. From the window I could watch the moon rise as its beams tickled the ocean." She gazed over at the back of the room. "Mom and Grandma Dorothy told us bedtime stories about Seraphina, and you would climb up to the top bunk next to me, and we'd spend hours staring out at the ocean until we fell asleep."

Lorelei's eyes met Halia's. "And we would sneak Daddy's binoculars up here to see a flicker of her tail. Gosh, I could never climb up to that top bunk now, with my knees!"

"We're blessed to have each other, the four of us. And this is bringing my daughter closer to me."

Lorelei sat down in the chair by the sewing machine. "This ceremony is different. I can feel it. The heart-shaped wampum shell Caroline found is no coincidence. The perfect match to Ida's, and you know what that means? Then, I found the mermaid wand at the bottom of Ida's dress bag. Something is up."

Halia walked over to Lorelei. "I'm always one to say yes to the flicker of lights. The cool air that finds a spot in the room with the air conditioning off and the wind chimes singing when there is no breeze. You know my daughter. She is no-nonsense, never believing in the tooth fairy or Santa from the moment she could talk. She is her father's daughter. For Caroline to see Ida is magic." Halia tilted her head. "Listen... is that a cell phone ringing?"

The cell phone ringing was not in her dream. Caroline realized it was her phone. Grabbing it, her eyes still closed, she said a sleepy, "Hello?"

"Oh no, did I wake you, sleepyhead?"

"Dillan? Wow, I have not slept like that during a nap in years. What did you do to me?" She rolled over onto her back and opened her eyes. "What did you put in my coffee?" Her eyes heavy, she yawned.

"*You* drugged *me*. I've been thinking about you all afternoon. Come over and finish our kiss."

"Mmmm. I wish I could." She twirled her hair.

"What did *you* do that made you so tired?" he teased as he sat on the sand, watching two boys skim boarding and tumbling as the tide was coming in.

"I'm not quite sure. I was at your cottage when this incredible man kissed me. I simply couldn't resist returning the kiss, and then suddenly, my aunts were wondering where I had disappeared to." Her heart raced as she sat up, drawing her knees tightly to her chest.

"Would you like to see this passionate man again? He's still at the cottage next door, or so rumor has it."

Caroline had an incoming call. Colton. She forced herself to sit up with her back against the pile of pillows. "Listen, I've got a call I must take. Call you later."

"What do we do now?" Colton sounded furious.

"We? About what?" She was still waking up.

"You don't know? Where have you been? On Mars? That witch did exactly what you said she would. I need damage control. Rumors are flying."

"Lawson and the team are on it. I warned you. But did you listen?"

"Caroline knows best. You need your own podcast," he snickered. "I have a call in ten minutes with you and Lawson."

"Lawson has it under-"

Colton cut her off. "I want *you*. Period. Seeing you the other night with the candles flickering and your mother so happy was heartwarming. I was home and I need you by my side. Can't see us with little kids and a puppy? Little Caroline or Little Colton running on the White House front lawn."

Caroline has accidentally put her phone on three-way calling. Dillan, silent, was still on the line.

"Admit it. This tug of war is fun, isn't it? You, me."

"And my mother makes three. Get your butt out there and do exactly what Lawson tells you to do."

"The only way I'm gonna save this is if we announce our engagement."

"Don't you dare! We are not getting married for the hundredth time. Why are you so desperate for a wife?"

Dillan pressed the red phone icon before Caroline said, *we are not getting married for the hundredth time.*

He'd heard enough.

Colton let out a long sigh. "Be on the call. I need you."

"All right. But next time you decide to get engaged, don't involve me."

"It will be you." Colton hung up.

"Oh, crud, Dillan." She dialed to tell him she had to be on a conference call in two minutes. He did not pick up.

Dillan was digesting what he'd heard. The words they were saying hurt, but the easy comradery between them hurt worse. He shoved his phone into his back pocket and made his way to his dad's cottage.

It was time to get out of bed. Caroline gave in to a wide stretch. She glanced over at the old clock on the end table. Time to be on the conference call.

The stressful call ended. Lawson was working on damage control.

The instant she was off the call, Caroline dialed Dillan, only to land in his voice mail. She texted. No reply. She brushed it off. He was busy.

Seashells and glitter lined the dining room table. Seafood in abundance occupied the table.

"This is a mermaid feast!" With excitement, Auntie Lorelei said as she arranged the steamed shrimp, scallops, and crab legs on a bed of seaweed. "Dig in! We need our energy."

Caroline sat down and yawned.

"Still tired? You took a lengthy nap," her mother commented while pouring herself a glass of iced tea.

"I'm good, Mom. Just relaxing."

Grams Dorea put on her glasses and looked over the buffet. "I think our mermaid had a busy morning and needed to nap." She winked at Caroline.

Caroline blushed. "Yes, Grams Dorea, I needed a rest. It was a long walk."

Once all the dishes were clean, it was time to prepare for the ceremony. The marigold sun was making its daily descent. The air was balmy, and a gentle breeze settled onto the island. Auntie Calypso was pushing tiki torches into the sand while Auntie Lorelei lined the path to the ocean with blue and aqua metallic painted scallop shells. Auntie Pearl was setting out candles in glass jars on the sand.

"Looking forward to learning my name and seeing my costume." Caroline said just as her phone in her pocket buzzed.

> Had a busy day.
>
> Hope your day was a good one.
>
> Dillan

No fun emoji? Caroline felt her face flush.

"Is that Colton? Look at your glow!" Halia cheered. "I knew this was going to happen."

Caroline turned her back to her mother and texted.

> Busy too.
> Tonight is special here at the cottage.
> Will you be around tomorrow?

She hit send.

Earl opened the fridge and grabbed two bottles of beer. He handed one over to Dillan. "Have you talked to Caroline?"

"Why?" Dillan's phone buzzed. He ignored it.

"The ladies have been acting strangely over there at the cottage. I've seen this before in late night movies. The coven is getting ready for something big," Earl said as he took a swig of his beer. "Then, in the blink of an eye, the menfolk disappear."

Dillan looked at his father. "Disappearing menfolk? Coven?"

"Yup, and they *are* up to something over there. Remember that crystal ball?" He snapped his fingers. "What in tarnation did she call it? Good golly, it was like a little dog, the way she carried on."

"Conchita. It lives in a pillowcase." Dillan chuckled. "That was strange."

"Ya see what I'm telling ya? How many people do ya know who do that?"

Dillan shrugged, enjoying his beer. "Few."

"Grams Dorea shooed me off the property today with a broom, of all things. I bet it's her witch's broom, and she uses it to cast spells. Why did she want me to cut the olive bushes and then she yelled at me to scat home? And Pearl has been avoiding me. She stole a look over the hedges and ran inside. Ya think the senator is going over there again. And if so, he just might disappear."

"Interesting facts, Dad."

"I'm telling you, son, there is something in the air."

Dillan shook his head. "Dad, it could be they're just enjoying their vacation."

Earl put his can of beer on the table. "Ya seen the news. Something 'bout the senator and a woman newscaster breaking up. She is madder than a marlin on a hook. And something about a tell-all book. Now the other fella running against him is all over it, saying the senator is bad news. Big debate in a few days should settle that."

"I'm not interested in his mess or debates, Dad."

Earl patted Dillan's shoulder. "I know you have taken a liking to pretty Caroline, but be careful, son. She has a lot on her frying pan. That senator is one big fish you can't fry."

Thirty-Five

The women gathered in the living room, and they laid the mermaid costumes out on the sofa and the chairs.

Caroline's eyes traveled over all of them and stopped at the one with her name on it. "Is this really happening?"

"Yes, my dear granddaughter, it is. Your hair looks amazing. Auntie Calypso did a gorgeous job. The weaving of metallic strands in your wavy long locks stands out. And your skin is all aglow in pink and aqua glitter gel!"

Caroline put her arms out. "I love this. I feel like a little girl again." She pointed at her feet. "My toenails are painted aqua, tipped in rhinestones. And we put some of that gold dust on my eyelids." She batted them. "Look at my aqua fake eyelashes! I love them."

"Put your toe anklets on now. Here, sit down." Halia led Caroline to a chair.

"I love these!" She held her feet up, wiggling her toes. "Sexy!"

"Yes, that it is." Auntie Lorelei came over with a gray dress bag. "It's time to unveil your mermaid costume. Are you ready? This is your special one."

The opalescent gown, dotted with white pearls and beige lace, shimmered. Strands of pearls on a halter top held two large scallop shells that were attached to the bodice by more strands of pearls. A slit up the front went up to the knee. The long-scalloped fish tail covered in gold sequins and pearls whispered to her.

"Oh my gosh, what a sexy gown! Wait, that is not the one you measured me for, Auntie Lorelei." Caroline's eyes followed the sparkles, causing her to gasp. "It's gorgeous! This looks vintage. It's simply stunning."

Auntie Lorelei blushed as she clapped her hands. "It's a surprise! This was Ida's and only worn by her. Grams Dorea completely forgot about it in storage, and I've been working on restoring it for months."

"Wow, Aunt Ida was something. What a sexy gown!" Caroline looked at her Auntie Lorelei and back to the gown. "I feel like a mermaid already! You did an amazing job! Thank you all so much."

Auntie Pearl met Caroline. "It was conservative, fit for that time, so Lorelei had it retrofitted it for a more modern woman. We hope you like it."

"I *love* it!" She cried, which had a domino effect. "I can't believe this is real. And the tail is stunning, scalloped and trimmed in miniature pearls. Who made this back then?"

Grams Dorea ran her hand over Caroline's arm. "That would have been my aunt Marie, the middle sister. She was an amazing seamstress. She designed and made all of them. Her mother was a seamstress."

"Are we all going to be in vintage costumes?"

"Unfortunately, we don't have them. If Marie stored them, we have no clue as to their whereabouts," Grams Dorea said.

Caroline frowned. "That's too bad. After the election, I will try to track them down, if they even exist."

Lorelei had chills rushing into her arms and said. "That would be wonderful! I would love to restore them." She picked up Ida's gown. "See this? I attached a cord to a wrist bracelet. This way, you can lift your tail to move around." She pulled on the cord, making the tail flutter.

"I love it!" Caroline cried out!

"Caroline," Grams Dorea reached for her hands, "I know our siren will sing over the waves tonight and her soul will finally reunite with Erasmus. It's time to get our costumes on, girls."

Caroline slipped into it, and after moments of fastening buttons and a long zipper, it fit like a glove. "This is so beautiful. I feel as if I'm stepping out of a fairytale. Or into one."

"You look so much like Ida," Auntie Pearl cheered as she dashed over to the sideboard and took a small frame out of the top drawer. "I've been saving this for this very moment. This is Ida in the same gown. You are her mirror image."

Caroline took the framed photo, tracing Ida with her finger. She looked up at Auntie Pearl. "It is amazing. I feel as if I'm looking at myself. Can I have a copy?"

"Of course, honey. Go out on the back porch while we put our costumes on. Imagine what it was like when Ida wore it. How it must have felt when she heard the siren and saw her tail flicker in the rising sun."

"I will. Thank you, Auntie Pearl."

The ease of movement surprised Caroline in her stunning mermaid outfit. She felt privileged and silly. If any of her colleagues could see her, what would they say? Colton needed to see her dressed up like a mermaid, dancing around a bonfire. Then he would find her unstable and leave her alone. Or would it turn him on?

The back porch door opened. Grams Dorea, in her costume, leaning on her cane, led the mermaid parade out of the cottage.

"I still got it, girls! My aquamarine tail is stunning. It has a shimmer, just like me. A little dusting off and I'm good to go." She stomped her cane and laughed. "It is almost midnight, and the blood moon is nearing its position. Let's get our party started!"

Auntie Calypso lit the torches.

Auntie Lorelei came out with a cooler. Inside was a large thermos of mermaid martinis, a cluster of huge yellow hibiscus flowers, and blue glasses sprinkled with gold dust.

In one of Pearl's hands was the wand, hidden inside a soft cloth, and in the other, a folding chair for Grams Dorea.

Calypso held the original rum bottle, letter, and journal.

Halia was last. She proudly held the box containing the crown in her hands. She turned to Caroline and asked. "Caroline, you have your heart wampum shell, right? The one you found after Ida visited you?"

"I do, Mom." Caroline was still wondering, was it really Ida?

The blue and green seashell path to the bonfire, now lit with small torches, guided everyone as they made their way down to the beach.

"The moon is almost above us, reflecting on the ocean ripples. This is splendid." Auntie Calypso said as she held the rum bottle.

Thirty-Six

Dillan had dozed off on the sofa. Earl had finished watching the old movie *Burnt Offerings* again by himself. He turned off the TV and got up and was heading to bed when he noticed a flicker of flames on the beach. Who would make a fire this late?

"Dillan, wake up." Earl nudged him on the arm. "Wake up."

"Huh? What's going on?"

"Come here, look at the beach. Someone is having a bonfire at this late hour. I sure hope they have a permit."

"Dad, it's well after midnight. Who cares? It's some kids having fun. Go to bed." He sat up, turning his head from side to side. "I'm gonna pay for falling asleep on this sofa. My neck is killing me."

"I bet it's that senator wooing Caroline down there."

That caught Dillan's attention. He got up and went over to the window. "It is a big fire." He looked up. "Dad, check out the moon."

"It's a big blood moon. We need to go on a mission and check out what's going on down by that fire."

"Dad, I'm not sure. What if it is *him?* Then what?"

"I'll tell you what! It's time to fry that fish! I see how Caroline looks at you. Like your mom used to look at me." Earl dashed off to get his night vision goggles. He came back with them around his neck. "All lights off. We're on the move."

"Dad, come on, don't you recall the last time you got caught by those security thugs? If the senator is here, they're here." He cracked a sarcastic smile. "And what if they *are* witches in a coven and they're looking to capture us menfolk?" He said, holding back a chuckle as he watched the flames flicker in the distance. "You know what? Now that I'm awake, what the hell, let's go check out what's going on."

"That's my boy! First, we check their driveway for those fancy black SUVs and steer clear."

"If we see an empty pillowcase, we're outta there!" Dillan grinned. "Us menfolk need to take care of ourselves and avoid misfortune." He rubbed his neck as he laughed. "Let me get the bug spray."

Once the women were down on the beach, they drew a large heart in the sand near the light of the roaring bonfire. Auntie Lorelei reached for Caroline's hand. "Let the magic of Hatteras begin. Caroline, step into the center of the heart."

Lifting her tail using the string on her wristlet, Caroline stepped inside it.

"Now, ladies," Grams Dorea intoned as she looked up at the moon, "take out your letter of intention and we will toss them into the fire and Pearl will add the colored powder. If it turns red, love will soon find our mermaid. If blue, then our siren will call out to us, and Erasmus will make his presence known."

They tossed their letters into the fire. Pearl added the magical powder, and flames reached up, turning red and blue! It has never happened in their lifetime.

Their eyes lit up as they stared at the dancing flames. Lorelei poured the mermaid martinis and handed them out. Caroline watched the flames, feeling a little silly as she drank hers in two gulps.

"The flames have spoken." Grams Dorea sat down in her chair. "My dear granddaughter, I hand you my heart wampum shell. Press it against the one you found. They will become two hearts beating as one."

Caroline had her shell in her hand. She took the one from Grams Dorea, pressed them together and held them close to her heart as all eyes were on her.

The women weren't the only one watching. Over in the dune path off Earl's place, the night vision goggles found the celebration.

"You ain't gonna believe what I am seein'." Earl smacked a mosquito on his arm. Can you get more bug spray?" He snapped his fingers. "Hurry, the dang skeeters are eatin' me up."

"Dad, what are you seeing?" Dillan sprayed the surrounding air with bug spray. "Is the senator there? Never mind, I don't want to know. I'm going back to the cottage."

"No, shhhh. It's far worse." Earl crawled forward on the sand.

Dillan crouched down. "Let me see."

Earl handed the night vision goggles over.

"What am I looking for, Dad?"

"Look at the fire. You ain't gonna believe it. They have their cloaks on. I ain't seeing this. Holy moly, they sparkle!"

"What? Sparkle?" Dillan adjusted the lenses. He was silent as he watched the women dressed in strange clothing toss something into the fire as vibrant colors met the night sky. He could see them holding hands around a bonfire and dancing. Caroline was nowhere in sight until he looked to the left. There she was, standing alone, also dressed in a strange costume. "What the heck is going on over there?"

"Let me see," Earl tapped Dillan's arm. "My turn."

"Wait, Dad, I need to see this." Lowering himself down until he was flat on the cool sand, Dillan whispered, "It's a ceremony of some sort. Now they're going down to the ocean, holding hands. Caroline is with them. Wait, are they wearing costumes with tails?"

Earl was running his time with Pearl through his mind. Was her chartie board to seduce him into one of these ceremonies? Is Grams Dorea the grand witch? Was there such a thing? He looked up at the heavens and back at Dillan. "Let me see this."

Dillan handed the goggles over. He remained flat on the sand, trying to figure out what he just saw. "Dad, we can't tell them we're spying on them."

"Heck, no, they might put a spell on us," Earl focused on Pearl. She was talking, but he couldn't hear anything at all. "They ain't tails. They are..." He adjusted the lenses. "Dillan. Ya ain't gonna believe this. Long cloaks are what they are parading around in. By golly, what is going on?"

Auntie Calypso cupped her hand behind her ear. "Can anyone hear our siren singing over the rolling waves? Her voice is sweet. Shhhh..."

Caroline waited, as did the others, when a soft whisper made her jump back. "Mom," she whispered, "did you hear that?"

Halia shook her head.

"You *heard* something, Caroline?" Auntie Lorelei looked around. "Are you sure?"

"Sure as I'm standing here."

Auntie Lorelei made her way over to Grams Dorea. She bent over and whispered, "Mother, Caroline heard her."

"Wonderful! Now we begin. It is time to read the letter. Gather everyone around the bonfire."

"*Begin*?" Caroline made her way back to Grams Dorea. "We're not done?"

"Back in the center of the heart circle." Grams Dorea pointed.

Auntie Calypso picked up an object on the sand and unwrapped it. "This is Ida's magic mermaid wand."

Caroline had to bite her tongue. *A magic mermaid wand? What's next? A handsome prince riding a seahorse with oyster slippers and a mankini of seaweed?* Oh, how she needed another mermaid martini!

Halia stood behind Caroline with a flashlight as they read the sacred letter, explaining how the crown was born. Caroline found this fascinating. How well over one hundred years ago, the words written by a sailor were to a mythical mermaid. She began accepting what was happening. This *was* magical, or maybe it was something in that blue drink.

After Caroline finished reading, they shared another mermaid martini as the blood moon watched from directly above.

Watching them closely, Earl maintained his focus on Pearl. "They're drinking again. I bet it is some witch's potion."

"Potion? Dad, you watch too many late-night movies. They're a bunch of women on vacation enjoying a drink. Although, why are they in strange clothing?" Sitting up, Dillan pushed aside a cluster of sea oats. "I'll give you that."

"Caroline is a lure to get us. They need to sacrifice someone."

Dillan burst into laughter and covered his mouth with his hand. "Wow, no more Netflix for you after midnight. My turn." He tugged on the neck cord. Earl handed them over.

Dillan focused on Caroline. Even in the green glow of night vision goggles, she was beautiful. The blood moon above and the flickering flames enhanced her. If they were witches, Caroline had him under her spell.

"What ya seeing, son?" Earl belly crawled on the sand. "I bet the senator is a king warlock. This country is going to hell!"

"King warlock? What the-"

Wide-eyed, Earl nodded. "I bet he drinks their potion too!"

"Dad, shhhh. We have to crawl closer. We can hide behind the sea oats and that sand fence to the left. What do you say?"

Earl looked back at his dark cottage and out over the moonlit ocean. "We gotta be silent and move like ghost crabs."

"Got it."

"Dad, stop, you're kicking sand in my face." Dillan said as he crawled behind Earl and made his way beside him. "We're getting too close. Did you hear that?" Dillan popped his head up. "Where's their dog?"

"Must be inside. If Wilbur were out, he would have already spotted us," Earl said as he stopped crawling. "Looks like they are not moving. Just standing there, staring at the fire. Bet they are chanting something. It's just like Betty Davis in

Burnt Offerings. The ghost of the old lady is living in the house. Grams Dorea is her."

"Dad, what are you mumbling about, Betty Davis? Let me see."

Earl handed the goggles over when they heard something rustling in the oat grass.

"No! Bad dog. Get out of here!" Dillan's face slobbered in slime. He pushed Wilbur back, only to have the dog think it was a game. "Dad, I told you the dog would find us."

"Let's get back home!" As Earl crawled, Wilbur's toenails dug into his back. Earl let out a yell. Wilbur took off.

"Shhhh!" Calypso looked around. "Did you hear that? It was a man. He cried out just as I asked for a sign."

"He heard us!" Lorelei's eyes widened as she looked south. "Erasmus heard us!" She moved away from the bonfire toward the voice.

"Don't frighten him away!" Grams Dorea warned.

"Oh, crap! Dad, one of them is heading this way. We gotta go!"

"I'm crawling as fast as I can. Darned dog."

They made it twenty feet to the walkway to their cottage.

Earl realized he'd lost his night goggles somewhere along the way. "I gotta retrieve them. The tide will take em out or they are gonna know we were spying."

"Dad, no. It's too late. They will see you."

Earl took off, as if he were running on hot coals, backtracking to find his goggles.

Thirty-Seven

"There he is! I see his silhouette in the moonlight! He's getting away!" Lorelei yelled, stumbling through the sand in her costume in the darkness, waving to her sisters to hurry. Pearl and Calypso ran behind her. Halia stayed with Grams Dorea.

Caroline went to step outside the heart.

"You stay right there," Grams Dorea ordered. "We have had nothing like this happen. It is magical! It was the wand that brought *his* spirit out to see you."

Caroline raised her wand to the moon. "Hello, sailor pirate man! Take me on your seahorse and to your seaweed kingdom. Mom, can you get me another blue drink? The last two were so awesome." She laughed, feeling light and free.

Halia shook her head. "You have had enough."

Caroline, feeling tipsy, frowned, and she waved her wand around. "Boo hoo!"

Dillan urgently called his dad over in a hoarse whisper as the women closed in. "Hurry!"

Earl snatched his binoculars. Breathless, with them in hand, he made it back to the walkway. "They're after us menfolk. We have no chance! Go!" he pushed Dillan.

"Watch out for the sand burrs, Dad."

"Ouch!" Earl yelped as he hopped and ran off.

Dillan, winded, made it to the back porch and sat down on the rear steps in the dark and burst into laughter, waiting for his father.

Earl, gasping for breath, made it to the porch. He put his goggles down and began plucking burrs from his feet.

"That was fun, I must admit! Whew. They came close. And when will you learn to wear shoes?" Dillan, still laughing, shook his head. "What did we just do? I felt like a teenager."

"Keep the lights off. There was enough moonlight for them to see." Earl sat down and took several deep breaths. "Whew... I'm too old for this. How am I ever gonna go over there again and face the coven? I need a beer. You want one?"

"Oh, yeah."

Earl limped inside and returned. He sat down next to Dillan. "Ya think they know it was me? Us?" Earl asked as he handed Dillan a beer. "We best keep a tight lid on this. I've lived a long time and ain't seen anything like that. Did you see their long cloaks?"

"I'm not sure they were cloaks, but it sure is strange." Dillan sipped his beer as he looked out past the dune. The blood moon was brilliant as it sat high in the sky.

"You still gonna see Caroline?"

Dillan rubbed his chin. "I like her a lot, but after the senator's visits and what we witnessed tonight, I have to say I don't know."

"I'm gonna reevaluate my liking for Pearl. She was dancing up a storm out there as if no one else on earth existed. A vision burned into my eyes."

"I'm going to bed." Dillan got up. "Night, Dad."

"Night, son. Don't turn your light on. We are in blackout conditions!"

From his window, Dillan could see the women. He heard one of them cry out in desperation, "He vanished! Come back to us!"

It was Lorelei. Calypso caught up to her. A little out of breath, she looked at her sister and out over the ocean. "We frightened him off. He's most likely terrified." She lifted her tail. "This is like running in a potato sack. I need to catch my breath."

"We scared the bejesus out of him." Pearl, out of breath, reached for her sister's hand. They had to have walked a half mile down the beach. "Did you notice he had a funny gate to him? A limp, hop, run of sorts. I bet he has a wooden leg. Oh, how did we let him get away?"

"Yes, I must have a wooden leg and an eye patch! His spirit vanished in the blink of an eye. I'm sure he went out into the ocean. He's looking for Seraphina!" Lorelei said as she gazed at the moon's reflection in the ocean's ripples. "That means one thing—his soul can now find Seraphina. This has never happened. This is exciting! Let's get back and crown Caroline. I know Erasmus will make another appearance."

Pulling the strings up on their costume tails, they made their way back to the bonfire.

"Was it the mysterious sailor in his mankini looking to take me into the depths of the ocean?" Caroline asked, fluttering her tail. "It's my costume. It's so sexy and sparkly. Can I have another martini? They are so good."

Grams Dorea cleared her throat, "Not yet." She looked over at Halia. "It is your turn to set the crown of seashells on Caroline's head."

The sisters circled Halia as she picked up the delicate box and set it on Gram Dorea's lap. She opened the lid and removed the vintage crown.

"My dear daughter, Caroline Anne Woodard, you are now one of the sisterhood of mermaids." Halia glowed. "As you cross the threshold of the Beach Heart Cottage, my love, I now forever declare you as..." she gently set the vintage crown on Caroline's head. "Seraphina."

"*Seraphina!* I love my mermaid name. It's so ethereal." Caroline cheered as she ran her fingers over the delicate crown. "Wait, isn't Seraphina the mermaid who saved the sailor?"

"It is the name we saved just for you." Grams Dorea smiled. "Yes, it is her name and now yours."

Caroline, feeling the weight of the crown, understood the responsibility it brought. She would one day place the crown on another relative, perhaps her own daughter.

"I feel like Miss America!" Caroline said as she ran her fingers over the crown of shells.

"How about Miss Mermaid! Our beautiful Seraphina," Lorelei said with cheer as tears rained down her cheeks.

With affection, Halia smiled at her daughter and said. "It is time to go down to the water's edge, toss our hibiscus flowers out to sea as an offering to Seraphina, and be thankful for all we have." She held her hand out as Caroline stepped out of the heart. "Then we can make s'mores and finish the mermaid martinis."

"Go on, Seraphina!" Grams Dorea sat back, opening the graham cracker box.

Hand in hand, they found their feet tickled by sea foam as they threw their flowers. Caroline reached for her mother's hand. "Thank you, Mom, thank you, Aunties and Grams Dorea. I'm so proud to be part of the sisterhood."

Thirty-Eight

It was after two-thirty in the morning when they went up to the cottage. They returned the crown to its box. They took group photos to grace the mantle and to remind all who came to the cottage of this magical night. The sisterhood.

Late that morning, and hung over, the women were dragging themselves around the cottage. They complained of aching muscles after their ghost chase. When Lorelei saw the damage to the costumes caused by chasing Erasmus, she felt horrified. Calypso reminded her how wonderful it was to get a glimpse of the infamous Erasmus. They could repair the mermaid costumes.

It wasn't until noon that anyone got dressed. Caroline was lying in bed with her thoughts roaming over the ceremony.

The beauty of it. Freedom. A belonging, and perhaps it was time to start a family to keep the tradition.

She texted Dillan several times. No response. Figuring he was busy working on his dad's many projects, she peeked at her laptop and checked her emails. That was a mistake. No one was paying attention to her. *I am away* message.

Closing her laptop without reading a single email, she went downstairs. Seeing her mother getting coffee in the kitchen, she went up to her. "Mom, thank you for allowing me to be part of this. It was magical, I admit, and it was funny watching you all chase down the spirit of a sailor! And that crown was heavy."

"It is a heavy responsibility you now have. Until the next mermaid is crowned, you are the keeper of the crown."

"You mean I must keep the crown? And costumes?"

"Auntie Lorelei keeps the costumes." Halia took her daughter's hands in hers. "As I imagined, you had the same ethereal aura in the moonlight as Seraphina would have had."

Caroline smiled at her mother.

The women spent the remains of the afternoon at the beach. Caroline stayed behind and sat on the sofa. With the clicker in hand, she turned the TV on. There was Colton on a few stations, and on others, his ex-fiancée promoting her new book. Caroline changed channels back and forth. She had to call Lawson and see how it was being managed. She turned off the TV and texted Dillan.

> Hi Dillan
>
> I have not heard from you.
>
> Busy?
>
> I'm home. How about going for a beach walk tonight?
>
> She hit send.

Her phone dinged within seconds.

Been busy.

Hope all is well.

Dillan

She texted back.

Beach walk tonight?

He texted.

Busy. Sorry.

Biting her lip, she let it go. He was most likely busy, or he lost interest. Should she go to his cottage?

Her phone dinged. Her heart sprinted.

Caroline Woodard MIA, where have you been?

I have been texting and left you several voice mails.

She texted back.

Colton, I'm on vacation. Talk to Lawson and the team.

He texted back.

I know you are on vacation.

I was there sharing dinner with your wonderful family.

The book is out. It's not bad.

She put me in a good light.

They stomped out rumors .

When can I see you?

Shaking her head, she smiled at his tenacity. Yes, he was a pain in her rear end. They were ying and yang. He knew how to break down her walls, brick by brick. She had to tease him.

She texted.

You miss my mother!

He texted.

And you. When will you go back to
DC?
She tapped the arm of the sofa, then
texted back.
Monday next week.
A second later, he texted back.
We can talk then. Dinner.
A car will pick you up at six.
She bit her bottom lip and texted.
Maybe.
A new text came in.
Hey, sorry. How about that beach
walk, say seven?
Meet me at the dune end of my
walkway. 🌊
Dillan

Her eyes lit up. There was an emoji. YES! She ran her
fingers through her hair. They got stuck. She sat back, laughing
as she pulled out metallic strands.

Thirty-Nine

The skies were restless as pink and violet marshmallow clouds swirled across the horizon. The remains of the day were clear. Caroline made her way to the path by Earl's cottage. Inhaling the sea mist with her head held high, she knew work madness awaited her in less than a week.

It had been a wonderful vacation. Although she was returning to DC, her mother, Grams Dorea, and the aunties would remain another week, then close the cottage. As she sat down and watched the soothing, sweet-sounding waves and the hush of the sea oats, she felt a hand on her shoulder. She looked up and back out at the ocean.

"Hi. I've been swamped with work. You, too?" Dillan asked as he sat down beside her and gently put his arm around her.

"We've been nonstop busy at the cottage. We had a late night."

"What were you doing that you had a late night?" His eyes met hers. "Partying?"

Caroline dropped her head. "Family stuff."

He nodded as he removed his arm from her shoulder. "I hope it was fun."

"It was fantastic. I feel refreshed." She leaned back on her elbows. "As if there's magic in the air."

"Magic?" Maybe Earl was correct. He had to probe as he narrowed his eyes at the remains of their bonfire. "What does a girl like you do to stay up so late?"

"Nothing much. Just an old family tradition we celebrate."

"Celebrate?"

"Yeah." She smiled mysteriously, looking out over the ocean.

Was that all she was going to say? He dug his feet into the sand. "I'm going to miss you. You have what I call pleasant vibes. I wish you weren't leaving so soon. Who am I going to share an iced coffee with at the café?"

"Think of me when you go there. It's back to the grind. I'll miss it here." With her finger, she drew little hearts in the sand. "I have commitments and a job that I'm not sure I want anymore."

"That's how I felt before I moved down here. I had enough of New York. Stay here."

"I can't. I have an apartment, a job. That would be a dream to live here, but people count on me."

He leaned over. Their lips met, but she pulled back.

"Dillan, six hours between us isn't too bad, is it?"

"Long-distance relationships never work." He pushed her hair back past her shoulder. "I wish it could. I really enjoy being with you and-" He stopped and looked out over the ocean.

"And what?"

"I can't compete with the senator."

Caroline reached for his hand, pressing it against her cheek. "There is no competition. Trust me. It's my job. My family was so tied to politics. It is all my mother knew, and she has a tough time letting it go. Colton and I will never be."

"So, you are not aiming to be our First Lady, Caroline?"

She squeezed her face. "Heck no. I have to help get him into the office. I guess we can chalk this up to a summer romance, the kind you read about in beach novels. She goes her way, he goes his, and twenty years later they bump into each other at a restaurant on the island. Kids and spouses in tow. We fantasize about how it would have been. We say we have aged little even though we have, and we fantasize about running off for a few special hours."

"Wow, when is this happening, since I need to make a note of this encounter? Did you say twenty years? Make it sooner. Like two years. No, two days." He tickled her ribs. "You know that those romance novels are unrealistic."

"Maybe not." She pushed him away, laughing. "I'm glad we talked." The tip of a wave met her toes. "Time to move!"

His phone beeped. "My dad. He needs a diversion other than me. We bought the cottage next to yours. Things need to be done."

"*We* bought it. As in *you*?"

"Yup, well, it's an enormous project. It will keep me busy."

"Awesome. Just make sure you get good people for the summer or Grams Dorea will... never mind." She tried to hide a yawn.

Dillan skirted around the question. "You must have had a wild time last night."

She stretched, tilting her head back. "We did. Too many martinis. I'm a wine girl."

"Maybe a moonlit beach stroll tonight?" Dillan's eyes lit up. "Full moon!"

"Maybe. I'll text you." Caroline said.

Feeling a coolness from her and disappointed, he got up and held his hand out. They kissed as they parted. Neither of them could escape the awkwardness.

Earl was on his back porch when Dillan arrived.

"Dillan, what did she say? Did you find out what that cauldron was all about?"

Dillan's eyes were on his father's neck. "No, Dad, and it was a bonfire, not a cauldron, and they are not... wait, what in the world is that on your neck?"

Earl tugged on it. "It's garlic cloves. I strung 'em. Miss Dottie said it would ward off bad juju and witches."

"Bad juju? What did you say to her? Come clean."

"I did not mention what we saw. I asked her what remedies would ward off witches that might be in the cottage we just bought. It's bruised up badly in the last hurricane and sitting empty." Earl pulled his garlic necklace to his nose. "I like it. Here, sniff."

Dillan stepped back, waving his hands. "I'll pass. Bad juju or not, let's head over to our project. We gotta start the cleanup. And hours ago, they connected the electricity."

"First, I have a job over at Grams Dorea's."

"What now? I thought you were never going there again."

Earl wiped his forehead. "Their kitchen faucet is leaking under the sink bad. Guess I didn't tighten something when I put it in. This here garlic will keep me safe. And I sure as heck I am gonna see if I can find those cloaks."

"If you say so. I'm going over to our cottage. I'll see you there," Dillan headed out.

With a wrench in hand, Earl knocked on the front door. Pearl answered it. Their eyes met. She smiled. "Earl, Grams Dorea mentioned you would stop by." Her eyes landed on his neck.

He responded, "Uh, don't ask."

Pearl gestured him inside and shut the door. "The faucet has been dripping terribly. We have a bucket under it and changing it hourly."

"I'll fix it. Just need to tighten it up." He was in the kitchen when Grams Dorea was standing behind him.

"Earl, what is that smell?" She moved in front of him. Her eyes narrowed. "For Pete's sake. Is that raw garlic strung around your neck?"

He looked down at the raw cloves. "I felt a cold coming on. Old family remedy and all."

Grams Dorea made her way to the stove and took out a large boiling pot. "The best kind of remedy is the old ones." She winked. "Earl, do I have to add you to my chicken soup stock list?"

He swallowed hard. "Soup?" His eyes found the pot.

Auntie Lorelei came into the kitchen. "Oh, thank goodness you're here, Earl. I've emptied the bucket several times today. I hope it's fixable. What is *that* smell?" she sniffed around when her eyes landed on Earl's neck.

"It's me, and that leak is nothing a wrench can't conquer." He held it up.

"Garlic! Is that what I smell?"

"Yup. Lorelei. It's garlic." Earl said, as his eyes watered. He held back a sneeze.

Auntie Lorelei turned to Grams Dorea. "Mom, you can make a delicious soup stock in that bigger pot out in the shed."

Earl eyed the back door. "Bigger pot? How big?"

Lorelei pulled her lips in and out. She had to say it. "Big enough to put you in it."

Earl's mouth fell open. He was correct all along. They were witches!

"Mom, I put Conchita on the coffee table. Please let her rest outside her pillowcase. I'm going to let her sit under the full moon. A recharge of energy." Lorelei tapped his cheek. "Earl, you look like a witch doctor."

His eyes grew as wide as saucers.

"He has a cold or something going on," Grams Dorea said loudly as she watched him squirm. "A big old pot of chicken soup is in order!"

Earl gulped. *Soup and Conchita. The vanishing menfolk tales could be true.* "I, um, yeah, uh, I felt a cold coming on. The cloves open my sinuses. I'll get this fixed quick and be on my way."

"And they certainly have opened mine." Auntie Lorelei's eyes watered as she pinched her nose.

Earl got under the sink and a minute later popped out. "All done, gotta run. Bye, ladies." With a quick hop, he was out the front door.

Pearl, chasing behind, stopped him outside. "Earl, how about a chartie board at your place later tonight?" She blinked her eyes as the garlic stung them. "And that necklace has to stay in your backyard."

How could he resist? So what? She dressed up in a strange cloak and danced around a bonfire under the moon? After mentioning the chicken soup, he feared Grams Dorea, and after discussing Conchita, he feared Lorelei.

Earl's eyes met soft-spoken, sweet Pearl. "Oh, sure, why not? Say eight? Just come on over."

Pearl batted her bright green eyes. "You are a catch, Earl. I may have you on my line."

Earl felt his face flush. "I had best be going. Got to meet with my son."

"Wait a minute, handsome." Pearl leaned in, pinched her nose, and kissed his rosy cheek. "See you later."

Sporting a wide smile, forgetting all about witches, Earl stumbled most of the way to the cottage next door.

Caroline was up in her room, toweling off from a shower, when a flurry of texts came in from Colton. He rambled on about how some things are meant to be. What a power couple they would be if she would only listen to her mother.

Ugh, listen to my mother? What about listening to her heart? That seemed to be neglected. She returned his texts with smiley faces.

Her phone rang. She answered. "Hey, Colton, shouldn't you be out campaigning?"

"I am. I just finished taping a Morning Sunbreak Show interview with Mason Goodson."

"How did that go?"

"Smooth, thankfully. He is on my side if you haven't been paying attention."

"Glad it went well." She was picking at the chipping nail polish on her pinky. "You are going to win by a landslide. Your ex's book did you a favor. I downloaded a copy and started reading it yesterday. She portrays you as a saint! My mother has already read it, adding her usual moans of discontent. How much did this cost you?"

"Not a cent. Her donation was solely her decision."

"She has something up her sleeve. I'll be back at the end of the week. My vacation is almost over, and we have a lot to do."

"Yes, *we* do. I miss your daily calls checking in on me. You know you are the best out there."

Caroline pressed the phone between her ear and shoulder as she got up to close the door.

"We have much to do. And that dinner date when I get back, seriously? You are tenacious. I know you're smiling at that photo of my father you have on your wall."

"Caroline, I will never give up on you. You broke up with me, remember? You said I was always on the go, but honey, *you* are always on the go. So why not make it a double on-the-go? Be by my side at the White House. We can do so much for this country. Your father came so close. It's in your veins to be our First Lady, Caroline."

"Colton, it is an immense responsibility, and being in the spotlight would be a change for me. I'm not the person you think I am."

"Okay, okay, you're right. Education. Stopping childhood hunger. Older voters will recall you in those photo ops with your father by your side, the pretty little girl giving out toys and stuffed animals to children in the hospital."

She sat down on the edge of the bed, draped in her towel, remembering every moment as if it were yesterday. It gave her a happy chill.

"Colton, FLOTUS is a tremendous responsibility, and I'm not the one for such an arduous task. I don't aspire to be in the public eye and analyzed for everything I wear and say. Just think about the criticism I would face if my decorating for the holidays did not please everyone."

"Honey, they will groom you. You know what to do. Your mom can be by your side."

"Of course she would."

She could not believe what she had said. He was removing another brick from her wall. How could he? Was it the mermaid magic taking over, sending her heart in the wrong direction? Dillan was the opposite of Colton. He was new and mysterious. She needed to delve into this new sexy mystery. That was Dillan. Colton was familiar and carried so many memories. She shivered.

As if he read her mind, he said, "Listen, I'm going to need someone there. When I win. There has only been one bachelor president, James Buchanan, right before Lincoln. We can solve the problem the same way he did—his niece was pretty much working beside him. We can do that if you like."

"I'm not your niece, but Colton. That's a beautiful offer."

"You get a choice ... hold on. Caroline, I gotta go. Call you later."

Caroline rolled her eyes. "Make it after ten tonight."

"You mean when your tanned body is in bed?"

"Colton. Bye."

They hung up. She fell back against the pillows, looking up at the ceiling, questioning why she went along with Colton. Maybe a stroll on the beach with Dillan would break the spell Colton seemed to put her under. What was she doing? This was not Caroline's behavior.

She ran it in her mind, over and over. Maybe he was the magic, and Dillan was a summer beach novel, the kind you read and then leave on a beach chair for the next dreamer to pick up.

Caroline, who rarely dated, was now finding her heart in two places. Going back to work was what she needed. Refocus and get her emotions in order. *Back to reality.* Colton was real. Solid. Like her father. Dillan was ethereal, like morning mist off the ocean. Mysterious.

Caroline was devoted to her career. Returning to D.C. and putting in hard work was the most effective way to break free from the small web she had been weaving around herself. And she would do just that, but only after taking one final moonlit walk along the shore.

Forty

"What a gorgeous night! It's going to be so difficult to go home to the chaos of Washington and work."

"Stay here. Work from the cottage. We can meet at the café early before we go to work."

"Dillan, that is a fantasy. Besides, Grams Dorea closes the cottage at the end of September. And you know what November fourth is."

"The day you say I'm done. And you move on to another client?"

Caroline shook her head. "My plate is full, and I have a lot to think about."

They kicked off their sandals and walked along the shore. The warm water washed over their toes as the moonbeams rippled across the ocean.

Dillan pointed at the sand. "Check out the ghost crabs."

"Where?" she looked, curling her toes.

"They are harmless little things, more afraid of us than we are of them." Dillan pulled her close. "I admit, I'm going to miss you. Your smile, laughter, and witty family."

"You'll meet another summer romance."

Dillan stopped. "Wow, is that what I am to you? A vacation gigolo? I'm guessing life in the political circle has taught you how to punch low."

"Oh no, that is not what I meant!" Caroline shook her head. "I'm *so* sorry. It came out wrong."

"No, your words said it all. Listen. This was a few fun weeks, and this gigolo needs to find a new vacationer. It was nice meeting you, Caroline Woodard. I wish you and Senator Jameson the best, and perhaps I will see you with the new president on TV." Dropping his head, he turned to leave.

"Wait, Dillan! Please!" She grabbed the bottom of his shirt. "I did *not* mean it. I meant-"

His lips met hers and, in an instant, she melted into his arms. He pulled away and brushed back her hair as a balmy breeze surrounded them.

"Dillan, I-"

"Shhhh. I know. You don't need to say what we feel."

She traced the outline of his face in the moonlight. "I can't make any promises, especially now. It is pedal to the metal time, as my dad would say. No pit stops."

He pulled her close. "I understand. All I ask is that you be honest with me."

Dillan knew somewhere in her heart there was Colton; he was not going away soon. He had to be careful with his heart. Caroline differed from anyone he had been with. Her serious, funny, relaxed, and free-spirited side emerged.

"I know what you're going to ask. As I told you at the coffee shop. Colton and I had a past. I need to leave it there."

"I had to check on that. You've changed since I first met you."

"Funny you say that. I *feel* different." She looked at the moonbeams rippling over the ocean. "I feel free. If mermaids are real, I'm feeling like one!"

Dillan recalled the costumes. "A mermaid. Hmmm... you would make a beautiful one."

"Yup, and you make me want to swim in briny waters. I feel as if I have known you forever."

Dillan was silent, then looked around and spoke. "Maybe we knew each other in another life?"

"You believe in that?" She tilted her head. "My Auntie Lorelei can tell if you did. She reads palms and is fantastic at that."

Dillan tightened his jaw as he looked out over the ocean and back at Caroline. "I believe things happen for reasons and we each have our seasons. And reading palms, interesting. As long as her pal, Conchita, does not come out, I'm cool with it."

"Hey," she tugged on his hand. "Come on, let's go see if she will read your palm right now. Come on!"

"Uh, what? Seriously?" Earl had told him to come home late because he was entertaining Pearl. "Sure, why not? But no Conchita."

The ladies were playing cards in the coolness of the back porch.

"Caroline," Halia greeted as she eyeballed Dillan who was next to her, "what have you been up to?"

Four voices cried, "Seraphina!"

"Oh, right, of course," Halia wore a tight smile, then let it go. "Hello, Dillan."

"Hi everyone." Caroline waved.

"Seraphina?" Dillan raised his eyebrow as he looked at the women and back at Caroline.

She smiled. "Just my nickname. Forget you heard it."

Dillan smiled, adding an uncertain nod. "Got it."

"Auntie Lorelei, can you read Dillan's palm?"

"Right now, Caroline?" Auntie Lorelei put her cards face down on the table. "Of course!" She pulled out a chair and asked him to sit down. "Give me your dominant hand."

"Huh?"

"The hand you use the most. The one you write with." Sitting down, he laughed nervously.

Curious, Grams Dorea got up and sat next to Lorelei and asked. "Relax, young man. Don't you want to know?"

He shrugged. "I guess." He looked around. "And where is Conchita?"

"She's out bathing in the moonlight," Auntie Pearl replied with a wink.

"I see," Dillan apprehensively opened his hand.

Halia got up and went into the kitchen to breathe, to let it go. *Caroline can be with whoever she wants.* She repeated her mantra ten times. To no avail. Faking a smile, she went back onto the porch.

Caroline sat next to Dillan, leaning in.

"Relax, Dillan, this is painless." Auntie Lorelei ran her index finger over the back of his hand, then turned it over, studying the lines. "Hmmmm. I see heartache. Recently. And past lives. Many. I see... a long life ahead. Oh, two children." She looked up at him and then at Caroline with piercing eyes. "That's all." She closed his hand. Her eyes found Halia's.

"How about we get back to our card game? Grams Dorea was ahead."

"That's it?" Dillan asked as he pulled his hand back. "Cool. Not too bad, right?"

Caroline rolled her eyes, knowing she was holding back. Something big. If it's negative, she usually turns pale. If good, her face flushed. Her face turned bright pink.

"How about you kids join us in our card game?" Grams Dorea suggested.

Halia's face twisted while she silently repeated her mantra.

Caroline reached for his hand as Dillan shrugged. "Sure, what are you playing?"

"A family game," Grams Dorea said. "It's called Oh, Hell. Do you play bridge?"

"I used to."

"This is a kind of cut-throat, free-for-all bridge," Auntie Lorelei chuckled. "We'll teach you."

Forty-One

Caroline packed after the card game—which Grams Dorea won, as she always did. Caroline went to bed with a lot on her mind. She wanted to head out early, ahead of the traffic heading to the interstate—a two-hour drive. Then, once she hit I-95 North, it was three-and-a-half hours more to her apartment.

Caroline's alarm woke her up as the early light of dawn approached Hatteras. She looked around her bedroom, feeling a little melancholy. The vacation at Beach Heart Cottage was her best. Now she held both the crown and the wand. She had received every item except the pearl ring. She wondered what had happened to it.

After getting dressed, she went downstairs and poured a cup of coffee. She looked around the kitchen, recalling when she had arrived. How Auntie Lorelei explained how

Grandpops' ashes had crashed to the floor and Earl had stepped on Wilbur's paw.

That night, Earl brought blue crabs, and Dillan brought lobsters. How they had too much wine when Earl and Pearl danced around the kitchen. Her mother's cancer scare. And Colton's memorable visit to the beach when he showed up wearing a wig and joined them for a pizza party. She laughed at the idea of Earl getting caught by security and her aunts picking burrs off his feet.

Then, during the rescue mission to Ocracoke, she held Dillan's hand in hers on his boat for the first time. Handsome, kind Dillan. He melted into her heart. Her aunties chasing the ghost of wooden-legged Erasmus, and then she was crowned Seraphina.

She needed to get back to the real world. And work. That was the only way to sort out her heart. She had just set her empty mug on the countertop when everyone, still in PJs, came in.

"Honey, we are going to miss our Seraphina!" Auntie Calypso said with tears in her eyes. "What a wonderful time we've had. I love you." She hugged her.

"Me too, now I *am* going to cry."

"It's okay to cry, honey." Halia reached for Caroline's hands. "We've all had a splendid time, and seeing my daughter crowned was beyond words. Do you have your shell, you know, to add to the wall plaque outside the front door as you leave? And did you give Grams back the heart wampum shell?"

"Yes, Mom. It's in the box inside the sideboard. And I glued my special shell on it yesterday. All I need to do is sign the plaque as I leave, right?" She put her hands over her cheeks and burst into tears. "I... I had a wonderful time, and I will miss you all. Am I being silly or what?"

"Now, now, my dear granddaughter, we all cry when we leave the Beach Heart Cottage," Grams Dorea held back her tears. "It holds a piece of your heart. It always will. You hold on to those memories, and we will all be back next August, God willing."

"Oh, Grams Dorea, I love you so much. That makes me feel better. This cottage holds my heart." She gave her grandmother a warm hug and a kiss.

"Don't forget to say goodbye to Grandpops on the mantel. He watches over us," Grams Dorea reminded her as she wiped her eyes. "You, Seraphina, are the most beautiful mermaid to date. Love will find you. Believe that, my dear. Keep your heart open and the crown safe."

Caroline wiped her tears as she hugged each of her aunties. She whispered in Auntie Pearl's ear, "Earl is a great guy. Keep him. And he loves your salami roses."

Auntie Pearl nodded as her eyes flooded with tears.

"Seraphina, never forget the night you were crowned," Auntie Lorelei smiled. "Your mermaid name is sacred, and as you will find out, the magic has already begun."

Wilbur trotted into the kitchen and barked at Caroline. She patted his head. "Bye, Wilbur, see you soon and be a good boy. And thanks for not humping my pillows!"

Everyone laughed.

"You drive safely and call us when you get home. I love you." Auntie Calypso held back her tears.

Halia took Caroline's hand. "Come on, we'll walk you out to your car. Oh, don't forget your marker for the sign, and did you leave your mermaid flip-flops upstairs?"

"I have the marker and my flip-flops are by the bed," Caroline replied as she took one last look around the cottage and blew a kiss. "Bye, Grandpops, see you next summer! Watch over everyone."

Outside, Caroline looked at her family as the sun rose out of the ocean. "Go inside! I'm leaving and no more tears. I will call later." She waved as she got into her SUV, as Halia blew a kiss and went inside.

Just as Caroline was about to leave, there was a knock on the passenger window. Her face lit up.

"You were going to run off without saying goodbye?"

"No, I... Dillan," she said as she wiped the tears off her cheek.

"This is for you. I picked it up minutes ago. The ice is still there." Dillan came around to the driver's side and handed her a cup of iced coffee. "Another sunny, hot day on Hatteras."

"That is so sweet. Thank you." She took a sip. "Perfect."

"If you stay, this could be every morning, you know. It won't be the same here once you leave."

Caroline nodded, fighting back her tears. His voice, his lips, his being melted her heart.

"Keep in touch, and, uh, work on taking those gloves off. Finger by finger." He looked away and back at Caroline. "Hey, drive safely, and try to find some time to relax with the election. And, uh, let me know you got home safe. Okay?"

Her heart was racing, and her throat was tight as she held back another tear. *Since when do I cry leaving the cottage?* These were new emotions, and she needed to get a handle on them.

"I will stay in touch. Promise. And I will text you when I get home." She looked away. Oh no, those salty tears found her and flowed out onto her cheeks. She could not escape what was happening.

"Are you okay?" He popped his head inside the vehicle.

She could not look at him. "Yup. I'm just dandy."

He turned her face to him. "Hey, it's okay."

She burst into a waterfall of tears, unable to speak.

He spoke for her. "I know, I know. Leaving Hatteras to go back to reality sucks! I'm gonna share something. It's a secret and don't tell my dad. I used to cry, too."

She laughed between tears. "You did not!" She sniffled, reaching into her glove box and found a small box of tissues.

"Come back when you have time. A weekend getaway. I'll be here." He smiled. "It's gorgeous here off season. Sweater weather. Or we can sit by a warm fire. How about that? And make s'mores."

Nodding, she dried her tears. "Is this a promise?"

"Promise." He kissed her salty lips. "You drive safely and let me know when you get home. I'll miss you, Caroline Woodard."

After a slow nod and many sniffles, she put the SUV in drive and waved as she drove down Sea Glass Lane.

Dillan's heart hurt. Caroline was one of a kind. The kind he would love to spend his life with. Still, how could Hatteras measure up to the dazzle of Washington? How could he compete with the possibility of her becoming First Lady, Caroline?

From the living room window, all the aunties watched Dillan. Even Wilbur perched himself on top of the sofa.

"I am learning to let my daughter go. It's her heart she needs to fill, not mine," Halia said softly as she broke into a smile. "Time for breakfast, girls. It is gonna be so quiet without Caroline here."

Grams Dorea agreed, holding back tears. "What happened this time? We're all crying and carrying on."

"Not sure, Mom. Maybe mermaid magic is getting stronger. We are all touched by something. The cottage feels it, too." Auntie Calypso looked around with a fond smile. "It's love. It's Ida and her sister's love for this island and cottage."

"We have another week here, and let's make it joyful. No more tears, girls! Blueberry buttermilk pancakes with fresh whipped cream is what we need!" Auntie Lorelei suggested. "Oh, and Pearl, I think you and Earl are having fun."

Pearl blushed.

Grams Dorea looked at Pearl. "Good heavens, you mean *you're* the one who's found love?"

Forty-Two

Caroline, exhausted, pulled up to her condo. The drive, which usually took less than six hours, took almost nine, with the end of summer traffic jams as everyone headed back to Washington. She should have known better than to come back on a Sunday.

Once inside, she opened the windows and let the room air out. Thank goodness for the delivery service. While waiting for her food, she kissed the tips of her fingers, pressed them on the top of the box that held the crown and the wand. She then put it on the top shelf in her walk-in closet. "Thank you for such a magical time on Hatteras, Great Auntie Ida. I know you are beside me."

She called her mother to let them all know she was home safe. It broke her heart when she hung up. Next on her list was to text Dillan. Someone knocked on the door. Her neighbor stopped by to drop off her mail. He mentioned how refreshed she looked. She smiled; if he only knew what a vacation it was!

She ate, took a shower, and put on her softest PJs and was just sitting down on the couch with a glass of wine to text Dillan when Colton phoned. She stared at his name with each ring and knew she had to talk to him. No way she could drive away from him and say, see ya next summer.

"Are you home?"

"I got home a little while ago. Oh my god, what a nightmare drive! What's up? Where are you? Still in New Mexico?"

"Not quite," he laughed. "I am in my car and about to get out and ring your doorbell."

"*What*!" She nearly dropped her wine glass as she looked at her door. "Stop it, you are not!" She dashed over to the window, and there was his car, with Alton standing by the passenger door. "Not tonight. I just got home a little while ago and I'm exhausted."

"Exhausted? *I'm* exhausted. You were on vacation while I was running around the country campaigning."

"Knock it off, Colton."

"I like when you get all fired up."

"I'm not in the mood for your nonsense. Save it for the campaign trail. My vacation will continue until midnight tonight. So be on your merry way with Alton."

"I will camp out if need be. And let's see what the press makes of that. Seriously, we must talk." He looked at his Rolex. "Give me ten minutes of your existing vacation time. I'll cede it back to you later."

Caroline let out an exaggerated sigh. "Colton, all right. I'll give ten minutes to the next President of the United States. Ten minutes."

"That's my Caroline," he laughed and hung up.

"That's *my* Caroline," she muttered as she closed the curtains.

She put on her robe, let him inside, and shut the door. Alton and two other security men remained in the hallway.

He kissed her cheek and stood back. "You look fantastic! And I bet your tan lines are amazing." His eager eyes roamed over her. "Do you have any bourbon?"

"Colton, what do you want? I can't have any rag magazines seeing you here. Did you watch your back?"

"Of course. It's all good. Scotch? Better yet, bourbon."

"All I have is something in the cabinet from last year's Christmas party. And I don't have those cutesy star-shaped ice cubes my mother makes. Follow me." She reached up into the cabinet and pulled out a bottle. "Is this good enough?"

"Heck yeah, that's very good. Straight, no ice."

She handed him a small glass. "There you go, help yourself. Now, what do you want?" She tapped her fingers on the countertop. "Well?"

"I want you to consider being by my side. We have to introduce you soon. The voters will go crazy seeing you with me."

She shook her head. "You don't listen, do you?"

"No. I don't." He sauntered into her living room and over to a collage of photos. He picked up one of her father, who was shaking hands with a president. "You know what he would say?"

Caroline twisted her lips. She knew her father would be proud to see his little girl beside Colton. "Well, that was my dad." Her phone buzzed. She picked it up. Of all times for Dillan to call. She put the phone down on the side table.

"Is that your beach bum? Oh, wait, a beach bum wouldn't have a seventy-thousand-dollar boat and own several ocean and sound front homes on Hatteras and Ocracoke. And he even has an apartment in New York on the Upper East Side. I would say he does well, wouldn't you, for a divorced handyman?"

"What? What are you talking about? He was an acquisitions lawyer for a financial firm. I am sure he did well." She recalled the look on Auntie Lorelei's face as she read Dillan's palm. "Where did you get this information, and why?"

"I have my ways and I wanted to make sure your beach bum was well..."

"Well, what?"

"Safe for you to be around."

"Wow," she realized Colton genuinely cared. She had to retort, "You should talk, with your ex-blabbermouth fiancée and her book. Did you do a background check on her? And yes, I heard about the movie deal."

He sipped his drink, avoiding her questions, never losing eye contact with her. "See what happens when you are with me? You will go places. Consider it. I know you still have a heartbeat for me."

Caroline was silent. She had a heartbeat, all right. She had to find out if these tales about Dillan were true.

Colton placed his glass on the countertop. "Caroline, let's give it one more try. What have we got to lose? No one will know. We can keep a lid on it for a few weeks, and if we make it, then we announce it. You can even write all our press releases. Get us on every morning, afternoon, and night show."

"I need time to clear my head, Colton, and get some rest."

"Time is something on which we are short. I still love you. I always will."

"Oh, gosh." *He loves me. He loves my name,* she had thought. "Call me tomorrow. I need to chill out. Good night, Colton." She took his empty glass and pushed him toward the door. He stopped her, pressing his lips to hers. It was all too familiar. It lasted a moment, then he pulled away.

"That is how it can be. Sleep well, Mrs. Colton Woodard Jameson."

"Stop it! Go!" She pushed him out the door, giving Alton a nod.

That glove, the one she was supposed to remove, wasn't going anywhere.

Caroline pressed her back against the door. She dropped her head, staring at her toes, still painted in aqua mermaid polish and rhinestones. Colton loved to stir the pot, and he brought this one to a near boil. This mermaid needed to surface for air.

She lifted her head and took her phone into the living room, and pressed Dillan's number.

"I guess you made it home safe and sound?"

"Hi, Dillan. Yes, I got home a little while ago. Just settling in. How is Hatteras?"

"Not the same without you. I'm down by the water. It's hot, the water is gorgeous, and your family invited my dad and me over for a cookout. In fact, it's in a few minutes. They gave my dad a list of projects for after they leave."

She could hear in her mind Grams Dorea telling Earl, *Get out! Did you get my list of repairs? Why is it so dusty in here? Here's five bucks. Clean the firebox. Help me with my puzzle.*

Laughing to herself, she walked to the window and watched Colton's car pull away.

"How are you?"

"Me? I'm doing okay. It rained earlier today. A passing shower, so I've been working on the remodel plans for the cottage next door." He looked out over the ocean. "I miss you."

"I miss the island." She bit the inside of her cheek as she went into her bedroom and sat down on a side chair. "Dillan, I need to know something and be straight with me."

Dillan waited for her to say she missed him. "Okay. Go ahead, ask."

"Do you own other houses on the island?"

"That's an odd question. I think I told you I do." He had expected so much worse. "I own my dad's house, and the cottage next to yours with my dad. And a handful of beach boxes I've had for years. My mother left them to me in her will and a couple of others up the beach that I'm selling. And I had an apartment in New York I sold recently."

She felt her shoulders tense up to her neck. "One more thing."

He settled into the sand. "Go for it."

She had to silently count before speaking. "Were you ever married?"

He tilted his head back to watch the clouds pass by. "No. I almost got married, and we ended it."

"Did you go through a divorce?"

"Kind of hard to do when you've never been married."

Her jaw tightened. *Colton, that liar!* "Sorry! But the boat, is it really yours?"

"It is. Why the third degree?" He laughed aloud. If she could have seen his face, she would have seen him blushing.

"I'm so sorry. I have had men lie to me in the past. You don't need to answer."

"No, I want to clear the air. The boat is owned by me and my dad's company to shuttle guests from Ocracoke to Hatteras. My dad owns several bungalows over on Ocracoke. There you have it. That is who I am and what I own. Now, should I ask you questions?"

"If you want to. Go ahead." *Here comes Colton.* "I deserve it."

"Did the senator's thugs really beat up my dad?"

Just as he had, she felt immense relief. "No!"

"I am being summoned to a cookout! One of your aunts is ringing that ship's bell. Can you hear it?"

"No. I wish I were there."

"Before we say goodnight, Caroline."

"I miss you, Dillan."

"Same here. And I'm wearing my white Vans to the cookout!"

They laughed.

"Bye, Dillan."

He waited. "Bye, Caroline."

Caroline had one more text to send before she fell asleep.

> I know why you are such a great politician.

> Colton texted.

> You could not stay away.

Her fingers were quick.

> Great politicians are also *great* liars.

She hit send.

Forty-Three

By mid-October, the cottage had been closed. Shades drawn, linens put away, furniture covered, air conditioning units taken out, and the doors locked. Earl had finally gotten over there to turn off the water and electricity. He stopped and looked around. His eyes landed on the fireplace mantle. He wondered why Grams Dorea kept her husband up there and not back at her home. A chill occupied the air. It was quiet. Too quiet. He went out the front door and locked it.

Pearl had invited him up to her home in New York to help her get the house ready to put on the market. She was buying the house next to Beach Heart Cottage, the one Earl and Dillan were fixing up. The plan was for it to be a peaceful sanctuary for guests to unwind with Pearl nearby.

The cooler air and colorful leaves occupied Washington. Two weeks to go, and Caroline's life could calm down a notch. Colton's lead in the polls left little doubt about his becoming the next president.

Caroline's mother was once again hosting politicians at her home. She held several fundraisers to aid his win. Caroline attended with the smile of Jameson's wife. At least that is what Halia wanted to believe.

It was a struggle for Caroline. Her heart belonged to Hatteras, yet her mind and body were firmly rooted in D.C. She had invested countless hours with Colton, promising him that if he emerged victorious, she and her team would be there to support him during his acceptance speech. Deep down, she convinced herself that she was doing this for her parents and to uphold the Woodard name in the public eye. The prospect of becoming FLOTUS was looming closer.

Temperatures dropped, and they predicted a surprise early snow for the evening of Election Day. Colton voted, exiting the booth to flashing cameras and wild cheers.

Halia was hosting an elaborate catered event at her home. Many of the who's who of Washington were attending. Once the election numbers were insurmountable, and the major news media called the race, Colton would make an acceptance speech at his hotel headquarters.

After he and his party would arrive at Halia's for the celebration. In his coat pocket, tucked in a velvet box, was a diamond ring. Halia had prayed for this night when Colton and Caroline would make the announcement she had been waiting so long for.

Halia had to drag Grams Dorea to the event. She sat in a corner recliner, enjoying the appetizers and champagne, shaking a hand or two, when Lorelei and Pearl found her.

Lorelei bent over. "Mom, I know this is not your thing, but thanks for being here to support us. What a beautiful job our sister has done. It's like being at the Ritz! You are being exceptionally silent."

Grams Dorea looked up at Lorelei with a bright smile, then sipped her champagne. "It's the night I prayed for."

"What? Mom, you despise Colton. Did you have too much champagne?" Pearl asked.

Grams Dorea continued to sip her bubbly drink.

"Halia went overboard. Especially with the surprise announcement," Pearl looked to Lorelei. "Where is Calypso?"

"She is stuck in traffic. She will be here soon. Where is Caroline? She should have been here an hour ago." Lorelei said as she looked around.

"She must be with Colton at the hotel, although I haven't seen her on camera," Lorelei said. "I can't wait to see her in that gorgeous dress Halia picked out for her for the announcement."

"I heard all about it. The media will bombard us. Caroline knows what to do and say. It's so exciting!" Pearl looked at Grams Dorea. "Mom, have fun. Let me get you another glass of champagne. We have a big night ahead of us!"

Grams Dorea, wearing a knowing smile, winked at Pearl. She knew why Caroline was late. It was her doing. She always had the final say. She is Grams Dorea.

Bundled in a thick wool sweater, scarf, and a matching hat, Caroline got out of her SUV. Her boots hit the crushed shells on the driveway. The dark night echoed with the sound of the roaring ocean. A storm was moving up the coast. Using her phone's flashlight app, she found the key hidden in the outside shower and opened the front door and set her bags down.

The Beach Heart Cottage was cold and silent. Its furniture was covered, and the electricity was shut off. In the pantry, she found a pile of newspapers and a box of matches. She made her way over to the fireplace and kneeled, opening the flue, and stuffed the crumpled newspaper under the grate. She reached into the kindling box and piled small logs onto the grate. With the strike of a match, a golden flame met the newspaper. She got up, rubbing her hands together to warm them. She put the fire screen securely in place. On the mantle, she lit a line of white candles. In the middle were grandpop's ashes.

"Thanks, grandpops, for this. I love you."

Next, she went to the sideboard, where Grams Dorea told her to look, and opened it. Inside, at the back, was a box. She reached for it and held it up, then pressed it against her heart. She then removed Ida's journal, letting the pages fall open. Over at the fireplace, she kneeled. Her eyes followed what Ida had written in ink.

When your toes find the sand, a smile finds your heart. It is under the full glow of the brilliant orb above that one day I will find my true love. With all my heart, I know this is true, as the waves crash on the shore. I know one day my love will find me as I open the cottage door.

The wind was picking up, and the door to the outside shower was banging. Caroline went out to shut it. Thick, tumbling gray clouds moved in, playing hide and seek with a half-moon. The wind swirled around her as she inhaled the chilled air. Feeling free, she sent a text. Then, pulling her sweater tight around her, she made her way down the path to the dune.

It didn't take long before she could see the wavering beam of a flashlight.

"Caroline! *What* are you doing here? It's your big night!" Dillan gathered her in his arms. "I missed you." He pulled her closer as the bitter north wind blew sand around them. "You're cold."

"Not anymore." She rested her head on his shoulder.

"My dad and I were watching the news. The senator is the projected winner, even without all the West Coast votes in. I hadn't heard from you in over a week."

"I know. Sorry. It's been beyond insane."

"You should be there. You've earned it. They mentioned a surprise announcement."

"The surprise is on them. I'm done. I did what I promised my father, what I would do. Colton Jameson will be our next president. I will not be his wife."

He pulled away. "Was that the surprise announcement?"

"Yes. I couldn't do it. My mother-"

"Shhhh." He pressed his index finger to her lips. "Truth? I was watching him in hopes of catching a glimpse of you. I've seen you in the background at his campaign speeches, and I looked forward to your daily texts."

"Serious? Well, he may have won the White House, but *you* won my heart."

"I fell in love with you that day we met at the coffee shop. How could I admit it when you were wearing Colton? That glove thing, you know?"

She giggled. "The glove thing." She stretched her fingers out wide. "I took them all off. I'm free."

"It wasn't hard, was it?"

"Truth? Yes, it was. It's a lot to give up, and I've been around that seduction of power my whole life." A gust of sea foam was blowing around them as the winds picked up, lifting her hat off her head and sending it flying into the darkness.

His lips met hers. "Let's go inside."

With his arm around her, he asked, "Wait, don't I recall you wanting to sit by a fire and roasting s'mores? Is that offer still open?"

"Yes, it is! Come on, let's get inside the Beach Heart Cottage. I have a fire started, and I brought the s'mores."

Dillan held her tighter. "You're always thinking. That's what I love about you."

"Love?"

"Yes, Caroline."

Caroline took his hand and led him inside. The living room was glowing. She lit a few more candles, went over to the sideboard, and took something out.

"What's that? A book? Should I turn on the lights?"

"The electricity's off." She pointed to the coffee table. "Grab that candle over there and sit next to me by the fire."

They found their bodies warming next to each other.

"Dillan, I have something I must read to you. It's been on my mind for weeks. I know it's why we met."

He brushed her windswept hair out of her eyes. "Okay."

Caroline opened the journal to a page that was marked with a feather.

"Before you go any further, I have something that has been on my mind since the day you were at my dad's cottage."

Caroline tilted her head, leaving the journal open on her lap.

"My ancestors go back to England. Seafaring people. There was a sailor named-"

She put her fingers to his lips. Now she knew what Auntie Lorelei had seen in his palm. She picked up the journal and read the passage telling of Erasmus and Seraphina, how one day they would reunite.

Dillan reached for her hand and kissed it. "It's destiny. Erasmus is the sailor."

Caroline felt chills rush up the back of her head to the tip of her nose. Her eyes met his. "I know. This is happening, isn't it? The magic of Hatteras. The blood moon, the ceremony."

"What are you talking about?" Dillan's fingers traced the outline of her face. "Dancing around the bonfire?"

She nodded. "I have a tale to tell you, Dillan." She leaned in, kissing his lips. She pulled back. "Grams Dorea said once your toes meet the sands of Hatteras Island, a smile finds your heart."

Dillan reached for her hand. "That's beautiful."

"I have something for you. It is something that my Grams Dorea said I could have and only share with the one who stole my heart."

"I stole your heart. I like that." He smiled, since he, too, had a surprise.

She pulled the box out of her pocket and opened it. Inside rested the two heart-shaped wampum shells. "Grams Dorea told me when you find your true love, the hearts need to be together." She handed Dillan the violet and white wampum shell and told him of the symbolism behind it. *The Croatan tribe's love story.*

He took it and held it. "The shell, the story, and you are beautiful." He kissed her soft lips. "Now I have something for you."

She looked into his eyes as he pulled a small green velvet box from his jacket.

"My dad and Pearl have a close relationship, and Grams Dorea has been in touch. She told me the beautiful story about a mermaid and a sailor." He smiled as he opened the lid of the box.

Her eyes twinkled in the flicker of the flames. "Are you serious?"

"It was your Great Aunt Ida's pearl ring..." he began.

"And they found the pearl in a bottle after a stormy night like this one, so the story goes," she continued, holding back tears of joy.

"A symbol of eternal love, our love, a pearl from the ocean."

Her eyes lit up as he slid the ring over her slender finger. "I love you, Erasmus." Her lips met his.

"I love you, Seraphina."

"May your toes find the Hatteras sand and a smile find your heart."

Discover the magic of the
Sea Glass Retreat

In book two, you will discover the Magical World of the **Sea Glass Retreat** on North Carolina's Hatteras Island. Pearl and Lorelei, with Earl's help, have revived the Sea Glass Retreat. A once dilapidated beach cottage, now transformed into a serene oasis.

At the Beach Heart Cottage, next door, they reveal new mysteries and witness the discovery of heirloom objects. Caroline, the newly crowned mermaid, has found herself in Hatteras, but what direction will her life take? Despite President Jameson's relentless pursuit, Caroline chooses not to marry him and starts over on Hatteras Island. Meanwhile, kindhearted Dillan is learning to live his life without competing with the president, a challenging task.

As events unfold, some hearts will break while others find mending. Grams Dorea is surprised when her sister Caldoria, who has been living in Italy, returns to Hatteras. It's time to mend the past and reveal the truth.

Explore the pages of the Sea Glass Retreat and immerse yourself in its world of wonder by the ocean. Laugh, cry, forgive, and love—it's all here.

About the Author

Diana loved telling stories even in childhood (much to my parents' disapproval.) A few years back, she came upon an abandoned antebellum mansion in North Carolina and began writing. The walls begged me to tell its twisted tale. The Eastport series (previously known as DuBois Manor) received five stars. It will be re-released. They invited me to a two-day book signing at the mansion. It sold out on the first day!

Since then, she has written several novels soon to be released. Adding a pinch of the paranormal, mystery, and romance to her books.

Living on the Eastern Shores of North Carolina, what better place to create beachside romance with a little humor? Diana is also an accomplished, trained artist and former owner of an interior design retail store. She has taught art and volunteered for the annual Labor Day Parade and Holiday Festival committees in Connecticut for many years.

"Stories are everywhere, and using my vivid imagination, I can weave them into my stories. I hope you enjoy this book and all the others I am writing. It is my passion to take you away with my characters and settings."

DianaBaxternovels.com for more information and new releases.

Upcoming books

The Mosaic Mermaid

A Hatteras Kiss - *Book 3 in the Beach Heart Cottage series*

You Left Me Once

Sapphire Moon